To: Leeann

I hope as you read my book, you realize more than you ever have just how important your role as a mother is.

Blessings in Jesus,
Brenda Rice
April 6th, 2012

Remmie, a Southern Heiress

Brenda Rice

WestBow Press books may be ordered through booksellers or by contacting:

WestBow Press
A Division of Thomas Nelson
1663 Liberty Drive
Bloomington, IN 47403
www.westbowpress.com
1-(866) 928-1240

ISBN: 978-1-4497-3617-0 (e)
ISBN: 978-1-4497-3618-7 (sc)
ISBN: 978-1-4497-3619-4 (hc)

Library of Congress Control Number: 2012902340

Printed in the United States of America

WestBow Press rev. date:2/17/2012

Acknowledgements

As a first time author, I was blessed with many wonderful friends who encouraged me to finish the manuscript that finally became, "Remmie, a Southern Heiress". The following people critiqued, proof-read and prayed with me about the book: Jo Christmas, Gayle Wade, Marilyn Adams, Gayle Tedder, Diane Chestnut and Mary McNeal. Harold and Betty Hansen took me and my manuscript into their hearts and their prayers as I worked to finish the final ten chapters.

Barbara Lee typed and edited the manuscript time and time again. I believe that God put Barbara in my life to keep me uplifted and at peace. She is a beautiful Christian through whom the peace of our Lord emanates.

Finally my family must be acknowledged. I am so blessed to have three adult children who live for the Lord. My sons, Brad and wife, Cilem, Heath and wife, Kim and my daughter Rusti have inspired me through-out their lives. They also gave me many experiences to draw from while writing this book. My six adorable grandchildren add plenty of sweetness and just the right pinch of spice to my life every day. To Hayden and husband Jason, Maegan, Taylor, Madelyn, Reece and Ezra, granny loves you.

Lastly, my father wanted me to finish the book so much that he bought me my first lap-top and pressured me to work on the manuscript that I had begun fourteen years earlier. My dad passed away in April of 2011, but he knew the book was finished. What a blessing he and my mom were to me.

I want to extend my heartfelt thanks to every person mentioned here, as well as to my entire church family. God is good…all the time!

Dedications

I dedicate this book to my husband, Nathanael Rice. He remains my most ardent supporter. He made sure I had time to finish the book, even if it meant he had to do the dishes or wash the clothes. God made you just for me. I would never have had the courage to do this without you by my side.

Prologue

Rebecca Elizabeth was adopted by Dr. Benjamin and Melissa Remington in 1971 at age eleven. After her adoption, she became Rebecca Elizabeth Melissa Remington, but she was known as Remmie from that day to this. In 1976, a change occurred that brought Remmie to maturity more quickly than expected.

It was a lovely spring morning at River Oaks. The birds sang cheerfully outside Remmie's open bedroom window. The pretty sixteen-year-old sat cross-legged on her bed, finishing some homework left from the night before. She spoke to her dad as he passed going from his study to his bedroom.

Everything seemed perfect in the Remingtons's home until Remmie heard a commotion down the hall and her Father's frantic voice call out, *Melissa, Melissa*!! Then she heard her father say, "Remmie go get Sarah and call an ambulance immediately."

Remmie ran down the hall to the kitchen to let Sarah, her mother's companion, know there was a problem. Then she called for the ambulance as instructed. When she finished, she raced back to her parents' bedroom door, which remained closed.

The smell of Sarah's homemade breakfast drifted through the hallway. Remmie could only wait and wonder what was happening. Finally, Dr. Remington came out of the room, walking toward Remmie. The look on his face caused fear to run through the teenager's body like a bolt of lightning.

"She's gone, Remmie. Your mother has gone to heaven. She died in her sleep." His voice cracked and great sobs came from deep inside him. He couldn't say anything for a few moments. Remmie didn't believe what she heard. Her mind reeled and from somewhere inside came a scream like nothing she had uttered before.

"I'll wake her. She's sleeping." Remmie bolted into the beautiful room which looked completely normal. Sunlight filled the room. A bouquet of fresh flowers sat on the table by the window. White lace curtains billowed out with the spring breeze.

There, on the big bed, lay her mother looking as beautiful as ever. Walking closer, Remmie touched Melissa's cheek, and then she laid her head on Melissa's chest, hoping to hear the comforting beat of her heart. So many times Remmie had taken refuge in that bed with her mom and often ended up with her head on her chest, hearing the steady beating of her heart. But not today---no beating---no breathing---nothing.

As Sarah prayed aloud for peace to come, it came in abundance, touching all three of them. In the distance, the siren announced the arrival of the ambulance, but the emergency was over. Now, only the reality of their situation remained.

In 1977, Remmie graduated from high school and junior college. She had been dually enrolled during her junior and senior years of high school. That fall she entered the University of Alabama. In the fall of 1979, Remmie entered medical school at the age of nineteen. She had already decided her specialty would be trauma surgery. So in 1985, Dr. Rebecca Remington received her medical license and reported for duty at a large hospital in Birmingham, Alabama.

For I know the plans I have for you, declares the Lord, plans to prosper you and not to harm you, plans to give you a hope and a future. Jeremiah 29:11 NIV

CHAPTER ONE

A concentrated beam of light pierced between the closed blinds right into the eyes of an exhausted nurse. The trauma unit was a mess---towels had been hurriedly tossed about. Pans, trays, and every other piece of equipment or instrument known to the emergency room lay this way or that.

Everything was quiet after a night of total bedlam. Pools of blood remained on the floor from an early morning accident victim. The place looked like something from *MASH*.

Dr. Remington made her way through the clutter on her way to the elevator. "Wha-T a dum-P."

The nurse gave no response. "Well, that's my best Bette Davis impression. I see you aren't impressed, Connie."

"Don't quit your day job, Doc," was the nurse's glum reply.

"I'm going to River Oaks to see my father for the week-end. Keep 'em in line, Connie. See you Monday night."

"Sure thing, Doc. Have a good time. Is Jesse going with you?"

"She sure is. As a matter of fact, she's waiting for me now. Bye."

As expected, Jesse was waiting under the canopy outside the emergency entrance. "Well, good morning, Dr. Remington. Must say, you look beat. Hard night, was it?"

"Don't worry about my looks. Just get this thing in high gear. The solitude of River Oaks is calling my name," Remmie said as she threw her bags in the back of Jesse's car, and slid into the seat beside her best friend.

"You got it, girly girl. You close those eyes while I navigate us safely to our week-end of country fun."

"Remmie gave a devilish grin and said, "You want my eyes closed so I won't have heart failure while you navigate. Just keep it between the ditches."

"You got it---Beam us up, Scottie," yelled Jesse as she sped away from the Medical Center.

Although Remmie's eyes were closed, her mind was wide awake. She had more than fun on her agenda for this visit with her father. She had plans that she knew Dr. Benjamin Remington would not approve of, but she was determined to give him the opportunity to help her answer some questions that had haunted her for a long time.

~~~~~~

River Oaks, a lovely Southern estate on the Chattahoochee River, was home for Remmie. Her father had purchased it many years ago. Once, she, her father, and her mother, Melissa, lived there all the time. The entrance to the estate was marked by a huge wrought-iron gate with a script "R" on it. The gate might have looked foreboding to some, but not to Remmie. The site of the massive stone and iron structure meant home to her. It meant safety with the only man she had ever loved, her father, Dr. Benjamin Remington.

Jesse drove along the narrow, winding lane bordered by kudzu-covered trees and bushes. They looked like some pre-historic herd of giant creatures trapped in time, becoming monuments pointing the way to River Oaks.

Remmie opened her eyes just as the car drove up to the gates. Jesse entered the code, and slowly the massive gates swung open, welcoming the visitors. The drive to the house was lined with huge spreading live oaks, their branches almost touching the ground. They looked so majestic, as if bowing to royalty. The manicured lawns and flower gardens were in full bloom. Wisteria, azaleas, bridal wreaths, dogwoods, and redbuds framed the house beautifully.

Jesse made the final turn into the circular drive that led to the front entrance of the spacious ranch-style house with large windows that faced the river, and the forest that surrounded the property. Jesse yelled out, "Sarah, we're here. Open up!"

The door opened to a gray-haired lady with a startled look on her face. "What 'n heaven's name is *yore* problem *chil*? Is somebody a *chasin' ya*? Is the law on *yore* tail? Maybe it's the IRS? That *yellin'* of *yores* is enough to send the squirrels *headin'* up river to safety."
~~~~~~

"Oh, Sarah, you are so funny. Look at you standing there with soapy water dripping on the floor. You could fall, and hurt yourself."

"Oh, no, honey *chil. Caus'en ya* are *a fixin'* to clean it up." Take my apron, and get busy."

Sarah handed her apron to Jesse, but her eyes were firmly fixed on Remmie. "Remmie, look *atcha. Ya* look so tired, and so thin. I *gotta* get some food into *ya,* and put some meat on them bones."

Remmie hugged Sarah, and kissed her cheek. "Well, Sarah, bones don't seem to be your problem. Maybe just seeing some bones makes you nervous."

"I'm the same pleasingly plump size I *wus* the last time *ya wus* here. Which, *wus* so long ago, *ya* don't remember what I looked like."

"How's my father?" questioned Remmie.

"Cranky---grumpy---full of aggravation."

"You know what I mean. How is he physically?"

"Dr. Carson *wus* here *yesterdy*; he said he's *bout* the same. I tried to tell him he *oughta* do *somethin' bout* his disposition, but he said the same *thang* he always says."

"And what was that?"

"He don't perform mercy *killins*. I'll have to call Kvorkiman or whatever his name is."

"Sarah, I declare you are too much at times. I'll go see for myself."

As Remmie walked down the hall toward her father's study, she tried to find the best choice of words to tell him what was on her mind. But she couldn't find the right combination of words to ensure that Dr. Remington would agree. In fact, she was sure he would never agree. So, she needed to find the words that would upset him the least.

The trophy-filled hallway brought so many happy memories, memories of frosty mornings cuddled up by her father, in the woods, near River Oaks waiting for a ten point buck to appear. She treasured those times because it was then that she had her dad all to herself.

At last, she entered her father's dark paneled study with book-lined walls, the distinct smell of wintergreen smoking tobacco, and the big mahogany desk. There sat a distinguished gray-haired man with a neatly groomed mustache, gently puffing on his pipe. The instant he saw her, his face broke into a wonderful smile that caused his sparkling blue eyes to come alive.

"Remmie, I'm so glad to see you," said the raspy voice as Dr. Remington stood to embrace her. "You look tired, and I do believe you have lost weight since you were here."

"For goodness sake, did you and Sarah rehearse how you would needle me when I arrived?"

"Rebecca Elizabeth Melissa Remington, how can you compare the loving concern of your father to the babblings of a gabby old maid?"

"Now Daddy, you shouldn't say things like that about Sarah. You know y'all couldn't get along without each other."

"You really think that I can't get along without that irritating old maid? I'll have you know, I can take care of myself, young lady!"

"Please Dad, lower your voice. Let's change the subject. Jesse came with me. We're about to take a walk by the river before lunch. Up to coming with us?"

"Not today, honey. Maybe…tomorrow."

"Dad, I need to have a serious talk with you while I'm here. I've made a decision, and I would like to have your approval."

"What's this all about, Remmie? There are very few things that you don't have my approval to do. So, which one of them is it?"

"Let's talk later, after lunch. Are you coming down to have lunch with us?"

"Puffing faster on his pipe, the senior Dr. Remington, stared into Remmie's eyes, and said, "I'll be down for lunch. And, I'll be waiting for this…talk."

CHAPTER TWO

In the kitchen, Sarah rattled on about the weather, the gardens, and about how she needed to fatten up Remmie. Jesse listened intently. Following Sarah around the kitchen with her shining black eyes, Jesse continued peeling the tomatoes that Sarah had placed before her when she stated firmly that idol hands were the devil's workshop. Not wishing to fall prey to the devil, Jesse peeled the tomatoes. When Remmie entered the kitchen, she was pointed to the tomatoes, also. Both ladies obediently peeled the messy vegetables.

Finally, Sarah declared they had peeled enough, and dismissed them to take their walk. Her final instruction was to be back at noon, on the dot. The two raced out the kitchen door, before Sarah could find another nasty task.

"Hurry Jesse, before she finds another awful job like cutting okra or removing corn from the cob. They are all methods of torture used by parents under the guise of 'life building skills.'"

As they looked across the picturesque lawn and flower gardens toward the river, the friends fixed their gazes on the natural beauty of their surroundings.

"This place is enchanted. I feel God's presence here more than anywhere else."

"I know, Remmie. I feel Him, too. It's an overwhelming sense of peace. A oneness. It's like being really in touch with yourself, the genuine you."

"That's it…the genuine you---the *you* not often shared with the world. I feel it sometimes when I'm performing surgery, and the odds are against me. Somewhere inside, I know that I'm going to succeed. I know the patient will recover. I believe God gives me those feelings. I believe He wants me to know that He is in control, not me or the marvels of modern medicine."

"I don't think I've ever heard you talk like this. You rarely talk about your surgeries. I'm surprised."

"There are volumes of things I've never talked about. I think the time has come for me to let them out. You are my closest friend, and have been since college. You've shared so much with me over the years. We've had such good times together. You and your wonderful family have been a source of inspiration for me. Even your brothers are so close to the family. I don't know why, but for some reason that inspires me. I feel like I've missed so much in life, even though I've had so much given to me. Sometimes I envy you, and your family, Jess. Even though, I know it's wrong."

Jesse looked at her friend with amazement. She knew she was seeing a part of her she had never seen before, and she wondered what secrets had provoked this introspective mood.

Remmie continued to purge herself of feelings she had buried beneath a façade of professionalism and sophistication. Jesse continued to listen to this woman she thought she knew so well. She was convinced there was plenty more to learn.

As they walked toward the river, Remmie told Jesse how much she loved her father. Somehow Jesse got the feeling there had been other fathers before him, other families, and other homes. Jesse couldn't quite put all the pieces together, but she remained silent. She feared if she asked questions, it would break the spell, and she might never learn the secrets her friend had carried for such a long time.

At a bend in the river where the dogwoods hung over the water with their white blooms turned upward, Remmie stopped beneath a large oak tree. "This was my secret place when I first came to River Oaks. I told this old tree all my secrets. I'm sure glad it can't talk or I could be in a lot of trouble."

"I had a secret place, too. I went to the attic of the old house where we lived, and hid myself among the things we no longer needed downstairs. I guess at some of those times, I felt un-needed myself, so I found a kin-ship with the things up there. Remmie, what do you mean by, when you first came to River Oaks? I thought you always lived here?"

"I've lived many places before River Oaks. You see my life as Rebecca Elizabeth Melissa Remington began at a girl's home in the city. Dr. and Mrs. Remington came to adopt a child. They had lost two babies shortly after birth to a rare genetic disease that Melissa carried, but didn't know it. Melissa was very depressed, but still wanted a child. My father felt that adopting an infant would be too hard for her, so he talked her into adopting an older child. That is very unusual because most people want infants with no memories of their past. But my father, being so wise, convinced his dear wife to adopt me. I am so thankful that they chose me. They gave me every opportunity life has to offer. I have been so blessed."

Jesse sat down and leaned back against the tree; her eyes stared seriously at her friend. "Yes, Jesse, I was adopted by the Remingtons when I was eleven. That was the beginning of my life as someone worth knowing. Before then, I had nobody that loved me. I existed in foster homes or shelters. Love meant some perverted, unspeakable act that caused excruciating pain, and left you feeling empty.

"Older children are rarely adopted. Their lives become living hells as they are passed from one home to the next. They never feel like they belong. Oh, some foster parents are nice people, but they have children of their own, and you know how the chips will fall in a crisis. You try to become the invisible person. You try not to be seen or heard, and you try for sure not to need anything."

"I can't imagine that you've ever felt like that. I mean, you are the most loving person I know. You give so much of yourself to others. I have to ask, why are you telling me this now?"

"Because, I need someone else to know about my life. Sarah is getting older, and Dad is old and sick. What happens when they both die? I'll be the only one who knows who Remmie is. That's not even what I mean, because I don't even know that. What I'm saying is everyone who knows about my life will be gone. I'll have no one to turn to. Can you help me by knowing that I have a past which is partially unknown even to me, and what I do know is disturbing? My past will shock you, Jess. It may change the way you feel about me. Can you do this for me?"

"Remmie, I'm blown away right now. You've just thrown a lifetime at me in a few minutes."

After a long pause, during which Remmie held her breath, Jesse spoke again. "First of all, you are my dearest friend. I love you, whoever you turn out to be. You will always be my Remmie, my friend. So, I'm here for the long haul. Do you understand?"

"Oh, thank you, Jesse. I love you, too. Give me a hug, please?"

"Come on Remmie, let's get back before Sarah turns the hounds loose on us. She said to be back by noon. I think it's getting close to that time by the looks of the sun."

They walked back to the house in silence. Lunch was waiting, and so was Sarah. "Well, it's about time *y'all* showed up. If *ya* don't eat this tomato pie while it's hot, you'll regret it." Sarah yelled down the hall to summon the elder doctor to lunch.

Dr. Remington entered the kitchen with his pipe in his mouth, and a half smile on his lips. "Hello Jesse, it's good to see you. You are as pretty as ever. Come give me a hug."

Jesse responded to his request, and she also gave him a peck on the cheek. "You look good, Dr. Remington. Why don't you come to the city so I can fix you up with a fancy city gal?"

"Come on now, Jesse. You know there aren't any fancy city gals who want to take care of an old man like me. You're trying to make me feel spry."

"Call it what you will. I still think you should get out more. You are a fine looking man. Who knows, there might be a nice lady out there who'd be willing to take on the challenge."

"Well, unfortunately, I have one of those, and believe me, one is enough." The doctor cut his eyes in Sarah's direction.

Feisty old Sarah picked up on his remark, and away she went with her acid tongue. "I'll have *ya* to know that the last *thang* I want to do, in my few remaining years, is take care of the likes of *you*!"

"Don't raise your blood pressure, Sarah. I was only kidding. I admit there are days I'd have a difficult time without you, but there are days I'd sure like to try."

"*Ya* ungrateful old rascal! *Ya* make me so mad I could spit!" spouted Sarah with her hands on her ample hips.

"Just look at you two arguing like a couple of school kids. Stop it. Let's have a peaceful meal," exclaimed Remmie.

Everyone enjoyed Sarah's fine home cooked meal of fried okra, splatter fried cornbread, tomato pie, and ice tea. Yum! Yum!

After the kitchen was cleaned to Sarah's specifications, the ladies retreated to the den while Dr. Remington returned to his study for a nap. "Sarah, that was a fantastic lunch. You sure do know your way around a kitchen."

"My maw started us out early *learnin'* to cook, clean, and sew. She said if *ya* want a good man, be a good cook. I believed her, and worked hard at *learnin'* all I could, and just look where it got me---*waitin'* on an ungrateful man who *don't* like *nothin'* I do."

"Sarah, you know better than that. Daddy loves you. He does appreciate what you do for him. He just isn't going to tell you. I know how stubborn he is, but I also know that you are family to both of us. You can depend on him, and on me."

"Oh now, now missy girl, don't let my *rantin'* get next to *ya*. But that old pooh in the study is a horse of a different color. He's so cantankerous, his hide won't hold him."

Jesse burst out laughing. "Sarah, you say the strangest things I've ever heard. Where do you come up with those crazy sayings?"

"They just come out. I reckon it's river talk. You know, I've lived here all my life. Folks talk different *round* here. I remember when I *wus* a *chil'*, *playin'* on the edge of a cotton patch while Maw and others picked all day. The *thangs* I *heared* them people say *kinda* stuck *wimme.* I went to school all twelve years, and the teachers tried to teach me proper English, but *everbody* talked like this, so I did too."

"Did you really live here on the river?"

"*Shore* did, Jesse. Just down the river a ways, in a little shack. It was *still a* standing last time I *wus* there, but that *wus* many years ago. *Ya* know they built *thang*s to last back then. I'll take *ya* down *there if'n ya'd* like to see it?"

"Oh, yes, I'd love to see it. Come on, Remmie. It'll be like when we were kids, and had an adventure. My brothers and I used to build forts in the woods, and pretend we were searching for hidden treasure. Did you ever do things like that?"

"I did a few things like that. You two go on ahead; I'll catch up by the bend in the river. I need to talk with my father for a minute."

Sarah and Jesse headed for the river path, chatting as they went. Remmie headed for her father's study. Dr. Remington was lying on the sofa. "What is it Remmie? What is on your mind? What decision have you made?"

"I've decided to tell Jesse about my life before I was Remmie."

With a stare that intensified, Dr. Remington spoke in tones that denoted his displeasure. "I'm not often angry with you, but I will be if you proceed with this plan. You know full well how I feel about anyone ever knowing about our family history. You are my daughter; you were Melissa's daughter, and that's that! Furthermore, you gave me your word about this a long time ago!"

"Well, unfortunately, it isn't that cut and dried for me. I am older now; I have many unresolved feelings, and many fears that I have to deal with constantly. You---you---won't always be here when I need to talk. Who will I turn to then?

"It's easy for you to tell me what is right for me, or how I should react to my past now, but what about when you are gone? Then who will I talk to? Who will care that I have all this pain locked up inside me, and who will help me, then? I didn't think you would have an answer to that,

Daddy. I made you those promises when I was a child. Well, I've changed. I'm almost thirty years old. You are eighty years old. When you leave me, I will be alone in a world where no one really knows me. Daddy, please release me from my promise."

Unrelenting, the elder doctor stared at his lovely daughter and in a strained voice said, "I will never give my blessing to you on this matter. Melissa and I are all the past you need. You are a Remington! You have a place of respect in this community as well as in Birmingham where you work. Leave well enough alone. Get on with your career. Find a good man, get married, and give me some grandchildren before I die.

"Remmie, I fear this will only cause you more pain. I truly believe you will come to grips with your past as you get older. Everything will be alright, honey." Dr. Remington embraced his daughter, patting her back, while he tried to encourage a consenting response from her. But Remmie remained silent.

Finally, Remmie stood, composed herself, and spoke in a quiet deliberate tone, "Daddy, you mean everything to me. I never want to hurt you, but you are wrong about this. I'll have to make my own decision about what it is right for me. I promise you that I will keep this secret from public knowledge as long as you live. But I am telling Jesse about my past. We will simply have to agree to disagree."

Remmie hurried to catch up with her friends. Her resolve was stronger than ever…*I will pursue this. I will tell Jesse, and one day, I will find out who I really am.*

CHAPTER THREE

In a couple of minutes, the three were together again, and off to find's Sarah's old home place. The atmosphere was cheerful. The day was magnificent. The smell of honeysuckle filled the river air. As they walked, they heard the river flowing over rocks, creating a tranquil sound.

The kudzu vine got thicker as they moved away from the river a few hundred yards. They were no longer on a path, not even an animal trail. Sarah knew she was near the old home place, so she kept searching. Remmie and Jesse stumbled their way through briars and vines of all sorts trying to clear the way so Sarah didn't hurt herself. Sarah was the scout, directing them to the left, then to the right until---there it was.

"*I be* dog! *Thar* it is! The *blamed old* kudzu has *bout* taken the place over. This place holds so many happy memories for me. I *wus borned* in this old house. My mother and a neighbor lady birthed me right yonder in that side room. Momma said I *wus* the most painful of her eight *young-uns* to birth, but the most joyful to raise. I reckon *y'all* find hard to believe." Sarah had a question mark in her voice as she looked back at Remmie and Jesse over her shoulder.

"Well, I *wus* a good *chil'*. I *done everthang* my folks wanted me to do. I went to church *ever* Sunday, I stayed away from wild boys, and I graduated from high school. Fact of the matter is, I *wus* the first of the eight *young-uns* to graduate. My folks *wus* so proud of me. I remember how they clapped and cheered at my graduation. The principal, a city *feller*, nearly had a fit when they stood up and hollered out my name as he handed me my diploma. I bet all his *kin-folk* graduated from school. He just couldn't imagine what it *wus* like to have the first high school graduate in the family.

I can still see my pa beaming with joy, and Maw just a *bawlin'*. I *wus* glad I had made them so happy.

"Ya know, *ya* don't have memories *floodin* back *everday*. It's good to have roots that go deep in a place like mine *does* right here. I buried my folks not far from here by the little country church where they got married. My pa died first, and Maw just couldn't go on without him, so she just gave up, and died a few weeks later.

"I thought my heart would burst out of me, the day I put her in the ground by Pa. She meant *everthang* to me. She *wus* what I wanted to be. So smart she *wus*, and sewed so *purty.* Maw always kept herself fixed up nice when Pa came home. She said a woman could keep her man at home *if'n* she wanted to. She *shore* knew how to keep Pa at home, *caus-en* that's where he *wus* or he *wus* at work.

"I stayed here day and night when they *wus* old and sick. They loved it here. Pa used to say, 'Listen to the river…it'll tell you all life's secrets.' Maw called him a dreamer and a poet. All she wanted *wus* to live out her days on the river, go to church, and pray for her family. That *wus* her life. Some might say she never *mounted* to much, but *thar's* eight *young-uns* that'll tell *ya* different.

"My two older brothers are preachers, and my two older sisters are teachers. They all had to work hard to catch up with their educations after *droppin* out of school to work. My three younger sisters all married preachers of some kind or the other. I'm the only old maid *amongst 'em.* I reckon if God had given me the man I prayed for, I wouldn't have been here to take care of my folks. I *wus* meant to be here just for them."

Sarah caught herself, and turned around quickly to find the two younger women crying their eyes out. "What *y'all cryin' bout*? Those *wus* the happiest days of my life. I didn't mean to go on like that, but *seein'* this old place just brought it all back in a flood."

"Sarah, I'm so touched by your story. I loved hearing about your parents, as well as about your life here on the river. It makes me wish I had those memories of my own," said Remmie as she hugged her friend.

Oh, now, *chil'*, you have some wonderful memories of your life here with the Remingtons. They've loved *ya* more than anyone else ever could. You've been so blessed by them in so many ways. Look at that beautiful home back yonder, your fine education, your financial security, not to mention the love and stability they've given *ya.*"

"I'm very grateful for all those things, and I do know how fortunate I am, but when I hear someone talking about their family, their childhood, like you just did, I can't help myself. I feel like I've missed so much."

"Now, now, you're a fine person, Remmie. You'll come to terms with this stuff. You'll be just fine. Lean on the Lord, honey. He knows what's best for *ya*."

Turning her attention to Jesse, Sarah said, "Come on over here, Jesse, and stop that *bawlin*. I never meant to get so sentimental."

"Sarah, that was so beautiful. You have so many sweet memories. Your family was obviously very special. I wish I could have known them, and somehow I feel like I do. You made me feel like a part of your family; I'll never forget it."

Remmie was the first to enter the old wooden house where Sarah grew up. She looked around, surprised to see pieces of furniture still in it. About that time, Sarah, followed by Jesse, came inside. "I *be dog*, this here is my momma's table that Pa built for her. She needed it to set a lamp on while she sewed at night. Pa built it one morning, put the stain on it that afternoon, and Momma sewed by the lamp that night."

"Let's take the table back to the house, Sarah. We can clean it up, or maybe refinish it. Then you can use it in your room, or anywhere you want."

"I don't know Remmie. Makes me *kinda* feel like I'm grave *robbin'* or *somethin'*."

"Nonsense, Sarah! Your folks are gone. They would rather you have it than for it to rot away out here, all by itself."

"I---I---reckon you're right. I would love *havin'* Momma's table in my *sittin'* room. Okay, let's do it."

~~~~~~~~~~~~~~~~~~~~

"I really enjoyed today. Did you, Jesse?"

"Well, let's say I learned things I didn't know before. Sarah's stroll down memory lane was very interesting. I admire her so much. She's one in a million."

"I'll never forget that either. She's a treasure all right. I know my mother loved her, and so does my dad. What Dad doesn't like is knowing he needs to be taken care of. That's really what gets his goat. He takes it out on poor Sarah, but for the most part, he's joking. Sarah gets all fired up, but deep down she knows the score with him.
~~~~~~~~~~~~~~~~~~~~

"When I was young, I used to hear my folks talking about what they were going to do for Sarah on special occasions. They also talked about their plans to take care of her financially for the rest of her life.

"I do feel sorry for Sarah, because she tries so hard to please him, only to be met with his bad attitudes. I know how he really feels, but I wish he would show Sarah. Dad kind of shut down after my mother died. He only had room in his heart for me."

"Do you think she'll stay on here if she becomes ill or incapacitated?"

"I sure hope so. I'll make sure she's well cared for as long as she lives. I know she'll never agree to come into the city with me, so, I'll make whatever provisions are needed to allow her to stay here.."

"What will you do with River Oaks after they both are gone?"

"I'll keep it. It's too special to let go. This is the only roots I have. I couldn't part with it. Anyway, I've got some far off plans for this estate that just might involve you. We'll talk about them, too. It seems my mind has been working overtime lately."

"Rem, I saw the look on your face while Sarah was talking about her roots. I knew what you were thinking. I want you to know that I'm ready to hear whatever you have to tell me. I'll be here for you, Rem."

"Oh girl, you don't how bad I want to tell you, but my dad is dead set against it. I tried to explain to him how much I need someone other than him that I can talk to, but he refuses to listen."

"Well, since when has that ever stopped you from telling me what you want me to know? I remember when he didn't want me at that big party, back when we were juniors. That didn't stop you from finding a way to have me here."

"That was pretty crazy, wasn't it? I can still see the look on his face when he realized the chick in the blonde wig under all the theatrical make-up was none other than, Jessica Elaine Morehouse."

"You, the person who pulled that off, is worrying about things her father doesn't want me to know? Give me a break."

"This is very different, Jess. I wanted to make a point with him, then. He was being so-so-so…."

"Prejudiced? Is that the word you're looking for?"

"No, I mean…yes. I suppose that word fits as well as any. I just don't like applying it to my father. This is very different. He could be hurt by my actions. I might change some history, and I might not like what I find. There could be consequences not only for me, but for Dad also.

"He's very wealthy. What if I locate people who think they have a right to some of his money? You know how the courts are right now. Anything is truly possible. I have no desire to cause Daddy any problems. Perhaps, I should wait until he's gone to probe into my past. I really just don't know anymore. I do know that I'm very tired; I think I'll go to bed early. We can talk more in the morning. Good night, Jesse."

"Whatever you say. Good night, sleep tight, and don't let the bedbugs bite," joked Jesse, trying to get her friend in a better mood before they parted for night. She wasn't sure it worked.

Remmie found sanctuary in her old familiar room among all the treasures she had gathered over the years at River Oaks. In her room and in this house, she had history, but outside of River Oaks, she felt disconnected and somewhat, alone.

Remmie got cozy in her bed with all her pillows. As she talked to the Lord, she told Him she didn't understand why she felt so strongly about finding her biological family. She told Him about her fears, and the uncertainty that plagued her mind. She also told Him how much she loved the Remingtons, and how thankful she was that they found her. Last of all, she told the Lord about her desire to share her story with Jesse. She asked Him to show her if that was wrong. Finally, after the "Amen," she was settled and fell asleep quickly.

On the other side of the hall, Jesse tossed in the bed with her eyes wide open. Her mind raced with what she had learned about Remmie, and with what she would hear in the morning. She, too, talked to the Lord, "Lord, I want to help Remmie. Will I be able to? Help me not to let her down." She lay quietly, but sleep wasn't coming, and staring at the ceiling wasn't one of her favorite past times. So, she got up and headed for the kitchen.

Earlier she had smelled a wonderful aroma coming from that direction. She figured Sarah had been baking, and that could only mean one thing, a serious bounty of something very delicious waiting for her there. From beneath the door, a light indicated someone else was already in the kitchen. Jesse paused. *What if it's Dr. Remington,* she thought. She didn't want to encounter him, since she knew Remmie had told him her plans. But before she could decide, a familiar voice came from the kitchen.

"Which one of *ya* is that? Come on in here and show *yoreself.*"

Jesse opened the door, and there sat Sarah eating a cookie and sipping on a cup of hot coffee. Sarah pointed to the cookie jar and said, "Have one. There's plenty of cold milk in the fridge."

"What are you doing up? I thought you'd be out like a light after all the activity today."

"Me? Well that shows what you know, young lady. I can stay up all night when I have to. Anyway, I got so excited *bout* my table that I *plum* got out of the notion to sleep. What's *yore* excuse?"

"I can't seem to get to sleep. I wore myself out tossing around until I remembered smelling those cookies baking. So, I decided they might help me sleep, or at least make the hours awake more fun."

"I have a *purty* good idea what's *botherin' ya*, and I think *ya* know too. It's Remmie, ain't it? She's told *ya somethin' bout* herself, *ain't* she?"

"Well, should I add mind reading to your list of talents? You're right, she has. I can't seem to get it off my mind, either. I hope I'm the one to help her with this."

"You'll do fine. I knew Remmie *wus* adopted, but the Dr. and his Mrs. didn't want it talked about, so I kept my mouth shut. That's all I know, but I have a *feelin'* there's lots more *comin'*. Remmie's too special not to have these questions answered. There may be someone somewhere who needs her, like she needs them. I personally hope she finds what she's *lookin'* for."

"Wouldn't Dr. Remington be very upset with you if he knew how you feel?"

"He *shore* would, that's why he don't know. He *ain't* right *bout* this situation. But it's not my place to tell him that. I do my *talkin' bout* it to the good Lord. He'll fix it. That I know for *shore*. I better go to bed or it'll be time to get up. You best stop *eatin'* those cookies or you'll be up all night in the bathroom. I fill *them thangs* full of bran, so the doctor can have regular eliminations."

Jesse stopped eating mid-cookie, and returned to her room.

CHAPTER FOUR

The sun had just crept over the oaks when Remmie woke up from a restful sleep. She felt peaceful, waking up in her own room, in a house where her life had changed so dramatically. Everything here made her feel secure enough to find out whatever it was about her past that her father didn't want her to know.

Standing before the beautiful beveled mirror her mother had bought on one of her trips abroad, Remmie brushed her deep auburn hair as she stared into her crystal green eyes. She studied her lovely face while her mind asked these questions: *whose eyes are these, whose nose, and whose hair? Mirror, mirror on my wall, whose child am I after all? Will I ever know the answer to that question? I wonder.*

Remmie heard a light knock on her door. "Remmie are you awake?"

"Come in, Jess, I'm up."

Jesse walked in, slightly slumped, and holding her stomach. "What's wrong, Jess? Are you ill?"

"I'm ill alright, but not like you mean. I couldn't sleep, so I went to the kitchen and ate several of Sarah's cookies. I'm mad, and well, I'm very uncomfortable."

Before Jesse could continue, Remmie laughed as she went into her bathroom returning with two small pills. "I know exactly what your problem is. I did that *once* myself."

"Once is right. I'll never eat another oatmeal raisin cookie as long as I live--- if I live. I've been in the bathroom all night. It's amazing that your father is still alive. I understand why he stays in his study all the time. It's right next to the bathroom."

"You'll be fine. Don't eat anything for about an hour. Your system should settle down by then. Come with me. I want to take a walk in the meadow behind the house."

"Are you sure these pills will fix me up? Otherwise, I better stay close to the house."

"I'm sure. You'll be fine. Come on. You don't want to miss this. It has always been my favorite early morning meditation spot. You're gonna love it."

~~~~~~~~~~~~~~~~~~~~~~~~~~

Leaving the house through the kitchen door, they walked across the backyard through a gate that had a trellis over it. The trellis was covered in morning glory, in full bloom. The dainty purple and yellow blooms hung so thick, the green of the vine and the trellis could hardly be seen.

The path on the other side of the gate was incredible, something out of a *Southern Living Magazine.* Rocks lay this way and that, covered with moss or miniature vines. There were bunches of daisies, clumps of daylilies, tiger lilies, violets, alyssum, and geraniums. It looked like a place from a movie set which was designed for lovers. Places that don't really exist, but here it was. The sun added just the right amount of brilliance in the form of light spears piercing the mist which lay near the ground. The birds gathered breakfast from among the rocks; the squirrels scampered about, retrieving hidden snacks from secret stashes. At the end of the path was the sprawling meadow, all decorated for spring. It was a wonderland for the imagination.

Remmie and Jesse walked further down into the meadow. Near the stream was a lovely tree with tiny blooms covering it like lights on a Christmas tree. The friends sat down in the shade, and Remmie's story began, again.

"By the time you reach age ten you are considered un-adoptable. People want infants or babies. A few will take toddlers or younger children. The system makes you feel so ugly, so rejected. No one says that you're ugly, but it's the way you feel. It destroys your self-image, and your self-confidence.

"I suppose I remember the worst of it, even though I do try to remember the good parts. But they don't make up for the bad. I mean, this system is supposed to help kids, protect them, and educate them. It's a train wreck, Jesse, and no one seems to be coming to the rescue. Maybe that someone is me."

"You? What do you mean? How can you help?"
~~~~~~~~~~~~~~~~~~~~~~~~~~

"That, I can't answer just yet. You know I told you, I had lots of stuff floating around in my head. Well, that's one of them. I can't let it go, or it won't let me go. Either way, Jess, something must be done for the children, who have no voice.

"I lived with strangers from the time I can remember until the Remingtons came to that home and adopted me. Most of the time, I didn't know the families I was with by name. As I got older, I did, but not when I was three and four years old. They were strangers, Jesse."

"I can't imagine how it would feel to wake up in a house full of strangers when you are so young. It has to be one of the most frightening experiences ever."

"You are right about that. The fear paralyzed me. I would stay in bed until someone came and made me get up. Then I would sit in the corner of the room as if something was going to creep up on me."

"Remmie, it is so difficult to hear how you grew up. How have you gotten passed it is my question? How were you able to cope with college, and now, your career?"

"Because I knew that getting my education and subsequent career would make me secure so that I never had to be at anyone's mercy again. I made myself believe that with time, education, and a successful career, I would forget the horrors of the past. That hasn't proven to be true so far, but I never want to be dependent on anyone for my security again. I have to make it for myself. Even after I was adopted, and I knew how blessed I was, the feeling of not being dependent on others didn't leave. I still feel that way, Jess. That's one reason I don't think I'll ever marry."

"Weren't any of your foster parents good to you?"

"Good to me? Yes, I had some who were kind people. They didn't beat me or yell at me, but they had kids of their own. That was a problem within itself. The parents were more sympathetic to their biological children. The biological children were jealous of the foster children. So when the mother was not there, her children were vicious. I ended up doing all the chores. But I never complained because I knew there were places where I could be placed that were far worse.

"Some of the mamas seemed very affectionate, but you better look out when something went wrong. She turned into a monster right before your eyes. This mama was usually un-employed, and she needed the foster care funds to make ends meet. In this situation, you never got new clothes or shoes. God forbid if you should get sick. Some of my worst beatings came when I was sick and needed to see a doctor.

"I remember a Christmas Eve when I was sick. I had a high fever and needed something to drink. So I tried to get to the kitchen without interrupting *Mom*, but I threw up in the hall. Being so weak, I just lay there waiting for her to come. I knew I was going to get it, and sure enough, she kicked me to the other end of the hall. After several additional kicks, I threw up again and fainted.

"The next thing I knew, she was rubbing my face in the vomit, and yelling in a drunken voice all kinds of obscene words that I promised myself I'd never say to anyone. When I got choked on my own vomit, I passed out again. When I woke up, I was in an emergency room. There was a bright light hanging over the bed, and a doctor leaning over me. His voice was so kind and he was saying the sweetest things to me. For a brief moment, I felt safe. Then the door flew open, and in came *Mom*. Although she seemed composed, she was obviously intoxicated. As she cried and slobbered all over me, she called me her little angel, and said how she wanted to take me home for Christmas.

"The horror I felt must have shown on my face, because the doctor immediately told her that I was being admitted for a few days. *Mom* didn't like it at all, but the doctor wasn't asking for her approval. Feeling great relief, I wanted to hug the doctor, but I knew all too well that kind men don't always stay that way. *Mom* left after a while, and the doctor returned with his nurse to escort me to my room in the pediatric ward.

"I was greeted by brightly colored walls with pictures of clowns, circus animals, and carousel horses painted on them. I hadn't seen anything that pretty in a long time. They wheeled me into a room with six beds, three on each side. Most were empty, but there was another little girl in the bed next to mine. The doctor told me the girl's name was Jenny. He also said the hospital always tried to get the children home for Christmas, but Jenny and I would be spending Christmas in the hospital. Reassuringly, the doctor told us everyone would do their best to make our stay as pleasant as possible. Believe it or not, it was the best Christmas I remember before coming to River Oaks. One nurse brought a tiny Christmas tree, which Jenny and I decorated with popcorn garlands and stars that we cut out of construction paper.

"On Christmas morning, we were surprised to find gaily wrapped packages all around the tiny tree. Some had my name, and some had Jenny's name. Our eyes were as big as saucers as we tore into the packages. All the nurses gathered around us to see our reactions.

"In mine was a Barbie dressed in a Cinderella gown. She had long red hair like mine. I also had a carrying case and additional outfits for her. In another package, I found an outfit just for me. No one had ever worn it. I couldn't wait to put it on. It fit like a glove, and I felt so pretty.

"Jenny had a blonde-haired Barbie like her, and an outfit that fit her like mine fit me. When we were all dressed, we stood looking at each other. Jenny was very pretty with long blonde curls, blue eyes, and a big smile. We didn't have to say anything; we knew we were foster children. I did notice that Jenny looked very pale, and she got tired so easy.

"Later that day, we had a real holiday feast with turkey, dressing, pecan pie, fruit salad, and red velvet cake. After lunch, we had warm baths in rose scented oil. We were put into clean gowns and into bed for a nap.

"Jenny got worse that afternoon, so she was taken to another room. I didn't see her anymore. Later, the doctor came in to ask me some questions about *Mom.* I was too afraid to answer them. He said he would have me moved to another home if I told him how I got the bruises on my sides and back. I just gave him my famous *I don't know* shrug. He encouraged me to tell the truth so he could help me. *The truth,* I thought, *is what gets you into all kinds of trouble.*

"Early the next morning, I was awakened from a deep sleep by an all too familiar voice. It was *Mom.* She was there to take me home. The kind doctor checked me over, gave me a reassuring pat on my shoulder, and reminded me of what he had said the day before. Of course, I had nothing to say about that, but I did want to know about Jenny.

"When I asked him about Jenny, his face grew strained, and his hesitation told me that he was searching for the right words to tell me something he wasn't sure I needed to hear. Finally, he spoke in that same kind voice, 'Jenny was a very sick girl, not like you. You only had a virus that goes away in a few days, but Jenny had a disease that we can't cure. She's well now; she's with God.'

"A smile came to my face as well as sense of relief for the little blondie with whom I had spent the happiest Christmas of my life. With God, how peaceful that sounded to me. I surprised the doctor when I said, 'I've thought about going to heaven many times. I wonder sometimes why God lets babies come here in the first place. Why can't we just stay in heaven with Him? Maybe Jenny will ask God that question for me.'

"Nearby *Mom* waited anxiously to take me away from the hospital. She pretended to be glad to see me, but we both knew the truth. As we walked down the hall, her grip on my hand got tighter and tighter. I was afraid to tell her that she was hurting me, but I think she knew. Just before we got to the exit, the doctor and two ladies appeared. *Mom* stopped in her tracks, and her grip got so tight my fingers were getting numb. Finally, one of the ladies said, 'We are from Child Protective Services, and we have a complaint against you.'

'Me?' came *Mom's* reply.

'Yes, I'm afraid so,' said the lady solemnly. 'We would like for you to release Rebecca into our custody right now without any trouble.'

"*Mom* dropped to her knees, making her eyes level with mine. 'Becca, have you told these people a lie about your mother?'

"My head was shaking side to side as fast as I could move it. Her grip let me know that I was in big trouble if I gave any indication of misconduct on her part. I was terrified!

"Calmly the doctor explained that I hadn't said anything, although he had asked me. He went on to say, he was making a professional judgment that I had been abused. He said the bruises on my body were from kicks, and he also felt that I wasn't given medical attention in a timely manner. The doctor stated that when I arrived in the emergency room, I had vomit caked on my face and in my hair in a pattern that he believed resulted from a deliberate act by someone.

"*Mom* was in shock. She pled her innocence, as well as her love for me. Thank God, they weren't buying it. After what seemed an eternity, *Mom* was taken away by one of the ladies, and I was taken by the other."

"Remmie, that's just awful! It's difficult to believe such horrible abuse is allowed by an agency designed for the protection of children. Were these isolated incidents?"

"I'm afraid not, Jesse. I haven't done an investigation, but I have seen examples of it since I've been a doctor. I've seen many young children in foster care come to the emergency room in appalling shape. I personally reported ten cases last year. Multiply that by the number of doctors seeing children each year and the number is astounding."

"How can we help the children?"

"That's a question that has haunted me for years. I don't know the answer, but I am sure I want to be a part of the solution."

"Me, too. Where do we start?"

"It won't be easy, I'm afraid. There's a whole lot of bureaucratic red tape to cut through."

"Perhaps my legal background can help us. I've really been considering returning to college to finish my degree. I love my work in the news media, but my first love was the law, and hearing this makes me want to do everything I can to fix it."

"Well, first of all, I have my father to contend with. He's opposed to any effort on my part that might lead to the truth about my past, which includes the foster care system. He has a point when it comes to his privacy. You know this is a small town."

"Yeah, I do understand about small towns. There's an old joke in our little town that says the women really don't know everything, but if the town is small enough, they just might."

"I'd say that's pretty accurate here, too."

"There has to be a way around these hurdles, Remmie. We have to try."

"I wish I knew the way. I'm at my wits end. I've tried talking to my father, but he's as stubborn as a mule. I just can't ignore his feelings completely. He and Mother have done so much for me."

"Of course, you are right, but you know me when a good cause comes along."

"Seems that I can remember a few *not so good* causes that captured your attention."

"Oh let's not talk about those right now. I'm serious about this. We have to find a way to help the children!"

"I agree, one hundred percent, but right now, we have to get back to the house or Sarah will be mad that we're late for breakfast."

The ladies talked about the possible solutions to the situation with foster care in the state as they walked back to the house. Sure enough, Sarah had prepared a feast: hot buttered biscuits, grits, ham, and homemade mayhaw jelly.

The remainder of the day Remmie wanted to spend with her father. She wanted to somehow persuade him to change his mind about her intentions to talk with Jesse.

"Lord, please give me the words that will help my father understand how I feel, and how important it is for me to know who I really am. Amen."

CHAPTER FIVE

After some hem-hawing, Remmie was able to talk her father into riding into Riverview. As it turned out, Dr. Remington needed to talk with his attorney, Hadley Markham.

Hadley Markham had been Benjamin Remington's attorney ever since the doctor had retired from practicing medicine in the city and moved to River Oaks full time. Although Mr. Markham was well thought of in the community, Remmie had never trusted him. In fact, she really didn't like him at all. It was one of those things you can't quite put your finger on, but you know something isn't right. Try as she did, she just couldn't shake her feelings about him. Unfortunately, Remmie wasn't the best at hiding her feelings. So, over the years, Mr. Markham had become aware of her dislike for him.

Remmie found a parking place right in front of Mr. Markham's office. She and Jesse walked to the general store while her father took care of his business. The general store had pretty much anything you needed, such as clothes, shoes, boots, guns, ammo, farm implements, seeds, and hardware. The old wooden building had lots of character, like the narrow wooden slats on the ceiling, walls, and floors, the potbellied stove in the middle of the store, which was the only heat, and the light bulbs that hung from the ceiling on long cords. There was also a string used to turn on the lights.

All customers were greeted by a pickle barrel and a jar of hard candy. It was very quaint and country, especially since the year was 1990. Remmie always visited when she came to River Oaks.

As the ladies walked toward the Victorian house that was Mr. Markham's office, they chatted about the restoration that had been done on the beautiful old home. When they entered, they were delighted with the lovely period furnishings, high ceilings accented by wide molding stained in cherry, and the chair rail around the room. It was like taking a step back in time. The long narrow windows with transoms over them were draped in mini-prints in shades of green and rose. A camel-backed sofa in maroon sat in the middle of the room. A Queen Anne chair sat near the fireplace.

"This is so elegant. Someone paid attention to every detail. Mr. Markham, or his wife, has very good taste."

"This room reflects more good taste than that of the attorney, believe me," said Remmie. "And he's not married."

"Sounds like you don't like him much."

"That's a fair assumption, but my feelings may not be fair to the man. He's tacky. He has a gross lack of manners. His personal hygiene is in question. I often find myself wondering how he can have such a fine education and still be so tacky. Don't judge him by me. I really can't explain why I feel this way, but I've never trusted him. Anyway, you make your own decision."

Simultaneously with Remmie's remarks, the office door opened and out came Dr. Remington, followed by Hadley Markham. Mr. Markham was short, slightly balding, with an overgrown mustache, but to say his eyebrows were overgrown was an understatement. It would be like saying the everglades were an overgrown lawn. They were huge, bushy, and swept upward making him look like he was in a perpetual state of fright. Comical would not be an exaggeration.

Jesse's observations, plus the look on Remmie's face combined to create one of those awkward moments when one can't help but laugh. Just as Dr. Remington was about to introduce his attorney, Jesse lost her composure. It was a moment if only captured on film, would bring thrills for years to come.

"Well, Hadley, you know Remmie, and this is her friend…

At that point, Jesse was laughing so hard she couldn't control herself. All she managed to do was nod to her introduction, which the good doctor was unable to complete. Remmie made some explanation about a joke they had remembered from college. Jesse fought to regain her composure, but the humiliating belly laugh kept coming. In desperation, she excused herself, and walked outside, followed by her annoying friend.

"You've done it this time. Your father will never want to bring me to town again. How could you just keep on until there he was, and more hilarious than you described?"

"You were pretty hilarious yourself. I doubt Markham had any inkling we were laughing at him. He is so smug; he doesn't know an insult when he gets one."

"Wow, you really don't like him, do you? One favor please, if you ever start having such feelings about me, you will let me know?"

"I'm sorry, Jesse. I'm sure the Lord isn't too pleased with me right now. But I can't shake my gut feeling about him. He and I have had disagreements over the years about my father's estate, but this is deeper than that. But my dad likes him, so what I think doesn't matter much."

Dr. Remington emerged from the building with a manila envelope in his hand, and a puzzled look on his face. "Got your tickle box turned over, did you, Jesse?"

"I'm so sorry. I'll go and apologize to Mr. Markham if you would like. I feel terrible about my behavior, sir."

"No need to apologize. Knowing my lovely daughter as I do, I wouldn't be at all surprised to learn that she had something to do with you finding Hadley so amusing."

Remmie stuck her pretty nose up and walked to the car. She never mentioned it again, and neither did her father.

~~~

All too soon the week-end came to an end. Remmie and Jesse had packed the car. Just the good-byes remained to close out two glorious days at River Oaks. Although the visit had uncovered secrets Jesse hadn't expected to learn, all in all, the visit had been relaxing.

Remmie gave her father and Sarah hugs and kisses. Jesse hugged them too, and expressed her gratitude for allowing her to visit. She also apologized one more time for her behavior at Mr. Markham's office.

Eventually, they drove through the massive gates, leaving River Oaks behind. But in the secret thoughts of both young women was the feeling that some way, River Oaks held them firmly in its grasp.
~~~

CHAPTER SIX

The city was like a war zone after the tranquility of the country. Sounds assaulted their ears as horns blew, car alarms screamed, sirens blared, and engines droned as they struggled to make it up the next hill. Additionally, the diesel fumes and other contaminates that filled the air were an unwelcoming, welcome for Remmie and Jesse as they returned to life in an industrial city.

Jesse parked the car in front of Remmie's condo. The ladies spent a few minutes talking about the events that had bound them closer together than they had ever been. "Thanks, Jesse. You really came through for me. I owe you a deep debt of gratitude."

"Hey, stop right there. You don't owe me anything. What are friends for, if not to support one another, believe in one another, and share one another's secrets? I'm still so shocked that I never had a clue about any of this before this week-end. I don't know how you do it Remmie. I would have caved in before now."

"All I know is I've tried with all my strength to honor my father's wishes, and keep a promise I made to him when I was very young. Now, at almost thirty years old, I find that I can no longer do what he has asked. Being able to finally talk about my life before the Remingtons has been such a relief. Jesse, I don't know how to explain what I feel now. But it's all good. I know Dad is wrong, but he hasn't ever required too much of me, so it was very difficult to go against him. I trust you, Jesse. I know you will keep my secret."

"I'll take it to my grave. You never have to worry about it."

"I know, and that's why we are best friends. I've always known your character. You have a pure heart. Thanks for letting me into that heart."

"Think nothing of it, madam. And just think of all the nay sayers, who said our friendship would never last. I guess we've proved them wrong."

"Yes, Jess, we have. Everyone, including my father, who thought our relationship was ill advised, was wrong. Our friendship is until death. That's not intended to sound matrimonial either."

"Neither race, nor creed, nor color can keep us apart," spouted Jesse, as if she were one of the musketeers---the two musketeers in this case.

The doorman arrived to help with Remmie's luggage, and Jesse drove away with a quick wave over her shoulder.

The message indicator on Remmie's machine was blinking. She motioned for Sam, the doorman to put down her suitcases, gave him a tip, and closed the door behind him. Then she pressed the button to retrieve her messages. But the voice on the recording was a complete surprise to her.

"Miss Remington, I need to see you right away. Call me as soon as you get this message."

Could she be right in her voice recognition or was she mistaken? It was obviously someone who knew her, and thought she would know them. Remmie replayed the message. After hearing the voice again, she knew she was right, but why was he calling her?

What could this mean? Why would he be calling me? Should I return the call? Should I call my father first? Finally, she reached the conclusion that when in doubt, wait a while. Trying to put the call out of her mind, she went into the kitchen to make herself something to eat. Just as she was about to take the first bite of her favorite sandwich, the phone rang. *Oh shoot! I'm hungry! I don't want to talk now,* thought Remmie with the sandwich to her lips. *I'll just let it ring.* So she took a big bite of the delicious turkey club. *Ummm, this is so good*, she thought, savoring every tasty morsel. Then, she heard the voice coming through the machine.

"Miss Remington, if you're there, pick up. I need to speak with you."

Well, I'm not ready for you yet, Mr. Markham, thought Remmie as she continued eating. After cleaning up the kitchen, Remmie thought that perhaps she should return the call. Surely, it was something about her father's business the other day, but she was puzzled as to why he had called her instead of her dad.

"Markham here."

"Remmie here."

"Oh, good evening, Miss Remington, and how are you?"

"Quite well, Mr. Markham, and to what do I owe the pleasure of this call?"

"I want to talk with you regarding your father's concerns about your adoption."

"I beg your pardon. Did my father ask you to call me?"

"Well, I certainly wouldn't be doing anything Dr. Remington was not aware of, now would I?"

"I suppose not, but I'm still confused about your need to discuss my adoption with me, rather than with my father. You said you were calling about his concerns, not mine. Explain, please."

"Miss Remington, I am well aware of your feelings for me, and I can disregard that. However, I am your father's trusted confidant and attorney, a position for which I would hope you could find some respect."

Remmie searched her memory banks for some shred of respect for this person, but a screen popped up, *Sorry no matching files*. Even as the words were forming on her tongue, she stopped herself and agreed to meet him, but only if he came into the city. Mr. Markham agreed to meet the next afternoon in the staff parlor at the Medical Center. Remmie's curiosity was overwhelming. But even her imagination couldn't conjure up what Hadley Markham could possibly want, or why her father hadn't told her to expect the call.

Monday afternoon at three o'clock Remmie reported to work. It appeared everyone had survived her absence over the long week-end. The trauma unit was unusually quiet, which can be boring for high strung professionals. But it was welcomed by Remmie. She felt distracted by the upcoming meeting with Markham, so it wasn't a great time for her to handle a trauma. It seemed four o'clock would never come.

Dr. Beau McCain was the other trauma surgeon on duty. Remmie told him about her meeting in the staff parlor. Since she was the senior doctor on duty, she told Beau to page her if she was needed. He agreed, and she left the trauma unit for her meeting.

Walking hurriedly through the endless maze of hallways, Remmie reviewed exactly what Markham had said to her. As she rounded the final turn, she wondered if Markham was already there. As she opened the door, her eyes scanned the room, and there he was in all his comical glory. She remembered Jesse's response to him, and almost burst out laughing herself, but that reaction was short lived. The conversation that followed was anything but humorous. Markham seemed smugger that usual today.

"Good afternoon, Mr. Markham. How may I help you?"

"Sit down Miss Remington. This may take some time."

"I don't think so, I'm on duty, and could be called away at any moment. So, please make this quick."

"As you wish, but I would prefer to give you some background before plunging in."

"Proceed, but be as brief as you can."

"After a recent conversation with your father about, shall we say mysteries in your past, your father asked me to look into your birth parents. He wanted to know where they live, and anything else I could find out that might cause you to have a better sense of yourself, and give you, as he put it, some peace of mind. Of course, I wasted no time in pursuing his wishes."

"Of course, you didn't. After all, he's probably your wealthiest client. And I'm sure you will be rewarded handsomely for your efforts."

"Now, now, Miss Remington, you of all people shouldn't be so cynical. You may be more common than you realize, instead of the royalty your father has insisted you to be."

"Just get on with it. You annoy me."

"As I was saying, I proceeded as your father requested, and the search didn't take long. Before I knew it, I had found out one of your family secrets, and well, being concerned for your father, I mean his health isn't all that good, you know. Anyway, I thought it best to share the news with you first. Perhaps, you and I can come to terms, and your father will never know about his only child."

Remmie's curiosity turned to anger. She let Markham have the brunt of her temper before she got control of herself. "You miserable little man. Have you come here to blackmail me? You ungrateful idiot. My father has put you where you are. Without him, you would be chasing ambulances. How dare you come here with this proposal behind my father's back, and assume that I will fall prey to the likes of *You*! *Get Out!*"

"Don't be too hasty, Remmie. You haven't heard my news yet. It's to your advantage to hear me out."

"Nothing you have to say is of any consequence to me. I am the daughter of Dr. and Mrs. Benjamin Remington. I should have left well enough alone. But my dear father cares so much for me, that he reached out to his so-called friend, and now look where we are! *No! No! Get Out!!*"

Remmie ran from the parlor, and down the hall in a fit of rage. By the time, she rounded the corner leading into the trauma unit, she was in tears, and failed to see Dr. McKinley approaching. They collided.

"Dr. Remington, my dear. What is it?"

Remmie was totally out of control and could not answer him coherently.

"Come into my office, and let's see what can be done to help you." Dr. McKinley led her into his office and closed the door. He sat down beside her on the sofa, waiting until the tears subsided. Gradually, Remmie began to calm down, regaining her composure. She was very embarrassed, but more than that, she didn't know what in the world she was going to tell him. One thing she did know, she wasn't telling what had just happened. This man was her boss, the Chief of Staff, and she didn't want him thinking she was falling apart at the seams, let alone that some horrible family secret was about to emerge that would bring reproach on the hospital.

"I'm terribly sorry, Dr. McKinley. I don't know what came over me. I don't usually react like that to anything. Please forgive me for allowing my emotions to take over that way. It won't happen again."

Dr. McKinley was a very distinguished looking man with a dark complexion, gray hair, and sparkling blue eyes. His eyes seemed to look directly into the soul. He was highly respected in the hospital for his skills as a doctor, as well as his administrative abilities. Since he had come on board, the quality of care given at the hospital had improved tremendously. Now, here he was sitting across from her, looking at her with those blue eyes that showed so much compassion. What was she going to say to him?

"Dr. Remington, I have known you for some time, and I know the level of professionalism you maintain. There is no excuse needed. I can see that you are distressed about something, but you do not have to tell me unless, of course, you desire to. I will do anything within my power to help you, but I will not pry into your personal affairs. Now, when you feel like it, you may return to your duties. Keep in mind, however, that I have deep regards for you, and don't let anything get too out of control before you handle it."

Remmie sat quietly for another moment. She would not let her mind think about what had happened. Her determination for perfection on the job took over. "I'm feeling much better, now. I should really get back to the unit. Thank you for your kindness, as well as your offer to help. I appreciate that very much."

As she turned to leave, Dr. McKinley spoke again, "Dr. Remington, you are an outstanding physician. If you weren't, you would not head up a shift for me. Keep in mind, that doctors are human, too. Maybe I should say mortal, just like everyone else, and sometimes we mortals need help. Those of us who are wise accept help."

Remmie paused with the doorknob in her hand, and with her face turned away from the older doctor, she said, “I may need your help, and I know you will be there for me. I have to deal with this myself right now. However, I won’t forget that I have people like you who care about me. Just knowing that makes this situation easier already.”

Remmie had absolutely no idea how to handle the situation that had been presented to her, but she knew one thing for sure: she would tell her father just as soon as she could get time to go to River Oaks. He would know what to do with Hadley Markham.

“Remmie, where have you been? I’ve been looking for you everywhere.”

“I told you that I had a meeting in the parlor. It took longer than I expected. Then Dr. McKinley called me into his office. Is there a problem, Beau?”

“No more than usual in this loony ward. I just like to see your smiling face around here. You are the prettiest boss lady I have ever had. Anyway, one of the nurses said she saw you, and you looked upset. Is there a problem? Old Blue Eyes doesn’t just call us in for chit-chat.”

“Well, believe it or not, today he did. Just plain chit-chat, that’s all it was.”

“You know what I think? I think he has eyes for you, lovely doctor. I suggest you meet with him in wide open spaces. That man-eating lush he’s married to has probably driven him over the edge.”

“Beau, you are so weird sometimes. Dr. McKinley is an honorable man. I’m stunned that you would say such a suggestive thing about him or his wife.”

“Stunned, are you? Stunning is more like it. You are a pretty woman, Remmie. I just thought I would throw that at you in the unlikely event someone hasn’t already told you. We should hustle our buns back to the loony ward.”

Almost the minute they entered the unit the doors flew open, and in came an accident victim. The team assembled. Each person knew their role, and they performed it to perfection. Remmie took charge. The initial exam revealed severe internal bleeding, possibly a ruptured spleen, or a kidney or liver laceration. A cat scan was ordered, but first his blood was matched and a bag was hung. Then Remmie followed the young man to the scanner, reassuring him that he would be alright. The man was frightened. He wanted to see his family. Remmie remained close, monitoring his vitals, checking for any signs that he might be going into shock.

The radiologist read the scan with Remmie observing. His conclusion was a lacerated liver and badly bruised kidney. Surgery was necessary to repair the liver, but the bruises would take care of themselves with time. Remmie gave the young man his prognosis. With his wife by his side, he gave Remmie the okay to do surgery.

Beau was to perform the surgery, with Remmie assisting. If all went as planned, it would take about two hours. The young man was still receiving blood, due the massive amount he had lost internally. When the laceration was repaired, the blood loss would be controlled. The abdomen would be flushed out several times to remove the blood that had collected there, as well as minimize the chance of infection.

Beau, a masterful surgeon, did a wonderful job on the man's abdomen and organs. Everything went like clockwork. The young man could expect to be back at work within six weeks. Beau was proud of himself, and Remmie was proud of him, too.

Time is everything in trauma situations. It's called the golden hour. If a patient can get help within the first hour, even though severely injured, they have a much better chance of surviving. That day, everything worked perfectly. Trauma medicine can be gratifying, but it can also be devastating when the pendulum swings in the other direction, and the outcome is not as good as it was that day.

The two surgeons got cleaned up and headed back to the unit. As they walked, they talked over the procedure they had just finished. Their conversation was interrupted by the arrival of another emergency, this time a heart attack victim. The other physicians had taken charge, so Remmie observed.

One of the Emergency Medical Technicians started reading out the person's chart: "White male, in his eighties, history of heart trouble."

For a second Remmie froze, then she took the chart and read the name. Thank God it wasn't her father. Everything possible was done for him, and he was eventually moved to the Critical Care Unit.

The shift proceeded with one emergency after the other, but none as serious as the first two. Finally, the shift was over. Remmie waited to brief the incoming physicians on the patients being left in the unit for whatever reasons. She was only there a few extra minutes, but the parking lot was empty when she walked out--a situation she tried to avoid. But she was in the lower level parking deck with only a few cars left in it. It was dimly lit and deserted.

For some reason, she felt uneasy tonight, even though she had done this hundreds of times. Remmie hesitated before stepping out of the elevator. She looked around but saw no one moving or heard any sounds except from the street above. She walked quickly toward her car, which was two rows back and over to the left. Each pillar caused her anxiety. Was someone there waiting to grab her?

I'm almost there, she kept thinking, *and everything is okay.* Suddenly, a shadow appeared, and she heard footsteps behind her. Freezing in her tracks with mace in hand, she turned to face whoever it was. They would remember this encounter for a long time. The shadowy figure moved into the light, and Remmie readied herself for a fight.

"Markham! What do you think you are doing? Creeping up on people surely isn't a skill you acquired in law school, is it?"

"I'm sorry I frightened you, but we need to finish what we started this afternoon. You don't seem to realize the seriousness of the information I have uncovered for your father. I want you to take this with you and read it before you tell me that you aren't interested."

Hadley Markham handed Remmie a folder filled with type written pages, plus some legal documents. He insisted that she read it before taking any further action, like telling her father. Remmie took the folder, got in her car, and drove away.

I was so afraid that I was going to be attacked, thought Remmie. *I wasn't considering that the attack might come in the form of this folder, and that tacky little man. But read it I will, and tomorrow, I'll know more about my past, be it good or be it bad.*

CHAPTER SEVEN

As Remmie drove through the streets of the darkened city, she pondered what might be in the folder lying on the seat beside her. The blanks in her life could be filled in today. For some reason, she wasn't as excited as she thought she would be.

What would she discover? What was it that Markham believed would make her strike a deal with him to secure his silence? All she wanted was the answers to the questions that had made her feel so disconnected all of her life. Whatever the consequences, she would have to deal with them, and so would her father. Markham would not only be out of luck, he would be out of a job when she told her father what he tried to do.

Sunlight reddened the horizon over the city, as streaks of crimson flashed toward the earth. Morning broke, sending the darkness scurrying into its secret place. As the light grew brighter, a figure could be seen standing in silhouette against the crimson sky.

On the balcony, Remmie stood motionless, arms folded across her chest, with her eyes focused on a far-away horizon where only moments ago night had captured the land. A sudden blast of a siren broke her hypnotic stare. She felt drained, but still her mind raced on.

How can the truth be so painful? How can people who were supposed to love you turn their backs, and walk away? How do I face this...this truth I wanted to know? How will my father face it?

Remmie walked into her living room, picked up the scattered papers from her table, and put them back in the folder. Her emotions gave way and she cried. Then she prayed aloud: "Father, I wanted to know about my past. I wanted to find my family. Now, I have found out their names, where they lived, and how I came to be in foster care. I thought it would help me to know. I thought I would feel more complete, if I knew. What do I do now? Will my father be able to handle this? I must have guidance, Father. You must show me Your will in all of this."

In the early dawn hours, Remmie sat with her head bowed, waiting for an answer to her prayer. She needed to know how to proceed or not to proceed. Maybe she should just let Markham do whatever he wanted with the information.

Remmie picked up the phone and dialed Dr. McKinley's number. She dreaded for him to answer. "Dr. McKinley, this is Remmie."

"Remmie are you okay?"

"I'm okay, but I need to ask for a few days off. I hate to do it, but as you saw yesterday, I am having personal problems. I need to get some things straightened out."

"You take care of whatever it is. I'll cover for you myself. Take all the time you need. Just let me hear from you by the end of the week. I want to know that you are alright."

"Thank you, Dr. McKinley. I wouldn't ask if it weren't important. I hope you understand that."

"I do. Say no more. I'll hear from you later in the week. Good-bye."

As she hung up the phone, she thought, *One hurdle, but how many more? Now what Lord? I did that, but what now?*

Ring…Ring. "Hello."

"Remmie what's wrong? I've been up for hours waiting for the time to call you. I know something is wrong. What is it?"

"Jesse, come here as quick as you can. You're right, but I can't discuss it over the phone. Come quickly!"

The phone was dead. Jesse had already hung up. Remmie sat down to wait for her friend. In about fifteen minutes, there was a knock at the door.

"You flew!"

"No, I didn't. The traffic was unusually quiet."

"Jess, I've learned a lot about my past."

"How did you find out?"

"Markham."

"Markham? What does he have to do with this?"

"Apparently, my father asked him to locate my birth parents. What he found interested him so much, he decided to tell me, not my father. He thinks I will compensate him to remain silent about what he found."

"You mean Markham is blackmailing you?"

"He tried, but I didn't go for it."

"Wait a cotton *pickin'* minute. Markham has uncovered information that he thinks you will pay to have him remain silent about? Even from your father, who pays him?"

"Bingo, Jesse."

"I'm not believing this. I feel like Rod Sterling is about to appear declaring that we have entered the *Twilight Zone*."

"I wish that would happen, or better yet, I wish I could wake up, and find out I have been dreaming for the last few hours. Jesse, why couldn't I leave well enough alone? Why did I have to bug my father about who I really am? I am such an ungrateful person."

"No, you aren't. It's perfectly normal to have the questions you do. Don't get down on yourself. Everything will be alright."

"You know, I've been praying for God to guide me. I was sitting here waiting for that guidance, and you called. You are supposed to help me, Jesse."

"I have no idea what you are supposed to do. I just know I was concerned about you, and I couldn't shake the feeling, so I called as soon as I thought you were home."

"Oh, Jess, I'm grabbing at straws. I will have to wait on the Lord."

"That sounds better. God might not like my solutions to your situation. I don't want to get in hot water with Him, or hot anything else."

"You make me laugh even when I feel like crying."

"What have you found out? I'm dying of curiosity."

"It's all in there, read it for yourself," Remmie said as she pointed to the folder on the table.

Jesse picked up the folder and began to read. Time passed. Remmie sat across the room watching Jesse's face. She was trying to decide what effect the story was having on her. Jesse was blank. Remmie's nerves were getting the best of her when Jesse finally laid the papers down.

"Well? What do you have to say about that?"

"I'm intrigued, but for some reason, I find it hard to believe, don't you?"

"I never considered that it isn't true. I guess I should have thought about the possibility of Markham concocting a bunch of lies. No, no, I'm sure it must be true. Markham wouldn't lie about this. After all, I can check it out. He gave me names, addresses--everything is right there."

"Yes, it is, and I suggest we do exactly that. Check it out. We can go to this Los Tripa, find these people, and see if what Markham says proves to be reality."

"Jess, I'm afraid. I never imagined, in my wildest dreams, anything like this. I never figured on such a sorted, ugly mess. I wish I had left well enough alone."

"Remmie, it's far too late for those wishes. Markham has put you in a position where wishing won't get it done. You must find out for yourself. Now, you said God wanted me to help, right? Well, I think you are supposed to find out if this stuff is true before you tell your father. If you give Markham a dime, you'll never be rid of him. He'll never stop."

"I know you're right. Okay, we'll do it. I've already taken leave from the hospital for the rest of the week. Can you get off? I can't do it without you."

"One phone call will take care of it."

CHAPTER EIGHT

As Flight 204 left the ground to float with the clouds, the young women sat motionless in their seats. Neither spoke for a long time. Jesse, from her seat by the window, gazed out into the billowing clouds of purest white. Her mind was gripped by the story she had read earlier that same morning when Remmie pointed to the folder filled with papers. It was mind-boggling to think of Remmie being a part of such a family. She tried to convince herself they would find it all to be a nasty lie conceived by Markham's perverted little mind to extort money from Dr. Remington, but realizing Remmie would probably end up being worth much, much more, decided to make her the target. Oh, how she hoped that would turn out to be the truth.

Remmie, with her eyes closed, remembered how she had felt on her first day at River Oaks. She had been excited to be in that beautiful place, but also frightened to death that she'd do something they didn't like, and she would have to go back to the group home, with all those mean girls who hated her because they said she was prettier, and got all the attention. For the life of her, she couldn't imagine anyone wanting the kind of attention she was getting. If that came as a result of being pretty, she often wished she was considered homely.

Her emotions were strained to their limit. At any moment, she might insult or offend these people. Nothing in her experience equipped her to handle the emotional stress of the excruciating fear - fear of failing to win the love of the Remingtons. What a tremendous burden to bear at age eleven. By the time night came, the pretty little auburn-haired girl was about ready to scream. She had tried to be little "Miss Perfect" all day. She hoped that finally being alone might offer her some relief.

Melissa came into the lovely room she had personally decorated. Lying still on the bed, Remmie waited for Melissa to speak. She spoke kindly to her in an effort to reassure her that everything would be okay. It would soon become her home, and then she would feel safe. She went on to say, that she had always wanted her little girl to be named after her. Melissa said she understood it would be very hard to take on a new name at age eleven. So, she had come up with a compromise. She said, "Since your name is Rebecca Elizabeth, how about just adding Melissa to it?" She said she knew it would be a long name, but not everyone would be fortunate to have such a distinctive name. She asked, "How does Rebecca Elizabeth Melissa Remington sound?"

Since Rebecca had always been called Becca, which she did not like very much, she wondered what would be the short version of this extended name. She just lay still with a slight smile on her face. Melissa went on to say she had thought of a nick name if she approved. She could be called Remmie. "R" for Rebecca, "E" for Elizabeth, "M" for Melissa, and put it all together with Remington and you have Remmie. Emotions overcame the little girl in an instant. She reached out with shaking little arms to embrace the lovely lady sitting beside her, finding ways to create a new name for her, and a new identity. She cried for a long time, and so did Melissa. When she was able to say what she was feeling, she said she liked the name, and she would be pleased to be called Remmie. She expressed her fear of rejection in words of an eleven year old. Melissa held her tightly. "This is not a trial living arrangement," explained Melissa. "This is permanent. You are here to stay," she said. "We want you if you are good or if you are bad. You belong here now. River Oaks is your home forever." Melissa stayed with Remmie until she fell into a restful, peaceful-looking sleep.

This ended the first day of Remmie's new life with the Remingtons. Now, she had a new family, new home, and a new name. Not bad, for just one day. As Remmie returned to the here and now, she realized how much like that scared little girl she felt. *Life is strange*, she thought, *One day you know who you are, and wonder who you were; the next you don't even know who you are anymore. I must be here for a reason. Things like this must have a reason. I will keep looking for that reason. Maybe then I can endure whatever lies ahead.*

Uncertainty was a familiar sojourner. She had traveled with it many times before. At least today, she was an adult, had her career, a loving father, and Sarah. *Let's not forget this beautiful person sitting next to me," she thought. "She has played a remarkable role in my life since college. Here she is making this journey into the unknown with me. She is one of the constants I can always count on.*

"Fasten your seat belts, please," announced the voice over the intercom.

Can it be, are we here already? Remmie's stomach tightened as did her grip on the arm rests. As the plane sank lower and lower in the afternoon sky, reaching for the tarmac, Remmie's mind wandered into the possibilities that lie ahead of her. With a quick jerk, the plane touched the ground. An immediate burst of speed pushed the ladies deeper into their seats until it slowed to a stop.

They stayed in their seats until everyone else had deplaned. Then, for a brief moment, they plotted their strategy - where they would go first, and how they would get there? Since neither wished to drive on this island, they decided to hire a taxi for the afternoon. The plane they planned to take out of here left at midnight, and they very much wanted to be on it.

Entering the country required nothing more than a show of an American driver's license, birth certificate, or voter registration, which they produced. English was the language of choice, so communication was not a problem. Engaging a taxi was not a problem either. However, deciding on a fair dollar amount took some horse trading, which Jesse handled nicely.

They squeezed into a mini version of a compact car. They were cramped, but they were determined to sit in the back together. Almost before the door was closed, they were moving. The 'G' force was worse than on the plane. The grimy looking fellow drove like a maniac. The ladies hugged each other as they prayed for the best.

After several minutes, the driver stopped in front of a broken down shack, and motioned for them to get out. They sat firm, looking the place over. What they saw, they found difficult to believe. There wasn't a front door on the thing. Chickens went in and out at will. "This your place. Americans get out," ordered the taxi driver. "I wait."

"You better wait, considering what I paid you to find this place," Jesse remarked.

"Wait here, we will be right back," said Remmie, wanting to make sure he stayed put.

"I wait. You get out, now!"

Both ladies stood by the taxi, not sure which way to move. Jesse, the adventurer, moved first, walking to the door (or perhaps *opening* would be a better choice of words). Just as she got near enough to enter, she put it in reverse, backing all the way up to the taxi again.

"What is it?"

"You aren't going to believe it, but there is a big, old hog sitting up on the sofa. I hope he isn't the one we've come all this way to see."

"Come on, Jess, let's get this over with."

Hand in hand, they approached the opening again, and sure enough, there he was – a big, old hog sitting upright on the sofa, Almost hidden in his shadow was someone or something else.

"Hello, are you there?"

"Who are you? What you want?"

"I'm from the states. I'm looking for Mr. Valdez. Do you know where we might locate him?"

"Don't know Valdez. Never heard of him. Go away. We going to miss the Wheel of Fortune. Snorter gets upset when we miss it, so go away."

"Are you sure you don't know Joseph Valdez? I've come a very long way, and I was given this address."

"I tell you, no one here but me and Snorter. We don't know him. Right boy?"

"Come on, Remmie. They don't know Mr. Valdez. If that hog starts answering him, I may lose it. Let's get back to the airport."

Reluctantly, Remmie walked back to the taxi. "I can't believe we came all this way for nothing, a dead end."

"Now, Remmie, what we may have found is the unraveling of Markham's lie. Let's not forget Snorter. He was a surprise. The biggest fan of "The Wheel" and I do mean the biggest."

Remmie forced a smile. "Jess, you are crazy. I hope I forget Snorter, and that shack. Dear Lord, it wasn't fitting for Snorter, let alone humans. Perhaps you are right about Markham. But for some reason, I feel like there is a piece of the puzzle here on this island. I'm terrified of finding it, and terrified of not finding it. What do we do now?"

"Perhaps we should read the information again. Maybe we overlooked something. Here, you take this part and I'll take this. As soon as we get to the airport, and out of this death wish, we will read it all again, carefully."

Sitting across the table from each other, they re-read every word. "There's nothing new. Same ugly story, just as I remembered it. What now, Jess? Do I just leave here? I feel I'm leaving something important. What time is it?"

"Ten o'clock. We have two hours before we leave. Let's get something to eat. I'm starving."

Gathering their things, they walked toward the restaurant. A young man approached them. He was tall, thin, neatly dressed, and well groomed. They side stepped to clear his path. He altered his course, continuing directly toward them.

CHAPTER NINE

"Miss Remington?"

"Yes, I'm Miss Remington. Who are you?"

"You don't know me, but I know why you're here, and I would like to speak with you if you have some time to spare before your flight."

"I asked who you are. Do you mind telling me your name? And just what do you know about me?"

"Come this way, please, and I'll tell you what you want to know."

The ladies traded glances, both with huge question marks in their eyes. Jesse nodded okay, so they followed the young man. In a nearby corridor, he opened a door to an office and the name plaque on the desk read, Joseph Valdez.

"Are you Joseph Valdez?"

"Yes, Miss Remington, I am. Your Mr. Markham contacted the local orphanage here in Los Tripa. I serve as a member of the Board of Directors there. Mr. Markham was referred to me, and I gave him some of the information he was looking for. You were placed in the orphanage here when you were approximately two years old. When you were barely three, you were taken to the states at the request of a family member who feared if you stayed here, you would never be adopted. That's where our records end."

"You aren't any older than I am. How do you know all this?"

"Research, Miss Remington. I researched old records. I felt you had a right to know. In your condition, I understand how imperative it is for you to locate any living blood relative."

"My condition? What are you talking about? Oh, let me guess, Markham."

"Yes, of course. Your Mr. Markham. He is devoted to you, and your adopted father."

"Devoted. Now there's a description that couldn't be further from my Mr. Markham. First of all, Mr. Valdez, I am a doctor, and to my knowledge I don‘t have a condition that requires blood relatives to treat it. I've wanted to know for many years who I really am, my origin, and the reason for my abandonment. More than anything, I just wanted to know why. I've consoled myself by thinking they must have had a very good reason to desert me."

"I see. This is much different from what your Mr. Markham told me. I'm afraid I have been taken in by your..."

"Please don't call him 'my Mr. Markham.' I'm not claiming him. He's not mine, and frankly, I don't want him."

"Surely he was representing your father, Benjamin Remington."

"Yes, I believe that is how it began. But somehow it all got twisted. For some reason, Markham saw a financial opportunity for himself, so he took it. The whys, I can't tell you just now, but I'll find out. That's a promise."

"I'm embarrassed to say that I've been taken in by Markham. I may have given out sensitive information about your biological parents. I hope this will not cause you or your father undue stress. I have acted with my heart, not my head."

"Unfortunately Mr. Valdez, it has caused me a great deal of stress. Thank goodness I've opted not to tell my father until I checked on things. May I inquire if you read the packet of information before giving it to Mr. Markham?"

"No, I did not."

"I see. Well, it contains my birth certificate, which has my birth mother's name on it. It also contains a written report from a state agency in Florida that indicates my grandfather wanted me off this island, as well as some newspaper clippings from Los Tripa that tell a sorted story about my grandfather. Then, it contains a note from Mr. Markham, in which he names you as his contact on the island. You are why we came here. I hoped that you could substantiate Markham's claims or lead me to someone who can."

"There is a nun who was here when you were born. She helped me locate the files. She remembers the situation surrounding your birth. She knows the whole story."

"You mean there's someone who can tell me about my biological parents, and why they gave me up?"

"Yes, definitely. She's very old, but still working in the orphanage. Her mind is sharp as a tack. Would you like to meet her?"

"Oh, Mr. Valdez, I would be grateful if I could."

"It's a long drive. You will miss your flight."

"That's okay. Perhaps you can tell us where we can spend the night near the airport."

"I wouldn't suggest that. You should stay in the tourist section by the coast. It's much safer for you there. I'll call the resort and make reservations for you. I have a friend there who'll make sure to take care of you. How will you get to the orphanage?"

"We rented a taxi earlier. I guess we can do that again."

"No, no! I will take you myself. Those taxi drivers are a menace to society. I will need to make a few arrangements before I leave. You may wait here if you like."

"One other thing before you go. How did you know I was here? How did you recognize me?"

"I became suspicious after Mr. Markham contacted me. I felt I had betrayed you, which turned out to be the truth. I told my cousin, the taxi driver, to be on the look-out for Americans who were looking for the address you went to earlier today. He called me and described you both to me."

"How did that address get into the folder with your name on it?"

"As I said, I was suspicious, so I used an address that no tourist would ever want to visit. Then I contacted the taxi driver as I've already explained, and just waited. I hoped you would come so I could straighten out this whole thing."

Soon the threesome settled in for their long ride into the interior of the island. At midnight on the dot, they saw lights in the distance. As they got nearer, the building slowly emerged out of the darkness. Remmie was filled with an eerie Déjà vu.

Stopping his car near a large arch-shaped wooden door, Valdez got out, opened the car doors for the ladies, walked to the door of the orphanage, and knocked. A small lady opened the door. She did not seem surprised by the late night visit. Once inside, the large room was sparsely furnished, but clean. Whispers were exchanged between Valdez and the woman. She hurried away without even speaking to Remmie or Jesse. Anxiety almost overwhelmed Remmie. She felt her emotions taking control, so she turned away, trying to focus on something out the window. However, she saw only darkness. Her eyes filled with tears. She wiped the tears away quickly, but they kept coming. Jesse handed her a tissue.

"Thanks, Jess. I just can't keep it together. It's all too much."

"Hey, I don't know how you've hung on as well as you have. This is heavy stuff. I think you are great. You are a strong person, Remmie. You'll make it."

Remmie reached out to embrace Jesse while they waited for the appearance of a woman who held Remmie's past in her memory.

Suddenly, there appeared a slight built, elderly woman in a white night gown with a sleep cap on her head. Gray hair hung down to her waist. The woman with a gentle looking face, and a kind smile, had her eyes fixed on Valdez. He spoke to her in a whisper, and her eyes moved straight to Remmie. Valdez continued talking to the little woman as she continued focusing on Remmie. When Valdez finally stopped speaking, the little woman moved across the room toward Remmie. She reached out to touch her hands. After a long moment of silence, she spoke in a soothing voice that reassured Remmie everything would be okay.

"Welcome, my child. You are a very lovely young woman. My name is Sister Anna Marie. I was here the day you first came. You were a beautiful little girl with all that pretty dark red hair, those questioning green eyes, and such a sweet smile."

Turning slightly, Sister Anna Marie acknowledged Jesse. She reached out her tiny, wrinkled hand to take hold of Jesse's hand, pulling her close to her. "And you, lovely child, are so pretty. You are Rebecca's friend?"

"Yes, I am. We have been friends since our first year of college. Remmie is very special to me."

"Remmie. Now that is a befitting nickname for you, Rebecca Elizabeth. May I offer you a room? We can talk more in the morning. It's so late, and you both look rather bedraggled."

"Well," began Remmie, "I am tired, but I am also extremely anxious to talk with you about my coming here. I certainly do not wish to keep you from your rest."

Sister Anna, realizing this intense young woman probably wasn't going to sleep anyway, quickly changed her plan, motioning them down the hall and into the kitchen. Moving swiftly about the pleasant looking kitchen, Sister Anna put on a pot of coffee, and set out three cups and a delicious looking cake that smelled of cinnamon.

Remmie and Jesse sat silently, watching the older lady's every move. At last, with the fragrance of fresh coffee permeating the air, Sister Anna Marie poured three piping hot cups, and sat down across the table from the ladies. Sitting silently, drinking coffee as they enjoyed the wonderful tasting cinnamon cake, the three women waited for the right moment to get on with the reason they were together here in the middle of the night. After what seemed like an eternity, Sister Anna Marie began to speak.

"Remmie, you were brought here by a distraught young woman who had nowhere to turn for help. She was indeed, at her wits end. Frightened and depressed, she came to this place looking for help, and acceptance for herself as well as for her little girl. That young woman, your mother, was as lovely as you are tonight. She had thick, black hair, and dark brown eyes, but you are amazingly like her, especially when you smile. I'll never forget how sorry I felt for that frightened young woman. She had come here hoping to find a refuge."

"She hadn't come intending to leave me on the doorstep to run away?"

"No—no, my child. That was never her intention. She was seeking a safe place. The reason you were left here came later. Your mother loved you, Remmie. She was a young, impulsive, inexperienced girl who had gotten herself into a very difficult situation. She had nowhere to turn except to us. We willingly accepted both of you.

"Unfortunately, she was in real trouble. Her father was a local strong man. He resented his daughter's involvement with a wealthy American, so he vowed to destroy the child. He made his threats so loud and so violent that your mother fled with you. Coming here in the darkness was a desperate act of love."

Remmie and Jesse sat spellbound. Tear-filled eyes were glued on Sister Anna Marie. Taking hold of Remmie's hand, Sister Anna Marie patted her hand reassuringly. Again, she began to speak in that comforting voice.

"Child, if you came here to fuel an inner anger about your birth mother, you came to the wrong place. Although she was young and foolish, she was a kind, gentle girl who loved her baby girl very much."

"Tell me about my birth father. Where was he? Why didn't he help her? You said he was an American?"

Sister Anna Marie paused, searching her memory for the words that would cause the least amount of distress to the vulnerable young woman waiting for her answer.

Sister Anna Marie decided to continue telling the story where she left off. "Your mother left here when she was eighteen. She wanted to get away from the lifestyle her father had brought upon his entire family. She didn't like the way he made all his money. Seeking her freedom, your mother went to the states where she eventually went to work as a domestic. From

Florida, she found her way to a large country estate of a doctor and his wife. It was located on a river near the borders of Alabama and Georgia."

Remmie's back stiffened. Jesse put her hand on Remmie's arm to steady her. Sister Anna Marie continued. "The doctor had retired from his practice in a large Alabama city. His wife was frail, so he advertised for a housekeeper. Your mother answered that ad and was hired. She came to love the couple, as well as her job with them."

Remmie could wait no longer. "What was the doctor's name?"

Sister Anna Marie paused, but without answering the question, she continued as if Remmie had not said anything. Remmie became very uneasy. Her stomach tightened and nausea set in. What was the elderly woman avoiding? Who was her father? She thought about interrupting again, but she was the reason this elderly woman was up in the middle of night. So, she decided to wait and listen.

"Your mother's name was Milea Marjoul."

"Milea Marjoul?" repeated Remmie, "I wasn't sure how to pronounce it. What is that, French?"

"You are partially correct. Your grandmother was from France, but your grandfather was an island native. That means he had many bloodlines. That's only one of the contradictory behaviors he exhibited. Although his bloodline was far from pure, he found it necessary to hate you for being as he put it 'a mixed breed.' "

"I don't understand. He considered me a mixed breed because my father was an American?"

"That's only part of it, my child. I know you want me to hurry, but if you'll be patient with me, I'll bring all the pieces of this story together. Your mother was at River Oaks working for your adoptive parents. In fact, she stayed there another year. But when she was twenty, she discovered that she was pregnant."

"My birth mother became pregnant while working at River Oaks?"

Nodding yes, Sister Anna continued. "That was about thirty years ago, and it wasn't as openly accepted as it is today. She hid her condition as long as she could, but the doctor's wife soon realized Milea's secret. Together they decided Milea should return to Los Tripa to be with her family.

"It wasn't long before her father discovered her condition. He demanded she abort the baby. Milea refused. His anger mounted. He felt her defiance was bad for his position of authority, so he vowed to destroy the child. Milea was horrified."

CHAPTER TEN

"The island is small; therefore, she had no place to hide. Her mother intervened, which she rarely did. She insisted that he stop his ranting and raving about destroying the child his daughter was carrying, threatening to take Milea and leave forever. Not wishing to find himself alone in his old age, he decided to stop his threatening. Milea stayed on the other side of the island with an old family friend, awaiting the birth. Things were calm until shortly after you were born. You were almost six months old when you and your mother were in town and ran into your grandfather. One look and he was infuriated.

"Milea fled with you to a remote part of the island. There she stayed in hiding for eight or nine months. She never left you for a second. Your grandfather was determined to find you. He had spies everywhere. Milea kept you hidden away until just before Christmas. Fearing she was about to be found, she brought you here. Even your wicked grandfather wouldn't come here."

"What about my looks turned my grandfather against me?"

"You were White, child. That's what disgraced your grandfather so. You were White."

The girls looked at each other for a long time. Remmie broke the silence. "I'm White, Jess, I'm white. My mother was a Black French island girl with a White man's child. Maybe now we know why we've always felt so close. We weren't so different after all."

Jesse put her arm around Remmie. With her head on Remmie's shoulder, Jesse whispered, "I love you. We would have been friends no matter our color or nationality. You are the best friend anyone could ever have."

"All those years my father resisted our friendship because of his prejudices. He couldn't bear the thought of my best friend being Black. Boy, what is this going to do to him?"

"He has been more understanding the last few years. But maybe you shouldn't tell him just yet."

"I have to tell him, Jess. Markham can't get away with his little scheme. Sister Anna, who is my birth father and where are my parents now?"

"Are you sure you are ready for this part of the story?"

"I'm as ready as I can get. Please tell me, I really need to get this behind me."

"This is the part I've dreaded telling you because this is the part that can cause pain for many people. Your birth mother is dead now. She was a victim of a disease for which there is no cure. She was only thirty-two when she passed. She loved you until the end, and she never stopped regretting the events that took you away from her. Your father has never known he fathered a child. Your adopted mother didn't know at first, but Milea called her in desperation.

"Melissa, being a kind and generous person, set out to find you. It took a long time, but when she located you in a group home somewhere, she and Dr. Remington adopted you. By then, Milea was extremely sick. It was as if knowing you finally had a family gave her the release she needed to succumb to her disease. She died seven months after you went to live with the Remingtons. She is buried here. When the light comes I will show you."

"I'm not putting the pieces together, Sister Anna. Melissa found me, because Milea told her of my existence, and needed her help. My mother was an unusually generous person, but something's missing in this story. What is it?"

Sister Anna Marie sat, head bowed for what seemed to Remmie a small forever. Finally, she raised her head, met Remmie's eyes with her own, and spoke. "My dear, dear child, the secret that sent your mother, Milea from River Oaks back to this island, the secret she kept until she was near death, the secret she knew would one day wound your very soul, is the secret she shared only with Melissa Remington and me.

"One dark, stormy day when Milea felt death's grip tighten on her frail, sick body, she reached out to Melissa, hoping against hope this gentle, southern lady would find it in her heart to forgive her, and rescue her precious little girl from a life in foster care. That secret went to the grave with those fine, strong women. I am the only one left who knows, and since death has not chosen to claim me, I am faced with this task.

"God be merciful, and give your servant strength. Rebecca Elizabeth, what I tell you now will change your life forever. The way it changes you is up to you. You can grow bitter, or you can rest in the knowledge that regardless of all circumstances surrounding your conception, birth, and life to this point, you were loved by your birth mother, and by the woman you called 'mother.' The choice is yours now, lovely child – make it wisely.

"One other thing you should know. Your father fell in love with you the moment he saw you, and he loves you now. Although you may have lacked the knowledge of who you were born to be, you have never lacked the love of the family God chose for you. Remmie, Milea's secret shared only with Melissa and me is...Dr. Benjamin Remington is your birth father."

Remmie's grip on Jesse's hands tightened, she took in a deep breath, and held it.

"For whatever reason, Dr. Remington, and Milea became involved sexually. You were the product of that union. Although Melissa knew Milea was pregnant when she sent her away, she did not know who the father was. When Milea contacted her just shortly before she passed, Melissa was very hurt, but she wanted to find you and give you a home and a family. She told Milea she would never tell you or the doctor the truth, and she didn't.

"When Mr. Markham came asking questions, Valdez looked up your files with my assistance. I'm afraid he now knows some of the facts, but not the secret. He knows you are half Black, and he knows about the money."

"Yes, I know. I saw part of the file but it didn't spell out the facts. It was vague, concentrating more on the wickedness of my grandfather, Marjoul. I never saw anything about my father or any money. It is so difficult to imagine my father being unfaithful to Melissa at all, but with a Black island girl! I'm in shock. He had such strong feelings about racial mixing."

"Perhaps it was not all out of prejudice; it was because of his relationship, and his inability to forgive himself. He tried to contact Milea many times, but she wouldn't speak with him. I spoke to him twice over the years. I believe he was filled with remorse and repentance for his unfaithfulness. I believe he had strong feelings for Milea. Perhaps, he wanted you to be spared the hurt he had endured because of his relationship with Milea. He was tormented by the affair. But he didn't know a child was produced, let alone the fact that he raised that child in his home for so many years. It is a strange turn of events, to say the least."

"You said Markham knew about the money. Can you explain that to me?"

"As I said, your grandfather made lots of money. However, it wasn't good money; it was evil money. He was the head of organized crime on the island. He did bad things to many people. When he was killed, he was reportedly worth millions, but no one knew where the money was. Your grandmother continued to live in the house, and was well cared for, but she had no access to the fortune either. Since her death, the house remains closed. I suppose everyone has forgotten about the fortune.

"When Markham came, he was looking for the heir, Milea Marjoul. Learning of her death, he seemed to think you would be the next in line to inherit your family's evil fortune. He said he had located it in a bank in Europe, but he had to be sure you were the rightful heir. That is one of the reasons Valdez and I assisted him. We wanted you to receive what is yours. So something good could come from all that evil. He also said you were suffering from a rare disease, and needed to find a blood relative for your treatment."

"Markham, unfortunately, is cut from the same cloth as my wicked grandfather. He only wants the money for himself. He has attempted to blackmail me. That's what brought me here. He'll tell my father the whole story unless I do. I won't allow Markham to have his way. I must get home and tell my father the truth. Sister Anna, it is through your memories that I have met my birth mother. Without you, I would have never known her. You say she was a good woman and that she loved me. How was I taken away?"

"When Milea became ill, she was put in a sanitarium for many months. You stayed here at the orphanage. We hoped we would be allowed to keep you until you were adopted. However, your grandfather petitioned the court to have you put in foster care in Florida, far away from here. The people came, showed the paper, gathered up your belongings, and took you away. Milea was devastated, but the courts said she was going to die, and the child needed a family. Since your grandparents did not want you, the court's ruling was upheld.

"Milea never saw or heard from you again until Melissa found you. I remember very well the day Melissa called to say she had located you in a girl's home near their estate, and that they were going to meet you. Milea was overjoyed. She waited anxiously for the next call. Melissa called to say you were beautiful, healthy, and that adoption procedures had been initiated.

"Milea lived for the phone calls and pictures from Melissa. With every passing day she grew weaker and weaker, but more peaceful than I ever remember seeing her. She knew the end was near, but she so desperately wanted to see you again. Melissa could feel that desire so she arranged for Milea to see you one more time.

"Do you remember a trip you made with your mother to buy rattan furniture from an estate sale? That plantation house is on the west side of the island. Melissa had Milea brought to the estate, and placed in a location where she could see you the whole time you were in the room.

"Milea told me you were near enough to touch many times. She said you even smiled at her once when you passed near where she was sitting. She was the happiest I've ever seen her that day. Melissa gave your mother the gift that helped her pass from this life to the next. That gift was love. Those two ladies shared the gift of loving you, Remmie."

"I do remember that trip, and the plantation house with all the beautiful live plants and big windows. I don't remember seeing my mother though."

Emotions welled up and overflowed. Remmie fell into Sister Anna Marie's arms and cried. Jesse cried, too. Although they were drained when the tropical sun peeked over the tall palms, they made their way to a desolate-looking hill overlooking the Atlantic. There Sister Anna Marie pointed out for Remmie the marker on which was written: "*Milea Marjoul - Resting Now With God.*" Kneeling beside the grave, Remmie and Jesse said a prayer in silence.

Remmie's tears ran down her face, dripping from her chin onto the slab covering the final resting place of the body that had brought her into this world. Many feelings triggered that flood of tears. They were cleansing tears, bringing pain from deep within to the surface, allowing it to spill out onto the cold, hard slab. Years of fear and hurt were washed away. Feelings of rejection and loneliness came out with the tears, too.

When the flood of tears ceased, Remmie felt at peace with her past, at peace with the present, and at peace with the future. She knew who she was. She knew where she came from. She knew it all. The sense of freedom was incredible. She was free from the uncertainty, from the sense of doom she had always carried. The truth had indeed set her free.

Rising to her feet, Remmie stood looking down at the grave of a woman who had made mistakes, but who in Remmie's eyes was a heroine, a woman of strength, of courage, and a woman she had felt inside her all these years, but could not identify. Today that woman had an identity. The woman in the grave not only had given Remmie life, she had imparted her strength and courage to her as well.

At that moment, on that hillside, looking out across the rolling surface of the ocean, Rebecca Elizabeth Melissa Remington knew herself for the first time. What she knew, she liked. She knew without question she was here for a reason. Finding that reason had given her life the meaning she had searched for. The void in her life was filled, she knew her purpose, and from this day forward she would dedicate herself to it.

Returning to the orphanage, the ladies and Sister Anna walked through a long corridor along one side of the main building. Coming to the end of the corridor, they entered a small room. Sister Anna opened the locked closet door, and beckoned Remmie to view the contents.

"These are Milea's things. She only had a few things. I almost got rid of them, but I had this feeling that someone would come who would consider these things precious. You may have them if you like, or I will continue keeping them for you. I may not be alive too much longer, then who knows what will happen to them when I am no longer here to stand guard."

Sensing perhaps Remmie would like to be alone as she went through the few meager belongings representing a life now ended, Sister Anna took Jesse and left Remmie alone in the little room.

Remmie was not immediately aware of their absence. She moved closer to the closet, surveying its contents carefully, touching the dresses hanging before her ever so gently. Something unusual came over her---a sense of another's presence, a protecting spirit or a guiding spirit was there in the musty little closet. Remmie felt no fear of the presence. So, she yielded to its leading. Pushing the clothes aside, on a shelf hidden by the garments sat a small, wooden chest. It was fashioned after an old trunk with a rounded top accented with metal strips and a fancy lock, protecting its contents from intruders. Touching the small chest with both hands, she lifted it, shook it gently not wanting to disturb anything inside; she could hear things shifting around. Carefully she checked the lock, and found it secure. *Well now,* she thought, *how do I open you, little chest? You may hold treasures from my past.*

She did not want to damage the lovely little chest, so she looked around for a place she thought a key might be hiding. Almost immediately, the guiding spirit led her to a ledge above the door in the closet. Running her fingers along the dusty ledge, suddenly she felt something within the heavy layer of dust she had just disturbed. It was a small, odd-shaped key, and it fit perfectly into the lock.

Instantly, the chest was opened, revealing the treasures within. It was like the little chest, the key, and the presence had all been waiting patiently for this moment when their secret could be revealed, and their treasure claimed. With ever so gentle movements, Remmie felt her way through an assortment of papers, some letters from Melissa, pictures of herself as a child, and a small box. Opening the box, Remmie saw a beautiful antique gold necklace. The chain was heavy and the medallion was heavy, also. It was unusual in design, a heart-shaped filigree with a solid gold circle in the center. Noticing what seemed to be a crack in the metal, she pushed her nail in and it opened. It was a locket. Inside the locket was a picture of a pretty young woman, and a small auburn-haired girl. They were smiling at each other. Tears came again from Remmie's eyes. *That's my mom and me, isn't it? That's us together?*

Without a sound being uttered, the guiding spirit acknowledged the questions Remmie was asking in her mind. She knew it was a picture of her and her mother. In that instance, she felt all the love she had desired to feel from her real mother. It was just there in that dismal little room, engulfing Remmie. Then suddenly, without explanation, she was drawn to the chest again. This time she saw a hand-written note. Opening it carefully, she read:

My precious child,

I have to believe that someday, someway, you will find this. And at last, I will have the opportunity to tell you how much I love you. I trust Anna Marie will tell you the whole story. I prayed every day of my life that you could forgive me, and love me. I loved Benjamin deeply, and he loved me. We were terribly wrong in our affair. I repented many times. You, my dear one, have been the light, and joy of my life. If only we could have been together longer. Life dealt us a cruel blow, but in eternity we will finally be together. Melissa was my guardian angel. She forgave me for my betrayal. And she found you, bringing you into her heart, and her home. You cannot imagine my excitement when I knew you would have a good family as well as the security that I could never provide.

I dreamed about how you would look when you are grown - how smart you would be, and how you would succeed in life. Somehow I've always thought you would be a doctor like Benjamin. I know you will have every advantage, so you can be whatever you choose.

My child, there is a special purpose for you to fulfill. I've known that since you were forming inside me. Often when I'd feel you moving about, I'd put my hand firmly to feel you better then, I would have this strong impression that you would be a special person. After you were born, when I looked at you, admiring your beauty, that same feeling came over me. I believe you have a special purpose. Find it, Rebecca Elizabeth and fulfill your destiny. There's so much I could say, so much I want to say, but there's no time left. The locket belonged to my grandmother whom I loved dearly. The picture was my constant companion. Keep it always, as my gift to you.

I Love You,

Your Mother,

Milea Marjoul

Fighting the tears that distorted the words of the note, Remmie sat holding the locket and the note. So much to absorb, learned so quickly, her mind was frantic to remember; to savor every bit of information she had heard. Carefully, she re-folded the only direct communication she ever had with her mother since she was old enough to remember. Placing the note gently in the chest along with the locket, Remmie closed and locked the chest. *This is what I came here for*, she thought. *Mother was right, I have a purpose, and now I know what it is.* Walking to the closet, she touched her mother's dresses once again. She looked around, making sure she hadn't over-looked something. Then she closed and locked the closet door. Remmie walked slowly out of the room. Before completely closing the door, she looked back, and near the window in the golden glow of the now bright morning sun, for an instant, she saw the angel outlined by the sun as it drifted up, and out of view. Remmie never felt it again.

Waiting just outside were Jesse and Sister Anna. Holding the chest as if it were worth a million dollars, Remmie stood smiling as the tears flowed freely from all three of them.

Loving good-byes were said, and Joseph, who had waited all this time, took the ladies back to the resort. He told them he would make flight arrangements, and would let them know as soon as he could. He suggested they get some sleep. Once inside the hotel room, the weary young women collapsed on the beds. They were awakened by a knock at the door. Remmie, wobbling around more asleep than awake, opened the door after hearing Joseph's voice.

"I'm unable to get a commercial flight for you, so I took the liberty of arranging a private flight. My associate will fly you out early in the morning. You will be home before noon. Is there anything else I can do for you?"

"I don't believe so, Joseph, you have done enough already. I will always be grateful to you for taking me to Sister Anna Marie. She filled in a lot of blanks in my life. Now it's up to me to fulfill my purpose."

"Of that, I am confident, Miss Remington. You will succeed at whatever you do. I will come for you at seven sharp. Good night."

"Good night, Joseph. We will be ready. Oh, by the way, we didn't bring more clothes because we weren't expecting to be overnight. Is there a cleaners or laundry where we can wash our clothes?"

"I will arrange for room service to pick up your clothes and have them cleaned."

CHAPTER ELEVEN

Seven o'clock came quickly. The girls were up and ready when Joseph arrived. The day was perfect for a flight. The pilot was waiting for them. Soon they were drifting with the clouds, looking down on a glassy sea. In no time at all, they were on the ground again heading for Remmie's car, then straight to River Oaks. Even though Remmie drove in excess of the speed limit all the way, it seemed like they would never get there.

Reaching the big iron gates, Remmie punched in the code, driving quickly past the bowing live oaks. Whipping the car into the circular drive, coming to an abrupt halt, she and Jesse jumped out, and ran to the door. Remmie used her key, not wishing to wait for Sarah. Once the door was opened, she called out for Sarah, but there was no answer. Hurrying into the kitchen she expected to find Sarah, but she wasn't there. The room appeared to have been left in a hurry. There was a carton of milk setting on the counter, half cooked grits, and eggs on the stove. Observing the condition of the kitchen, the ladies turned around quickly, heading down the hall. Sarah's room was empty and so was the study.

"Oh, my God – something's terribly wrong, Jess!"

Picking up the phone, Remmie used speed dial to reach Dr. Carson. But before she got an answer, Hadley Markham appeared. "Remmie, put down the phone."

"Where's my father? Is he alright?"

"He's critical, Remmie. It's the heart again. Sarah's with him. They've been looking for you everywhere. I know where you've been."

"You haven't told my father anything, have you? If you are responsible for this, you'll need a lawyer!"

"I haven't told him anything. Just calm down, and let's get you to your father. Come with me quickly. I have a chopper waiting to take you to the Medical Center."

Within an hour, Remmie and Jesse were running through the halls of the hospital, heading for C.C.U. Bolting through the doors, Remmie stopped suddenly.

"We can't go running in there. We'll frighten him. Let's get control of ourselves." Walking slowly, they entered the unit.

"Dr. Remington, we have been trying to reach you for twenty-four hours. Come with me. Your father's in this unit," said the nurse, motioning with her hand toward where the senior Dr. Remington lay.

Entering the room where her father was, Remmie moved to his bedside. Tubes and gages, monitors, and IV pumps surrounded him.

"Father, I'm here now." Dr. Remington opened his eyes to acknowledge her.

"I'm sorry I wasn't here when you came in. Jess and I took a couple of days off. I should have let you know, but you were doing so well over the week-end. I never expected this."

Dr. Remington tightened his grip on her hand. Remmie caught herself rambling on, and stopped. Just then Sarah rushed in.

"There ya are. I thought I *wus gonna* to have to call in the FBI. Where in *tarnation* have *ya* been?"

"That's a long story, Sarah, but we're here now. Tell me what happened."

"Well, we got up Monday, and he w*us* grumpy as usual, so I thought he *wus* alright. I went into the kitchen to cook breakfast. Well, before I could fry a couple of eggs and cook grits, he called out for help. I ran to him and called 911. We *wus* here a few hours later. That's *'bout* it."

"What does the doctor say? Did he have another heart attack?"

"Yes, he did, but he's gonna be okay. He'll be *yellin'* at me within the week."

Turning her attention to her father, Remmie leaned down and kissed his forehead. "Forgive me for being gone when you needed me."

His eyes told her she was forgiven, but they also showed the relief of having her there.

Jesse's eyes noticed how tired Sarah looked. "Sarah, come go home with me. I'll fix you something to eat, let you take a hot tub bath, and then you can get some sleep."

"No thanks, Jesse. I *ain't* left him. I think I'll stay. As a matter of fact, young lady, you look *kinda* haggered. You better be *gettin'* some rest *yoreself.*"

"Sarah," Remmie called out sharply, "Jess is right. You need to go with her. You can relieve me in the morning. Please don't argue, just go with Jess."

"Come on, Sarah, and I'll tell you all about our trip."

"Okay, okay, Jesse, I'm *comin'*. Remmie, *ya* take care of that grumpy old man. I'll see *ya* tomorrow."

Remmie asked for a dinner tray as she settled into a chair by her father's bed. Hours went by. She could see the sun setting behind the city's tallest buildings. In her mind, she wondered how her news would affect her father, or if she should tell him at all. About that time, the doctor came in. After checking her father, he motioned her into the hall. "Where have you been, Remmie? We've had a close one. Ben almost checked out of here. I think your absence was the only thing that kept him hanging on."

"I'm very sorry. Something came up suddenly. He was doing so well over the week-end. I just never expected this. What's your prognosis?"

"He's improved, he's determined, and you're here. All those things are in his favor. But he can go anytime. You should prepare yourself as best you can. If he's still improving tomorrow, you can take him to your place, and if he does alright, maybe you can take him home by Sunday. Are you staying here tonight?"

"Yes, I am."

"You look as if you need rest as much as he does."

"I'll rest better right here. Don't worry about me."

"Whatever you say, Remmie. I'll see him again early in the morning."

The room was quiet. Dr. Benjamin Remington lay quietly, eyes closed, with his daughter holding his hand.

Meanwhile, over at Jesse's house, Sarah sat up to her neck in rose scented bubble bath. *"Hep, hep* me, Jesse! I can't *git* out of this *thang.* My knees are weaker than freshly churned butter. Come on in here, and *git* me out before I swivel up like an old prune. Jesse! Are *ya comin'* to *hep* me or do I have to call 911?!!"

"I'm here, Sarah. You're alright. Just take hold of my arm with both your swiveled little hands, and I'll pull you up. Once you're on your feet just walk up the steps. I'll help you."

"Okay, here goes. But if I bust my behind on that cold tile floor, you're in big trouble. And don't be *lookin'* at my body. You probably *ain't* old enough to see a body like mine."

"I'm not looking, Sarah. Just get up so I can get you dried. Now see there, you're okay. Get your gown on while I fix you a cup of hot cocoa."

Finally, Sarah was asleep. And Jesse crawled into bed, exhausted from her adventuresome two days. Sleep came easily.

A sudden burst of light woke Remmie from a restless sleep. "Morning. I'm making rounds early today. How'd our patient do last night?"

"He slept some, but not much. He seems pain free, and the monitor was steady every time I looked at it."

"Good morning, Ben, how are you feeling? Can you tell me if you had any pain?"

Struggling to speak with the large throat tube, the elder doctor managed to let them know he wasn't in any pain. After examining Dr. Remington, the cardiologist, Dr. Walt Shannon, made some notes. Then he spoke with the elder Dr. Remington while Remmie listened.

"All the signs I have to go on indicate you are improving. If all goes well for the next twenty-four hours, we'll entertain the idea of you going to Remmie's for a few days before returning to the country. I'll see you or hear from you later today. Oh, I almost forgot, Dr. Carson called, checking on your progress this morning. He said to let him know when you are coming back to River Oaks so he can arrange home health services for you."

"Thanks, Dr. Shannon," said Remmie, "but I'll be there until he's able to be on his own."

The next twenty-four hours passed without incident, so early the next morning Dr. Shannon released Dr. Remington to Remmie's house. She had him transported by ambulance. Once he was all set up in her guest room, Remmie relaxed in her living room. Drifting into a half sleep, her mind recalled the events she had just been through. She could see the tiny little room where her mother spent her final days. She could see the chest, the locket, and the handwritten note. All her questions were answered. Jarred from her nap by her father's voice, Remmie ran down the hall and into the room to find her father sitting on the side of the bed.

"What are you up to? You know Dr. Shannon said stay in bed."

"I need to talk to you. I have done something I want you to know about. I asked Hadley to try to locate your birth parents. He is working on it right now. I want you to have answers to some, if not all of your questions. I won't be here much longer and I want to know you are happy and fulfilled before I leave you. I'm sorry I showed such insensitivity to your needs. I thought about it, and realized you have a right to know all you can about yourself.

"Today so many genetic disorders require family history to diagnose or treat. You don't have that information, but there are other reasons as well. Melissa urged me years ago to let you do this if you wanted to. She always felt there was quite a story behind you coming to us. She felt you should know the truth. And, she didn't want me interfering."

Although Remmie thought it strange that Melissa would encourage him to allow the search, she masked her intrigue as she listened to her father's weak voice. When he finished speaking, she had decided she would not tell him what she knew until they were at River Oaks. The elder Dr. Remington made progress, and on Sunday morning the ambulance came to transport him to his beloved home, River Oaks. Remmie followed in her car with Sarah. Sarah talked all the way. Finally, they were home and settled in. After dinner that evening, Remmie walked across the back yard to the fence that was covered with honeysuckle. Leaning against the fence, she gazed out across the meadow as the sun was sinking low in the sky. Lost in her thoughts, she was unaware that Sarah had joined her.

"Beautiful, *ain't* it? I often spend the last hours of the day *standin'* right here. What's happened, Remmie? And don't say *ya* don't know what I'm *talkin' bout.*"

Not wishing to discuss the subject that was weighing heavily on her mind with Sarah at that time, Remmie continued gazing at the glorious sunset without saying a word.

"Okay, *chil'*, I can see *ya* ain't ready to discuss it just yet. I want *ya* to know I'm here when *ya* need me."

Hugging Sarah tenderly, Remmie whispered, "I do know that, Sarah, I've always known it. I love you."

The two stood arms wrapped securely about each other until the flaming ball disappeared, pulling its fiery glow into the velvet blackness it left behind. The crickets, frogs, and cicadas sang their symphony to the night while Sarah and Remmie walked back to the house.

At last all was still. Remmie was alone in her room. Her father was sleeping, as was Sarah. The time had come to take out her precious treasures, to feel them in her hands once again. First she placed the little chest on the bed and unlocked it with the special key. Then she opened the small box that held the locket and the note. Tenderly unfolding the treasured find, Remmie read the words of her beloved mother again. So many questions now vanished with every reading. *She loved me*, thought Remmie. *She always loved me. She never meant for me to be alone. It wasn't her fault.*

Relief flowed through her body, relief to know the mystery was over. She had a mother who loved her. Even at the point of death, she found a way to rescue her from foster care. Caressing the locket near her heart while holding the note as gently as she could, Remmie sat for hours letting her mind run free, imagining what life would have been like if they could have been together. Her mind played out an enchanted video of playful romping in lush island meadows or along the exquisite shore. Remmie lay down, still holding her treasures as she tried to fall asleep.

Your mother was Black, you are half Black. Thirty years ago, you would have probably been exiled to an island, and even today the truth you now possess will not bring you glory, and certainly will not enhance your father's memory, Remmie heard Hadley Markham saying to her.

Suddenly all the happiness she felt romping with her mother was gone. *How do I approach my father with this truth? How do I, his daughter, tell him, a man of eighty years old, 'you fathered a child by your domestic island girl and I am that child'? Will it be too much for him? How will he accept the fact that Melissa knew and never told him?* Her weary mind was filled with questions, but she fell asleep in the midst of it all.

Waking abruptly, Remmie sat up in bed. What had awakened her so suddenly? Hearing nothing in the house except her own rapid breathing, she lay down again. Before her eyes could close, she heard it again. Sarah's loud yell pierced the stillness, and Remmie knew something was wrong. Hurrying out of her room, trying to determine from which direction Sarah was calling, Remmie called out to her, asking where she was.

"I'm here with Dr. Remington," Sarah replied.

Remmie's heart leaped in her chest as she dashed toward her father's room. Sarah was standing by him, holding his hand. He was pale, sweating profusely, and his breathing was labored. Grabbing his wrist she quickly checked his pulse and respirations. Turning to her medical bag, she took a stethoscope, put it to his chest, and immediately knew what was wrong. His chest was full of fluid. Her father was in respiratory distress. Quickly she propped him up with pillows. This allowed him to breathe somewhat easier. She also increased the oxygen as she administered a dose of his medication. Within an hour he had stabilized, but she knew the end was not many hours away.

Coaxing Sarah into her bedroom, Remmie told her the elder doctor was dying. He had requested no resuscitation, so there was absolutely no need to transport him back to hospital. Remmie told Sarah that she expected him to pass within twenty-four hours. She also told her that this is what her father wanted. He wanted to die at home, not in the hospital.

Sarah became emotional, but soon regained her composure. Then she went off to start the coffee pot. Remmie returned to her father who was resting more comfortably now. Inwardly a battle raged: *Do I tell him? Do I let him go without knowing?* She found no answer within herself. Bewildered and sensing time was short, she looked up to heaven, and asked God to give her direction. Almost immediately, Dr. Remington opened his eyes and spoke.

"Remmie, has Hadley found out something about your birth family? I really would like to know before I go."

Pausing momentarily before speaking to give the Lord a *thank you*, Remmie spoke softly. "Yes, he has. I have found out even more than Hadley Markham told me. I was waiting to get you home before discussing it with you, then you had the episode which made me I think that perhaps I shouldn't bother you with it at all."

"Please tell me. I want to know, and I'm running out of time."

Beginning with Hadley Markham's blackmail attempt all the way to her island adventure, Remmie told him everything except the most sensitive pieces of information. She left out Milea's name, Melissa's involvement, and the birth father's identity. The elder doctor thought carefully about what his daughter had said, and he realized Remmie hadn't told him everything. So he pulled her near, and said in a weak voice, "Tell me everything – *you must*!"

Continuing, Remmie groped for words, hesitating until finally she blurted it out. Afraid to look at him she kept her head on his chest, waiting for a response from him. After several minutes of silence, he stroked her hair and cried, "My own child. What a thing to learn just before you leave this world. Oh, how true the Word of God is when it says, *'Be sure your sins will find you out'*. That incident was well hidden in my long forgotten past - such a foolish, insensitive thing for me to do. Milea was so young, so impressionable, and so in need of love. When I realized she was infatuated with me, I was flattered, but I never intended to return the feeling.

"Melissa wasn't well then. She had become addicted to medication her doctor had ordered for depression. I had to put her in a rehab program to get her straightened out. It was such a painful ordeal for both of us. During the three months she was away, Milea and I grew extremely close. I loved her, Remmie, and she loved me. But it was terribly wrong, so we ended it before Melissa came home. I missed Melissa so much that when she returned I threw myself into making her happy and poor Milea went back to her island. And that was that.

"I always regretted hurting her. She was a wonderful person, but Melissa well…she had always been the love of my life. And, I remembered our vows before God. So I asked God to forgive me, and I spent every minute loving her. Remmie, I must be honest with you. I loved Milea, too.

"Melissa had always encouraged me to allow you to pursue your search for your family. She was something, wasn't she? She knew the truth about me, but she didn't let that influence her love for you. She was a very complex woman, but a strong woman in her later years. You meant the world to her. I often thought that we couldn't love you any more if you had been naturally ours. Now, I know why. You were ours, or at least mine, and loving me as she did, Melissa would have moved heaven and earth to find you. How are you feeling about all this? Are you disappointed in me? Have I become a failure in your eyes?"

"Father, you could never be a failure to me. Surprised and shocked pretty well describe how I felt at first. But right now, at this moment, I feel at peace with myself for the first time ever. I know who I really am, where I came from, and I know without a doubt that I was loved by all my parents. Knowledge truly is power. I feel empowered by what I know. I'm not at all ashamed. You are my birth father, and if you don't care for the world knowing, I certainly don't care."

"I am indeed troubled by Hadley's attempts to blackmail you, and I will handle that in just a few minutes. As for the world knowing, that's something else. I won't be here much longer, but you will. Have you thought it through? Have you considered how you will be affected professionally, as well as personally, by this part of your history? That's my only concern. You do with this knowledge what you will. You have my blessing. Now, as soon as eight o'clock gets here, I'll take care of Hadley."

Within four hours after Dr. Remington's call, Colin Forrester, an attorney from Atlanta arrived. After spending a while with the doctor, he had legal papers signed and notarized by his assistant who came also. Hadley Markham was summoned to River Oaks. Surprised to see Mr. Forrester, he had absolutely no idea what he was about to hear. As he entered, everyone else was already in the room waiting. After greeting Dr. Remington, he inquired as to the nature of the visit. Dr. Remington, with a burst of strength, told Hadley he was being relieved of his services. Mr. Forrester was now his attorney. He further instructed all his records be turned over to Mr. Forrester that day. Hadley stood there in complete shock, stammering for words. Nothing was mentioned about the blackmail attempt, Remmie would handle that in her way. After the entourage departed for Hadley's office to finish what Dr. Remington had started, Remmie and her father were alone again.

Remmie sat holding her father's hands. They were at peace with each other, and with the past. There wasn't really anything left to say, so they just sat there enjoying the peaceful silence. Dr. Remington broke the silence by telling his daughter how proud he was of her, and how fortunate he was to have been loved by two fine women like Melissa and Milea. He went on to say most couples today look only for reasons to end their marriages. Forgiveness is not, as he put it, a *popular activity* anymore. He spoke about how happy he had been, and about the devastation of losing Melissa when they were still so young.

Remmie had been his only joy since then, and River Oaks, of course. Fondly he spoke of his estate, and he asked Remmie to keep it always. "Make provisions for it to bring joy to others for years to come," was his statement exactly. Then he spoke to Remmie about her future. He expressed a strong desire for her to look beyond her medicine for her fulfillment. It was as if he knew she had another calling, another purpose for her life. "Do it, Remmie, whatever it is – go after it. You are strong and wise beyond your years. You can do it," urged the weakening doctor.

The day had turned to night again, and Dr. Benjamin Remington's days on the earth were coming to an end. At that point, he requested Sarah to be brought in. In came Sarah with head high, and hands folded behind her back. Moving closer to his bed, she waited for him to speak.

"Are you just going to stand in perfect silence? I find that so hard to believe. You always have something to say. Can it be my faithful friend that you are all talked out?"

Reaching out he took Sarah's hand. She began to cry. "Now, now, Sarah, there's no need for tears. We both knew this time would come. What is that verse you quote so often to me: *This is the day the Lord hath made. Let us rejoice and be glad in it.* Rejoice with me, faithful one, for today I go to be with my Lord, my dear Melissa, and the children we lost so long ago. I have only one request of you. Take care of Remmie. She has much to do now. She will need you. Wherever she is, please take care of her and be with her, even if it means leaving the river for a time. Is that way too much to ask?"

Shaking her head, Sarah indicated it wasn't. Then she found her voice, "I will do whatever *ya* ask of me, just like always. Remmie is like my own *chil'.* I feel I belong with her now. She has a *callin' ya* know, and I'll be right *there hepin'* her do it. That *ya* can count on. Just as long as the good Lord leaves me here, I'll be *hepin'* her. Don't *ya* worry *bout* that

"I've always been able to depend on you, Sarah. You've been as faithful as a member of this family could ever be, and although, we've been hard on one another, we knew we loved each other. I want you to know you will be taken care of financially. Remmie will see to it. Even if you should retire, you will be taken care of always. Thank you Sarah, and God's blessings be upon you. Remmie, are you still here?"

"I'm here, Father. I'll be here. Don't be concerned."

"The morning has come again, sending the night away to rest. Oh, how lovely it is to see the glow of morning coming in that window. It's like a warm golden glow filling this whole room. Y'all see it, don't you?"

Looking at each other, the daughter and the friend saw only blackness in the pre-dawn hours. They listened to hear what else he would say.

"It's the most beautiful sunrise I've ever seen. I'm feeling so peaceful now as if I could sleep, and sleep, and sleep. Y'all get some rest now. I'll be alright."

Releasing his grip on their hands, he folded his hands across his chest, positioned his head on his pillow, closed his eyes, and went to sleep. In only minutes, his vital signs were gone. He now slept the eternal sleep of death. Remmie noted the time for the reports she would need to do later. Standing there for quite a while, they didn't speak, or cry, or move. They simply stood in peace, just as he had left them. Sarah broke the spell of silence.

"That's how I *wanna* go. Just go to sleep. I *thank* that was the most peaceful death I've ever seen. He *wus* ready, *chil'*. He *wus* ready."

Tears came to Remmie's eyes as she touched his motionless face. "Yes, Sarah, he was ready. He was the only man who ever loved me. I could feel desperately alone right now, but I feel like I'll never be alone. He'll always be there. Let's leave him now. He's sleeping. We need to make some calls, don't we?"

"We *shore* do. There's plenty to do. We better *git* busy. Come on."

Walking from the paneled study where Dr. Remington had spent so much of his time over the last ten years, the two women were calm and serene. As

Remmie turned to close the door, she noticed a single ray of sunlight forcing its way through the wooden shutters and illuminating her father's face. "Sarah, look, the sunrise Father saw in the darkness has come."

"My goodness, *chil'*, he looks like an angel. That's the brightest beam of light I've ever *seen.* I *thank* God let him have a little glimpse of heaven, and now the *afterglow's a lingerin'* on."

~~~

The church was filled, and people stood outside as the service for Dr. Benjamin Remington began. The pastor spoke of Dr. Remington's loving service to the rural community. He told how the clinic Dr. Remington built and staffed in Riverview would accept whatever the patient could afford. He reminded those present that Dr. Remington's wealth or position never caused him to feel he was better than any other human being. In the early years of the clinic, un-conventional methods of payment, such as a chicken or a pig, were often accepted. Dr. Remington or one of the other doctors would graciously accept the animal, and mark their accounts "paid in full."

He went on to say that the chicken or pig would be passed on to the next patient they saw with a need. Medicine wasn't Dr. Remington's only contribution, however. He gave financially to assist many victims of the flood a few years back. He was concerned with the whole person: body, spirit, and soul. The Pastor stated that this little town was blessed to have had him, and today he felt sure Dr. Benjamin Remington's account was marked "paid in full."

Remmie and Sarah sat straight, inspired by the many acts of kindness being remembered on this solemn occasion. The casket of cherry wood was covered with Alabama wild flowers, which were her father's favorites. Many other floral offerings filled the front of the church while still others lined the walkway to the crypt where Dr. Remington would join his beloved Melissa. Now and then a tear would spill from their eyes, flowing quickly down their cheeks. Remmie held in her hand a single yellow rose. This would be her final gift to her precious father. At the appropriate time, she walked to his closed casket, placed the rose, and returned to her seat.

The organ played *It Is Well With My Soul,* as slowly the casket was rolled down the center aisle, then across the cemetery to the crypt standing open to receive the body of a beloved father and friend.
~~~

Remmie and Sarah greeted all who came, weeping with those who wept, and remembering with those who remembered. The outpouring of love was tremendous. Near the end of the line of mourners, Remmie saw a familiar face. It was Hadley Markham. He approached as if she wouldn't want to see him, shook hands, and murmured his condolences, leaving quickly. She also saw Colin Forrester. He gave a benign hug, and reassured her all was handled on the legal front. Then, last, but certainly not least was Jesse, standing there bawling like a baby. Remmie's calm, composed facade faded. Falling into each other's arms they cried together. Sarah encouraged them to get control. Together they walked to the crypt where they touched the head of the casket one last time.

"I wish I could have gotten here sooner, Remmie, but it was impossible. You must have had everything planned to be able to have the funeral so quickly."

"Yes, Father had pre-arranged everything. I had very few decisions to make. Jess, I wish you could have been with us those last hours. It was an awe-inspiring chain of events. He was so peaceful, so content. I was amazed at his resolve to die at River Oaks in his room.

"Sarah, and I were there holding his hands when suddenly he said he saw the most beautiful sunrise he'd ever seen. He felt the glowing warmth of the sun on his face. Then he folded his arms, and went to sleep. Jesse, it was pitch dark outside, not one single ray of sun was showing."

Jesse, crying continually, couldn't find words to express how she felt. She just cried more and hugged Remmie tighter.

~~~

About dusk, the last visitor left and the house was finally still. Remmie, Jesse, and Sarah sat down at the kitchen table for a moment of reflection. They had seen so many old and dear friends. Many of them they had not seen in a long, long time. Recalling who said what, how they looked, how old they had gotten, the threesome talked on and on about all the gestures of kindness they had received. And the food! My goodness gracious – the kitchen and dining room were full of food.

"They must *thank* we eat like horses," exclaimed Sarah. "I don't know *what'n* the world *we gonna* do with all this stuff."

"Eat as much as we can for the next couple of days and freeze some, I suppose," said Remmie.
~~~

Jesse had spotted the ten layer chocolate cake. "This one is mine. I'll take it back to the city with me."

"Take whatever you want, Jess. We'll never eat all this food before it spoils."

"Well, ladies, let's eat supper, and clean up *everthin'* before it gets dark. We can watch the sunset behind the meadow *if'n* we hurry."

CHAPTER TWELVE

Morning came quickly for Remmie. Upon opening her eyes, her mind immediately alerted her that things weren't the same today. She wondered how many times she would awaken with that empty feeling and that mental reminder. *Time is truly our friend in situations like these. It may not heal, but it does allow for adjustment to take place. All I need*, she thought, *is some time, and I'll be just fine. Some things are the same*, she thought as the alluring smell of Sarah's breakfast crept into her room. *Some things are the same, at least today.*

After breakfast Jesse returned to the city, which left Remmie and Sarah putting the big old house in order. Around ten that morning, Colin Forrester called to set up a meeting with Remmie regarding her father's will. He was coming out at three. Sarah wanted to go to the graves of her parents, so Remmie asked a neighbor to take Sarah about the same time the attorney was coming. She needed to ask some questions she didn't want Sarah to hear. After all, a decision did have to be made regarding where Sarah would live now.

The neighbor picked Sarah up at two-thirty, and Mr. Forrester arrived at three sharp. Inviting him in, Remmie offered coffee and cake, but Mr. Forrester seemed all business this afternoon. "I have many things to discuss, Miss Remington, and my time is limited. May we begin?"

"Please do, Mr. Forrester."

"Your father's will is cut and dried. You are his only heir, so everything is yours. He had stipulated that Sarah be provided for, but if you out-live her, that will be your responsibility. That is most likely the outcome in my opinion. Should you die, however, I will make sure Sarah has everything she needs. Will she be staying on at River Oaks?"

"That's my question. I'm not sure exactly what Father had in mind for her. Can you help me with that?"

"His only comment to me was that you would take care of her. He did seem to feel she would be here in this house, though, and for that matter he felt you would be, too."

"That isn't possible at this particular time. My work requires me to be in the city. However, I believe before long I'll be here full time. But Sarah, now that's a different ballgame. She can go to the city with me. I've plenty of room or she can stay on here. I'm afraid she'll be lonely in this big old house. I'll have to speak with her about this."

"Well, as I said, you own everything now. Uh, his financial holdings may surprise you. He was a wise investor. His diversification made him very wealthy. You will not need to work if you should decide not to."

This caught Remmie's attention. She felt her father had accumulated a nice amount of money, but she had absolutely no idea he was wealthy enough that she didn't need to work anymore.

"Could you give me an amount, Mr. Forrester?"

"It would be a rough estimate at this point, but I'd say ten million. That doesn't include this estate or the clinic in town."

All Remmie heard ringing in her head was ten million. Never in her wildest dreams did such an astronomical amount enter her head.

"Did you say ten million?"

"Yes, I did. You are a very wealthy woman, Miss Remington. This kind of wealth carries with it some major responsibilities. You will be approached by every money-grabbing con-artist in these parts. You need careful management of this fortune. With careful management, your successors for generations will benefit from it."

"Please forgive me, Mr. Forrester, but I'm blown away by that amount. My father never indicated to me he had accumulated such a vast fortune."

"It's possible he didn't know. Mr. Markham handled all his investments, and he may have hidden the size of his fortune from your father. I have discovered some rather strange practices he used to mask where the funds were. It took me a good bit of time to run down all this information I'm giving you now. To be frank, Hadley Markham wasn't much help. I found him to be a rather annoying person."

"You and I will get along just fine, Mr. Forrester. You are an astute judge of character. There's another large amount of money to which I've been told I am the heir. Can you check into that for me?"

"Certainly, if you'll provide me with the information I'll get on it tomorrow. Miss Remington, if I may be somewhat pushy, you need an attorney to manage your estate. It isn't an easy thing to do. I will present you a figure for my services annually, but you should get other estimates as well before making a decision."

"I will entertain that idea, and I will get additional bids before making my decision. I have the information regarding a bank account in Switzerland. I've been told my grandfather put his ill-gotten wealth there. I believe I'm his only heir. That's about all I know to tell you. It's all here in these letters. Please handle them carefully. They are fragile, and I'd like to have them back."

"As you wish. I'll be going now, but we'll talk tomorrow. Good afternoon, Miss Remington."

"One thing before you go, could we call each other Colin and Remmie? Mr & Miss is too stuffy for me."

"Okay, by all means, Remmie, let's do that."

Early the next morning Mr. Forrester called to request another meeting, but this time he asked Remmie to come into the city to meet with him in his office. She agreed to be there at one o'clock.

It was a lovely day. Fall was coming, so the breeze was just a bit cooler than it had been. Remmie drove away from River Oaks with the top down on her car, headed to Atlanta and her meeting with Colin. Driving along and listening to the radio, she thought over all the events of the last few days. People had been so kind. It really made her feel good to know how much they loved her father. His life had meant something to others, not just her. He had given so much to their rural farming community, and they remembered it. That meant a lot to this young woman who now faced life without a family again. Remmie thought about Sarah and what would be best for her. Life in the city would be absolutely foreign to her. She couldn't walk by the river, watch the sun come up over the meadow, hear the clicking and chirping of crickets, cicadas, and frogs in the evening, or go to her little country church with long-time friends. Life in the city would not be the best thing for Sarah, she concluded. But alone at River Oaks didn't seem right either. After all these years of taking care of the family and having Dr. Remington to yell at and cook for, Sarah would be alone there. That didn't seem like the right answer. Well, she obviously wasn't going to find an answer for this one before reaching Colin's office.

Colin, thought Remmie, *now there was an interesting man – very professional, compassionate, and not bad looking either.* She wondered if he was married. Yes, she was sure he was. Men who look like him were usually married with five kids. Their wives have built-in radar able to detect a flirting client several blocks away. She decided to get her mind on business by bringing her imagination to a screeching halt. *Oh well*, she thought, *window shopping doesn't cost anything.*

Taking the next exit off the interstate, she drove into the downtown area. The tall, distinctive looking building where Colin's office was located wasn't hard to find. The elevator was on the exterior of the building, giving every rider a tremendous view of the South's largest city. Not caring much for elevators, Remmie faced the doors and watched the numbers as thirty-seven floors sped by. Getting off on the thirty-eighth floor, she walked into an extremely plush office, done in brown and gray, with muted green and spicy gold mingled about. It was most impressive. The receptionist led her back to Colin's office, which was itself something to see. His oversized golden oak desk sat in front of a huge window. There were no drapes or blinds, so the view was spectacular.

The secretary greeted her and asked her to sit down at a small conference table. Colin joined her. He laid out several documents in front of her. She looked them over, waiting for him to tell her exactly what she was looking at.

"I've located the Swiss account you told me about. Right now, it appears you will be the only existing heir to this money. There is some question, though, about another child, a boy born to the same woman you believe to be your mother. Do you know about him?"

"That's not possible. My mother was very ill with a terminal disease just shortly after my birth. That's why I was put in foster care. She couldn't have had another child."

"The lead I have says there was another child alright, but he's not younger than you – he's your twin."

"My twin! I can't believe that. Sister Anna Marie never mentioned it. And my letter from my mother said nothing about a brother."

"Can we contact Sister Anna Marie to see if she can verify this claim?"

"Yes, we can. I have her number right here. I'll call her now if I may use your phone."

Colin motioned for her to make the call. It seemed the phone would never be answered. Finally, the comforting voice of Sister Anna came over the line. Remmie quickly told her what she had just learned, asking her if she possessed any knowledge of a boy baby. Sister Anna Marie assured her that she had no knowledge of any other child. But she did remind her that Milea did not give birth at the orphanage. She said a local mid-wife helped Milea give birth, and she was still living. Remmie asked if she would speak to her to find out if she remembered Milea, and if she had one child or two. Sister Anna agreed, assuring Remmie she would call back within two hours with the answer.

The wait was difficult, to say the least. Colin worked at his desk while Remmie sat staring out across the immense city, lost in her thoughts. Of all the things that she had learned over the last few weeks, this had been the biggest surprise. A brother, a full-fledged blood relative – she couldn't wait to find out if it were true.

As it is with any wait, time stood still. After watching the anxious young woman, Colin decided to do something to distract her until the call came in. Calling his favorite restaurant, he made a reservation, requesting his usual table. That was the easy part. Talking his guest into leaving proved much more challenging. After convincing Remmie the call she expected could be forwarded to him on his cellular, she consented to have lunch with him.

Colin and Remmie were greeted and escorted to a secluded table in a corner by a very large plant. A nearby window offered a view of an enclosed area between buildings that had been turned into a quaint little garden. It was so lovely, so private, and so inviting. Remmie couldn't take her eyes off the garden - pots filled with impatience in every color, ivy climbing the brick fortress surrounding the garden, unusual shaped boxwoods, and daisies blooming everywhere.

Colin watched Remmie as she carefully observed every detail of the private garden. His eyes scanned her beautiful face. Becoming aware of his attention, Remmie turned to face him. "You are a very lovely woman. I hope I am not making you uncomfortable by saying that. I don't often express myself so directly. When we first met at your father's bedside I noticed what a devoted daughter you were. Again at the funeral, I observed your strength while facing one of the most distressing events in one's life, and here today discovering yet another unknown about yourself. I can't help myself, I admire you. You are not a typical nineties woman."

"Is that a compliment? What is a typical nineties woman?"

"I'm not touching that one. I'll just say you are the most attractive and interesting woman I've met in a long time. You have a purpose, and a sense of yourself that I've not seen in the women I've dated recently."

"I assumed you were married."

"Me? No Ma'am! I've never been married. I've helped a lot of people end their marriages, which has given me a fairly negative view of the institution."

"I can't imagine you practicing divorce law. That's a fancy office for a divorce attorney."

"That was a while back. I've expanded my practice. I do, however, handle a divorce or two every year. It helps me remember why I'm not married."

"So you never plan to marry or have a family? Who will take care of you in your old age? You can't want to be alone always. I surely don't. I really can't say I've seriously considered marriage, but I don't have a negative view of it. My folks had a wonderful marriage. I think I'd like to marry and have a child or maybe two. I just don't know when I'll find the time."

"Medicine is a demanding career in itself, but trauma medicine must be totally consuming. Do you seriously think you will ever find time to be a wife and mother?"

"Yes, I think so. I think..."

At that moment, Colin's cellular rang. Remmie stopped speaking as Colin answered the call.

"She's right here. Just a second."

"Hello. Sister Anna Marie did you speak with the midwife?"

The aging lady told Remmie she had indeed spoken with the mid-wife.

"Did she remember my mother?"

Again the comforting voice answered, "Yes...Yes, child, she remembered Milea. She said the girl was very afraid of her father. He was going to hurt the baby. She wanted to protect her child from him."

"That sounds like my mother, doesn't it?"

"I'm sure it was your mother. I remember Milea told me about the mid-wife, and about the ordeal in giving birth. She said the mid-wife helped her a lot. She was very patient with your mother during the eighteen hours of labor."

"Tell me, Sister Anna, was there a second child? Was it a boy?"

"Yes Remmie. It's true. There was a boy baby born just after you were. Your mother indeed had twins. The boy baby was small and not breathing correctly. His color was deep blue. He didn't cry. There was something wrong."

"Sister Anna, what happened to him? Why did my mother keep him a secret?"

"The old mid-wife said she felt great compassion for Milea. She said the woman had a torturous labor and birth. She fainted when the first baby came out. She was bleeding badly when suddenly, another baby came. This one was in bad shape. She said she felt so sorry for the woman that she took the sick baby boy away immediately. Milea only knew about the first one, the girl. The mid-wife believed the boy would die soon, so she wanted to spare the distraught young woman the heartbreak. But the little boy didn't die, so the next day she took him to the clinic, telling the nurse he was abandoned by a woman she never saw before. The baby was taken to a special hospital in the states. That's all she knows."

Remmie found this story very hard to comprehend. After thanking Sister Anna for her help, she hung up.

Colin took her hand across the table. Silently they sat for a while. Remmie resisted the story she had just heard, trying to make herself believe it was impossible. She struggled with her feelings about an old woman who would tell such a fabrication, and why? She found no answers for her questions.

"How can I believe this story? It's so bizarre! How do we find the person if he does exist? I'm confused, upset, and angry!"

"All those emotions are normal, Remmie. This situation did not happen today. We just learned about it today, so we don't have to solve it today. You need a little time to absorb this before you decide how you want me to proceed. I'll make arrangements for you to stay in my firm's suite at the Hilton. We can talk again tomorrow."

Remmie and Colin walked out of the restaurant onto the busy street, heading back to Colin's office. In a flash it hit Remmie, like a bolt out of the blue. She stopped, stared at Colin, and demanded to know his source. "Who told you about the second child? If my mother didn't know, and the mid-wife acted alone, who told you?"

"Come on, Remmie let's talk about it in my office."

"No! I'm not moving an inch until you tell me who told you about my brother!"

Pausing, weighing the consequences of continuing this discussion on a public sidewalk or provoking this obstinate young woman to lawyer battering, Colin decided he better fess-up.

"Okay, Remmie, when I contacted the bank in Zurich, I was faxed a document naming the woman you call your mother, Milea Marjoul, as heir to the fortune contained in the account. The document indicated she was the only child of Manuel and Margarita Marjoul. It was believed she had given birth with the help of a mid-wife to twins, one girl, one boy. The boy baby was taken to a hospital in Florida, and it is believed may not have survived. The girl baby was healthy and remained with the mother. The document stated further that these children had been fathered by a White American. Therefore, they were a public disgrace to the Marjoul family. However, being half Marjoul, there was a family obligation to see to their welfare. This document was signed by your grandfather, Manuel Marjoul."

"He knew all the time about the babies, but he never told my mother. He let her die without knowing she gave birth to twins. What a wicked man he was. My mother would have found my brother just like she found me if she had only known. Now, I may have a brother out there somewhere, but I have no idea how to find him."

Wishing to console her, Colin opened his arms to embrace her if she would allow it. She did. Having strong arms around her made her feel secure, at least for the moment. *Tomorrow*, like Colin had said, *we can deal with this tomorrow*, thought a fatigued and emotionally drained Remmie.

The next morning, awakening to the sound of a busy city below, Remmie got ready. Then she waited for Colin to call. He was prompt. By nine she was in his office where together they mapped out a plan of action. She wanted to find her brother, and she felt confident Colin could find him. With a plan in place and high hopes, Remmie returned to River Oaks.

CHAPTER THIRTEEN

The all-observing Sarah was sure she sensed something in Remmie's voice when she called to say she would be staying over-night. She knew something had happened, so she was waiting with a fresh cup of Remmie's favorite coffee. Remmie wasn't in a talking mood. She had her coffee, but it didn't loosen her tongue. Without any explanation she left again.

This time she went to the cemetery. The flowers were wilted now. Remmie traced each letter of her father's name with her finger. She missed him so much. This was news she needed to share with him. How she wished she had known this sooner. They could have searched for her brother together. Seeing Melissa's name there beside her father's made her think about what a remarkable woman she was - keeping Milea's secret, raising her like her own, even after knowing she had been betrayed. Melissa had not allowed her feelings to keep her from reaching out to a little girl who needed a family. Remmie found herself overcome with pride to have known and loved the two people buried in the crypt. She realized how fortunate she was to have been so deeply loved by three parents. All the sadness that she had endured in foster care was overshadowed by the realization she had at that moment.

Now she must find a way to do for other foster children what her parents had done for her. Standing for a few silent moments, collecting her thoughts, Remmie walked away. The feeling of loneliness was replaced by the knowledge of how fortunate she was. She was determined to be as courageous and generous as her parents had been. Whispering to herself, and to her parents, "I won't let you down. I'll make a difference, like you did for me."

Returning to the house, she found Sarah in a bad mood. She was feeling the emptiness of the house, and Remmie's silence had hurt her feelings. Knowing Sarah as well as she did, Remmie felt words would only open the flood gates of tears, so she decided to initiate a distraction. Heading into the kitchen, she got out pots and pans, rattled silverware, and slammed cabinet doors, in general she created racket. She snickered to herself as she waited for the very predictable Sarah to charge in, protecting her domain. Sure enough, she heard Sarah coming down the hall huffing and puffing, sounding a bit like a runaway locomotive. Standing there among all the pots with all the cabinet doors wide open, Remmie waited to spring her trap on Sarah.

"What in heaven's name are *ya doin'* in my kitchen? It *shore* seems like *ya* are *tearin'* the place up!"

"Well, Sarah, I've decided we should remodel, update things, put in some big windows over here, add a pantry over there, paint everything white, and buy all new appliances."

"What!!! Have *ya* taken leave of *yore* senses? I like my kitchen just like it is. I don't want *new fangled* appliances. They're all plastic now. These are made from real stuff. Paint *everthin'* white! You can't keep white clean. I *ain't* got enough energy to wash *'em ever-day*. I can't believe *ya wanna* put big *winders* in over *yonder* and a pantry over *thar*. I like it just fine like it is right now. Get busy, young lady, and help me straighten this mess out. *Ya* can make a bigger mess quicker than anybody I know. You're faster than a Banty chicken with a rooster in the pen. Get *movin'* now, and put this place in order."

"Let's cook something, Sarah. I'm in a mood to cook. You want to help me?"

"Any suggestions, or are *ya* just *gonna* throw *thangs* in a pan and give it a name?"

"How about an Onion Casserole? We haven't made that in years. Or maybe a Tomato Soup Cake? I know, let's do an Onion Casserole and a Tomato Soup Cake. What do we need? Let's see now, we have onions, mushrooms, saltines, cream of mushroom soup, and I'll make the bread crumbs. What do we need for the cake? We have flour, sugar, spices, tomato soup, cream cheese, and nuts. Come on Sarah, let's get going!!"

Assembling everything they needed, Sarah and Remmie cooked away the evening hours, forgetting all about the lonely feelings and the empty house. After the food finished cooking, they cleaned up their mess. Then they fixed themselves generous helpings of Onion Casserole, but they saved the cake to give to the neighbor who took Sarah to the cemetery. Making their plans to deliver the cake early the next morning, Sarah and Remmie finished their casserole and left their dishes in the sink.

They walked out back and sat down together in the ivy-covered trellis swing. The night was still, but cooler than usual. The crickets and frogs were singing their top forty hits while a big old hootie owl kept the beat. Sarah pulled her apron up, covering her arms. Remmie sat arms folded, watching the moon come up over the meadow.

"Sarah, we need to discuss some things. I realize I haven't been a wealth of information the last few days. I've had to deal with a few overwhelming facts about myself. I just needed a little time to sort through my feelings before making any decisions.

"I am concerned about you. I'm afraid you won't be happy in the city, but I hate to think of you here all alone. I can't be here all the time right now. I have to finish my schedule in the trauma unit. I just can't figure out what we should do."

"We, *did'ja* say? When do I get to have my say? Seems to me you've *done'n* shouldered this whole burden as if I *wus* some senile, old woman. I'll have *ya* to know, I *ain't* ready to have *ya,* or anyone else, make my decisions for me. So, I'll relieve *ya*, my dear, of this heavy load. You don't need to resign *yore* position or drive back and forth *seein' bout* me. I can see to myself, thank *ya* ma'am. To be exact, I've been *a seein'* to *ya* for some time now. So, with that weight removed from *yore* shoulders, get on to the next decision, *causen* I'm *makin'my* own, and I'm *a stayin'* right here.

"I'm at home here. People know me here. I feel much safer here than I would in your house. I can't imagine *havin'* to go down ten floors to take out the garbage. Lordy be, all I do is walk over to the back door. *Ya* can't leave a door open to catch a nice breeze; *ya* can't even open a *winder*. I don't know how much *ya* pay for that place, but I hope it *ain't* much. Don't get me wrong now, it's *purty*, but it *ain't* homey.

"My favorite part is that little *fella* who opens the door for *ya*. I remember the first time I came there without *ya*. I nearly *'bout* fell flat on my face. I *wus* all set to push the door open when he stepped up and opened it. I asked if he *wus tryin'* to kill me. He said he *wus* paid to stand *thar* to open the door for folks. I *couldn't hardly* believe some city *fella wus payin'* him to open the door. We all got hands! We can do that for our own selves.

"No, Remmie, my place is here, where I understand the ways, speak the language, and I can *hep* folks out and take care of *thangs* here. If I weren't here to see to *thangs,* the blamed kudzu would take the place."

"Okay, okay, Mother Superior, you've made your point. I hear you loud and clear. I'm sorry I left you out. That wasn't my intention at all. I guess I do feel a responsibility to take care of you."

"I appreciate that, but just wait a while until I need it. Then I'll be the most cooperative little *ole'* lady you've ever seen."

"Somehow I doubt that, but I agree. We'll wait until the appropriate time comes. I don't blame you for wanting to be here instead of in the city. However, I'm concerned about the isolation of the place. Perhaps we could hire a fulltime maintenance man. He could live in the garage apartment, fix whatever breaks, tend the grounds, and be security. How's that sounding?"

"Who's boss, me or him?"

"You, of course. You tell him what to do, and he does it."

"Well, then, it has possibilities. But who could we hire?"

"I'll run an ad in the paper. We'll interview and make a choice together. I'll have Colin check out his background and references."

"Let's do it! But remember *ya* said, 'We interview.' Don't *ya* be *forgettin'* that."

Remmie chuckled to herself, thinking that was probably her big mistake. *Sarah would be hard to please. He'll need to know how to shoe horses, cure meat, and plow a mule. Poor fellow,* she thought.

Sarah's mind jumped to another subject. She hadn't forgotten all the strange goings on of the past few days, and she knew something was being kept from her. "Now, Rebecca Elizabeth Melissa, *hows bout tellin'* me what's happened over the past few days? And don't try to tell me that *nothin' happened.* I *ain't* blind or stupid. Your father *a changin'* lawyers on his death bed, *yore* mysterious trip, whispers – it all adds up to *somethin'* in my book."

"I never considered you blind or stupid. As I said before, I needed some time to think things through. I always intended to tell you everything but, then again, I wonder just how much you already know. It occurred to me how you encouraged my pursuit of my birth family. Oh, you were subtle, but you were getting the message across. What did my mother tell you anyway? Did she tell you to encourage me? Maybe she told you more. Do you know who my birth mother was? You do! I'd recognize that look anywhere! You know!"

"Oh, now, what look are *ya a talkin' bout*?"

"That deer in a headlight look. The one's that all over you at this moment. You are full of secrets yourself, my friend. Maybe we should just compare notes before I tell the entire saga. You know that my real mother was a domestic here, an island girl pregnant out of wedlock?"

"Yes, I know, Remmie. Melissa told me how Milea contacted her before she passed, *beggin'* her to find her little girl."

"Well, then do you know who my real father was?"

"No, Melissa would never discuss him, even if she knew."

"Okay, do you know that Milea was Black? Sarah, the deer in the headlight look is back plus, your mouth is hanging open. I take it you didn't know that?"

"*Yore* father would have had a fit! *Ain't* we the lucky ones, he'll never know all this?"

"He knows. I told him after we returned here the day before he died."

"Lord, have mercy, I'm surprised he didn't just die *right out* when he *heared* that."

"Well, there's more, much more. Are you sure you're up to it?"

"I'm as strong as a mule. *Let'er* fly!"

"Milea and my father had an affair while my mother was in a rehab program. I was the product of their union."

"Sweet St. Peter! *Yore* father and a Black girl? He admitted to that?"
"He certainly did. He even said he loved Milea, but it was terribly wrong, and they ended it before my mother came home. Father never knew about the pregnancy. My mother knew, but she had no idea the identity of the father until Milea called her years later."

"*Chil', chil'*! This *oughta* be a book or a movie maybe. *Them* stories on day time television *ain't* a bit more bizarre than what *ya* are *a tellin'* me. *How'd* you find all this out anyway?"

"Hadley Markham found it out. He tried to blackmail me with it. That's why I went down to the islands to find out if it was true. Father asked Hadley to find my birth family so I could get on with my life. Hadley, being the obnoxious little worm he is, saw opportunity knocking."

"I bet he never thought it would knock him out of a job! I never liked him much."

"Nor did I. Father replaced him with Colin. He's a fine attorney. He found out my father was worth ten million dollars! Can you believe that?"

"Ten million? What in the world are *ya gonna* do with ten million dollars? You *ain't thinkin'* of *hirin' no* high priced maintenance man, are *ya*? Shoot, we could hire *ever* one of *'em* in the whole states of Alabama, Georgia, and Florida for that, and have some left over."

"Sarah, I have bigger and better plans than that for the money. I'm not ready just yet to talk about those plans. I think you'll like them. However, getting back to my trip to the island, I found an aging nun who knew Mother and me when I was a small child. She filled in all the blanks for me. Why I was orphaned, who my parents really were, and there's one other story you won't believe either."

"Well, get on with it before my imagination kills me dead."

"I had a twin brother. He may not be living. Mother gave birth to twins. A local mid-wife attended her. Realizing the boy was seriously ill and that the young woman was already in a bad situation, she hid the boy. Mother was so weak she fainted, and never realized she had given birth to a second child. Later, after the baby survived the night, the mid-wife took him to a clinic and left him.

"My wicked grandfather knew all this. He had me and my brother brought to the states to protect his reputation. We are half White, you know. And in his distorted view, we were a disgrace. Mother was never told. She died believing I was her only child. Colin is trying to find my brother now. Oh, Sarah, it would mean so much to me to have a living blood relative. Maybe he would come here. Maybe we could be a family."

Sarah put her arm around Remmie's shoulders, consoling her. "Maybe so, sweet one, maybe so."

Rising early, Remmie went for a walk along the river. The mornings were so busy there. All kinds of wild life made preparations for the day. Squirrels and chipmunks scurried around, chattering messages only they could decipher. Then there were the birds. They came in a rainbow of colors and sang a variety of melodies. The trees never seemed more alive than in the mornings.

The largest animals on the river were the white tailed deer, the bobcat, and the panther. Some people believe the panther is extinct, but folks living there knew better. There's nothing on the river that made a noise like that big cat. It sounded just like a woman screaming. Many a young camper had packed up and gone home after hearing those blood curdling screams coming out of darkness.

Remmie remembered the time she and her father had been hunting way back in the woods and it got dark before they could walk to the jeep. Sticking close to her father, Remmie could feel something near. Turning around, she saw green eyes piercing the blackness that encompassed them.

Tugging on her father's sleeve, she pointed to the eerie eyes following a few yards behind. The tone of her father's voice made her even more afraid. Speaking in a monotone voice, he said, "Whatever you do, don't run! We're almost there. We'll be okay. Just keep walking!"

Remmie never looked back after that. She just walked searching the path ahead for the jeep she hoped would appear any second. Taking shape out of the darkness, the jeep appeared, offering safety for Remmie and her father. Once inside the jeep, her father turned on the head lights and there they were not one, but two big cougars. They stopped straight ahead of the jeep on the path where moments before Remmie and her father had been. Chills ran up her spine as she sat spellbound, watching the magnificent creatures. Slowly they disappeared into the night. That was the only time she had ever seen them, but she had heard them many times. All Remmie knew was that she admired their beauty and power, but she could do that from a distance. She hoped she would never see them that close again.

Returning to the house to get Sarah and the Tomato Soup Cake, Remmie drove over to their nearest neighbor's, Cupideen Smitherman. Cupideen had lived on the river all her life. She was eccentric, to say the least. Sarah liked her though, and she was a good neighbor.

"*Yo ho*, Cupideen. It's Sarah here!"

"Come on in, Sarah, and take a seat. I'll be *thar* in two shakes of a lamb's tail. Well, good *mornin'* to *ya,* too, Miss Remington. I didn't know *ya wus* here."

"Yes, Miss Smitherman. I wanted to come along with Sarah to express my appreciation for all your kindnesses over the last few days, especially for giving Sarah a ride to the cemetery at Quail Ridge."

"*Wern't nothin'*. I *wus jest* tickled to do it. She's a real friend. I owe her many good deeds. So that's that. *How's ya'll* doing over *thar* by *yoreselves*?"

"We're okay. It's lonely, of course. We miss Father, but life does go on. Sarah wants to remain at River Oaks. She doesn't think she can adjust to living in the city. I'm afraid that I agree with her, but I'm finding it difficult to leave her alone."

"Yep, I *kin* understand that. River Oaks is a big *ole'* place. I *shore* wouldn't stay *thar* alone. No ma'am, not me. Sarah, are *ya right shore* you *wanna* stay *thar*?"

"It's my home, Cupi. I don't know *nothin'* but the river. I just can't move into the tenth floor of that fancy buildin' with a man that does *nothin'* all day but open doors for folks. I wouldn't fit. *How'd ya* like to move into the city?'

"No, no, not me. I *ain't leavin' har.* But I'm young and strong. I can take care of myself."

Remmie closed her eyes, and waited for the explosion.

"Are *ya sayin'* I'm some old *hepless* woman who can't take care of herself? I'll have *ya* know I can handle *thangs* very well over at River Oaks. I just might challenge *ya* to a wrestling match to see how strong *ya* are."

Cupi burst out laughing. After a second or two, so did Sarah.

"Didn't mean to get *yore* dander up, Sarah. It *wus* a bad choice of words. What I *intentioned* to say *wus thar's* a lot of work at River Oaks and it's off to itself. You may need some *hep.*"

"You're right, Mrs. Smitherman. Sarah and I have talked about hiring a handyman to live in the garage apartment to keep things up and provide a little extra security for her."

"Well, *thar's* a fine *idear.* She'll keep him busy, alright. I'll pay *ya* regular visits, Sarah, and we can take rides to Quail Ridge anytime *ya* want. Thanks *fer* the cake, but I've *got'a git* in the yard now to milk my goat."

Remmie left Mrs. Smitherman's house feeling much better about Sarah's future at River Oaks. She knew the handyman idea was right. With visits from Cupideen, Sarah should be able to make a good transition to living alone.

CHAPTER FOURTEEN

"Hello. Yes, I'm Miss Remington. Alright, Mr. Kinkaid, I'll be interviewing several people this afternoon at River Oaks. Can you be there at four o'clock? Very well then, I'll look forward to meeting you at four."

Remmie worked the graveyard shift in the trauma unit. Then she drove straight to River Oaks. She told Sarah she had received several applicants for the job, but she had narrowed them down to four, and now, they would make the final decision. Sarah was pleased even more than she let show. The truth be known, she hadn't rested well at all since Remmie had been in the city. Every odd noise had awakened her. So the thought of having someone around was most comforting. The four applicants were prompt. *Nice looking and healthy, too,* thought Sarah as she showed them into the living room. One by one she took them down the hall to the study where Remmie sat in her father's brown leather chair behind his big, old desk. *She's a Remington, alright,* thought Sarah. *She looks like she's in charge.*

Each applicant was interviewed by Remmie, with Sarah chiming in all along. After the fourth man left the room, they conferred with each other, and to Remmie's surprise, they liked the same one. Stuart Kinkaid was a tall outdoorsman who loved country living, and was familiar with farming, ranching, and fixing things. Standing 6'4" with broad shoulders and dark, tanned skin, Stuart looked like a security person or a body guard. Remmie thanked the men for coming, and said she would notify them within two days, one way or the other.

After the applicants left, she called Colin to request a background check on Mr. Kinkaid. Colin assured her he would have it completed as soon as possible. Then, without warning, he asked if he could bring the results out personally and take her out for dinner. She surprised herself by accepting. She anxiously awaited Colin's arrival the following afternoon.

Remmie was a vision in a flowing lavender raw silk dress with a V-neckline, and tiny pearl buttons down the front. Her hair was pulled up with curls hanging on her neck. Pearl teardrop earrings and a single strand of pearls accessorized perfectly.

The entry gate sounded an alarm, and Remmie gave clearance after hearing Colin's distinctive voice on the intercom. Waiting by a window, she could see his red BMW coming up the drive. She was very excited. Then it occurred to her, she had never felt this way about a man before. Opening the door, Remmie welcomed Colin.

For the first few seconds he could not take his eyes off of her. When he did speak, he let her know what an eye full she was. Remmie seemed somewhat shy, but very flattered. After sitting down in the living room, Colin gave her the report on Mr. Kinkaid. Reviewing carefully, Remmie was pleased with what she read. Colin confirmed her decision to hire Stuart Kinkaid. That left Sarah. Remmie's promise would be honored. Sarah would have the final word.

Remmie took the report into the kitchen to Sarah. She asked her to read it and be prepared to give an opinion when she returned from having dinner with Colin. Sarah started reading right away. Remmie and Colin drove away to a quaint restaurant not far from River Oaks.

The restaurant was built with large windows facing a lake. Lights were all around the edge of the lake, creating a shimmering mirror. Colin chose the table nearest the lake. Then he assisted Remmie into her seat. The meal was delicious and the conversation was more personal than professional. Leaving the restaurant in the glow of a gorgeous full moon, Colin opened the car door for Remmie. Before she could get in, he stopped her to gaze at the moon with him one more time. His gaze was more on Remmie than the moon. Colin surrendered to his impulse and kissed her gently. Though somewhat caught off guard, Remmie was responsive to his kiss, so he kissed her again.

Both Colin and Remmie were quiet during the drive back to River Oaks. Colin was concerned that he may have been too bold. He thought he should have waited to kiss her until they knew each other better. Remmie was a little uncomfortable about the whole event, but she had not protested in any way. However, she decided that she would stop his advances if he tried it again. She also knew she liked it very much, maybe too much.

"Sarah, we're home." Remmie and Colin headed into the kitchen where Sarah was busily writing something. She acknowledged them but continued writing. They sat down at the table to wait for her to finish.

"There, now I've got Stuart's job description all written out. He's *gonna* be a busy boy. I have plans for a vegetable garden in the spring, some greens this fall. And then, I want the barn painted, and the flower gardens cleared out."

Remmie and Colin looked at each other and laughed. "I guess this means we have a winner. You want him to work here. Is that right?"

Sarah nodded yes.

"Then pray tell kind, gentle woman, why are you trying to work him to death?"

"I *ain't tryin'* to work him to death. I want him to feel needed. I *ain't gonna* have him *sittin'* around here *watchin'* me all day long. He's a big, strong *fella*, and he likes to work. We're *gonna* turn this place into a real farm."

Remmie and Colin looked at each other, then at Sarah, then at each other. Remmie's face reflected her total amazement.

"A real farm? Is that what you said?"

"Yep, a real farm. We're *gonna* have livestock, crops in the fields, chickens and fresh eggs, pigs to fatten, and to butcher. I can hardly wait to get going. Stuart is *gonna hep* me turn River Oaks into a real farm. You know it once *wus* a farm. It can be again. And after all, you've got all that money and *nothin'* to do with it. We might as well use some to turn this place into a real farm."

Sarah stood arms folded, looking very determined. Remmie, on the other hand, was completely caught off guard. She didn't know what to say; she really didn't know how she felt about this idea. It was so unexpected. Deciding to leave it for now, she told Sarah that she and Colin would talk about her plan and develop a budget. Happily, Sarah retired to her room for the evening, leaving Remmie and Colin in near shock.

Remmie told Colin she couldn't believe her ears. A farm of all things! Why in the world would she want a farm? Colin had no answers of course, so he decided to divert Remmie's attention to the gorgeous night they were missing by standing in the kitchen pondering Sarah's unusual plan. Taking Remmie's hand, Colin led her to the door, coaxing her along while she continued recanting all of Sarah's visions of farm life.

Once outside, he and his confused lady friend sat down in the swing. Looking up, he saw the same lovely full moon they had seen earlier. Trying to refocus Remmie's attention, he pointed upward as he put his finger to her lips. She was silent, at least for that moment.

"You aren't planning to drive back to the city tonight, are you?"

"I was unless you need something else that would keep me here longer."

"I do, but it may not be what you have in mind. I would like to explore the farm idea as well as another idea I've been thinking about for some time. Colin, I want to be honest with you about myself. There are still many things you don't know about my life. I realized something earlier when I was waiting for you, something I hadn't realized before. I was excited about you coming here, about our date, and about the fact that you find me attractive.

"There have only been a few men in my life because that's the way I've wanted it. I don't find it easy to trust men. I'm not sure that will change easily. I'm attracted to you. I enjoy your company. I admire your professionalism, and I hope you'll ask me out again. But I'm not a party girl, and I don't have affairs. I'm inviting you to stay the night, but I'll be in my room and you'll be in the guest room. That's the only way for me."

"Well, Miss Remington, I've learned even more about you tonight. Frankly, I am surprised that a woman with your looks, personality, and background hasn't had many men in her life. Knowing you as I do, I know you are telling me the truth. So, that means I either accept or reject your terms for a relationship. I'll be as honest with you as you've been. You are not exactly a nineties woman in the relationship department. However, that is not a disappointment to me. If you are entertaining a playboy image of me, you are wrong. I am a one woman man, but unfortunately I've not found my one woman. I have strong spiritual beliefs about relationships. I wasn't inviting myself into your bed. I was inquiring about your reason for asking if I intended to return to the city tonight."

"I'm embarrassed, Colin. I'm sorry. It's just that I've been approached so often, by so many men that I barely knew. I just assumed, and I was wrong. I feel like you do. Relationships must be based on something more than our basic human instincts. That, to me, puts us right down on the level with the animal kingdom. Don't get me wrong. I'm anticipating the time I'll fall in love, marry, and have a fulfilling physical relationship with my husband. But in that order."

"Well then, Miss Remington, we are in agreement. So, shall we proceed with our evening as well as our friendship?"

"Yes, Mr. Forrester, we shall."

Later in her room, Remmie thought about the conversation she had had with Colin. She thought it was so unusual to find a man with his standards. Her admiration for him intensified. *Tomorrow,* she thought, *Colin, Sarah, and I will see about turning River Oaks into a farm.*

Remmie woke up early before anyone else was stirring. She dressed in jeans, her favorite football logo T-shirt, and sneakers. Pulling her hair up into a ponytail of sorts, she headed out for a walk. The Deep South had a slight chill in the air---just a hint of fall. This was her favorite time of year. The leaves along the river were as beautiful as the foliage in the mountains, especially if there had been a lot of rain. Walking briskly, she reflected on all the events of the evening – Sarah's plans, Stuart Kinkaid, Colin, the money, etc. Her mind was full of what to do's.

The farm idea had somehow grown on her overnight. She was beginning to connect the farm to the plan she had for her future. It seemed to fit somehow, but there was much yet unknown. Her career, which until recently had been her whole life except for her father, Jesse, and Sarah, now seemed only to encumber her. She knew she loved medicine. She knew nothing challenged her like the trauma unit. But now, she felt more challenged by the purpose she had felt so clearly while on the island. Those feelings, those emotional ties to her mother gave her a new sense of purpose that was undeniable. But she still questioned, *Is it time? What's the first step? Who do I contact? What if they say no?* On and on went the questions. Picking up her pace to a jog she tried to leave the questions behind, but they followed.

Running now, she was becoming exhausted, but the questions were keeping up with her, stride for stride. Suddenly, Colin appeared running beside her. He looked very handsome in his jeans, T-shirt, and sneakers. The only problem she saw with this good-looking fella was the logo on his shirt. They were obviously for opposing teams - opposition like the north versus the south, serious rivalry.

They ran on however, refusing to be competitors with each other, until all at once she found a burst of energy leaving him in her dust. Shocked by her swiftness, Colin responded with a quick acceleration, catching her at the big old oak tree. Panting for breath, Remmie leaned against her special tree, trying to catch her wind. Colin joined her as he, too overcame the effects of their unplanned foot race. No winner was declared. After resting for several minutes, Colin could finally speak.

"What are you trying to do, kill me for wearing this shirt?"

"No, it's just when I wear this shirt the pride of champions comes out in me."

"I see. Is this going to be a hindrance to our friendship?" "Surely not. I refuse to hold your choice of football teams against you. I'm just for the better team. Let's leave it at that."

"No can do, I'm afraid. The better team is the one who wins a certain game every November. If my memory serves me well, we won."

"I don't remember seeing that on television for some reason, but I think the overall record of wins is in our column. Although, you may have won a battle, you still lost the war."

"Hmmm, I think we better get off this subject quickly. Let's make a deal to wear our team shirts when we aren't together."

"I guess that diplomacy helps you in the courtroom, and it makes good sense. You've got a deal."

Colin noticed something carved in the old tree. It said, Rebecca Elizabeth with the date October 4th, but there was no year. Remmie told him she had done that the day she came to live at River Oaks. It marked a new beginning, she told him. It was the day her life changed forever. He asked why there was no year inscribed. She explained she was only eleven at the time, and years weren't significant. But on October 4th she began a new life, and she felt it should be inscribed. She considered every October 4th the beginning of a new year with a family of her own.

Colin asked about the home she was in when the Remingtons adopted her. She explained it was a group home for girls. She said it was probably the best place she had been in years. Briefly she described the horrors of foster care she had experienced. He was appalled to know how out of whack the system had become.

"That's what I want to talk about. That's why I asked you to stay. When I was on the island, I found a sense of purpose that I haven't had before, not even about medicine. Colin, I believe everything we experience is for a reason. Whether good or bad we have a choice in how it affects us. I got through some pretty awful times by telling myself it wasn't so bad or it could be worse. I've had it both ways, and I've learned from both.

"I want to spare children what I went through. I want to make a home for foster children - a permanent home with parents, pets, their own rooms, and clothes - all the ordinary, everyday things you and I take for granted. I want to give ordinary lives to children who have never had them. Sarah's farm may be the exact way to do it. The families of yesteryear grew up that way. That generation has a strong sense of family, patriotism, loyalty, and hard work. What better way to teach our children than to work as a family - growing food, tending animals, hunting, fishing, playing in the woods? All those things create a world where children can grow up strong, healthy, as well as happy. They learn all too soon how the real world works. Some delight in their childhood can help make the transition easier. Do you think I'm crazy?"

"Crazy? No. Ambitious? Yes. You really have this etched in your spirit, don't you? So it really doesn't matter what I say, you are going to proceed. I think the wisest move for me is to begin some research into the child custody laws. It won't be difficult to find a loop hole. We will need to put a detailed plan together, including finding the right helpers for you. Every detail must be thought out before we do this. You should expect opposition.

"Remmie, I want you to realize this may not happen overnight--it may not happen at all. With your experience and determination, you can present a powerful argument for change in the system. I can't guarantee the results, but I'll put together the best legal team I know, and we'll give it our best shot. It will also be expensive. It won't cost ten million, but it won't be cheap. We may consider putting together a foundation to help fund the legal battle as well as the home itself."

"I'm not sure about that, Colin. I don't want a Board of Directors running my home. Let's look at my money from investments. I prefer to do this without anyone else's money. I'd like a preliminary plan drawn up for my review. I'd also like to get a private investigator looking for my brother, and I'd like to get the Swiss Account turned over to me as quickly as possible."

"Okay, anything else, Miss Remington?"

"I don't mean to sound so bossy, but I want to move on this now. You are my attorney, and I just can't waste time beating around the bush. There are children in this state and this country who are suffering as we speak. I can't forget that. Help me do this, Colin, or help me find someone who can."

Pausing, Colin rubbed his chin, looked Remmie straight in the eye and said, "I'm the one to handle this, and I will, but it will take time. Get ready for the fight. I can tell you some obstacles now:

1. Single woman, never married, no children.

2. Racial background. We are still in the south...some things haven't changed as much as we'd like to think.

3. Child Protective Services are a formidable foe.

"Remmie, we may have to go to the State House with a bill. I don't know at this point what we'll face. I just want you prepared. Get back to work, occupy your mind, work on your plan, enhance your vision, and trust me. I'll do everything I can to make this happen.

"As for your brother, I've already got someone working on that. The money is coming. The wheels of banking institutions grind slowly, but they grind. An agreement of sorts may be necessary to ensure your brother a share. I told the bank that wasn't a problem. The exact amount I don't know. They are vague on that, but I believe it will be in excess of twenty million dollars."

"I can't fathom that kind of money. I'm glad to know you are already working on the money, as well as finding my brother. I think I've found the right attorney. Consider yourself permanently retained."

Remmie took Colin's arm, "Let's head back. I'm starving. Sarah was in her favorite domain when I left. I'll bet she has created something wonderful by now."

Colin returned to Atlanta that afternoon. Remmie sat down with Sarah to talk about the farm. Sarah was gung-ho about it. She was sure River Oaks would be a workable, productive farm. She wanted Remmie to bring Stuart in right away.

Deciding the time was right, Remmie told Sarah about her plan to create a home for children in foster care. She explained how she thought the farm and the children could fit together. Sarah sat quietly for several minutes while Remmie waited for what she hoped would be a positive response. As she studied Sarah's intense-looking little face, she wondered what she would do if Sarah hated the idea. Sarah was very important to Remmie. She wanted her to be happy, but she also knew she had to do this thing. It would be so much easier with Sarah's help. Finally, Sarah spoke.

"I like it. It's a real good plan. My farm, and *yore* young-uns. Yep, we'll do it, Remmie."

"Uh um, your farm and my children? How about our farm and our children? We'll do this fifty-fifty, all the way."

Pausing again, Sarah had no immediate response.

"What is it, Sarah?"

"My farm will be a difficult *thang* to share. If I agree, *ya* won't try to run *everthin'*, will *ya*? Stuart needs one boss…me."

"Sarah, I don't know anything about farming. You and Stuart can manage that all by yourselves. There will be areas I will have to coordinate, but I won't boss you or Stuart."

"All right, then. When's the *young-uns comin'*?"

"That will take some time. I don't want to have a group home. I want to adopt the children. I want a permanent home for them when they come."

"That's probably a good *thang, considerin'* me and *ya* know absolutely *nothin' bout young-uns.* Maybe we can get a nanny."

"Colin and I will take care of all those details. You and Stuart get the farm going. I think we will need to remodel the house. We'll need more bedrooms and bathrooms, and I know you don't like it, but we will need to put in a commercial-style kitchen or you'll be cooking all day. However, we'll wait on those things until I know for sure the children can be adopted. I want each child to have a room. That's important in creating an identity for children who are not naturally related. I remember how I felt, always sleeping in someone else's room. You feel portable, like it's only a matter of time until you'll be moving. I never want our children to have that feeling. They'll know from day one they are here to stay, for better or worse. There'll be no disposable children at River Oaks!"

"You've given this a lot of thought, haven't *ya,* Remmie? Does *anythin'* ever really undo what's done to children who *ain't* adopted? Can we really *hep 'em*?"

"Sure we can. Sarah, I'll never forget my childhood, but then came my parents, and River Oaks. That changed my life forever. I want to do that for other children. They'll always remember, but they'll know they are loved and wanted. That will make all the difference, believe me, I know. Okay, Sarah, I'm calling Stuart about coming out tomorrow for lunch so we can talk terms."

CHAPTER FIFTEEN

Stuart drove down River Road heading to lunch at River Oaks. His red Ford four by four passed through the deep shadows being cast across the road by the kudzu monuments, beckoning him on. As the iron gates swung open, Stuart proceeded up the drive, past the huge live oaks, and into the circular drive, stopping near the front door. Stepping from the truck, Stuart's large frame almost seemed to unfold. Reaching back into the truck, he retrieved his cowboy hat, placed it on his head, straightened his shirt, and stomped his feet to make his jeans fall smoothly over his rattlesnake boots. With everything in place, he walked to the door. Before he could ring the bell, Sarah snatched the door open, grabbed Stuart, and pulled him into the house, babbling about her plans for the farm. Stuart was completely caught off guard. He was yes ma'aming and no ma'aming, and looking like he wished someone would show up to rescue him. Watching momentarily from the hall, Remmie came to his rescue.

"Mr. Kinkaid, how nice of you to come for lunch. Sarah is just a bit excited about things, but she's harmless. Come into the dining room, and have some iced tea."

"Yes, ma'am, that would be good. I appreciate the invitation and the job offer. Miss Sarah is quite a talker, isn't she?"

"Now that is probably the understatement of the year. She can be somewhat overwhelming, but she is a dear lady who is generous to a fault. I think you two will get along very well. After lunch, you and I will speak privately in the study, but right now let's enjoy one of Sarah's greatest talents, her cooking. Please sit here."

In rushed Sarah. She began pouring tea while helping Stuart's plate. All the time she was babbling ninety-to-nothing about farming, animals, *fixin'* the barn, on and on.

Remmie smiled at a very bewildered-looking Stuart, who just nodded as he occasionally got in a "Yes, ma'am."

"Sarah, sit down, and slow down. Let's enjoy our lunch before we talk business. Mr. Kinkaid can't take in all our plans at once. Give him a little time to digest his food before he digests your plans for River Oaks."

Sarah calmed herself as she began eating her lunch, but she was watching Stuart closely. This was making him very uneasy. Remmie, trying to put Stuart at ease, asked him where his family home was. He quickly answered that he was from Texas, but had lived in the southeast for many years. He went on to say he had been running a large cattle ranch in the panhandle of Florida for the last five years until the owner died and the ranch was sold.

"I'm sure you observed that this land hasn't been farmed in years. How long will it take to get it ready to farm?"

"Well...ma'am...that depends on exactly which part of the land you are intending to farm. If you want the land along River Road, it'll take a year or more just to clear the timber. If you've got some open land behind the timber, it could be three or four months. I'll need to survey the property, test the soil, decide which crops we need to plant, assemble the equipment and..."

"Great Scotts! I never knew there *wus* so much to *farmin'*. What happened to *plowin' plantin'* and *pickin'* it? We never surveyed, tested, and all that stuff. Poppa just planted the seed then *us young-uns* picked the cotton."

"Yes ma'am, that's how it used to be, but not today. There's no way to produce a good crop without proper preparations. Otherwise, you might as well just throw your money out in the field, and hope a money tree grows up. So, we need to prepare before we do anything else. Y'all do have some open land, don't you," asked Stuart in his slow Texas drawl, "Or are y'all planning on clearing timber?"

"Absolutely not. That timber stays! There are several fields behind the meadow. You can see it all after we finish. We have pastures with ponds, horse stables, as well as equipment storage buildings. Keep in mind, they've been unused for some time now, so they will need some clean-up. As for equipment, you will have to decide what you need, get some prices, and we'll get it."

"Miss Sarah that was a mighty fine meal. I've not had cathead biscuits like those in a long time, and those potatoes were as light as air. Country fried steak with onion gravy is one of my favorites."

"Thank *ya,* Stuart. Do *ya* have room for some of my blackberry cobbler?"

"Oh, now I think I could handle that, but just a small portion please. Otherwise I'll have to take a nap before we can tour the property."

Sarah decided to stay behind to clean up while Remmie took Stuart around the property in her jeep. Sarah hated the jeep, especially topless.

Remmie stopped on top of a rise behind the meadows. From there the pastures, stables, and equipment building could be seen. Beyond that lay the rich bottom land covered in heavy weeds. The farming acres in this plot alone totaled more than three thousand. Stuart was impressed with what he had seen, but anxious to examine the soil more closely. Maneuvering the jeep around the large pond, Remmie drove into the field. Stuart got out, walked across a few yards, pulled up a big clump of Byhalia grass, and grabbed a handful of rich, black topsoil. He took a plastic bag out of his pocket, put the soil in, and sealed the bag carefully. After repeating this process several more times, they rode on across the terraces to an access road which led back to River Road. Remmie turned the jeep onto River Road to the right. She drove passed the entrance gate for half a mile. There was a metal gate across a drive row. Stuart opened it so Remmie could drive in. Slowly they proceeded down the drive row, which was badly overgrown. As they rounded a sharp curve to the left, they came into a clearing. Beyond the clearing, huge fields spread out in all directions. Surveying them quickly, Stuart estimated it to be three to five thousand acres. Again he took soil samples, labeling them carefully.

Re-positioning his hat and tugging at his belt, which was a habit of his, Stuart spoke. "Well, Miss Remington, you appear to have some fine farm land here. It just needs working. I'll take the samples to the Extension Service to see what they need, if anything. We'll have those results in a few weeks. All I can say is, we'll probably be planting these fields come spring."

"What will you plant?"

"That depends on several things. One thing to consider is the fact you don't have any equipment to use. Now, we can hire the crops planted and harvested. That way we avoid buying those expensive tractors and combines. But it's not cheap. You don't always get to decide when your crops get planted or picked. The hired equipment people tend their own crops first. That can mean that we get a late start or get harvested later, which translates into lost time, poor crop quality, as well as loss of money. If we have our own equipment, we decide when to plant and pick. That can mean getting our crops planted at the right time for a maximum harvest at the right time. Cotton comes in later than peanuts, so with as much land as you have here, we could split it between the two big money crops. Chances are, one will bring in a yield, but if we're lucky, both will. I'll do some checking around with neighboring farms. It may be we can rent a picker, especially if they are rotating their crops. There's several ways to put off big purchases your first year."

"Could you prepare me a list of things you absolutely must have to get started, along with the prices? Then a list of things you'd like to have, including their prices. I'll leave the crop decision up to you. I know nothing whatever about farming. I want this to become a real farm, supporting itself as well as a home for several children that I intend to adopt one of these days."

Straightening his hat, and tugging his belt again, Stuart cut his big brown eyes around at Remmie. "Several children, did you say?"

"Yes, will that be a problem for you?"

"That all depends, ma'am. If I'm to tend to ‘em, and farm this eight thousand acres, then yep, it just might pose a problem. I don't know much about children, but what I know convinces me I'd be better off with some distance between us."

"I see. That concerns me a little bit. I have no plans to ask you to tend to the children, as you put it. I was hoping that you would be able to use them on the farm. Perhaps, I was wrong in assuming farming is a good way to raise children these days."

"It, uh--it's not the life it once was. Farming is much more automated these days. The children would need to understand machinery and be old enough to drive. The huge tractors and combines are dangerous, as are the other pieces of equipment used today. I think the farm life Sarah has in mind will be better for your children. Then as they get older, they can be taught safety."

"Yes! You are absolutely right. The vegetable garden, the animals, including horses for learning to ride – that's the chores to involve the children in, then, gradually introduce them to the bigger farming picture. Stuart, you are going to be a big help to me and to Sarah. There are some things I should clarify where Sarah is concerned."

"I think I get the idea, Miss Remington. You're the boss, but Miss Sarah thinks she is."

"Can you play our little game without going nuts? It's important for Sarah to feel needed. This farming idea has really captured her imagination. That's really important right now. My father died two weeks ago. Sarah's been with him for twenty-five years. They were the odd couple for sure, but they loved each other deeply. Sarah's feeling somewhat displaced, I think. I've offered her a chance to live in the city with me, but she won't even consider it. This is her home. She was born up that road, back on the river. Her roots are deep in the soil of the Wiregrass. She's a true, blue river person, as stubborn as a mule, but as good as they come. If you can help me with this, I will appreciate it."

"No problem for me. I like her already. We'll get on just fine, ma'am."

"We still haven't discussed salary. My attorney has an annual budget drawn up for the farm. It's in the study. When we get back, you can look it over to be sure you think you can live with it."

Stuart sat at the big desk in Dr. Remington's study reading the budget. Remmie came in carrying a tray with coffee and cookies. "How's that look to you? Can you run the farm for a whole year for that?"

"Ma'am, I can buy a good size farm for this, and have some left over. This is a peck of money. What'd y'all do, discover oil or gold?"

"Oh no, Stuart. My father made some wise investments over the years. So, he left us in pretty good shape." Remmie decided not to mention the ten million dollars. If Stuart thought the farm budget was excessive, he would probably keel over if he knew how much she really had.

"Miss Remington, we can set up a real fine operation on this budget. My salary is just fine. Will I be paid weekly, monthly, or how?"

"I thought bi-monthly if that's alright with you. I'll be going back to work next week so, I won't be here that much, but twice a month I can get out here or I can mail your check if I need to."

Rising from the desk, Stuart stuck out his hand offering to shake on their understanding. Remmie shook his hand. The deal was made. Stuart left with plans to move in the next afternoon. Upon hearing that, Sarah began to clean the garage apartment. She washed the curtains and blinds. She cleaned the bathroom and kitchen. She washed the towels and sheets. The floors were hardwood, so Sarah mopped, waxed, and placed area rugs to protect them. Finally, she was finished, not to mention worn to a frazzle. Returning to the house, she showered and fell into bed.

Remmie sat down in the den to catch up on some reading. Just about the time she got settled in, the phone rang. Answering on the cordless phone she had with her, she heard Beau's voice.

"Hello, good looking! When are you planning to improve the appearance of this place by coming back?"

"Hi, Beau. As a matter of fact, I'm planning to come in Monday night. I just about have things under control here."

"That's good news for me, gorgeous. I've missed you. I've realized how much you mean to me. I've made a decision I'll share with you when you get home."

"Who is this impersonating Dr. Beau McCain," joked Remmie. "You were convincing until you decided to get serious. You've blown your cover."

"I am serious, Remmie, and it is me. Haven't we been toying around with a relationship for three years now? Don't you think it's time we did something about it?"

"Beau, you are one of my favorite people, but it's not the time for me to discuss this right now. I'll be there Monday night. We can have a donut brick with a cup of rot gut coffee while we talk this over. See you Monday at six sharp. Good night, Beau."

Remmie couldn't believe Beau's attitude. He had never wanted a serious relationship before. She remembered when he first came to the Medical Center. She thought he was about the best looking guy she had ever seen, but he couldn't be serious about anything. So she quickly decided friendship was the best route for them to take. He was still the best kisser she had ever dated though. Maybe he deserved a chance to be taken seriously. Suddenly, she remembered Colin. Now that was a man to be taken seriously, and he wasn't a sloppy kisser either. *Oh well, tomorrow is another day*, she thought, *I'll make this decision tomorrow.*

Stuart arrived the next afternoon with his pick-up loaded high and wide. Sarah was waiting to help him get everything in order. Remmie helped him, too. All three carried boxes up the stairs leading to the apartment. After everything was taken up, they proceeded to make it look homey. Stuart placed the overstuffed wing chair near the front window, the plaid camel-back sofa sat in the center of the living area, separating the dining room. Directly behind the sofa sat a drop leaf oak dining table with three chairs. Sarah had put a cloth on the table with red, navy, gray, and white colors in it. It matched the sofa very well. In the bedroom, Stuart put his bed on the long wall by the rear window. In the corner, he placed a side chair with a small table beside it. On the table he set his reading lamp that had a big buck as its base. On the wall, over his bed he hung a large painting of a beautiful black horse. He placed a pair of duck decoys on the oak chest. Finally, on the small wall near the bathroom door he put up a hat rack. Anyone could guess what went up there. Everything was perfect. It was easy to tell that it was a man's space. Stuart was pleased.

Remmie insisted they leave him to get acquainted with his new home before dinner. He surprised them both when he announced he would be preparing his own food for now. It didn't set just right with Sarah, but he was a grown man.

As they walked through the garage into the house, Remmie told Sarah how much better she felt about returning to the city since Stuart was there. She reminded Sarah of the intercom that could summon Stuart with the push of a button. Sarah was glad, too. Even though she wasn't ready to admit it to Remmie, she felt safer now. Sarah was glad that Remmie could return to her home and career in the city without worrying about her every minute. She knew Remmie had things to settle before she could begin the plan she had to adopt the children. Sarah didn't want to be an obstacle.

Just as they walked into the kitchen, the phone rang. Sarah answered, spoke briefly then handed the phone to Remmie.

"Hi, how are you?"

"Missing you. Can you come up this weekend? I would like to see you before you go back to work."

"I don't think so, Colin. I would like to see you too, but Stuart moved in today. We have some things to take care of before I leave."

"Is that it, or is that tall, slow-talking Texan beating my time?"

"Ha! You are insecure for such a confirmed bachelor. Anyway, Stuart may know the difference between male and female horses, but not humans. He *ain't* interested."

"Don't kid yourself, pretty lady. He's a man, and you are a beautiful lady. He's interested. If he's not, we need to have his hormones checked."

"Stop it, Colin. Stuart's a perfect gentleman. I think he'll be a big help to me here. By the way, the budget was acceptable. In fact, he seemed to think it somewhat excessive."

"Then tell him not to spend it if he doesn't need it."

"He won't He's very cost conscious. He'll work out well here. He understands Sarah. What more could we ask for?"

"I'd say that's definitely in his favor, but I'll be watching him. Since you can't come here, I'll come down Saturday. I want to talk to you before you go back to work. See you then. Good night."

Colin arrived just after lunch carrying a big bouquet of yellow roses with baby's breath. Remmie took the flowers and gave Colin a big hello kiss.

"I've missed that. How about putting those flowers down so I can show you how much I've missed you?"

"I don't think so, not just now. Come to the kitchen with me while I put these in some water."

"I see, you haven't missed me at all."

"That's not true! I've missed you alright, but Sarah could pop out at any moment. And we do have a resident farm manager now. I just don't like feeling as though I'm on display."

"You're right. I'm sorry. I'll try to be more subdued when I'm around you. We wouldn't want anyone to think we liked each other or that we might occasionally kiss each other, especially not Stuart. He might see something that gives him an idea."

Remmie stopped arranging the flowers, turned to face Colin, threw her arms around his neck, and kissed him long and hard. Of course, in came Stuart which neither, Colin or Remmie observed. They continued kissing, oblivious to anyone or anything. Stuart tried backing up quietly. Unfortunately, Sarah was coming into the kitchen carrying several boxes which were stacked one on top of the other, obstructing her view. Sarah did not see Stuart, nor did he see her. At the moment of impact, Sarah yelled as boxes flew all over the place. Poor Stuart didn't know if he should catch Sarah or the boxes. He chose Sarah. After steadying her, he gathered the scattered boxes while apologizing profusely.

Remmie and Colin stood startled and embarrassed. When everything was settled, Stuart went on his way without another word. Sarah proceeded into the laundry room with the boxes. Nothing was said about their exhibition in the kitchen. Carrying the vase of flowers, Colin followed as Remmie headed down the hall to the living room.

"See, that's exactly what I thought would happen. Are you satisfied now?"

"Not quite, but I think one more kiss will do it."

"You are impossible!"

"You are probably right, but I am fun, aren't I? Come walk with me, I want to talk to you."

They walked out the patio door and across the patio and pool area into the yard. They were finally alone, hidden behind a trellis covered with clematis vine. As Remmie sat down in the glider, she motioned for Colin to join her, which he did. Remmie waited for Colin to speak. He didn't. Instead he began kissing her again. When she could free herself to take a breath she said, "I thought you needed to talk to me."

"In a minute. I'm busy right now."

"You just became un-busy, sir. Speak to me."

Sighing deeply, Colin gathered his thoughts. "It occurred to me that you are planning to return to the trauma unit Monday. You will be very busy working nights, sleeping days, and I won't be able to reach you as often to say hello. I'm not looking forward to this arrangement. I miss you terribly already. So, while wallowing in self-pity, I made a decision. I decided that I must do something to remind you every day of the heart in Atlanta that's thinking of you."

From his pocket, Colin took a small black velvet box, and placed it in Remmie's hand.

"Colin! I'm, I'm…I'm overwhelmed. I never expected..."

"What? What did you never expect? Open it before you expect too much."

Remmie's eyes were glued on the box. Inside was a lovely heart pendant studded with tiny diamonds. Colin fastened it around her neck. Remmie touched it with her finger tips, to make sure it was in the proper place. "Colin, it is lovely. I love it. I'll wear it every day, and it **will** remind me of you."

The look on Colin's face revealed how pleased he was with himself. He had impressed her, and he knew it. He had staked his claim. The necklace would be a constant reminder that this territory belonged to someone. All was well in Colin Forrester's world that early fall afternoon at River Oaks. He stayed only a short time longer, before he drove back to the big city, feeling confident he had made progress with this unusual young woman with deep auburn hair and crystal green eyes.

CHAPTER SIXTEEN

While driving back into the city Sunday afternoon, Remmie called Jesse. The two had not spoken in a couple of weeks. Jesse had been out of town on business. Remmie had been busy with her father's final details, as well as hiring Stuart and getting the plans for River Oaks under way. She had had little time to touch base with her best friend.

Hearing Jesse's happy-sounding voice made Remmie feel better. She always had that effect on her. In only a few minutes the two weeks of silence between them had merged into the present, and as always, it was as though they had never been apart. They had so much to say to each other that the conversation lasted until Remmie was almost home. By the time she parked in her space, the two had covered a great deal of territory, ranging from the trip to New York Jesse had made to represent the television station at a media conference, to the new plans for River Oaks, which included the hiring of Stuart.

Jesse said she couldn't wait to meet him. Maybe he would like a city girl to show him around. Remmie assured her that Stuart was all business, and the city was low on his list of places to visit. As Remmie described him, Jesse decided she better stick with womanizing city fellows. She understood them, after all. Stuart sounded like a rare breed that might not have been broken just yet. As usual, Jesse's terminology was colorful, but on target. She concluded that she didn't have the time or energy to whip him into shape.

Remmie confided her loneliness for her father. She told Jesse that Sarah had become so sensitive, wearing her feelings on her sleeve, crying or brooding easily. All this she contributed to her father's death and Sarah's displacement as his companion. She told Jesse how she had suggested remodeling the kitchen.

Jesse replied laughingly, "I'll bet folks around there thought a bomb had gone off at River Oaks." Remmie laughed, confirming it was pretty loud for a few minutes, but it diverted her attention away from herself and the loneliness of the house.

Jesse asked about Colin. Remmie said he had been there several times, and that she had gone to Atlanta a couple of times as well. Probing for details, Jesse pushed Remmie to say more. Deliberately dragging her feet, Remmie hemmed and hawed, saying little or nothing to satisfy Jesse's curiosity. Becoming more curious, Jesse sensed a romance in bloom, and she was going to have the full story. So probe she did. Remmie played dumb for a while, coy for a while, skirting all the things Jess wanted to know. She could hardly keep from laughing out loud at her precious friend. Finally, Jesse couldn't stand it anymore.

"Okay, smarty, you've had your fun with the minority today – let's have it! I want the facts ma'am – just the facts! Are you interested? Is he interested? Tell me--tell me--tell me!!!"

"I am interested. He is interested. We have common goals and value systems. He's a good person, strong and caring. He knows about my background, but he isn't adversely affected by it. We are strongly attracted to each other. I have never felt as excited as I did the first time he came to River Oaks to take me out. I waited by the window like a teenager on her first date. It's a new experience for me, Jess, and to be honest I like it. I like him very much."

"Does he bring flowers and gifts? Does he call daily? Does he say, 'I miss you' or things like that?"

"All of the above. Yes, Jess, he brought me yellow roses, he called, and he missed me. I know he's really interested, but I'm probably not the only woman he's seeing."

"Why do you think that? Have you some proof?"

"Well, just common sense tells me a man like Colin probably has plenty of lady suitors. Women aren't exactly shy or demure these days. When they see a good man, they pursue."

"That's true, but some men don't like to be pursued; they are the hunter. Perhaps Colin is that kind of a fella. He is the hunter. Are you the prey?"

"Sounds like a line of narration from *Wild Kingdom*. I'm not his prey, but you may be right. I think Colin would be turned off by a pushy female pursuing him vigorously. I like mystery. I figure he does, too."

"So, you haven't actually seen evidence of another woman in his life?"

"No, but I haven't looked too close. I guess I really don't want to know. It's none of my business anyway."

"Girlfriend, you make it your business! Shoot, I would! I'd know more about that man than he knows about himself. I'd be closer than his razor is to his face every morning. I'd..."

"I'm not you, Jess. That's not my style. If it's meant to be, it will be. But I'm not targeting this man for a trophy case. He's special to me, no doubt about that, but I'm not in any hurry to be locked into a relationship for the rest of my life. I've waited this long. I don't intend to rush it now. Time will tell."

"You are something, Rebecca Elizabeth Melissa. You never cease to amaze me. I'd be all over that man like white on rice. I'd turn him every which way but loose. I'd..."

"Jesse, you know, and I know that is a bunch of bologna. You are letting your Whoopie Goldberg mouth overload your Michael Jackson behind. We are more alike than you care to admit. That's why we're both single. We aren't the hunter type. We like to be pursued."

"As much as I hate for you to be right, you are. I'm all talk and no action. But good men are hard to find these days. So play your hand carefully, my friend."

"That's advice I will accept. You and I are both looking for a *Fantasy Island* romance, but we may have to settle for *Green Acres.* Come over here. I've got something to show you, and I hate to eat alone. We can order Chinese and talk about you for a while. I need to stay up really late so I can sleep tomorrow in preparation for my 12 hour shift tomorrow night."

"I'll be over in an hour. Have my food ready. I'm famished."

~~~

"That was great, Remmie. Thanks for asking me over. Now, what is it you have to show me?"

Remmie pulled the dainty, gold, diamond-studded heart from beneath her shirt. "This. How do you like it?"

"Oh, Remmie, it's beautiful! Did Colin give you that?"

Remmie smiled and nodded yes. She was going to let Jesse's imagination run away with her by saying as little as possible, while letting Jess answer her own questions and draw her own conclusions. Jesse had a very active imagination. She rambled on about how pretty the necklace was. She just knew he would be bringing a ring soon. All the while Remmie sat smiling, waiting for her friend to run down.
~~~

"Why aren't you talking to me? You're just sitting there with that silly grin on your face. Haven't you anything to say about this?"

"As a matter of fact, I do. I could tell you exactly what Colin said when he gave me the necklace, but you were having so much fun rambling on, I didn't have the heart to interrupt. Are you finished now?"

"You make me act so silly. Why do you do that? You could have said something to start with instead of sitting there nodding your head and feeding my wild imagination. Tell me what he said."

"He called to ask if he could come down Saturday, saying he needed to talk to me before I came home and went back to work. He brought yellow roses with baby's breath. We walked into the yard to be alone. We were sitting in the glider near the trellises when he took this box from his pocket and put it in my hand. He said he wanted me to think of him every time I saw it, and remember that he cares for me."

"How romantic. He sounds like a wonderful man. When do I get to meet him? I haven't had a chance to pass my approval on him yet. I may not like him, then *whatcha gonna* do?"

"You mean you may want him for yourself. I see through you like Saran Wrap."

The girls spent several more hours talking about Colin, the plans for the farm, and the children. Remmie told Jesse about the search for her brother. Jess was blown away by the mysteries that continued unfolding around her best friend. She was so excited to think Remmie might have a brother, realizing what her own brothers meant to her. It was two o'clock in the morning when Jess finally left.

Remmie stayed up until 4:00 a.m. just piddling around in her apartment. She rearranged some of her furniture in the living room and sorted through a box of photographs she found in a cabinet. There were pictures of her folks and Sarah. There were also pictures of her and Jesse taken on a trip to Mexico right after graduation. She wished she had found the pictures while Jesse was there. They would have had quite a time reliving that trip.

They both got a bad case of Montezuma's Revenge. It is very difficult to try to explain one's symptoms at a pharmacy when the pharmacist speaks a different language. It is mucho embarrassing to point to the affected body parts while locals stand nearby staring in amazement. Jesse, as Remmie recalled, was much more animated in her description than she had been. It paid off, however. The pharmacist finally got the message and gave them something. As Jesse put it, "Who cares what they thought, we're tourist.

They'll never see us again." Jesse was remarkable that way; she never sweated the small stuff.

In Remmie's estimation, she couldn't have found a better friend. Jesse had always inspired her. She had a great attitude about life. Remmie remembered how smart Jess was in college. She made it look easy. Jesse had always been fiercely loyal. No doubt about it, she was blessed to have a friend like Jesse. Remmie put the pictures on the table in the foyer. Tomorrow she would get together with Jesse so they could revisit Old Mexico.

Remmie arrived at the Medical Center at 5:30 p.m. sharp. Entering through the employees' entrance near the emergency room, she headed for the dressing area. Suddenly, she was surrounded by her co-workers. They were dressed in scrubs with masks on their faces. Two male nurses picked her up while the others clapped and chanted, "Remmie, Remmie!" She was carried into the lounge where they had prepared a party to welcome her back. Even Dr. McKinley was there. It was a special moment for Remmie. When all the chanting, clapping, and merry-making had subsided, Remmie stepped up on a chair, getting everyone's attention.

"Thank you all. I appreciate your show of support. These have been difficult days for me, but knowing there are those who sincerely care makes everything easier. My father's death has helped me see clearer than ever before how much medicine and my friends have motivated and inspired me. You are a great group of people! I love you. I thank you! Let's go to work!!"

Before she could get out the door, Dr. McKinley asked her to stay for a moment longer. Everyone else left. Dr. McKinley inquired about her emotional condition. He wanted to be sure she was ready to handle the stress of the trauma unit. He was satisfied with her response. She was prepared mentally and physically. She had the respect of her staff. Dr. McKinley personally welcomed her back. He told her there was a new doctor coming in on Wednesday, and that he'd like for her to be present for the orientation. She agreed.

Monday nights in the trauma unit were unpredictable, but with football season underway, anything could happen. It was a busy shift, but uneventful. Remmie read over some articles in current medical journals. She was always updating her knowledge of trauma medicine. It was a demanding specialty. In many hospitals, there were no trauma specialists. The emergency rooms were staffed with general practice physicians, internists, orthopedic physicians, or whoever was available. The Emergency

Medical Technicians in the rescue vehicles often had more appropriate training than the physicians in the emergency rooms.

Trauma medicine was demanding and extremely stressful, but it had the potential to save many lives every year. Auto accidents, plane crashes, or motorcycle accidents produced the most devastating injuries, which were often fatal. A good trauma team was prepared for those situations.

Remmie's team had successfully managed several major accidents by using all the facilities and physicians available in the city. The Medical Center became the command center when a major incident happened. A trauma team was dispatched to a triage area near the scene. From that point the injuries were triaged by severity, and then sent to the appropriate facility.

The most critical were transported first to the trauma unit at the Medical Center. If all worked as it should, the golden hour was achieved, the people recovered, and they returned to their normal lives.

It was almost 6:00 a.m. and the unit was quiet. Everyone was getting ready to pass the baton to the next team. Remmie walked to the reception area where several staff members had gathered.

"Where's Beau? I've been meaning to ask all night, but I always got side-tracked."

Each one looked at the other, but there was no answer to her question.

"Well, has the cat got your tongues? Where's Beau?"

After another pause, Connie, an RN who was a twenty year veteran at the Medical Center, spoke up. "He took a leave of absence, Dr. Remington. That's all we've been told. Beau never said anything to us. He just wasn't here one night, and that's all McKinley would say."

"Have you all tried calling him?"

"We did, but he didn't take our calls. All we got was the machine, and he never returned our calls. We were hoping you knew, but when you never said anything about him not being here, we decided we shouldn't ask."

"I have absolutely no knowledge of this. I can't imagine why McKinley didn't tell me or why Beau didn't tell me. I'll find out. That's a fact!"

Remmie headed straight to the phone to call Beau. Just as expected, the machine answered. She yelled into the received, "Beau McCain, pick up the phone, and talk to me!" There was nothing. She dialed Dr. McKinley. He answered, sounding groggy. "Sorry to wake you, Dr. McKinley, but it has come to my attention that Dr. McCain has taken a leave of absence. Why wasn't I notified? He is on my staff."

"Hang on, Dr. Remington! I was told you knew, and approved of his decision. I took his word. I had no idea you didn't know. When you didn't ask about him last night, I thought it was because you knew. That's why I have a new doctor coming in Wednesday."

"I didn't know anything. Beau called once, but he was not his usual self. He was strange-acting, but he never mentioned any of this. I can't believe he's pulling out of trauma medicine. He's one of the best we've had. He's making a big mistake!"

"I agree, Remmie, but there's a little more to his mistake than you know. The decision wasn't totally Beau's. I had a part in it. I would prefer to talk to you about this in person, but I know you need to get home, so I'll briefly explain. Beau has apparently become addicted to prescription medications. While you were away, it came to my attention that he had written and filled several prescriptions for codeine or Demerol to himself or to a relative. The hospital pharmacy reports monthly on employees who fill their prescriptions at the hospital. That concerned me. Since you weren't here, I brought him in to ask him about it. He was defensive, but he would not admit to a problem.

"I went to Dr. Merrick in the trauma unit to see how Beau was performing. I got a negative report. He had been late repeatedly, he was irritable, unsociable, and he fell asleep often. However, his medical decisions were correct. I called Beau again. This time, I gave him a choice--get help or else. He took a leave, but he never said he would get help. He also told me he had talked with you about the whole situation."

"That is not true. He called me, but he never mentioned any of this. I am shocked beyond words. This isn't the Beau I know. He is totally opposed to drinking and smoking, let alone drugs. There's something we don't know. I must get to the bottom of this. I'll keep you informed, Dr. McKinley, and thanks for handling this discretely."

"I have no desire to keep such a fine doctor from practicing medicine, but he must get help. I'll wait to hear from you. Have a good day."

Hanging up the phone, Remmie stood stunned by what she had just heard. How could she have missed the warning signs of addiction? It didn't happen overnight. She must have overlooked things that would have let her know Beau was in trouble. She walked back to the group, not knowing what she would say. They were all looking at her, waiting for an answer.

"I spoke with Dr. McKinley. He didn't appreciate my early morning call. I will have to meet with him before I have anything to report to you. Beau took a leave of absence, but why isn't exactly clear. I will do my best to get in touch with Beau today. It's time to go. See you all tonight."

CHAPTER SEVENTEEN

Remmie drove directly to Beau's apartment. His car was in the deck, but she got no answer to the doorbell. She called out his name as she knocked loudly, but still no response. An older man came out of the apartment next door. He told Remmie he hadn't seen or heard from Beau in several days. He said he usually knows when Beau is at home, because he plays his stereo very loud or because he comes over to borrow something. He said Beau must never shop because he's always out of something. The old man said Beau looked tired and pale the last few times he had seen him. Then he added that Beau had not been as friendly as usual.

For a second, Remmie decided to go on home and try later, but something prompted her to act now. She asked the man where the manager lived. Pointing across the courtyard, the man indicated which apartment was the manager's. Remmie made a beeline for the apartment. She rang the bell rapidly. A man appeared, looking somewhat disturbed. She quickly explained she was a doctor, and she expected a medical emergency had occurred in unit ten. He quickly opened the door for her. Following her inside the darkened apartment, they went down the hall. Remmie called out to Beau as they went. When they entered his bedroom, they saw Beau on the floor beside the bed. He was sitting up, but he was out of it. Remmie rushed to him, checked for a pulse, checked his pupils, and immediately grabbed the phone.

"I need an ambulance at unit ten Cambridge Place. I am a doctor. This is a Code 3 situation. After hanging up the phone, she laid Beau over on his back, cleared his airway, and began CPR. It took the ambulance ten minutes. Remmie was exhausted, but she kept going as the useless building manager stood watching.

As soon as the ambulance pulled away with Beau, she called the hospital, telling them she was coming in behind the ambulance to take charge of this case. She briefed the physician on duty about what she expected to find. She also told him it was a staff member. Remmie stayed with the ambulance as it raced across the city, reaching the hospital in six minutes. Once inside, she rushed to get Beau hooked up to monitors as the Emergency Medical Techs performed CPR. By the time she drew his blood, he was breathing on his own. His heart was in a good sinus rhythm, but he was in serious condition.

Preliminary tests revealed a high concentration of Demerol in his blood, along with some morphine. Anti-dotes were administered to counter act the effects of drugs, and Beau quickly responded. But suddenly, he went into convulsions and agonizing pain. Fearing a grand mall seizure might be more than his weakened heart could take, Remmie started an IV drip with a controlled dosage of morphine. Beau settled down, but remained in severe pain, floating in and out of consciousness.

More diagnostic tests were performed. Within a few hours, Remmie knew what was causing his pain. It wasn't good news. She changed his medication again, adding some different things that she hoped would relieve his distress.

It was about an hour before Beau regained consciousness and recognized her. He was upset. She gave him all the support she could as she explained everything to him that she felt he could comprehend. She asked him how long he had known about his illness. He said six months. She asked what his prognosis was. He replied six months again.

She thought that was a little optimistic. Her tests indicated a significately shorter time. Beau read her face and knew he was much worse. He asked her how much time he had left, but Remmie avoided answering him by saying all the tests weren't in yet. As she turned to leave Beau's side, she thought how easy it was to blame a test result, when in fact the patient may not able to deal with reality. She wasn't ready to deal with the hopelessness of Beau's situation. Considering his actions, she didn't think Beau was either.

Telling him to rest, she left his room. Once outside she stood statue-like, trying to grasp all the events that had brought her to this moment, to this painful moment. Her conclusion was she hadn't been there when Beau needed her. He was a genuine friend. There was a point in time when he could have been more than a friend.

Dr. McKinley approached the fatigued looking doctor standing so helplessly outside Beau's room. Taking her arm, he led her away to the lounge where he fixed her a cup of coffee.

"I take it you couldn't go home. You had to have answers immediately."

"Yes, Dr. McKinley. That's right. I had a compelling feeling that Beau was in real trouble, so I had the manager let me in, and we found Beau. He was almost gone. Dr. McKinley, he's terminally ill. He has bone cancer that is far advanced. He took the medications to be able to work in an effort to keep a normal routine for a little longer. He's known for two months that he's dying. The addiction is secondary to the cancer. Beau may not leave the hospital. It is very bad."

"I'm so sorry. This is one of life's unexplainable turns. We didn't even see it coming. Beau has always been the picture of health."

"He didn't want us to know. He couldn't deal with our feeling sorry for him."

"What about his family? Surely they know."

"I don't know about that. I didn't ask him that, but I will. I should get back to him now. I'll be admitting him. I'll turn his care over to an oncologist. Unless he responds quickly, he won't make it to leave the hospital. Life's unexplainable turns...that's for sure."

Within the next few hours, Beau seemed to respond well to the intense IV therapy. His body attempted to launch an attack on the disease that was draining his life away. He was moved to the fourth floor where Dr. Jennifer Evans took over his case. She told Remmie that there wasn't anything more she could do but keep him comfortable. His immune system was too weak to keep up the fight for very long. The improvement was temporary.

Remmie had many unanswered questions. Beginning with why wasn't Beau treated more aggressively with chemo or radiation? Dr. Evans expected his disease was too far advanced when discovered and that Beau, wishing to remain at work, declined any last ditch efforts to prolong his life. He knew the treatments would substantially weaken him, forcing him to give up medicine sooner. That was only a guess on Dr. Evans' part, but knowing Beau, Remmie thought she was probably right. He didn't want life if he couldn't be a doctor. Satisfied that she knew the answers to some of her questions, Remmie went into Beau's room.

"Hey, good looking. I was hoping I could see you again today. You came to my rescue in the nick of time, didn't you?"

"Did you even want to be rescued, Beau?"

"By you? Anytime."

"Be serious for once. After all, we are talking about your life."

"My life or the ending of my life. Either way, pretty lady, I'm glad you are here. I wasn't trying to kill myself, Remmie. I was trying to ease the pain, but I overdid it. That's all there is to it. I took too much morphine, and I wasn't coherent enough to know how to help myself. If I had attempted suicide, I'd have taken enough of something in one dose to end all this pain forever."

"Does your family know?"

"They know I'm sick, that it is serious, but they don't know I'm dying. I haven't admitted that to myself, let alone to anyone else. 'Immortal Beau McCain dies in sleep.' How's that for a caption in the obituaries?"

"You need to tell them. They would want to see you, Beau. Let me call them?"

Beau dropped his head in silence. "Okay, Remmie. You can call my father, but him only. He will tell my mom. My mom isn't a strong person. She won't handle this very well. Tell him I'll send them a ticket if they can come. They can't afford to fly across country. Thanks, Remmie. Oh, one more thing, tell 'em to hurry."

Over the next twenty-four hours Beau's fever went up and his body weakened. Dr. Evans called Remmie to let her know that it wasn't going to be long before he could lose consciousness for good.

Remmie called the airport to see if the flight from California was on schedule. It was. She drove out to pick up Beau's family. They spoke very little as they rode to the hospital. Remmie felt so helpless. All she could do for these people was offer them a place to stay and plenty of tissues. It seemed so little, so insignificant, and yet it was all she could do. Beau's parents were calm, but his father was obviously the stronger one. His mom looked so sad. His sister, Adrian, was a tall blonde California girl. Her expression revealed some anger. Remmie couldn't blame her. It was extremely hard to deal with the death of someone you love so much.

Beau was a young man, in the prime of his life. She could understand the anger that was showing on the face of Beau's sister. She remembered how she felt after her mother died at forty-eight years old. The tense silence was broken by Beau's father.

"Have you known Beau a long time?"

"Yes. I've known him since we were residents, and he decided to specialize in trauma medicine. He is a fine doctor and a great friend."

"Are you Dr. Remington, the head of his shift?"

"Yes, I am."

"My, my, you are so young. I thought perhaps Dr. Remington was your father."

"To be exact, my father was a doctor. He died a few weeks ago."

"I'm sorry to hear that. You and your mother are going through a difficult time."

"My mom died when I was sixteen. It's just me now." In her mind she thought, *at least until I find my brother.*

"Forgive me; I seem to be dredging up all your difficult memories. We appreciate you for picking us up and inviting us to stay at your home, but we'll get a motel near the hospital."

"I sincerely hope you'll reconsider that. My place is near the hospital. I have plenty of room. If you choose to stay somewhere else, I'll make arrangements for you to stay in a hospitality suite. It is pretty much like a dormitory, but the essentials are there, and it is courtesy of the Medical Center. I would like to have you, but that is your decision."

"Let us talk it over, and we will let you know. Tonight we definitely want to be near Beau."

"That's understandable. It can be easily arranged."

Leading Beau's family down the hall was difficult for Remmie. The closer to his room they got, the more emotional she became. She was literally fighting the tears. Opening the door, she motioned for his family to enter. She waited near the door. All three walked near his bed. His mother reached out first to touch him. As Beau opened his eyes, he smiled. He was glad to see them. It was his father who spoke first, but momentarily they were all talking. They had a lot to catch up on. Remmie slipped out the door, leaving the McCains to spend the precious moments with their son.

To everyone's amazement Beau made it through the night. He actually showed some improvement. His family never left, neither did Remmie. She had now been up thirty-six hours. Remmie knew she had to get some sleep. Heading to Beau's room, she hoped to convince the McCains to go home with her. They were all still there around Beau's bed. Beau was sitting up, eating breakfast while talking ninety-to-nothing. It was a relaxed atmosphere, to Remmie's surprise.

As usual, Beau greeted her with, "Hey, good lookin'. How about giving me a big ole kiss this morning? Don't mind my folks. They won't care."

"You are a sight for these sore eyes. If you aren't careful, I just might give you that kiss. Let's talk about your family. We'll get around to the kissing. Have y'all thought about going home with me? I know you are exhausted after flying most of the day and being up all night."

"We are exhausted. Since Beau is so much better, we could use a hot bath, as well as a few hours of sleep. Are you sure we won't be too much for you?"

"Absolutely sure. I've taken the liberty of ordering breakfast for you. It is ready down in the nurses' lounge on this floor. As soon as you eat, we will go to my house."

As soon as Beau's family left the room, Remmie approached Beau's bedside. "How are you, kiddo?"

"Hanging in--hanging on, doc. I really do feel stronger since my fever went down. Who knows, I may end up being a bona-fide miracle. I hope it won't upset you or Dr. Evans if I pull through this."

"You crazy man! You know nothing would make me happier."

Lifting his head up to be nearer to Remmie as if telling a secret, Beau continued his foolishness. "Well, I've heard Dr. Evans doesn't like patients to prove her wrong. She might just bump me off to prove she was right."

"You never stop, do you? I'll keep her under surveillance. You are safe here; don't worry about the notches on Evans' guns. I'm taking your folks home so we can all get some sleep. You try to behave until we get back."

Beau gestured he would try, but Remmie knew that wasn't true. He was full of mischief.

Remmie showed the McCains into the guest room. She helped Mrs. McCain unpack a few things. She ran Adrian a hot tub filled with rose-scented oil. Mr. McCain was first in the shower, and first in the bed, followed closely by his wife, Ellen. Adrian spent a good while in the hot tub in Remmie's bath. She looked much more relaxed when she came out. She thanked Remmie for everything before heading down the hall to the study where Remmie had prepared the daybed for her. Soon they were all sleeping.

It was six o'clock when Remmie and the McCains entered the hospital. Remmie reported to the unit while the McCains went directly to Beau's room. Things got hectic for Remmie very quickly. It was ten p.m. before she had a chance to check on the McCains. To her complete surprise, Beau was still improving. He was sitting up, alert, and looking much stronger than the day before. He and his family were still enjoying their time together.

After visiting with them for a few minutes, she left to review Beau's chart. It revealed a remarkable improvement. Dr. Evans' notes indicated that he appeared to be going into remission, but she feared this to be a temporary improvement, and that his immune system was not strong enough to sustain him. *Any minor infection could be fatal,* read Remmie.

Beau's life as he knew it was over, at least for now, thought Remmie. He'll be a prisoner in a sterile environment. He wasn't going to like that, and he wasn't going to be an easy patient.

The next few days Remmie was busy with work and boarding the McCains. They were no trouble, so unassuming. It was Remmie who wanted to do everything for them - home cooking complete with fancy desserts and buttermilk biscuits.

Mr. and Mrs. McCain were so kind. They appreciated Remmie's generosity. They liked her a lot. Adrian was a little harder to please. She found little things wrong with Remmie. Adrian believed that Remmie thought she was better than them, because she was a doctor, and she also felt Remmie was a bit too high and mighty.

In reality, Adrian was jealous of Remmie, but try as she did she couldn't dislike her. Adrian's secret thoughts were of how pretty Remmie was, how sophisticated, how well she dressed and spoke, but mostly how generous she was. Something deep within Adrian wouldn't let her admit how mesmerized she was. She could see why Beau liked her so much.

Remmie thought Adrian was lovely. She attributed her coolness to the stress of the situation, as well as being in the house of a total stranger. It never occurred to Remmie that Adrian was jealous. Part of Remmie's charm was that she was so ordinary, so down to earth. She was herself – nothing more, nothing less.

Beau gained strength as his condition improved with every passing day. Dr. Evans was cautiously optimistic. The chemo was working well. Beau had few side effects, which was in itself unusual. Then again, no one ever said Beau was usual. Dr. Evans felt Beau could leave the hospital soon, but he would have to be very careful. His bones were so brittle that he could easily have a break. There were many risks involved with keeping him in remission. He couldn't tolerate another series of treatments as strong as those he was taking. Although everything was stable for the moment, Beau was still very ill, and the future for him was at best uncertain.

The apartment was quiet when Remmie came in at 6:30 a.m. from work. The McCains weren't up yet. Tired and a little depressed, Remmie walked across the living room to the balcony overlooking the awakening city. Looking down on the surface streets where traffic was getting heavier each moment, her thoughts rambled. She missed her father and River

Oaks. She wondered how Sarah and Stuart were getting along, well Stuart anyway. She knew how Sarah was--in charge and enjoying it. But more than anything, she missed Colin. He made her feel secure. Turning around, she walked to the phone in the kitchen to dial Colin's number. It seemed as if the connection would never go through. She was about to hang up when Colin's very groggy sounding voice came on the line.

"This better be good."

"Colin, I'm sorry. I forgot how early it is, and how late you sleep. I just needed to hear your voice."

"Rem, is that you? You don't sound like yourself. What's wrong?"

"I'm trying not to disturb my house guests, so I'm talking softly. Colin, what's your schedule like tomorrow?"

Realizing something was not right, Colin answered, "I was planning on hitting I20 South and taking you to an early dinner. Can you pencil me in?"

There was a long pause. Remmie fought to control her emotions, but she lost. Breaking into tears, she asked him to come as soon as he could.

To hear Remmie sobbing was very touching to Colin. He knew what an inner strength she possessed. So Colin grabbed his things, and rushed to get to Remmie.

Remmie lay down, but sleep didn't come. She got up, showered and dressed, expectant of Colin's arrival. Now the McCains were up getting ready to head out to the hospital. As they headed out, Colin headed in. The entourage met at Remmie's front door. Hearing the voices, Remmie came to investigate just in time to make the proper introductions.

Everyone was gone. Colin and Remmie were alone. Struggling to be composed, she poured coffee as she tried to make small talk. Colin cooperated, drinking his coffee while observing every move she made. After several minutes of her rambling on about this or that, Colin reached over, touched her hand, and looked into her green eyes. Remmie tried desperately to avoid eye contact, to stay in control. He didn't have to say anything, just his gentle touch conveyed to Remmie how he felt. That was enough to open the flood gates.

Her emotions were so frayed that she needed to let it out. Tears ran freely down her cheeks, dripping off her chin. Occasionally, she would wipe the tears away with the back of her hand, but others rushed to replace them. Colin listened patiently.

Eventually, Remmie had released all of her pent-up emotions. She vented about all the decisions she had to make, the truth about herself, her still missing brother, and last but certainly not least, was Beau. She felt so helpless in the face of Beau's condition. He was a good person and a talented doctor. It seemed unfair, and yet, she had always tried to deal with every situation life dished out as a part of a bigger, more important plan or scheme.

As Sarah had always told her, God is in control of everything. At times like these, mortals really want their own way with God's blessings added on. It's hard to relinquish our wills to His will when what we see is defeat or death.

What God sees, however, is a new beginning, total healing, and eternal joy. One's perspective is everything. Many feelings surfaced, and many fears became apparent to Colin as he listened. His admiration for Remmie grew. She was indeed a remarkable person. He felt very fortunate to have the opportunity of sharing this small part of her life with her.

Most people would have taken their inheritance and headed off for a life of leisure, but not Remmie. Even as she struggled to deal with the ordeals of her past, she longed for ways to reach into the lives of helpless children. Her desire to help others was intensely strong--intensely pure. Colin saw no indication that she wanted or expected anything in return. She wanted the pleasure of serving others.

"Remmie, you don't have to have answers to all the questions floating around in that beautiful head of yours. You have been a true friend to Beau. His fate is not yours to control. No doctor can achieve the outcome they want every time. Beau is in God's hands now. Find comfort in that. Find peace in knowing you have done everything you can."

Remmie grasped Colin's hand with both of hers. "You are right. When I hear you saying it, I feel it deep inside me. You are very convincing. Did I say thanks for coming? It was so comforting to know that I could call you and you would come to me. I need you, Colin. I am thankful to have you as a part of my life."

"You are welcome, but I'm the fortunate one. To find a woman like you isn't easy. You have filled a void in my life that has been empty for a long time."

CHAPTER EIGHTEEN

Remmie sensed there had been someone significant in Colin's life. She encouraged him to continue. What followed was more than she expected to hear. Colin poured himself another cup of coffee, sat down on the huge white sofa, and proceeded to tell Remmie about the only woman he had ever loved.

They met in college, dated steadily, and planned to marry right after graduation. Her name was Alesa. She was as beautiful as she was brilliant. She was going to be an attorney, also. They had planned to go into practice together.

They were inseparable, studying together, playing together, and shopping together. Alesa excelled in everything she did. Everybody loved her. Colin related how much in love he was. She was the center of his life. Everything revolved around Alesa. All his plans for the future included her.

Alesa was from a very wealthy South Carolina family. She had the best of everything. Colin said he was from a working family; they weren't poor, but neither were they wealthy. He appreciated simple things, but not Alesa. She liked fancy clothes, cars, and high-priced activities.

She traveled often to New York to buy her clothes. She drove a Mercedes, and lived in an expensive apartment away from campus. His plans included how he would provide her with the things she was accustomed to having.

He had an offer to join a firm in Atlanta as a junior partner, but he would only be making $150,000 a year. This wouldn't be enough to support Alesa. That's when he got the idea to introduce her to the senior partners in the firm to see if they would hire her, too.

That would double their income, and they would be working together as well. Colin said he arranged a meeting of the firm's partners with Alesa. They were impressed, and offered her the job.

Everything was set. Colin and Alesa would live in Atlanta and work together for one of the largest firms in the city. All his dreams were coming true. He was living a fantasy. But as is often the case with fantasies, they disappear right before your eyes.

Remmie was sitting beside Colin, listening intently as he continued, revealing more about himself than he ever had before. The expression on his face let her know these weren't fond memories. This was something long buried inside him, but now, for some reason, he needed to exhume it so it could be put to rest, forever.

Colin continued by saying their fantasy lasted until just weeks before graduation. The firm had asked Alesa to come down to do some interning with them before she returned to school for her final quarter. Colin had already done this, so he would stay at college. Alesa, as he recalled, was very excited about the trip. She bought a new business wardrobe, got a new hair cut, and she even changed her make-up. It was like looking at a different woman.

She was in Atlanta for six weeks. Colin went down several times, and they spoke daily on the phone. She was learning a lot. Alesa had found an exclusive condo near downtown that she wanted Colin to see.

When she returned to school at the start of their final quarter before graduation, she was different. Colin related how he noticed it immediately, but thought it was one of the phases a woman goes through. She spoke less often of their plans as a couple. She spoke more about her plans with the firm.

During Christmas break, Colin gave her a new engagement ring, replacing the smaller diamond he had given her earlier. For a few days, she was her old self again. Their plans for the future were renewed. Colin felt secure in their commitment to each other. He put his re-occurring doubts about Alesa out of his mind.

They had a wonderful Christmas, traveling to Charleston to see Alesa's family, before returning to Tallahassee on Christmas Day to be with his folks. Everybody's excitement about their wedding in the spring was mounting, but no one's more than Colin's. He adored Alesa. He confided, he could hardly wait to make her his wife.

It seemed the holidays had only been over for a few weeks when finals were looming. Colin again noticed changes in Alesa. She was distant, restless, and distracted, not at all the way she had been during the holidays.

He blamed it on finals. Sometimes he wouldn't see her for a week. When they would talk on the phone, she would say everything was okay, but she would avoid seeing him. It was very confusing to him. Here they were, two months away from the biggest wedding Charleston had seen in a while, and he wasn't even having dates with the bride-to-be.

Several times he tried to talk with Alesa about their odd relationship, but she would change the subject or find an excuse to hang up. Then came the day she didn't show up for graduation practice. The sponsor was furious.

Right after practice, he went straight to her apartment. Her car was there, but her newspapers had not been gathered in three days. He remembered he had spoken with her on Saturday, but she wasn't feeling well, so he didn't come over. On Sunday, her machine answered but she never returned his calls. Now it was Tuesday. He had neither seen nor heard from her since Saturday.

He rang the bell, but there was no answer. So he took out his key, opened the door, and called out her name. There was still no answer. Colin related how he walked down the hall into Alesa's bedroom, back into the living room and kitchen, but she wasn't there.

In the bathroom he noticed a man's toiletries, plus a small bag with a few clothes in it on a chair in the bedroom. He decided to wait for a while to see if Alesa came home. It was almost midnight when Colin was awakened by voices and someone unlocking the door. To his amazement and theirs, there stood Alesa and Blake Dunsmore, one of the partners in the firm.

The scene was pretty obvious to all involved. Alesa had been away for a couple of days with Blake, and it wasn't on business. She was uncomfortable and somewhat irritated that Colin had let himself in to wait for her.

Blake wasn't disturbed in the least. Basically, his attitude was, "You're a big boy, Colin. This sort of thing is commonplace, so get with the program." Colin was hurt and disappointed, but he was rapidly becoming very angry. Alesa realized he was getting angry, so she took him into the bedroom, leaving Blake in the living room. Colin said she offered him lame excuses at first. But then she just blurted out the truth. She had become involved with Blake shortly after Colin introduced them, but intended to break it off and marry Colin. However, Blake had fallen in love with her. His persistence had finally paid off. He had won her heart.

She apologized, handed Colin the ring, and said, "It's over, good-bye." Colin only had one question, what did they intend to do about the wife Blake already had? Alesa said he would be divorcing her soon.

Clutching the ring he had given her, Colin left with some of his dignity intact, but over the next few days, he became devastated by the loss of Alesa. He became totally aimless as graduation grew near. He had no fiancé, and no job waiting. He had gone from every detail planned out to absolute chaos. He said it took him a year to put the puzzle together, and get his life on track again.

Remmie wanted desperately to know if Blake married Alesa, but she really hated to make him tell her that. When it looked as though Colin was going to leave out that bit of information, she asked him if Alesa was still in Atlanta. He responded, "Yes, she's in Atlanta, but she never married Blake because he never divorced his wife. Alesa is still his junior partner and his mistress."

Maybe Alesa wasn't as brilliant as Colin thought, was the conclusion Remmie reached. It was obviously difficult for Colin to relive this unhappy time in his life. *So why now,* thought Remmie. What had brought this up now? Being Remmie, she asked Colin, and he replied that Alesa had contacted him, wanting to see him, and wanting him to give her a job so she could free herself from Blake. This was not exactly what Remmie wanted to hear, now that she had decided she was interested in Colin. But she couldn't stop now. She had to know what Colin was going to do.

"Are you going to help her?"

With a somewhat puzzled look on his face, Colin looked at Remmie and said, "I'm not going to give her a job, but I can't ignore her request for help. She meant a great deal to me once. Even though our break-up was completely her doing, I must try to help her."

"I see, well just how do you plan to help? Are you sure she's really breaking it off with Blake?"

Still looking directly at Remmie, Colin replied, "I don't know, Remmie. All I know is this woman has made some pretty bad choices. One of those choices hurt me deeply, but she needs help, and she's asked me to help her. What would you do if you were me?"

Oh boy, now the shoe was on Remmie's foot, or perhaps the foot was in her mouth. What should she say? How should she answer? Part of her wanted to say, *Leave her alone. Remember how she treated you.* But then the real Remmie blurted out, "By all means, help her."

This was a human being who had made mistakes, but who hadn't? Now, she needed help. Colin should help her, no matter how insecure it made Remmie feel.

"I'm fighting my evil alter ego that wants me to say let her help herself, but I know better. You should help her. Colin, that's what I would do, and I'm sure that is what you are going to do. I have no right to interfere in your decision. So whatever you do, I'll accept."

Colin's solemn stare was softened by a little bitty smile that curled his lip a tiny bit.

"You are a real find, Rebecca Elizabeth Melissa, and I'm the fortunate one to have someone who can understand how I feel about this. Alesa caused me more grief than I care to remember. I don't know exactly how to proceed, but I promise you, I'll give it careful consideration. All I intend to do is get her an interview and give her a good recommendation. What she does about Blake is her business. I won't be getting involved in it."

"I'm sure you'll handle it all just fine, Colin. I just want you to remember that this little heart (Remmie pulled the diamond heart from beneath her blouse) says you and I have a special relationship. And I, Mr. Forrester, keep my commitments."

Colin reached over, touched the little heart, and kissed Remmie.

"You and I do have a special relationship. And I, Miss Remington, keep my commitments, too. It's getting late. I must get back to Atlanta. I'll keep you posted on this situation. Thanks for understanding."

"Drive carefully. Call me at the hospital when you get in. I'll work much better knowing you are home safely. And by the way, do keep me posted on Alesa. I'm very interested to know if after all this time, she really does end her affair with Blake."

Colin was feeling much relief because Remmie had handled this so well. As Sarah would say, he was full of foolishness. Walking to the door, he paused a moment and gave Remmie a curious look. "You really don't have to worry about Alesa. You are prettier, smarter, more trustworthy, and did I mention, richer?"

"I should have known you are only after my money. If you weren't so good at managing it for me, so dependable, and did I mention cute, I would get another attorney."

Colin blew Remmie a kiss as he closed the door.

Remmie dressed and left for the hospital. First she checked on Beau and his family. Then she went in to see Dr. McKinley. With all the excitement of the past three days, Remmie had not met the new doctor. She wanted to apologize to Dr. McKinley for being so distracted, and see if she could assist in some way with the new doctor's orientation.

Dr. McKinley's secretary told Remmie to go right in. Upon entering the office, she saw Dr. McKinley, who welcomed her, and then she saw the new doctor. McKinley introduced them. "Dr. Caren Rabon, this is Dr. Rebecca Remington, our second shift director."

For some reason, Remmie was surprised to see another woman standing there. Dr. McKinley had never mentioned the new doctor was a woman. After their introduction, they spoke about Caren taking over for Beau.

Caren was a trauma surgeon with five years experience in a trauma unit in South Florida. She would be an asset to the Medical Center. Remmie was pleased to know Dr. McKinley had hired Caren without letting the fact she was a woman become a factor. She was sure the hospital Board would take him to task over this decision, but she felt that perhaps it was a positive sign.

The ladies spent a good portion of the shift together. Remmie was very open with Caren, explaining everything she thought would help her make a quick and easy transition into the program. Caren seemed to be able to adapt quickly. Remmie foresaw no problems and conveyed to Dr. McKinley her support of his decision.

With the arrival of morning, Remmie clocked out and headed to Beau's room. Mr. McCain was with his son. Beau was still holding his own, even though his final round of chemo was producing some pretty nasty side effects. Dr. Evans had indicated that Beau might be leaving the hospital in a few days. This was good news, but Remmie couldn't help thinking what he'd do all alone. She was certain his family would have to return to California soon. Who would take care of Beau when that happened?

It was about 7:30 a.m. when Remmie got home. Mrs. McCain was up making coffee. The two sat down together for a fresh cup before Remmie went to bed. Remmie learned from Beau's mother that they intended to take Beau back to California with them just as soon as he left the hospital. That was a surprise for Remmie, and yet, she thought it was probably the best move right now. If Beau did fully recover, he could come back to the Medical Center. She made a mental note to discuss it with Beau.

Remmie arrived at the hospital early, going directly to see Beau. He was cheerful and although very pale, he looked good. After making small talk for a few minutes, Remmie asked if he was indeed returning to California. He acknowledged he was, stating it was the best thing for his parents.

He was concerned, however, about becoming a financial burden on them. Remmie assured him he would remain on a leave of absence, which would keep his insurance active. That was a tremendous relief for him. Remmie left, feeling that Beau was dealing with his illness very well. She hoped he would beat the odds and come back to the Medical Center. *I sound like a bookie,* thought Remmie. Speaking out loud she said, "Lord, Beau is a young man. He needs to be healed from this awful disease. Heal him in Jesus' name. Amen."

Dr. Rabon was waiting for Remmie when she entered the unit. She was concerned about the way a case had been handled the night before. After hearing her complaints, Remmie assured her she would review it and get back to her. The unit was extremely hectic that night and Remmie never thought about Dr. Rabon's complaint again. She left the hospital at 6:00 a.m. driving straight to her condo to check on Beau's family. If they were okay, she was going to River Oaks for a couple of days. They were fine, and Beau would be in the hospital until she returned. Remmie pointed out the frozen casseroles she had prepared for them to have while she was gone, encouraged them to feel at home, and left for River Oaks.

CHAPTER NINETEEN

It was a gorgeous morning. Autumn's canvas was painted flamboyantly with brilliant oranges, rusts, and browns against the deep blue sky. There were vibrant touches of yellow, gold, and red all mixed together, creating a collage of color along the roadways.

Remmie enjoyed her ride more than usual today. The crisp, humidity-free air of early autumn was very pleasant. The summers were so hot and muggy that it was always a relief when autumn arrived.

Remmie let her mind relax as she enjoyed the scenery. She wondered what she would find at River Oaks. Would Sarah and Stuart still be getting along, or would she be driving him crazy by now? Perhaps she had already worked him to death, and all Remmie would find would be a shell of his former self. Laughing at herself and her silly wonderings, Remmie drove farther away from the industrial city and deeper into the country.

The freshness of the air became more apparent the farther from the city she rode. The roadsides and fields were filled with goldenrods waving in the breeze. Butterfly weeds yielded their bright orange blooms to the delight of the butterflies that feasted on their sweet nectar. Persimmon trees laden with golden fruit outlined cotton and peanut fields. All these familiar sites made Remmie thankful she was from the southeast. It was truly a lovely place to live.

River Oaks was also decorated with color. The kudzu vine provided the dark green background on which had been added all the colors of fall. It was a love feast for the eyes. Remmie drove slowly, trying not to miss anything. The entrance was so pretty. Mums of bronze, yellow, and purple along with red and yellow salvia adorned the flower beds on either side of the gate. Perfectly trimmed boxwoods added the right touch of permanence to the setting. Once inside the gate, the welcoming live oaks bowed respectfully as she drove past. Up ahead, Remmie saw lovely things happening in the gardens - the stately sculptured evergreens, the splashes of color from mums, gladiolus, the pale pinks and whites of sasancquas, all cooperating to produce a scene perfect for the cover of a major magazine. It appeared, at least from this point of view, that Stuart was getting the job done well.

After getting a positive report from Sarah, Remmie went up to the equipment building to speak with Stuart. Stuart was busy working on some odd-looking piece of equipment. He didn't see Remmie driving up or walking over to where he was.

Remmie didn't realize Stuart was so enthralled in his work that he didn't know she was approaching. As she reached the equipment where Stuart was working, she slapped the side of the machine. Stuart, believing he was alone, jerked upward, hitting his head on the motor covering of the large contraption. Turning around quickly, he smashed his knee into a large metal drum filled with axle grease. Shocked by all the commotion, Remmie thought, *I wish I had not done that little slap.* Poor Stuart was hopping around on one foot, holding his head, and mumbling to himself.

"I'm sorry, Stuart. I guess I thought you saw me coming."

"It's alright, ma'am. I just wasn't expecting anyone to be here. When I heard that noise, I thought for sure I'd done messed with the wrong thing, and it was gonna blow."

"Let me see about your injuries."

"Shucks, ma'am, I'm alright. Don't worry yourself about this thick skull of mine."

"How are things going? Have you been able to keep up with Sarah's demands?"

"Miss Sarah and I are getting along just fine, Miss Remington. She's a slave driver at times, but I work pretty fast. We are making some progress. Did you notice the front gardens?"

"Yes, I did. Everything looks lovely. I also noticed how orderly this place is. What is this thing you are working on anyway?"

"It's a peanut picker. I bought it from a local farmer who is retiring. I got us a really good deal. It only needed minor repairs that I can do myself. Come next fall, we will be picking five thousand acres of peanuts. All my soil tests are back, and there's not a whole lot I'll have to do to the soil. I'll be planting in the spring. We should be bringing in a good crop next fall.

If prices are up, we can make enough money to run the farm on its own next season. I'm very optimistic about this being a profitable operation for you, Miss Remington."

~~~

Remmie returned to the city Sunday afternoon. To her surprise, Beau was sitting on her sofa surrounded by his family. Adrian was waiting on him hand and foot, and enjoying every minute of it. Beau saw Remmie first, calling out, "Come in and welcome! We are pleased you could drop by."

"Not as pleased as I am that you could drop by. How are you feeling?"

"Oh, the freedom is fantastic, the view from here is stupendous, and if I can stay germ free, I might have a fighting chance at staying alive a little longer. So all in all, I'm feeling great."

"Beau McCain, you are remarkable. You have the best outlook on life I've ever seen. The world needs more attitudes like yours. I have a feeling God may need you right here to show some folks that life isn't so bad after all."

The McCains told Remmie they were leaving the next day with Beau. She accepted that decision, realizing from a medical view point that Beau's chances were slim, and he needed to be near his loved ones. From a spiritual view point however, Remmie was content to leave this matter in God's hands. Ultimately, His will would be done.

Reporting for duty at 6:00 p.m., Remmie found a note on her desk from Dr. Rabon. It was a steamy reprimand. Dr. Rabon was very upset that Remmie had not reviewed the case from earlier in the week as she had said she would. Although Remmie found the note very annoying, she put her feelings aside to first see if she could find a reason for the original complaint. She would deal with the personal side later.

After spending the first couple of hours reviewing the case in question and interviewing the charge nurse with whom Dr. Rabon had found so much fault, Remmie found absolutely no cause for the complaint. In her opinion, the case had been well managed by all involved. The patient had later been dismissed. Remmie even called him to get his opinion on how he had been treated. He was fine and had no complaints. *Very puzzling*, thought Remmie. Why was Dr. Rabon making so much noise over a very routine case which had obviously been handled extremely well? The nurse in question had been on staff eight years, and had never had a single doctor's complaint before. What was going on here?
~~~

After careful deliberation, Remmie decided to think it over a while longer before personally dealing with Dr. Caren Rabon. She did write Dr. Rabon a brief report, stating she found no basis for her complaints. She put the note in Dr. Rabon's box and went on with what turned out to be a very busy shift.

As the clock reached midnight, the trauma unit doors flew open and in came a paramedic carrying a small child. He was shouting, "Code Red! Code Red!" This meant that everyone should assemble STAT! Converging around the tiny form the medic had placed on the bed, what they saw was so disturbing, that a general, "Oh, Dear God" went up in unison from the trauma team. Everything became automatic. They each had a job to perform, and they had to do it right if this tiny life would be saved.

Remmie was team leader. She tried to keep her mind clinical to hold back the tears that wanted so desperately to free themselves from her stinging eyes. All tests revealed serious head trauma, internal bleeding, not to mention the numerous cuts and contusions covering the little girl.

"Her name is Lisa," someone said. Someone else asked the blood-covered paramedic how she was injured. He just stood there looking helpless with tears streaming down, wetting his uniform shirt. Composing himself, he said she had been beaten up by her stepfather, and then thrown from a moving car. The mother and stepfather had been arrested for substance abuse and reckless endangerment of a child. If she died, the charges would change to murder.

The entire trauma team was quiet for several moments. Busily working to save the little girl, they all pondered what they had just heard. Dr. Rabon appeared to be totally unaffected by the heart-wrenching situation. Although she functioned well as a physician, her total lack of emotion troubled Remmie. The struggle went on until 2:00 a.m. when little Lisa lost her battle. The room was still when Remmie called out the time and cause of death. Everyone left the room except Remmie. Standing over the body of what once was a beautiful little blonde-haired girl with big blue eyes, she was reminded of Jenny and the Christmas spent in a hospital ward so long ago. Speaking out loud, Remmie made a promise to Lisa.

"I'm so sorry I couldn't help you, little one, but I promise you I will help others like you. Your death at such a young age will not be in vain. Other children will live because of you."

Tenderly Remmie touched Lisa's forehead before pulling the sheet up to cover the tiny body. As she turned to leave, Dr. Rabon was standing there watching her with a look on her face that made Remmie shudder.

Then, in a voice as cold as steel, she said, "You are too emotionally involved, doctor. If you can't maintain a professional demeanor in the unit, perhaps you shouldn't be here."

All the hurt and remorse Remmie felt at that moment for Lisa kept her from saying anything to Caren, but she made a mental note that they would be having a talk. Remmie dried her eyes as she walked passed Caren without responding to her statements. The other team members had gathered in the lounge. Each member sat quietly, sipping coffee. The mood was very somber.

Remmie poured herself a cup of coffee then turned to face the trauma team before she spoke. "You all did a magnificent job. The task was too great for medical science. That precious child will never know the brunt of human anger again. She'll never feel pain again, but most importantly, she'll be loved. Our grief should be for a society where our children are casualties of domestic violence. We, as doctors, nurses, and para-professionals must find ways to channel the emotions we are having right now, to make sure we never see another Lisa. Search your hearts, your minds, and ask God to reveal to you how you can stop the violence in our homes. This problem will never go away unless every citizen makes it a personal goal to see that it does. There was little hope for Lisa when she came through the door, but we shared our hope with her. We gave her every opportunity medically possible to make it. It was not meant to be---you did all you could. Now, there's another emergency coming, and we must be ready to give it all we've got."

At that instant a clap-clap-clap rang out through the room. Everyone turned to see Dr. Caren Rabon standing there clapping as if she had just seen a wonderful performance. Startled, Remmie told her to stop.

"That was great coaching, Remington. Let's go out and win one for the grim-reaper. You are a pathetic group, allowing your emotions to hang out all over the place. I've never seen such un-professionalism in my career. What kind of hospital is this, anyway?"

"That will be enough, Dr. Rabon. You are out of bounds! You can finish this with me in private, but you cannot continue this with the team. It isn't the time. We have an ambulance arriving in thirty seconds. Dr. Williams, you are team leader. You are all dismissed."

When everyone had left the room, Remmie turned her full attention to Caren. "Please feel free to finish your speech, Dr. Rabon. I'm anxious to hear the rest of it."

Caren stood glaring at Remmie. Such hostility she had rarely seen in a person's eyes. "Don't patronize me, Dr. Remington. You are so high and mighty or perhaps I should say so self-righteous. You are the one who is out of bounds - talking about God and His will. We didn't do enough or that child would be alive! You aren't a doctor; you are some kind of faith healer!!"

"I know I said you could finish your speech, but you've said enough, Dr. Rabon! You may clock out; you are finished for the evening. You and I will meet with McKinley at five tomorrow afternoon. Good evening, doctor."

Remmie waited for Caren to leave the room. She watched as she clocked out and left. *What in the world is wrong with that woman*, she thought. *Well*, she concluded, *McKinley hired her. He can figure this one out.* Dismissing the whole situation, she returned to the unit.

The shift was busy, but there were no more fatal injuries for which Remmie was thankful. She called the team before they clocked out.

"I want to tell you all again how well you performed your duties tonight. I'm proud to work with such a fine team."

From the back of the room came a voice Remmie didn't recognize. Moving to her left, she tried to get a clear view of the person speaking.

"Dr. Rabon is a very distinguished physician. She is highly respected. How do you explain her remarks?"

"Your name, please?"

"I'm James Hooker, lab technician. I'm not a member of the trauma team, but I was in here last night, and I heard what was said. She's right, you know. You've no right to push your religious beliefs on these people. You shouldn't be deciding a patient's fate when they are wheeled in the door. You said that little girl didn't have a chance when she came in. You don't know that. Maybe you didn't do everything you could have, because you had already decided she was done for."

"Mr. Hooker, your presence here is inappropriate. I have no intention of discussing this with you. Would you please excuse us? We need to finish our meeting."

Hooker reluctantly left the room.

"Well, I'm flabbergasted. I've never encountered so many negative remarks during a single shift before. Is there anything anyone else would like to say?"

Dr. Williams spoke up, "I agree with you, Dr. Remington. We did all we could for the child. She was mortally injured when she got here. It is always devastating losing a child, but I feel we can all take comfort in knowing we did our best."

"I've been here longer than any of you," added Connie. "This hospital has a long standing reputation of integrity and sound medical practice. There was nothing wrong with either as far as I saw. I don't know what mental ward Dr. Rabon escaped from, or how she connected with the technician from hell, but we all did a good job. I for one have never felt that you pushed your religion on me. To be frank, I take comfort in knowing you have a strong faith. At least you don't think you are God like some doctors I've known. One other comment and I'll hush. You should not take this lightly, Dr. Remington. Follow all procedures on this to a 'T'. I've got a nagging feeling you may not have heard the last of Dr. Rambo, I mean Dr. Rabon."

Remmie slept very little. She tossed and turned, reliving the treatment given to Lisa. She reviewed every procedure, but she still felt confident there was absolutely no basis for any mal-practice claim. As for the remarks concerning religion, she had a right to speak about her personal beliefs. In her opinion, she had never tried to convert a soul to her way of thinking, not directly anyway. She had only offered comfort to people experiencing tremendous pain or loss, or encouragement to a fine trauma team when they were feeling low. No! She absolutely denied any wrong doing regarding her spiritual beliefs. The more she thought about it, the angrier she became.

Dr. McKinley was waiting for Remmie at the employees' entrance. He looked strained, not at all his usual self. He proceeded to tell Remmie what had transpired since she left the trauma unit that morning.

"We've got a mess, Remmie, and it's all my fault. I hired Caren, but I had no idea she was so vicious. She came highly recommended. Her credentials are impeccable. She is a highly qualified trauma specialist."

"I suspect they recommended her to get rid of her. She's a miserable human being, Dr. McKinley. I'd hate to know I had to go through life with her disposition. We are clear on any mal-practice claim. She's all wet on that. I just don't understand her. What is she after?"

"Your hide, and your job, I'm afraid. She not only claims irregularity last night, but earlier she reported an incident to you that she says you ignored completely. She claims you are preaching to the trauma team, and deciding the fate of patients based on your religious experience rather than medical evidence."

"What! This woman has no proof of any of this, Dr. McKinley. I reviewed the nurse she complained about. I wrote her a brief report. I found nothing to substantiate her complaint. I am a sound medical practitioner. I follow the rules of my oath, and I believe in God. When do we settle this?"

"That's what I'm trying to tell you. We don't settle it, Remmie. She's gone over my head to the Board, and I'm afraid she has some support."

"Support! What do you mean, support? We aren't running for office."

"She is, Remmie. She's running hard for your job. She has found favor with two very powerful Board members. You have to take this very seriously now. Get all your facts together. Be prepared to answer clinically every charge. Keep calm and professional. She is a force to be reckoned with."

"When, Dr. McKinley, when do I meet my formidable foe?"

"In two weeks."

"*Two Weeks!* I've got to put up with that insufferable, pompous..."

"Yes, Remmie, you do. The Board decided the charges are so complex that you both need time to get your information together."

"Well, may I at least have a description of the charges?"

"I have that for you in my office. I wanted to prepare you before you read it. It will make you extremely angry. I want you to take some time away from the hospital to digest it before you prepare your response."

"No can do, Doc. I'm not leaving her to take over in my absence. I can deal with this. I've been through a lot recently. I've learned a lot about myself. I'm not intimidated by her at all."

"Okay, if you are sure I won't have to come to the unit to separate you two."

"You will not be called to referee. That's a promise."

"Dr. Remington, you know I have total confidence in you as a person, and as a doctor. You can overcome this. I'll be by your side all the way. I'll use every legal and ethical means at my disposal to make sure you are treated fairly."

"Is that even in question? Are you telling me the deck is stacked against me? I've been here five years. Never have I been accused of wrong doing. How can this be?"

"Politics, Remmie. It's a dirty business that has no place in medicine, but it's here, and we have to deal with it. You'll come through this, my special friend, and you'll be better for it. Now is the time to call on that deep faith of yours." Dr. McKinley hugged Remmie reassuringly, and she nodded her understanding.

The next few shifts were very difficult for Remmie. Dr. Rabon was arrogant, which put the entire team on edge. To top it off, she was lonesome.

Beau and his family had left for California. Her condo seemed so big and so empty. Sarah had called to say everything was fine at River Oaks. Jesse was away on business, and Colin was in court every day. She hated to call him when he was busy with a case. The days were dragging by. For the first time since becoming a doctor, she hated going to work.

Finally, she gave in and called Colin. He was very understanding. He assured her everything would be okay, but to make certain he would come over Saturday to review the claim himself. Remmie felt so much better after speaking to Colin. Now she had something to look forward to.

Colin arrived about lunchtime. Remmie was ready for him. She had fried chicken salad with pecans, topped with ranch dressing. For dessert, she had banana pudding – Colin's favorite. Colin carefully reviewed the information Remmie gave him regarding the claims made by Caren Rabon. His final conclusion was that he should represent her at the hearing. The claims were much too serious to go into the hearing without legal representation. He told Remmie to stop worrying and let him handle everything. Those were comforting words, so she agreed.

They spent the rest of the weekend at an art festival in the park. Colin bought several lovely paintings from local artists. Remmie felt relaxed and confident by the time Colin kissed her good-bye and returned to Atlanta Sunday afternoon.

When Remmie reported to work, she called the team together for a brief meeting. The day shift had been horrendous. She suspected they were in for a difficult night. Ignoring Dr. Rabon without being obvious, Remmie encouraged the team, and then she appointed team leaders for the shift. Dr. Williams and Dr. Logan would head up the teams, alternating with each other. Everyone seemed in good spirits except the wicked witch of the ER. She was as obnoxious as usual, questioning every decision Remmie made.

Taking it all in stride, Remmie proceeded as she planned. Dr. Williams would take charge of the first case, then Dr. Logan the next. They didn't have to wait long. Remmie's instincts were right on target. One after another all night long, it was total bedlam. Everyone held steady. Things went well. Remmie hoped things with Dr. Rabon would turn out as well.

CHAPTER TWENTY

Finally, the day of the hearing came. Remmie dressed in a gray flannel suit with a mid-calf straight skirt and a deep purple blouse. She wore gray suede pumps and silver jewelry. She put her hair up loosely. She did her make-up conservatively, with earth-tone shadows. Then she added a touch of pink lipstick. She thought she looked professional.

Colin met her in the hospital parlor. Together they went up to the meeting room where Dr. McKinley was waiting. Moments later Caren came in, followed closely by her two Board members. Eventually, all seven Board members were present. The chairman called the meeting to order. Dr. McKinley introduced everyone before reading aloud the complaints of Dr. Rabon. She was allowed to present her side of the story, which was distorted, to say the least.

Then it was Remmie's turn. Colin reminded her of everything they had discussed. He encouraged her to tell the truth, reassuring her that the Board would recognize her integrity. She was to respond to each accusation calmly and precisely. The questioning began.

They all seemed interested in learning what really happened. Their ultimate goal was to find out if the hospital had been compromised in any way. There came a point when Dr. Rabon realized her two cronies were not going to be able to sway the other five Board members. She became infuriated, lashing out at everyone. The chairman called her down. She had not helped her case at all. The questioning continued for another thirty minutes.

The Board members had apparently satisfied their curiosity. They conferred with each other privately for a few minutes. When the findings were announced, Dr. Remington was cleared on all accounts. The Board had decided that she and the trauma team followed all hospital procedures to the letter. As for Dr. Remington's religious beliefs, they found no conflict between her faith and her performance as a physician. All of Dr. Rabon's charges were dismissed. She was livid.

The two Board members Caren had enlisted in her scheme had also been swayed by the evidence in its entirety. She was alone in the room, but she was determined to make her feelings known. After several minutes, the Chairman again called her down, stating emphatically that the decision of the Board was final. Caren stormed out. Remmie thanked the Board. She, Colin, and Dr. McKinley left the meeting room.

"I'm so thankful that's finally over. This has been a most difficult two weeks."

"You handled yourself well, Remmie. Now, put this behind you. Get on with your work," stated Dr. McKinley.

"I'm not convinced that it is over. That woman is volatile. Anything can happen when a person is that angry. I want you both to be aware of her at all times. She may try again. As an attorney, I'm advising you both to watch out."

"Colin, you don't think she would try this again? After the Board voted against her one hundred percent?"

"I think she's much too angry to think rationally. People like that can be dangerous. That's all I'm saying."

"Mr. Forrester, I appreciate you being here today for Remmie. This whole charade was uncalled for. I'll deal with Dr. Rabon myself. I'm moving her from the trauma unit."

"Are you sure, Dr. McKinley? She is not going to take that well."

"She'll have to take it the best way she can. My mind is made up. I'm not leaving her in trauma to sabotage an operation we've worked years to put together. Most hospitals don't have trauma teams like ours. No, we aren't going to jeopardize it because of a power hungry doctor."

"Is that really all there is to this? She's power mad? You don't think there's something mentally or emotionally wrong with her?"

"No Mr. Forrester, if I did, I'd insist she seek professional help. If she refused, I'd dismiss her. I must be careful not to put the hospital in a libelous position by false accusations, so I'll move cautiously on this."

"My experience with people who display such an intense degree of hostility is that they are emotionally unstable. That's the reason for my warning to you, Remmie, because she views you as the obstacle between where she is, and where she wants to be.

Dr. McKinley, you are the force keeping her where she is because you allied yourself with Remmie. You represent the power. And she knows where you stand. That's why she went to the Board. They were not easily swayed either, so now she's back to square one – a subordinate of Remmie's. No, in my opinion she isn't finished. Be on guard is my advice."

Remmie tried to forget the whole thing, reporting for duty as scheduled. Dr. McKinley summoned Dr. Rabon to his office just before the shift ended. He told Remmie to clock out and leave before he released Dr. Rabon. He wanted to avoid a scene in the trauma unit.

Remmie left with other members of the team. They paused in the parking deck a few moments to shoot the breeze. Then they all drove away before Dr. Rabon emerged from the building.

When Remmie arrived at her condo, Jesse was waiting in the parking deck.

"Hey girlfriend!"

"Hey yourself. What's up?"

"Oh, I wanted to see you before you settled in for the day. I wondered if you could be off this week."

"As a matter of fact, I am taking off Saturday and Sunday nights."

"Great! Let's go to the ballgame Saturday, and spend the night talking girl talk."

"You have a date. As a matter of fact, I found a box of pictures I've been dying to show you. There's been so much going on, and you've been away for so long."

"Has Colin found your brother?"

"No, it's hospital stuff. Look, I'm really beat, so let's talk about it all Saturday night."

"Okay! Now, I need a favor. My car has to go to the shop. You know how I hate public transportation, so I wondered if I could pick up your car Friday evening while you are at work, and use it to make several meetings. I'll finish up about midnight. Then I'll return your car, so you'll have it Saturday morning. I'll take a taxi from the hospital."

"Sounds fine to me. When will you get your car back?"

"They promised me I can get it Saturday morning. So Friday night is my only problem."

"I'll give you my spare set of keys now so we won't have to connect Friday night. That's usually a wild one in the unit. You get the car when you need it. I'll see you here Saturday morning by eleven-thirty." They said good-bye. Remmie went to bed.

Upon arriving at the hospital, she ran into McKinley, who had plenty to say about his encounter with the tempestuous Dr. Rabon. He had moved her to surgery. Her first shift would begin the first of the next week. His reasoning was the only times their paths would cross would be entering or leaving the hospital. Dr. Rabon had been plenty mad.

Dr. McKinley advised Remmie to avoid her as much as possible. But if the situation became unbearable, she was to let him know right away. She agreed as she walked toward the trauma unit, dreading her meeting with Caren.

In the orientation session, Remmie appointed team leaders as usual. This time she appointed three because it was Friday night. She suddenly realized Caren was not there. She asked if anyone had seen her. Connie said she had seen her pull into the parking deck at the same time she had, but she had driven away in a hurry.

Maybe she forgot her broom, Remmie thought to herself.

The evening was getting underway without Dr. Rabon. This puzzled Remmie. *Why would she fail to report? She must know that carries some pretty tough consequences.* Her concentration was interrupted by a police scanner. There was a massive pile-up on I-20 at I-65 – Malfunction Junction.

The police were requesting the Mobile Intensive Care Unit to the scene. Remmie, along with two support staff, left on the MICU. The driver had to go past the accident, which was in the north bound lanes. Then he had to cross a grassy median in order to get to the scene. It was a mess. There were MICUs from three other hospitals arriving. Remmie jumped out, found a state trooper who was in charge, and asked if a triage area had been established. A trooper said, "Yes," and pointed.

Following his directions, she headed toward a group of paramedics who were busy working on several injured people. Identifying herself, she let them know the intensive care units were available. Then she began examining the injured. The nurse who came with Remmie, as well as the Emergency Medical Technician, began offering assistance also. After briefly checking the injured on her side of the wreckage, Remmie told the EMT to help the nurse get an elderly woman into the unit as quickly as possible. By then, three other physicians with their support staffs were assisting.

"Are you a doctor," someone yelled at Remmie.

"Yes. What can I do?"

"Come with me immediately. We have two people trapped in the worst part of the pile-up. Don't think they're going to make it until we get 'em out," shouted the intense trooper.

Remmie followed him through a maze of crumpled vehicles. Smoke and fumes filled the air. Portable lights lit the area as bright as day. Paramedics, firemen, and police officers worked feverishly, trying to extricate the two injured people. Walking closer to the vehicle, she thought, "That car is like mine. Boy, it sure didn't handle a collision very well." The car was completely demolished. It looked flat. *How could anyone survive that*, was Remmie's first thought.

"Come around to this side. You can get to her better," said the police officer.

Kneeling down, looking into space no more than a foot and a half high, he showed Remmie where the victims were trapped. As Remmie knelt, she caught a glimpse of the tag on the front of the car. Her heart stood still. The tag read, *Doc R.*

"Oh my God! It's Jesse!"

Remmie was screaming as she struggled to get into the car to help, but she couldn't. The space was just too small. Seeing her hysteria, the trooper pulled her back.

"Do you know her?"

"Yes, this is my car! She's my best friend – Jesse Morehouse. I've got to get to her. Please let me get to her. Jesse, Jesse!!"

The trooper pulled her even further away.

"Ma'am, I don't think you need to help here. This is too stressful for you. You can help the other lady. She's in real bad shape, too. From the looks of it she hit your car at full speed, causing it to flip several times. With traffic like it is at 6:00 p.m., several other vehicles got involved. But these two cars got the worst of it."

"I'm not leaving her, officer. She's my best friend."

Realizing he was fighting a losing battle, he allowed Remmie to return to the side of the demolished Mercedes with Jesse inside. By this time, her nurse had found her. Together they struggled to reach Jesse, offering some human contact. The nurse was petite which allowed her to get further inside the wreckage than Remmie.

"I've got a pulse, Dr. Remington. She's still alive. In fact, it's a good pulse."

"Hang on, Jesse. We're here! We'll get you out."

The Jaws of Life were cutting the car apart to reach Jesse. But the gas spills made this a very dangerous procedure. Everyone had been moved away for their protection except Remmie and the little nurse. They refused to leave. Firemen were standing far enough away that should the wreckage ignite or explode, they would be able to extinguish the rescue workers if they caught on fire.

If Remmie had not been so frightened about Jesse, she would have been long gone. It was an extremely dangerous situation. At last, one final cut, and the car was apart. Jesse was so tangled in the wreckage that great care had to be taken to assure she wasn't injured further. At least Remmie could see her and could touch her. It wasn't easy to look at her. She was a broken, twisted mess, but she was alive. Calling out to the EMTs, Remmie ordered an MICU be set up for Jesse immediately. She knew every second counted if Jesse was going to survive. Moments later, Jesse was carefully lifted free of the wreckage, immobilized, and placed in the MICU on her way to the Medical Center.

Remmie began preliminary evaluations on Jesse. It was so painful seeing her in such a state. Jesse remained unconscious. She had multiple breaks in her leg, ankle, and foot. Her pelvis was most likely fractured. The condition of her back and neck were not known. Internal injuries began to manifest as her blood pressure plummeted. Remmie knew Jess was in deep shock. Her skin was cold, clammy, and her respirations were rapid and shallow.

Realizing Jesse was in a life-threatening condition, she prayed for God's help and mercy.

She started an IV to control the shock, which would also stabilize her respirations. Phoning ahead, she alerted the hospital to what she knew. She wanted to get as many pieces of the puzzle as she could in place before Jesse arrived. She asked what senior physicians had been called in. Waiting to hear Dr. McKinley's name, she prayed that he was there. *Yes! Yes!* He was there waiting to take charge of Jesse's care.

The MICU backed in slowly. As soon as it stopped, the doors were opened and Jesse was wheeled into the trauma unit. McKinley was waiting with a team in place with a portable x-ray, a cat scan, and an MRI all ready to help them pinpoint the most critical injuries. Blood was hung because she was losing a lot internally. From this point on, all Remmie could do was observe.

She had a strange feeling that this wasn't real. She wasn't seeing Jesse at all. It was a weird sensation. But the big knot in the pit of her stomach was telling her something else.

Suddenly, her concentration was broken by someone calling her name. "Dr. Remington, trauma room three-- STAT! Responding, Remmie walked into the room where, to her absolute horror, she saw Caren Rabon on the table in front of her. Someone said she had been the last wreck victim extracted.

The doctor in Remmie took over. This was a person who needed help. For the next hour, she was too busy to think about what was happening. Caren's injuries were devastating - massive head and chest trauma. Remmie called in Dr. Blalock, the best neurosurgeon on staff. He took over, with Dr. Williams assisting.

Completely exhausted, Remmie went to check on Jesse. McKinley was performing surgery to repair her badly lacerated kidney and liver. He had removed her crushed spleen. When he observed Remmie at the viewers' window, he gave her thumbs up. That reassured her that Jesse was holding her own. She collapsed on a sofa in the lounge to wait.

McKinley came in about an hour later with a fairly good report. Internal damage was under control. She would need a few more units of blood. The orthopedic surgeon was working on her leg, knee, and ankle. He estimated another hour before Jesse would be put into the Surgical Intensive Care Unit.

"Caren's in surgery with Blalock and Williams. She was also a victim in the same pile-up."

McKinley stared at Remmie. "She should have been on duty. How was she involved?"

"I really don't want to speculate, but I have an awful feeling she caused the whole accident. Jesse drove away from here about 6:00 p.m. in my car. Connie saw Rabon drive into the deck, but she drove away again in a hurry. I think she thought Jesse was me, so she followed my car onto the interstate at rush hour, where she rammed Jesse from behind. That caused my car to flip, involving several other vehicles. Jesse never knew what hit her. She was after me. Jesse was in the wrong place at the wrong time."

"Remmie, are you sure?"

"No, but a state trooper said my car was hit from the rear which caused it to flip over several times. He indicated Caren's car was the one causing the accident. And as you said, she should have been here. Something odd happened. Colin said she wasn't finished, but I never imagined anything like this."

"I want a police report – now!"

McKinley left to locate the police officer who came in with the victims. He wanted to know exactly what had happened. This could be attempted murder by a member of his staff.

Remmie waited to hear from surgery. McKinley returned and confirmed what Remmie had suspected. It appeared to the police that Caren had deliberately rammed into the red Mercedes, causing the pile-up. Several motorists gave the same account of the accident. Before McKinley could finish speaking, the orthopedic surgeon came in to report on Jesse.

Remmie jumped to her feet, anxious to hear. He reported the surgery had gone very well. He said he expected the knee and ankle would take a long time to heal. Jesse would need extensive physical therapy to regain use of her foot and leg. He believed she could recover eighty to eighty-five percent usage, but he felt she would have a limp.

Both doctors headed to recovery. Jesse was not waking up as quickly as expected. She was still unresponsive. Without warning, her blood pressure dropped. The crash cart was summoned. After working feverishly for about fifteen minutes, Dr. McKinley ordered Jesse back to surgery. Something was very wrong. He had to get in there to see what it was.

Again, Remmie was left to ponder all these unexpected, tragic events alone. She had waited to call Jesse's folks until she was sure Jesse would be okay. Now she had a sinking feeling in the pit of her stomach that told her she should make the call.

It was so difficult telling Jesse's father. He was frantic to learn all he could about what had happened. Panic stricken and horrified, he told her he was coming, and then the line was dead.

Memories passed through Remmie's mind. One after another, they paraded across the years of their friendship. Jessica Elaine Moorehead, a beautiful Black girl introduced herself on the first day of college with all the warmth and charm of a much more mature woman. So energized, so excited about life, so sure she would make it. Those were the characteristics that endeared her to Remmie in the beginning, as well as today. She was never arrogant or cocky, just confident. Jessica Elaine Morehouse had a place in this big old world that she intended to occupy.

Remmie was determined and sure of herself, but for a very different reason. She had to make it. She knew all too well what Jesse didn't know. She knew how it felt to be alone with no help in sight, with the whole world resting on your shoulders. She had to make it so she could be safe and secure, no matter what else life tossed her way. But on the first day of college so long ago, when she met Jessica Elaine Morehouse for the first time, she knew they were destined to be a part of one another's lives. Not since that day had she been plagued with that overwhelming feeling of loneliness, until tonight.

A gentle touch brought Remmie back from the sweet memories of happier days. Seeing Jesse's parents with eyes full of questions, Remmie released her tight grip on her own emotions. She fell into their arms, and together they had a good cry.

The whole story of Caren, including the borrowed car, the pile-up, and the injuries Jesse had sustained, was told in between her sobbing. Jesse's mother held her like a little child upon her breast---a child who needed comforting.

"Remmie, my dear, you are the best friend Jessica has ever had. She truly adores you. The years you have had together are precious memories for Jess, and for us. Because I know you so well, I know this is causing you deep pain, but I also know you are a woman of great faith. Release your faith, Remmie, and peace will replace the fear. We did that before leaving to come here. Long, long ago we gave each of the children back to God in a gesture of faith, letting Him know we are aware they are a gift, and we are thankful for them. If He chooses to take Jesse, my heart will be broken, but I have no fear for her. She will be safe forever."

Remmie lifted her head as she wiped her tears. The love she felt from Jesse's parents was so comforting. She should be consoling them, and yet, here they were consoling her.

"You are so strong, Mrs. Morehouse. I've always admired your quiet strength. It reminds me of my mother. She was like that, so much in charge, but so inconspicuous about it. Thank you for being so encouraging. I should be the one encouraging you both."

"Nonsense! We are in this together. Your loss will be our loss. You are not alone, Remmie. Jesse has told her mother and me so many times how important you are and how no matter what, we are to be family to you."

The hours slipped by. Daylight brightened the room where the three sat waiting for news that could change their lives, forever. Over the intercom Remmie was summoned to Surgical ICU. The Morehouses accompanied her down the long corridor. Dr. McKinley was waiting and the look on his face was grim.

Remmie introduced Jesse's parents. Dr. McKinley motioned them into a small waiting area. His report was clinically detailed. The bottom line was that Jesse had hemorrhaged severely, losing almost all her blood internally before he could reopen her incision to locate the bleeder. It was a perforated artery near the sight of the original liver laceration. All was repaired, but Jesse had slipped into a coma. He was concerned that her brain had been injured from the lack of blood. Time would tell. He said they could see her, but he encouraged them to speak positively while they were in her room. He said that it is not known how much an unconscious person hears, but he believed they could hear everything.

The room was small. The space was filled with equipment of all kinds. Taking positions at the sides of Jesse's bed, they touched her arms and her face in an effort to make personal contact with her. She was pale, but otherwise no visible injuries. Her leg and foot were supported by a sling. They weren't in a cast yet, but they were bandaged. Her foot was badly swollen, and almost black. After careful inspection, their attention turned to talking to Jesse. Each one had a turn, first dad, then mom, and then Remmie.

"Hey, you better open those eyes and talk to me. You know how I hate being ignored. I could order some horrible procedure that would expose you to the mercy of the world."

They all laughed. Remmie knew how Jesse hated medical examinations. She had often said that modern medicine is unable to help anyone with their clothes on. Someone must be naked if they want a diagnosis.

After a while, they ran out of things to say, so they said good-bye and left. Once outside, they group hugged each other good-bye, knowing full well they'd be seeing each other in four hours when visitation rolled around.

The first few days went by. The hope that Jesse would suddenly wake up was gone. Every day Remmie sat by her side for hours, talking about things they had done, places they had been, or things they planned to do. Her parents and her brothers came daily, too. The strain was showing on her parents. They were physically exhausted, but still they came.

Remmie had been unable to work a complete shift because she was so fatigued. Dr. McKinley had filled in for her. Early one morning, Remmie came up from the trauma unit to see Jesse. It was just like all the other mornings. Everything looked the same and sounded the same in the room.

"Good morning, Jess. It is going to be a beautiful day. The weather is cooler now. It was only seventy degrees yesterday, and then it dipped to fifty-six degrees last night. Great football weather, Jess. The Tide won again, but Florida State University lost. I'm sorry we missed Homecoming, but I couldn't do it without you."

With no warning, Remmie fell apart. She laid her head on Jesse and cried her heart out. She just couldn't pretend anymore. It was too much.

"Jess, I need you, please wake up. You can make it back from wherever you've gone. Everything internally is healing fine but your leg needs therapy. You must wake up so we can get you walking again. Jesse, please, please, hear me!!"

With her face buried in the covers, Remmie did not see as Jesse slowly moved a hand toward her. All she knew was that someone was patting her head as if to say everything would be okay. Looking up, she expected to see a nurse or Jesse's folks, but what she saw was exhilarating. Realizing it was Jesse, she grabbed her hand as she moved her eyes to see if Jesse was awake. Oh, yes! There she was looking somewhat confused, but it was Jesse alright.

"Welcome home. You have had quite a hibernation. How are you feeling?"

Slowly, very slowly, Jesse attempted to speak. "Where have I been? I don't remember anything."

"How do you feel? Are you in pain?"

"No pain. I feel strange, but I guess I feel okay. What are you doing here? Shouldn't you be at work?"

"Oh, I've been working less and less these days. I've had more important things to do. Exactly, what do you remember?"

After taking a couple of minutes to concentrate, Jesse said, "I borrowed your car to go to a dinner meeting. It was rush hour. The traffic was horrible. I heard a loud noise then I woke up here. Are you going to fill in the blanks for me?"

"That's great, Jesse. You remember just fine. I will fill in the blanks for you, but first I need to call your folks."

Compared to the last time she called the Morehouses, this ranked number ten! She related her news from the phone in Jesse's room.

Jesse continued to progress. Within a week she was ready for therapy to begin on her badly damaged leg and foot. Everyone had tried to prepare her for how serious the injuries were, but when she actually saw her leg, she almost fainted.

The therapy was to keep the muscles from atrophying, but she was totally exhausted after thirty minutes, so she was returned to her room. This was only the beginning of what lay ahead. The pain, the struggle, and the determination of this courageous young woman won the hearts of all her caregivers. She was admired by the therapists who knew from the beginning she would have permanent damage. Somehow Jesse found a way not to concentrate on how much damage was permanent, but to record her daily victories.

Remmie was there constantly, offering all the support and love she had to give. She cheered for every victory and minimized every effort that failed. She was a one woman cheering squad. Together those two could conquer the world. One day, Remmie was pushing Jesse in a wheelchair roller derby style through the halls, turning sharp corners –just in general acting crazy. They were giggling like a couple of school girls. Remmie pushed Jesse into the doctors' lounge to have a cup of coffee.

"It occurs to me that you and my folks have carefully avoided telling me about the accident. What really happened?"

"You were mistaken for me by a colleague of mine. You may recall I told you about the new doctor who was Beau's replacement. She was abnormal, to put it nicely. She brought charges against me. When she was overruled by the Board, she took it personally, focusing her anger on me. Believing I was driving my car, she followed you from the parking deck onto the interstate, eventually ramming you. That sent you flipping several times, involving several other vehicles. When the pile-up came to rest, my car with you inside, and Caren's car were hopelessly entangled.

"When I arrived at the scene with the Mobile Intensive Care Unit, I realized it was you, but I didn't know it was Caren until later when she was brought into the hospital. I was the only trauma surgeon left to handle a case. She was critical with severe head and chest trauma. I stabilized her while a neuro-team assembled. I turned her over to the best neurosurgeon on staff."

"Jesse, I am so sorry. I feel responsible for this. I should have realized how dangerous she was. I should have done more to defuse the situation, but I didn't. Colin warned me, but I didn't listen."

"Come on, Rem! How could you have possibly known she would do something so ridiculous? You can't hold yourself responsible for what others do. I asked to borrow your car. You didn't put me in it and shove me off toward disaster. The crazy doctor is the one, and only one to blame for this situation. Maybe she couldn't help herself. How is she doing?"

This was the one question Remmie did not want to answer. Her uneasy pause alerted Jesse that there was something she hadn't been told. She restated her question.

"She didn't make it, Jess. She died in surgery. Everything possible was done for her, but she was too seriously injured."

The always compassionate Jesse was touched. "Now we'll never know what really motivated her to do what she did."

"Hate, Jess. Hate motivated her, but who put all that hate in her we will never know. I wish I could have seen it coming, and somehow intervened."

"Remmie, no one could have predicted what she would do. We just have to make our peace with this so we can move on."

"You're right. We do have to move on. Buckle up and hang on – this capsule is blasting off."

Away they went. The dynamic duo was on their way to another adventure together, always together.

CHAPTER TWENTY-ONE

Winter had come to the Deep South. It was freezing outside. The damp, chilling wind blew hard across the gardens where only weeks ago flowers bloomed. River Oaks looked very different in winter. Although snow was rare, it did snow sometimes. Sarah was hoping for a white Christmas this year.

"Lordy be, it's colder than a well digger's feet in Montana. I think I'll make a big pot of refrigerator soup and hot cornbread. I'll just bet Stuart will enjoy that. How's that sound to *ya* Remmie?"

"Sounds delicious, Sarah. I'm sure Stuart will be glad to warm up with your refrigerator soup. He sure is working hard. I don't know how he stays out in this wind."

"He's a tough one, alright. *Ya* could do worse than him, *ya* know. He's a real fine man."

"Sarah, I don't want you to get started on that subject again. Stuart and I are business associates. That's all. I'm not interested in a romance right now anyway."

"*Ya ain't inner-rested. Ya* were *inner-rested* in Colin until Jesse got hurt. Then *ya* spent all your energy on her *til ya* left him right out of *ya* life. All *ya* have to do is give him a sign. He'll be here in two shakes of a lamb's tail."

"It's all for the best, Sarah. I'm not ready for a serious relationship. I may never be ready. Colin is a terrific guy, but I'm all wrong for him."

"Well *tar-nations*! Why don't *ya* let him decide that? He's plum crazy about *ya,* Remmie. *Ya* are the most *aggervatin'*, pig-headed woman I've ever come in contact with."

"Let's don't discuss this, Sarah. It only gets you upset. Let me help you fix lunch. Jesse will be getting hungry soon. You know how she just loves your cooking."

Down the hall, Jesse practiced walking on the ramp Stuart had built for her. It was a struggle, but she was determined to make that foot and leg work right again. Time after time she walked the twenty feet, turned around, and walked back again.

Jesse had come down to River Oaks at Remmie's constant urging. She planned to stay a month. She had put her career on hold in order to make a full recovery. Remmie had also taken a leave of absence and turned her attention to Jesse's rehabilitation. She was so determined to see Jesse fully recover that she didn't have time for anything or anyone else.

Sarah was right, she had pushed Colin away. She had not intended to at first, but as time went by, and he pursued her less and less, she realized it was the right thing to do. She wasn't ready for a serious relationship, let alone marriage. In reality, it was intimacy that horrified her. Besides Jesse's therapy, Remmie wanted her at River Oakes so she could talk to her about her fears and about the horrors of her past.

Remmie had also decided to spend her time researching the child protective service and foster care systems in the state. She felt her plan to adopt children would never be a reality until she gave it her complete, personal attention.

Colin was still working on the legal end of adopting older children. He was also still looking for Remmie's brother.

~~~

In winter, darkness came early on the river. Many of the trees were already bare. Since there were no street lights or illumination from passing traffic, no neon signs or lighted billboards, it was dark as pitch outside after the sun went down. When the moon was full, light could be seen reflecting off the river.

The house was quiet. Sarah had gone to bed early, as she often did in winter. Stuart was up in his apartment. Remmie sat by the roaring fire in the den. Jesse sat in a big, overstuffed recliner with her feet up. Knowing her friend as well as she did, she knew the past was tormenting her again. She also knew she needed to let Remmie know that she was ready to listen.

"I love big fires. I look into them, and imagine all sorts of things. They are hypnotic, aren't they?"
~~~

"Hypnotic, yes, I would agree with that. Jesse, I need to talk to you about my past."

"I know, Remmie. We've got all night, so when you're ready, I am."

It wasn't easy to tell the sorted, painful story of abuse Remmie related to her dearest friend. She struggled with it time and time again, looking for the words to make it easier to say or easier to hear. Being a doctor, she tried to be clinical, impersonal, but it didn't work. It still happened to her, regardless of how removed from it she tried to be. She was talking about things that happened to her, things that should not happen to a child.

Jesse sat motionless, trying to prevent her feelings from showing. Her mind was torn by thoughts of how anyone could do such things to a child. Anger and remorse for her friend's suffering were overwhelming. She fought the tears, staring into the fire. Images danced in the fire---images of demons pranced and gloated over their victories won long ago in the life of a helpless child.

Remmie talked on, revealing more of the hideous secrets she had hidden away. She focused on an incident that happened when she was ten years old. She was living in the home of an older couple who had a grown son, Hector. Hector didn't live in the home, but he visited often. Remmie remembered hating his visits. The couple would go to a movie or out to dinner, leaving her at the mercy of Hector. He would usually start by sitting extra close to her on the sofa. When she moved away, he would move too, until she was at the end of the sofa with no place to go.

Hector would laugh this snickering, snorting kind of laugh. He would then put his hand on her leg and move it slowly upward, snorting like some kind of pig. Her screams were unanswered. No help ever came. No one ever heard her desperate cries.

When Hector finished, he would make popcorn as if nothing out of the ordinary had happened. The old couple would return and Hector would go home. This went on for months. One day at school Remmie told a teacher that it hurt when she went to the bathroom. After talking with her about her pain, the school nurse referred her to a doctor. Remmie was immediately removed from the home.

The whispers at school let Remmie know everyone knew she had been sexually abused. They looked at her like she had a disease. No one was kind. She felt like everything was her fault. She felt that it was only a matter of time until the same things would happen again.

Remmie told Jesse that she remembered times with some strange dad lying next to her, fondling her while talking baby talk to her, telling her how much he loved her and what a pretty girl she was. She didn't feel pretty. She felt ugly and used and alone. She felt if these were fathers, she was just as happy not to have one.

Jesse couldn't stop the tears from spilling out of her eyes and running down her cheeks. The tears glistened in the fire light, catching Remmie's attention.

"Are you okay, Jess? I'm sorry. You have been through so much you may not be up to hearing my story."

"Remmie, I'm the one who's sorry. I am so ashamed of a society that allowed children to suffer the way you've had to suffer. I detest what has happened to you, but it is so difficult to hear. I want to share this with you. Please go on."

"I could tell you many more episodes just like those I've mentioned, but I won't. The fact is I was never a child when it came to sex. I've always known about it. As a child, I couldn't explain sex, but I knew. I knew what certain looks meant. I knew words that I shouldn't have known, and I knew submission was the wisest thing I could do. Fighting, crying, screaming, and begging only made it hurt more or made them angry, which caused me to get whipped.

"So, I submitted. I literally hate that word. It stands for feelings that haunt my soul. I was forced to give away pieces of myself to men who meant nothing to me, who thought nothing of raping and robbing me. Submit is an ugly word to me. All the promises made to secure my submission were forgotten very quickly after desires were satisfied.

"I'm terrified of intimacy, Jesse. I'm so afraid that I'll never be free of the memories. I'm afraid I'll feel the way I used to when my husband requires sex from me. How will I ever put those horrible, ugly feelings to rest and be free to be intimate with my husband?"

"I can't answer that, Remmie. I don't know. I do know the right man will be the key to unlocking the door to your feelings. The right man will be able to help you overcome those ugly feelings and tragic memories. Have you ever considered counseling?"

"Hundreds of times, but I've never sought out a counselor. To be perfectly honest, I don't have a lot of confidence in counseling. This talk with you is therapeutic enough for me. Sharing all this with a stranger isn't something I like to think about. I always feel there's someone to protect. I guess it's me.

"My father was completely against counseling. I guess I could come to terms with all the abuse if I could overcome the fear of intimacy. I really do want to get married and have children, but I think it would be very unfair of me to marry a man, and fail him so miserably. I don't think I could face that. So, I'm not taking any chances."

"Again, let me repeat, the right man can help put all your fears to rest - a kind, gentle, patient man who loves you with all his heart. Wait for the right man. You'll be alright. You are as stable or normal as anyone I know, in spite of all you've endured. You can overcome your fear. I know you will. You simply haven't met the right man yet."

"I hope you are right. I cared for Colin, and he for me. I just couldn't let it go beyond a certain point. When I felt his passions intensify, I retreated. I know he doesn't understand, but I don't know how to explain it. We are all business now. I'm much more comfortable with that. He's an excellent attorney. His advice has saved me a lot of money. I know he'll find my brother one of these days, too. He's a real good guy. He'll make someone a great husband."

Rising from her comfortable chair, Remmie placed another log on the fire. The fire responded by flaring in great yellow and orange flames, cracking and popping in a noisy display. Settling in again, the reflecting young woman continued her thoughts on love and marriage.

Jesse listened, but never broke her concentration on the fire. In her mind, Jesse wondered what life for her would have been like without her wonderful parents and her loving but aggravating brothers. She remembered feeling so loved, so secure each night as she was tucked in by her parents. Each morning she awoke in the safety of her own home. It was incomprehensible to visualize what it must be like to wake up surrounded by strangers. It was even more horrifying to think about trying to sleep with strangers. And the other possibilities were just too horrible to ponder. Jesse felt so incredibly blessed.

There was another feeling dominating Jesse's thoughts. It was an overwhelming feeling that she must do something to help the children who, like Remmie, were silent victims. They had no voice. They screamed in silence – their cries were never heard, except when courageous people like Remmie gave them a voice others could hear. Jesse knew that Remmie was destined to be the voice of the silent sufferers – the children that haunted her. She knew also she had a role to play. She wasn't here by accident – maybe the children, the silent victims, were haunting her, too.

The month went quickly. Jesse's folks arrived to take her back to the city. It was hard to leave Remmie, but she had a plan of her own that no one knew about. She needed to get home to work on it. After a long hug, the friends said good-bye.

As the car disappeared through the gates, Remmie waved one final time. Jesse turned to take another look at River Oaks, which now was captured by winter's grasp. In her mind, she vowed to herself, a vow conceived out of love for her friend, and empathy for what she had suffered. The vow was a way of giving rest to the silent voices only she could hear – the silent voices of the children.

CHAPTER TWENTY-TWO

Jesse's recovery proceeded at a steady pace, but to her it seemed to go very slowly. One good thing about it was the time it gave her to research child custody cases in the tri-states area of Alabama, Georgia, and Florida. Her interest grew with each case she researched.

Colin was also engrossed in his own research. He hoped to find adoption cases from the southeastern states where a new precedent had been set. A new precedent could open doors for broader rulings, which is exactly what was needed if Remmie was to be allowed to adopt children.

In Birmingham, Remmie pulled the night shift from Monday through Thursday, but from Friday until Sunday, she worked on renovation plans for River Oakes. She and Sarah tossed around a number of ideas that would make the old ranch house cozier and more convenient for a family.

After attending a series of meetings on raising children who had been abused, Remmie set up an appointment for herself with a prominent child physiologist. She was determined to acquire as much knowledge about the children she planned to adopt as possible.

Jesse, Colin and other experts in adoptions collaborated by phone during the week, and they met with Remmie at River Oaks on the week-ends. Their plan was coming together. When it was ready, it would be presented to Child Services, and an adoption hearing would be scheduled.

The courtroom was large and austere. The judge was also large and rather bored looking. His hair looked as though it hadn't been combed that day. The twig of hair he kept twiddling was sticking straight up, making him appear rather stupid. All of this, Jesse observed while waiting for court to begin.

Dressed in a dark gray suit with a white shirt, Jesse looked very distinguished, indeed. She was nervous, but one certainly couldn't tell it by looking at her. The attorneys for the state who were contesting Remmie's request looked like two comedians for *Comedy Zone.* They were disheveled, wrinkled, hurrying around dropping papers, and muttering to each other. "*Laurel and Hardy*," thought Jesse as she casually watched them from the corner of her eye. Within a few minutes, Colin arrived, as did Remmie and Sarah.

Colin and Remmie greeted each other formally, as if they hardly knew one another. Jesse handed Colin some paperwork, which immediately captured his attention. It pertained to a couple in Florida who had children of their own, but had adopted fifteen children of all races, ages, and several with impairments. They were a huge permanent family, not a half-way house or holding pen for children. The success of this couple would be helpful to Colin as he argued Remmie's case.

The big difference between Remmie's case and the Florida couple was that she was single, and not a biological parent herself. The state would use that against her, sighting no experience as a parent, and no husband would make this not only unconventional, but in fact, a single parent home. The media was filled with stories about the difficulties of single parent homes. By and large, they were considered dysfunctional by professionals, except in rare incidences.

Colin hoped to present enough evidence to convince the judge of Remmie's stability as well as her capabilities. He would show her as a professional person with high morals and deep convictions about marriage and family.

The religious aspect he would be careful about, fearing she would be branded a fanatic. That wouldn't help her case at all. He had rounded up witnesses from Remmie's past, including a school teacher, her first employer, which happened to be a day care manager Remmie had worked for her first year in college, as well as Dr. McKinley, and last but certainly not least, Sarah. Colin intended to show Remmie as a strong, but kind woman, who had been a victim of the foster care system, but one who had been victorious. Finally, he would call Remmie to the stand to testify for herself.

Remmie's deep love for children would be emphasized, as well as her strong determination to make life better for children who would never be adopted otherwise. Colin had studied and prepared well.

Jesse had worked long, hard hours as his assistant. She had begun her research immediately after she returned home from her convalescence at River Oaks. Jesse's talent for investigation had helped her do the necessary research for Remmie's case. Just as soon as they won this case, she planned to return to law school full time. She could finish her law degree in two years if she worked very diligently.

The bailiff entered the room to announce that court was in session. After the introduction of the judge and some logistical announcements, the proceedings began. Colin called Mrs. Oakley, Remmie's high school science teacher, as his first witness.

Mrs. Oakley was a petite, elderly lady with a beautiful smile and a kind, Southern drawl. She answered each question thoughtfully. From her recollections, as she put it, Remmie was a bright student, a caring person, and a lover of children. She recalled an incident that occurred one day during lunch break. She was leaving the dining hall when she caught site of Remmie assisting a little girl with her lunch. The little girl was finding feeding herself difficult because she had a broken arm. Remmie, who was just passing through, saw her difficulty, stopped, and fed the child her lunch.

Mrs. Oakley also recalled one cold February morning while driving to school when she saw Remmie rescue a child who was being beaten up by the neighborhood bully. At this point, Colin thanked Mrs. Oakley for her testimony, motioning to the state's attorney that it was his turn. "No questions," responded the attorney.

Colin then called Shannon O'Neil. Shannon owned a day care where Remmie worked when she was a freshman in college. She described Remmie as a beautiful young lady with an infectious smile and a genuine love for children. Colin asked if she ever suspected abuse in Remmie's past. She replied, "No." She went on to say Remmie approached each crisis with the children with kindness and patience. After making several more technical points with the witness, Colin again turned over the witness over to the state's attorney.

This time, the state's attorney did cross examine Shannon. They asked about her education and training in child care. She responded by saying that she had a degree in early childhood development, and she had also had training in identifying signs of child abuse, which seemed to re-enforce her testimony. With her credentials clearly established, the attorney asked

Shannon if a person with Remmie's background of abuse could truly overcome it. Without a hesitation Shannon said, "Yes." In her opinion, Remmie had overcome it when she was a freshman in college. With her medical training and successful career history, there was no doubt in her mind that Remmie was a mature, caring individual who should be a parent.

Realizing he was making great points for the other side, the lawyer gave up. "No more questions, your Honor."

Dr. McKinley was the next witness called on Remmie's behalf. He re-enforced the testimony about her maturity. Dr. McKinley stated firmly that he felt Remmie was the most gifted physician he had ever known. She also possessed a genuine compassion for the sufferings of others; a combination not often found in a physician. In his opinion, Remmie's character was impeccable. He considered her concern for the older children in protective services genuine. Being a father himself, and a pretty good judge of character, he felt she would be an excellent parent, single or otherwise. His only regret was that she had chosen to give up medicine, at least for the time being. That was a great loss for the trauma team at the Medical Center.

On cross examination, the state's attorney asked Dr. McKinley about the incident that caused Dr. Rabon to bring charges against Remmie. Dr. McKinley was emphatic that the entire episode was caused by a deranged individual. Dr. Remington was cleared of all charges. In fact, according to Dr. McKinley, only two of the Board members ever seriously considered the charges. The others merely allowed procedures to be followed as a formality. They knew it was a hoax.

The final character witness was Sarah. Saving the best for last would be the best way to describe this testimony. Sarah looked lovely. She was all decked out in her favorite black dress with an ecru lace collar and covered buttons down the front. Sarah was her usual testy self. It wasn't long before Colin asked the right question, so away she went. The question that motivated her was, "How long have you known Miss Remington?" Sarah began a trip into the past twenty-five years during which she had worked at River Oaks.

She recalled the day Remmie came home with the doctor and his wife. She was a frightened little red-haired child with the biggest green eyes she had ever seen. Sarah recalled how Mrs. Remington devoted every second to the child, and Dr. Remington, when he came home, took over where she left off. It was a month or more before they put the child in school.

They took that much time to bond with her and to make sure she knew they would always be her family.

Sarah continued by saying, "Remmie was a good girl, absolutely no trouble at all. The house was always filled with friends. Dr. and Mrs. Remington were so very proud of their beautiful, young daughter." Sarah told how Remmie would always take charge of any visiting children. "She was mother to *'em* all. Their parents could visit as long as they liked because she would take care of the children just as long as they would let her. It came natural to her. She just loved children."

Finally, the state's attorney got his turn at Sarah, but it seemed that he got a little more than he bargained for. In his opening remarks, he described Remmie as a spoiled little rich girl who thought only of herself. Sarah stopped him in the middle of a sentence. Rising slowly to a standing position, she let him have it with both barrels blazing. The judge ordered her to sit down and calm down.

"I'm awful sorry, *Yore* Honor, but *them* are *fighten'* words on the river where I live. He's got no right to paint such an ugly picture of Remmie with his words. She's a fine person who loves children. All she wants is to make a home for *young-uns* nobody wants anyway. Lordy be, it seems *kinda* stupid for the state to spend taxpayers' money *findin'* ways to keep children they can't find homes for from being adopted. That makes no sense at all."

Realizing he had gotten off on the wrong foot, so to speak, the attorney turned his attention to the other subject that Sarah would take exception to - Remmie's real parents. This time Colin objected. He stated that subject would be dealt with by Miss Remington herself. He assured the judge no attempt would be made to conceal anything, but he felt Miss Remington had the right to do that herself. The judge sustained Colin's objection and the state's attorney had nowhere else to go. He quickly decided that he had no more questions for Sarah.

Colin requested an opportunity to ask her one more question. "Sarah, in your opinion, is Miss Remington self-consumed, as the good attorney has suggested?"

"No sir, she *shore ain't.* Remmie is without a doubt one of the most generous and *unassumin'* people I've ever known. She is always *helpin'* one charitable cause or another - most of *'em havin' somethin'* to do with children. No *sir're*, she *ain't* what he said at all," exclaimed Sarah, pointing to the state's attorney.

"Thank you, Sarah. For my next witness I call Dr. Rebecca Elizabeth Melissa Remington."

Remmie rose from her seat with her shoulders back as she walked to the witness stand. She was a stately young woman, dressed in a teal suit with a short high-necked jacket and straight knee length skirt. Her long, thick, auburn hair was pulled back in a 40s style, rolled loosely and caught at the nape of her neck with a tailored bow. Pearl drop earrings and a broach covered in pearls were the only jewelry she wore. Colin controlled the powerful urge to drag her away to a hiding place where he would never have to share her with anyone again. He still loved her very much, but he was victorious over his urge, so no one ever suspected how strongly he felt for Remmie that day.

Sarah and Jesse sat straight up in their chairs, eyes keyed in on Remmie, ears a-tuned to her every word, waiting anxiously to see how telling her story out loud for all to hear would affect her. Colin led her into the story slowly, deliberately establishing the pertinent facts as they went. Remmie cautiously followed his lead, letting him take her where she needed to go.

Why can't she be so obliging in her romantic life, thought Sarah, *instead of being so pig-headed*! *She could let the poor feller lead her a little bit. Oh no, not Miss Stubborn-as-a-Missouri Mule! She's got to be in control at all times when it comes to men. Look at 'em, he's so* handsome *in his navy suit. Sometimes Rebecca Elizabeth Melissa, I could knock a knot on yore head a show dog couldn't jump.*

Dear God, please help my friend today. She's going to need your strength, and your wisdom to get through this, prayed Jesse to herself as she intently listened to every word of Remmie's testimony. *I wonder how the local people will react when they learn the whole story of River Oaks and the Remingtons. Will they act differently toward Remmie or will they accept the past as it was? Maybe they won't even find out. Don't be naive, Jess, of course they'll find out. Remmie can handle it, whatever happens, she'll be okay. God, I know you haven't brought her this far to leave her now.*

"Miss Remington, you are aware of certain facts concerning your birth parents that we need to reveal to the judge. I'm sure this information will not sway the outcome of his decision one way or the other. However, I do believe certain facts pertaining to how you received this information may interest him a great deal. Will you tell the court who your birth parents were, and how you came to know this information?"

The courtroom was silent. Only the sounds of Colin as he paced pensively across the front of the room, and the clock at the back, tick-tock, tick-tock! The old wooden floor of the courthouse creaked with each step.

The smell of sweeping compound and musty old books filled the large arena where only a handful of on-lookers waited for Remmie to speak.

Jesse and Sarah held hands tightly, breathing silent prayers for this courageous woman they loved so much. Dr. McKinley sat nearby, his eyes glued on Remmie. The other witnesses had left after they testified. All the other faces were strangers. Remmie's eyes scanned the room. She focused on Sarah and Jesse. They were sources of strength for her. "*I can do this. I must! Dear, dear Father, forgive me if I bring any reproach upon you. You were the dearest thing in my life for so many years. Now, I sit here about to reveal the most secret things about our lives. You know, I only do this to give myself the freedom I need to fulfill what I believe God has called me to do. If I don't tell our story, they will, thanks to Hadley. I must tell our story, Father. It will sound much better coming from me. There will be no secrets to hinder me anymore.*

Suddenly, Remmie felt the slightest brush against her cheek. She lifted her hand to her face on the spot she felt the touch, but nothing was there. Then, without explanation, papers flew about on the judge's bench. Again, the touch caressed her cheek and an ever-so-slight nudge on her back as if to indicate, "Get on with it." Remmie almost laughed out loud, but she managed to control herself. Her spirits were suddenly lifted. She knew this was the thing she must do. This would forever end the secrets of the Remingtons from River Oaks.

CHAPTER TWENTY-THREE

"Some time ago, my father's attorney, Hadley Markham, came to me with some information he had found during an investigation into my past. My father, Benjamin Remington, had instructed Hadley to locate my birth parents shortly before his death. Although I loved my adopted parents dearly, I wanted to know why I was given up by my biological parents. So, at my insistence, my father instructed Mr. Markham to look into my past.

"As I said, Hadley came to me with his finding and offered to conceal the information from my father for a price. He felt the information would be so damaging that I would be willing to compensate him for his silence on the matter."

This information caused the state's attorneys to take notice. They poked each other under the table, and whispered back and forth. Remmie's testimony definitely had their attention.

Remmie continued, "I was infuriated with Hadley, so I refused to compensate him. I fully intended to tell my father immediately. When I read the brief Hadley gave me, I decided to check the story out for myself before going to my father with it."

"Did the story check out, Miss Remington?"

"Yes, it did. I learned more than Hadley knew. I met the man who gave Hadley his information, but when he realized how Hadley had used him by trying to blackmail me, he took me to a person who could tell me the whole story. This woman filled in all the blanks in my life. I was finally a whole person."

"Please tell us who your mother was."

"Her name was Milea Marjoul. She grew up on a small island off the coast of Florida. Her mother was French and her father was from the island. He was a local crime boss, so to speak. He was a powerful, corrupt man who controlled everyone around him except his French-born wife. My mother left the island in her teens, coming to Florida to work as a domestic. Eventually, she came to River Oaks to work for my parents, the Remingtons.

"Melissa, my adopted mother, had recently lost a baby and was in very poor health. Emotionally, she was a wreck; therefore, my father felt she needed help with the house. Soon after my birth mother arrived at River Oaks, Melissa Remington was hospitalized for medication dependence. My father, Benjamin Remington, and the young girl, Milea, had a brief affair while my mother, Melissa Remington, was in the hospital. Realizing the harm that could be done by their relationship, they ended it, and no one ever knew. Shortly after Melissa came home, she discovered Milea was pregnant, so she sent her back to her family.

"Years later, Milea came into my mother's life again. This time she wanted her help in finding the child she had birthed. Milea was terminally ill, and wanted to know her child had a permanent home before she died."

"Now, Miss Remington, please tell us who that child was and who the father was."

"I was the child born to Milea Marjoul when she was nineteen; Benjamin Remington was my biological father. He never knew Milea was pregnant. He grieved for his mistake, and confessed to me before he died that he had loved Milea very much. He loved Melissa more. He had made a vow to be her husband - a vow to God; a vow he would keep."

"Did Melissa Remington know Milea was carrying her husband's baby when she sent her away?"

"No. She only knew she was pregnant, and felt she should be with her family. She had no idea about the father of the child until Milea contacted her just before she died."

"Why were you given up?"

"My wicked grandfather hated me. When my mother was found to be ill with tuberculosis, he seized the moment to have me taken away to the mainland."

"Why did your grandfather hate you?"

"I was White and my mother's family was Black. My grandfather hated me because I had a White, American father, and I was White in appearance."

"Let me sum this up for the court. Your dying birth mother turned to Melissa Remington, the woman she had betrayed by having an affair with her husband, for help in finding her child. Your adoptive parents, the Remingtons, found you, adopted you, and raised you as their own. Your father, Benjamin Remington, never knew who you really were until shortly before his death. Hadley Markham discovered that you are racially mixed, and attempted to extort money from you to insure his silence. You found a person who told you everything about your secret past. All of this, you told to your father, your friends, Jesse, and Sarah. Is that correct, Miss Remington?"

"Yes, that is correct."

"Did any of this change your life for the better or for the worse?"

"No, I can't say that it changed my life at all. It completed my life. I now know that I had a mother who not only brought me into the world, but loved me very much. She spent her life, brief as it was, making sure I was rescued from the system and given a proper home. The Remingtons were, without a doubt, intended by God to be my family. I couldn't feel more at peace with who I am."

"Now, Miss Remington, tell the judge how you feel about being racially mixed."

Thoughtfully, Remmie began to speak, "I was surprised, obviously, but that's about it. I have no strong bias toward any other race, color, or creed. I find all people to be basically good.Even those who are the worse among us have some good in them. Furthermore, I don't believe race is what makes a person good or bad. I am who I am. To be frank, I'm proud of who I am. My biological parents were human beings capable of making huge mistakes, but capable also of loving deeply. I'm a product of those two people, as well as the gentle, kind, and forgiving woman who raised me as her very own, even though she knew the truth. I'm extremely blessed to have had so many to love me so much. My race is now public record. If it harms me, so be it. I have nothing to hide, nothing to fear. I hope I have disarmed those who would use the past against me."

"Can you help the judge understand why you have such a strong desire to adopt children?" asked Colin.

"Being a product of the state's childcare system gives me an insider's viewpoint. I know what the older children are going through. I know how it feels to be told you are not adoptable. The realization of growing to adulthood in the system is devastating, because you know at age eighteen you are released into the world. You probably won't be able to go to college.

You never really belong. You never feel secure. There was always that nagging feeling that at any moment you could be moved again. It's like living out of a suitcase your whole life.

"I want to save children from that kind of life, from those kinds of fears. I have more to offer than financial benefits. I have love to give, time to share, and understanding to offer. I can remove the stigma of being unwanted from children who deserve the chance to develop in a loving environment. Permanence is essential to these children, because they've never had it. They feel portable. They have been moved from one home to another for years. I can give them a permanent home. I can give them their own room, their own clothes, their own toys, an education, but most importantly, I can give them their own identity.

"They will be accepted and loved regardless of behaviors, failures, inadequacies, or appearances. They will live as a family, cooperating, sharing, working, and playing together. They will worship as a family and be taught strong, moral values, good citizenship, proper work habits, and kindness to others. I've had everything, and I've had nothing. I know the benefits of being financially secure. I can provide financial security for the children I want to adopt. I can educate them, but more than that, I can help them start their own lives. But far, far more importantly, I can love them, because they are here, because they deserve love. To have nothing is to be without someone who loves you...my children will never have that problem."

"Tell us, Miss Remington, where do you plan to live with the children you adopt? And, how you intend to support them?"

"I own more than ten thousand acres of farm land on the Chattahoochee River. The land is farm land, open pastures, and woodlands. There is a ten thousand square foot home on the land that I will remodel to accommodate the children. There is also a stable with horses, animals of all kinds, and plenty of farm chores to do. I have a full-time housekeeper-companion and a farm manager who cultivates approximately eight thousand acres of land. Last year we made two hundred thousand dollars from peanuts, cotton, and soybeans. I plan to employ additional household staff to meet the needs of the family. My personal holdings exceed thirty million dollars.

"At some point, I will return to the practice of trauma medicine, but on a limited basis. The farm will be a source of funding for the family, but my holdings will be the long term security of my family. I hope to generate enough money each year on the farm to support the children plus the staff comfortably. Then I will educate the children with trust funds from my own monies."

"I have no more questions at this time. Your witness."

"Miss Remington, being the mature, educated woman you are, please explain to the court how you plan to fill the role of mother and father to the children. Would I be correct in assuming that you aren't interested in men, since you are so self-sufficient?"

"You, sir, may assume whatever you like. I have no control over your assumptions. You would however, be wrong. I don't plan to be "father" to my children. I plan to be a strong, devoted parent who firmly disciplines as well as generously rewards. I had a strong father; I still miss him every day. My mother died when I was sixteen, so my father finished raising me alone. He never once tried to be my mother. He was my father...my only parent. That's how I'll approach being a single parent."

"Don't you think boys need a father?"

"Yes, I do, and so do girls, but these children have neither. I believe they will be much better off with one parent than no parents."

"Do you intend to adopt racially mixed children?" questioned the opposing attorney.

"I don't plan to allow race to be an issue at all. I want to adopt several children, regardless of race."

"I see. Well, how do you plan to keep race from being an issue? Will the children also be blind?"

"I will not allow a handicap to keep me from adopting a child," stated Remmie, ignoring the attorney's facetious remark. "So, yes, they may be blind, deaf, immobile, or mentally challenged. They won't however, be tainted by the prejudice that scars history. Children are children! They need and respond to love, regardless of color or race. Love, sir, will bind us all together into a family."

"Miss Remington, you don't expect this court to believe that you can adopt a hodge-podge of racially mixed or handicapped children, and then somehow create a proper environment in which they can develop. You know the chances of that being successful are slim to none."

"I know that children in the system are children without homes or families. They are not adoptable after about age ten. They remain in the system until age eighteen. The statistics will show that more than fifty percent of these individuals never achieve a normal family existence. The rate of suicides is higher in this group, as well as alcoholism and drug abuse. Emotional and mental disorders seem to occur more often. All this tells me that someone needs to help these children before age eighteen. I want to help them.

"I will not allow the narrow-minded views of a few bigots to influence my decision. I believe I am living proof that almost every obstacle can be overcome with love, kindness, and strong guidance. I will not be swayed. My mind is set. I hope this court will agree with me. Furthermore, sir, I wonder who sets the standards of normal families in this state anyway. Surely not the system that allows children to be ware-housed like non-perishable cargo while they are indiscriminately moved about with no regard whatsoever for their well-being or feelings. I wish someone could define what a normal family is for me in light of what we see happening every day in this state, and in this nation.

"The system tolerated my abuse. I ask this court, is that normal? Was I the only one? No, I was not! The children my heart bleeds for are the children no one else wants. If that's not normal by some pre-determined formula known only to the state, then so be it. The outcome, I assure you, will be better for the children as well as the state. The children I adopt will never be a drain to taxpayers again. They will be financially supported for the rest of their lives. They will have a place to call home. They will have people who will love them. Isn't that more than they have now? My petition to this court is based on one thing---love. I love the children. I can feel them with me even now, and my sincere hope is that this court will grant my petition, and perhaps someday fully embrace my family, be it 'normal' or not. It will be functional, and it will be full of love."

In a gesture of frustration, the attorney for the state threw up his hands to indicate he was finished with the witness. Colin said he had no further witnesses.

The state began its feeble attempt to prove Remmie unable or incapable or whatever it was they were trying to prove. One after another "experts" testified about children's needs, the problems of single parent families, and on and on. The racial issue was discussed with the state presenting Remmie as a rich do-gooder, only trying to make a name for herself by taking in un-adoptable children. The claims became more outrageous as they proceeded. Colin objected often, and the judge ruled in his favor often. Still, the state continued with its attack on Remmie by questioning her real motives. They went as far as to insinuate that her real desire was to use the children as a promotional tool, drawing attention to herself and her so called 'model home' for the un-adoptable.

It was ridiculous. Jesse and Sarah sat there with looks of total disbelief on their faces. Colin was furious! Remmie was quiet, but focused on the judge. She set her eyes on him and never looked away. He was about to decide the future of River Oaks and the family she wanted to raise. He would have the final word. Whatever his decision turned out to be, Remmie would be looking straight in his eyes when he delivered it.

Long, amber shadows filled the courtroom as the sun began its downward journey. Still, the attorney paraded back and forth, flinging his arms, pointing at Remmie, at the audience, at the judge.

Shut-up, you babbling idiot, Sarah thought. *Ya are without a doubt the most word-filled wind bag I've ever seen, and ya ain't said a thang worth hearin'. Too much gush, and not enough substance.*

Finally, it was over. The attorney rested the state's case. It was totally dark outside. The judge looked exhausted. After a moment of silence that everyone in the courtroom desperately needed, the judge explained that he intended to review the case overnight. Court would reconvene at nine o'clock sharp.

Soon the room was empty except for Colin, Remmie, Jesse, and Sarah. Colin reassured Remmie that things had gone well. He was confident the judge would not be influenced by the personal attacks made by the state's attorney.

Sarah invited Colin to stay at River Oaks instead of the local motel, which was a little mom and pop operation down by the highway. He was reluctant until Remmie insisted on him staying. Jesse was also staying over, so the four left together, splitting up outside. Sarah, Remmie, and Jesse rode together, leaving Colin to follow them the six miles to River Oaks.

CHAPTER TWENTY-FOUR

Sarah made a beeline for the kitchen and began fixing supper. The girls went to their rooms for a little quiet time. Colin went to the study. They all appeared again when Sarah called out that supper was ready. Remmie only picked at her food. Her mind was filled with the events of the day, and the possibility that the judge might decide against her.

Leaving her chair while the others were clearing the table, she walked outside. The night was cool, with a stiff breeze rustling the few leaves remaining on the oak trees. Winter's hold on River Oaks was almost over. Soon everything would be green and fragrant again. But tonight the fence was bare, no honeysuckle to hide it.

The breeze cut a little more than it would in a few weeks. The meadow was quieter than it would be in the spring. The owl near the barn stayed all year, so he made his lonesome questions echo through the meadows...who-o-o.

Who, indeed, thought Remmie, *Who will help the children if I fail them?* Turning her face upward, Remmie looked into the black sky filled with sparkling stars. "My Father in heaven, I reverence Your name. You are the creator of all I see. I give praise to You alone. So much rests on the decision I will hear at nine in the morning. I felt You leading me today as I have throughout the years. But now, I have fear in my heart, fear that I will fail the children, fear that the judge will decide against me, and fear that I will not be strong enough to handle that decision. I know you are not giving me this fear. I am bringing it upon myself. The battle that rages within me tonight has been building up for a long time. Let me be victorious over my fears. Replace the fear with peace. Strengthen me for what lies ahead tomorrow, and beyond tomorrow. You have shown me a path to walk. You have burned a desire within my heart. I ask You to finish in me the work You have begun."

At that moment, a hand was placed on her shoulders, and the calming reassuring voice Remmie heard was Colin. "You have such strong faith, Remmie. You will not fail the children. The decision will be in your favor. I, too, believe God has called you to this purpose. He will make a way."

"Thank you, Colin for your reassurance. You have done a magnificent job with the case. I wouldn't be this far without you and Jesse." Turning to face him, Remmie gently touched his cheek. "Colin, I realize this hasn't been an easy relationship for you to maintain. I am sorry that I let you down, but there's so much more about me I've never shared with you. I found myself struggling with the idea that our relationship might become more serious. I'm not ready. It's me, not you. I hope we can always be friends."

Taking hold of Remmie's hand, Colin kissed it tenderly as he stared deep into her green eyes. "I honored your wishes because I care for you so deeply. That has not changed. I know there's much more to your abuse than you have verbalized. You will put it all behind you one day, and I'll be waiting. The decision is yours, my dear Remmie."

"No, Colin. I won't leave it that way. You must not be waiting for something that isn't going to happen. I care for you far too much to allow you to be deluded. My life will be dedicated to the children for many years to come. That's the way I want it. Please understand it's what I must do... it's my purpose. No waiting now; you get on with your life." Embracing each other tightly, the two stood for a long time, and without speaking further, they returned to the house.

The first light of morning revealed Sarah kneeling by her bed, asking God to intervene in Remmie's behalf. Down the hall, Remmie was praying as she stood by the window watching the sun make its first appearance of the day. So much rests on the events of this day. River Oaks could become a happy home again or it could be silent forever, filled only with what might have been. *Well,* thought Remmie, *the day has arrived, and we can't send it back, so let's get on with it.*

The drive into the little town seemed to take forever. Sarah and Jesse made small talk while Remmie stared out the window, focusing her mind on every scene flashing by. Small country houses with clothes lines full of overalls or blue jeans lined the back road Jesse had taken into town. She saw chickens in the yards, tractors in the sheds, smoke coming from the chimneys, and families out doing morning chores. Children were waiting for the school bus as mothers waved good-bye. She wanted to be an ordinary parent, watching her children leaving for school or playing in the yard or doing chores. The difference was her children would be chosen, rather than biologically conceived.

As each little settlement passed by the window, Remmie saw herself on the porch waving good-bye or hanging clothes on the line or raking the yard. Oh, the ordinary things that become the sublime so easily when viewed through the eyes of one longing to be ordinary.

Suddenly, the scene changed from rural countryside to a town. The houses were closer and the streets busier. The courthouse was only a few blocks away now. Soon the answer would be known.

The walk to the entrance of the courthouse seemed much longer today. The wooden floor creaked louder today. The musty smell of old books mixed with sweeping compound was more noticeable today. With the courtroom just ahead, Remmie, Jesse, and Sarah stopped as they took hold of each other's hand. "This is it. However it goes, I want you both to know how thankful I am for your encouragement, devotion, and support."

Jesse and Sarah hugged her tightly. Remmie faced the courtroom entrance, walked head up, shoulders back, and heart pounding into the courtroom, taking her seat next to Colin. Immediately the judge was announced and he took his place on the bench. Silence filled the room. Every eye was on the judge.

Finally, the silence was broken as the judge began to speak. "After careful review of my notes, I found my decision rather easily. The issue upon which I must maintain a clear focus is the welfare of the children who are wards of this state. I will not allow anything to deter me from fully protecting those who cannot protect themselves. Miss Remington, you obviously have a negative opinion of this state's efforts and abilities to protect our children. I do not intend to fail them as miserably as you seem to feel they have been failed in the past."

That statement struck fear deep in the hearts of Remmie and Jesse. Was he saying Remmie's opinions were unfounded? Exactly what did he mean? Exchanging glances was all they could do.

"As for you, Mr. State's Attorney, you may have missed your calling. Your flair for drama is profound, but it doesn't change the facts in this particular case, nor did it make me forget them. Although, I do admit to being somewhat entertained by your flamboyant performance, I never lost sight of the overwhelming fact that you seem to have absolutely no sincere concern for the children who are cared for by this state every day. You were so intent on painting a verbally destructive portrait of the lovely Miss Remington here, that you carelessly overlooked the children you were hired by the state to defend."

Sarah all but giggled when she heard that. She wanted to shout, realizing the judge had not been swayed by the outrageous antics of the attorney for the state. Jesse breathed a little deeper, and Remmie looked relieved. Colin reassuringly patted her hand. The state's attorney dropped his head in frustration as the judge continued.

"Mr. Forrester, your presentation was professional and appropriate. Miss Remington, you were an excellent witness for yourself. It is quite obvious to me that you are a sincere and determined young woman. Many in your position would not have proceeded, knowing family secrets would be revealed that might be considered controversial. In light of the size of your fortune, you could obviously pursue many endeavors other than raising children with their own unique set of problems. I trust you do fully realize that loving someone will not prevent or erase problems, attitudes, or behaviors. You will face many challenging events in the years ahead, should you adopt the children you now have plans to adopt. They have strong recollections of painful or even disturbing memories that most certainly will not disappear merely because you love them.

"I must be extremely honest with you, Miss Remington. I have concerns regarding the bringing together of males and females who are not related in the same house, merging them into a setting normally reserved for individuals who are blood relatives. I can see troublesome possibilities that you may not be equipped to handle. Add to that the possibility of racial integration, which poses other problems in the home, as well as out of the home. This is the Deep South, Miss Remington, and struggle as we do to overcome an ugly history I feel the children would be ostracized, as would your whole family unit if you adopt children of all races. Since you and those already living in your home are White, at least in appearance, I feel strongly that I should urge you to reconsider any plans you may have of adopting racially diverse children.

"As for the fact that you are an unmarried woman, I must say it is not the ideal family situation. I agree with you, however, that one parent who loves and nurtures is better than none. You are, in my opinion, a capable and courageous woman who has faced her own demons head on, and won. You have a lot to offer children.

"It is therefore my decision to allow you, Rebecca Remington, to adopt children from the state of Caucasian background, and raise them in your home for the duration of their lives. I will not, however, sanction racial mixing in your home. This court considers all adoptions final after one year. There will be no unnecessary scrutiny of your home and children.

Like all families, problems will arise. You, as a parent, will be expected to handle each crisis with wisdom. All resources available to the family in this state will be available to you. Miss Remington, you have my respect and admiration. I have rarely met a woman or man with your strength of character. God bless you is my prayer. This court is adjourned."

For an instant, Remmie was frozen. Her mind locked on the words of the judge. Suddenly, she realized Sarah and Jesse had grabbed her crying. "It's over, finally over. You've won. Thank God! You've won, Remmie."

Their jubilation came to an abrupt halt when the state's attorney came over and made it very plain that he didn't consider this a closed case at all. He stated that Remmie would be hearing from him in the very near future. He went on to say that he considered this an outrage, as well as a destructive ruling on the part of a senile judge who had no business remaining on the bench. Remmie was horrified. After all this, it wasn't over. How much longer could she go on like this? All these hours spent in this courtroom for nothing. Where would she find the inner strength to go on? Colin came quickly to the rescue, sending the arrogant attorney on his way pronto!! But it was too late – the damage was done. The moment was ruined. Colin quickly escorted them to the cars and ordered them back to River Oaks.

Dinner was a solemn affair. Very few words were spoken. Sarah tried to be her usual aggravating self, but it was no use. Finally, everyone retired for the evening.

Remmie couldn't close her eyes. The ceiling of her room seemed to close in on her. After hours of tossing around, the tears came. Alone in the darkness of her bedroom, she allowed all the hurt and disappointment she felt to overflow. After what seemed to Remmie an eternity, she got up, put on a robe, and walked to her car.

Driving through the gates, she remembered so many times when she had left River Oaks feeling so blessed to have such a wonderful place to call home. As she drove out into the darkness, Remmie recalled many happy days with her parents. Then she recalled so many terrible days with strangers in foster care. She felt very alone. How could this happen? She knew she had heard from the Lord. She knew He was the One who had impressed her to go in this direction. Why?? Why, God was this happening? Questions, fears, and doubts filled her mind as she drove farther into the blackness of the river's night.

Remmie drove to the cemetery where her parents were buried. As she walked toward their crypt, she felt like an orphan again. She knew if she called out, no one would come to help her. Old feelings flooded her, feelings she thought were long ago dead and buried. No, they were very much alive. When she reached the crypt, she touched each letter of her parents' names. Emotions overwhelmed her.

Alone with the fear and doubt, Remmie reached out to God, crying out loud to Him all her feelings, all the whys, and all the hurts. When all was said, she sat down beside the crypt to wait for her answer. Sitting with her silent pain, she watched as the sun came up behind the trees and the thick mist began to shrink back toward the river.

As morning arrived, she stood by the graves of her parents in silence, hoping to suddenly know all the answers she desperately sought. Hearing nothing but her own mental questioning, she walked back to her car. Turning around once more to look, she saw a radiant beam of sunlight pierce the mist that surrounded the cemetery and illuminatedg the word "Peace" on her mother's marker. "The Lord will keep thee in perfect peace whose mind is stayed on Thee." This verse was engraved on the marker, but only the word "Peace" was illuminated. *How strange*, she thought, as she watched to see if any other word would became involved in the beam of light. Only the word "Peace" – nothing else. *Peace*, she thought to herself, *peace.*

How do I have peace when all my dreams are being threatened by a carelessly run system that doesn't protect the children? At that instant, without any hesitation, the beam of light illuminated ...whose mind is stayed on Thee. *Well, I guess that answers my foolish question*, she thought. *I should keep my mind on God and off the petty little circumstances that are trying to rob me of my peace and my purpose. I will take your advice, Lord. Thanks for arriving at just the right moment today and for having the right answer. I'm sure You'll be hearing from me again, since I always seem to get so full of self-pity.*

As she drove back to the house, she wondered how crazy everyone would think she was if she told them about the amazing beam of light that had just turned her grief into confidence, confidence that God was still in control of this whole world, and yes, of her situation, too. "Well, I guess I'll just let them wonder what has changed my mood." Remmie said out loud.

"Where have you been, missy? You've had me scared nearly *bout* out of my mind. I was *bout* finished *plannin' ya* funeral and *everthang.* Remmie, don't *ya* ever go *traipsin'* off in the middle of the night again."

"I'm sorry, Sarah, I was upset. I couldn't think about anybody but myself. I won't do it again. Do you forgive me?"

"*Ya* know *good'n* well that I forgive *ya* for *anythang*, young lady. I just don't want to be scared into an early grave. Get on in the kitchen and have some breakfast. *Ya* look like *somethin'* the cat drug in."

"Colin left early this morning, but he said not to worry so much. He thinks *everthang* will be all right. He feels confident that the judge made a valid ruling that will stand up to the higher courts."

"But can I still get my children? And if I go ahead with adopting, will they take them away from me when some judge overturns this ruling? Don't you see, Sarah, I can't take that chance. I can't adopt a child and live with the fear of losing the child back to the system. I will simply have to wait until the last gavel falls on this issue. I am not going to wake up one morning to find someone here to take my children away from me. That isn't something I could live with. I will have children someday soon, but I will have to learn patience while I wait for final ruling."

At that moment, Jesse came into the room. "Where have you been all night? I've been up for hours. I couldn't find you anywhere. I didn't know what to think."

"I just needed some time alone to have a pity party. I think I've got it all out of my system now. Wasn't a pretty sight. Be glad I spared you."

"I don't know how you do it. You seem to find a way to come through every trial stronger, and more at peace with yourself than you were before."

"I'm sorry Jess. Give me a hug, and let's eat breakfast." With arms entwined, they walked into the kitchen where together with Sarah they enjoyed breakfast.

"Well, what now, Remmie? Are you going to proceed with your adoption plans?"

"No, Jess, I can't continue with the state planning to fight me in a higher court. The last thing I want to have happen is for children I've adopted to be removed from my care and put back in the system. That would cause the children too much pain. It would break my heart. I've waited this long. I'll just have to wait a little longer.

"I'm going back to work. Dr. McKinley wants me to take over the first shift. He's not going to work in the unit at all. He's just going to work as an administrator and train the trauma physicians during their residency. It's a tremendous opportunity, an increase in salary, a new challenge, and a rewarding way to fill my life. So, I'm going to do it. I'll be home every Thursday night and Sarah can stay in the city with me some if she wants to.

I'll be here on weekends. Stuart will continue farming the land and looking after the place. The only change will be our plans to have children here by Easter, but Easter comes once a year, so who knows, maybe next year."

"Wow, you have done a lot of thinking, haven't you? One thing for sure, you should be at work. You're too good of a doctor not to practice. I'll enjoy having you back in the city, even though it's been great spending so much time at River Oaks. Sarah won't go with you. She has her garden and animals now. She'll stay here to look after things and to take care of Stuart."

"I'm sure you're right, but I'll make the offer anyway. She's not getting any younger, Jesse. I hope things work out while she's able to enjoy the children. She has so many plans."

"Who's *ain't gettin'* younger?" asked Sarah, entering the kitchen suddenly. "*Ya ain't talkin' bout* me, are *ya*, missy?"

"No…no…of course not. You're a mere youngster. Your hearing is certainly holding on just fine."

"Okay, missy smarty, *ya* best not try my patience any more today. That stunt *ya* pulled last night is enough for a while. What's *ya* next plan of action, Remmie? I suppose you'll be moving back to the city to start working again."

"You know me very well, Sarah. That's exactly my plan. I hoped perhaps you'd..."

"Don't even finish that statement, missy. I'm just plum satisfied right here. No need to go *runnin'* off to the city, *fillin'* my lungs with bad air, my stomach with bad food, my mind with bad news, and *ruinin'* my nerves in that forsaken rat race. No ma'am! I'm staying here with the river, the animals, the clean air, and the tranquility. Stuart's here. I'll be fine. *Ya* just go on, and be a doctor like *ya wus* intended. Stop *tryin'* to get me into the city. I *ain't comin*!"

"Yes-um. I get the message. You are special, Sarah. No frills, no thrills, just plain Sarah."

"Don't be sassy, missy. I may be plain, but I'm a sensible person. I'm staying where I'm needed, where I'm happy. You don't need me, but these animals do. I've got a calf *comin'* in a few weeks and goats due anytime. They need me."

"I can't argue with that logic. If I have to be pregnant before you'll come with me, you probably won't be coming for sure."

"Now, you listen here, Remmie. I'd come in a second if you really needed me, but truth is, I've taught *ya* too well. You're as independent as I am. *Ya* don't need me."

Walking to Sarah, Remmie embraced her aging companion, kissing her gently on the cheek. "You are so special, Sarah, and you are right to a point. I don't need you to take care of me here or in the city. I do need you, however. Without you I'd be terribly lonely. You are my family...I need you."

Sarah, returning the embrace and the kiss, agreed with that definition of *need*. They needed each other, they loved each other.

CHAPTER TWENTY-FIVE

The trauma unit was hectic when Remmie arrived at seven o'clock. The doctor in charge was Tim Archer. He was a veteran trauma surgeon who had come to the Medical Center shortly before Remmie took the leave of absence. Everything was chaotic, but what else was new? This was life in a trauma unit - nurses rushing about, doctors shouting instructions, technicians hurrying about with x-ray machines, and people...waiting for news.

"Good morning everyone," shouted Remmie. "Where do I need to be first?"

"Here."

"No...here."

"Over here," came three replies simultaneously.

"Okay, that shouldn't be too difficult to be in only three places at once," replied Dr. Remington. At that moment, Dr. Archer called "Code 3", sending all playfulness away. The team assembled quickly and began CPR on a man who had been brought in after an explosion and industrial fire during the late afternoon hours. He had been trapped for hours by twisted metal beams and was severely burned over most of his body.

Remmie observed as the team worked to bring the man back from the brink of death. Finally, a rhythm appeared on the monitor, then a pulse, and a positive response from the man. After stabilizing him, the team faded away to finish the tasks they were doing before assembling to work on the man. Remmie stayed with him.

"I'm Dr. Remington. You've been in an accident. You've been burned and you've breathed in a lot of toxins. We're trying to clear your lungs. Is there someone we can contact for you? Do you have family?"

That question brought terror to the man's eyes. He immediately became agitated and began fighting the tubes and the equipment near his bed. Remmie leaned over to restrain his arms.

"Sir, please relax. You'll only make matters worse. If there's someone you are concerned about just tell me. I will notify them about your situation."

The man tried to speak, but the tube made it very difficult. Reaching into her pocket, Remmie found a pad and pencil, which she gave the frantic man. He struggled to write something, but his hands were badly burned and he couldn't do it. Carefully, Remmie moved the breathing tube to the side of his throat, freeing his vocal cords as much as possible. Feeling the relief in his throat, the man slowly called out the name Tenille. "She's alone. She's alone. Please help her."

"Is that your wife?" asked Remmie.

The man began shaking his head in frustration.

"Okay, okay, just hold on. I'm trying to get it. Is Tenille a child? Your daughter?"

A look of relief came over the man's face, as he realized he had communicated to someone that his child was alone somewhere.

"Is she at your home?"

Again, the answer was, "Yes."

"There's no one with her that we can notify?"

"No," was the frantic reply.

"How old is she," was Remmie's next question.

The man replied, "Six."

Leaving the distraught father, Remmie ran to the desk, searching for the accident report that should have arrived with him. Locating the report, she scanned for the man's name, address, and contact person. There it was: 702 Stargel Place, and a phone number. Dialing the number, Remmie waited for an answer. After several rings, the machine picked up. "Hello, Tenille, are you there? Please pick up. Your father asked me to call. I'm Dr. Remington, and your father, Jeremy Ryans, has been in an accident. He wants you to talk to me."

"Hello," came the timid little voice. "I'm afraid. It got dark and daddy didn't come home. He always comes home before dark. Tell him to come home now!"

"Okay, Tenille, I'll tell him, but I was hoping you might want to come here to see your daddy. If I come after you, will you come with me? I'll bring your daddy's work badge with me. I'll be driving a red car. I'm kind of tall with red hair, and I have on green clothes. Will you open the door when you see me? Remember now, I must have your daddy's badge or don't open the door."

"Okay, but hurry. I'm very scared. I want to see my daddy."

"I'm coming right now. It'll take me about fifteen minutes to get there. I'll call you from my car so we can talk the whole time. Maybe then you won't feel so afraid."

Remmie flew out of the parking deck while hurriedly dialing the number. Tenille answered, sounding more comfortable than before. "Is my daddy sick," she asked.

"He's been burned on his hands and arms. That's why he can't call you himself."

"I'll take care of him like I always do and he'll get better really fast. Last winter he got the flu and I took care of him then."

Remmie's heart ached for the little girl on the phone. She resisted the hot tears that were fighting to spill out of her eyes. "I'll bet you are a great nurse. Your dad is very lucky to have you. I'm getting closer to you. I'm turning on your street. Is your porch light on?"

"It's day time, but I'll turn it on, then you can see the wreath I made for our front door. It has yellow sunflowers on it. Daddy says it's the prettiest one on the whole street."

Remmie saw the light come on. She turned into the drive. There on a green door hung a pretty wreath with three yellow sunflowers. "Okay, Tenille. I'm outside. You can open the door now."

"You said I had to see my daddy's badge first. Come near the door so I can see it better."

Remmie got out of the car and walked to the door. There were glass panels on either side of the door. From inside she could see a tiny face peering out, waiting to see proof of her identity before opening the door. Squatting down, Remmie placed the badge near the glass so the little girl could see. The tiny face disappeared, then door opened and there stood a lovely, little girl with long black hair, big brown eyes, and an angelic face as beautiful as any Remmie had ever seen.

"Hi, Tenille, I'm Dr. Remington."

"Hello. Will you take me to see my daddy now?"

"Yes, but first you need a jacket, something to sleep in, and a change of clothes. We probably need to secure the house, too."

"Oh, I can set the alarm when we leave. I'll get my overnight bag. I know what to get. You wait here. I'll be right back."

Scurrying away down the hall, Tenille disappeared into a room. Remmie could hear her gathering things. Walking toward the patio doors, Remmie checked to be sure they were locked. Then she picked up the remote to turn off the television. Leaving the den area, Remmie walked into the hall leading out to the garage. The door was locked, so she looked into a very clean kitchen, making sure everything was off.

"I'm ready. Let's go see my daddy."

Remmie turned around and there stood the beautiful little girl with bag in hand, looking like she was off to grandma's house. Little did she know the trip she was about to take would bring major changes in her life.

After safely buckling Tenille in, Remmie drove toward the Medical Center to reunite a father with his child. As she pulled into her parking place, Remmie called the unit to get an update on Mr. Ryans' condition. She also alerted the staff that his child was coming in to see him. She didn't want anything said that might be disturbing to Tenille. The nurse told Remmie that Mr. Ryans was in a great deal of pain, but refused more medication until he saw his daughter.

As the two walked down the hall, Remmie tried to prepare Tenille for what she was about to see. She didn't want to frighten her, but she did want her to realize that her father would look different, and she wanted to reassure her that he was getting the best treatment available. What she wanted to say was that he would be okay in a few days, but she didn't want to make any promises, realizing she might not be able to make good on them.

Just outside the door of Jeremy Ryans' room, Remmie knelt down to be at eye level with Tenille, and then she said, "Your father is not feeling well. He's hurting really badly, but he's very anxious to see you. There are a lot of machines around him, some tubes in his throat, and he has a needle in his arm. Are you ready, Tenille?"

Nodding her head that she was, Tenille straightened her back as she entered the room where her severely burned father lay waiting to see her. The moment she saw her father, she broke free from Remmie's grasp and ran over to the bedside. She was too short to see her daddy's face, but she reached up and touched him as she quietly called out, "Daddy, daddy, can you hear me?"

Jeremy Ryans struggled to speak to his daughter, but produced only garbled sounds. Remmie picked up Tenille, holding her close to her father so they could see each other. Then she carefully moved the tube so he could speak more easily.

There was obviously such closeness between them. They both became more relaxed. Mr. Ryans' vital signs began to improve. After several minutes, he became exhausted. Remmie took Tenille to the nurses' station. She instructed the staff to keep her busy for a while so she could find out what Mr. Ryans' wishes were regarding her care. Tenille busied herself with the nurse's stethoscope and tongue depressors to the complete delight of several onlookers. She was definitely an eye catcher with her long, black curls, bisque complexion, and dark brown eyes.

Remmie returned to Mr. Ryans' room, finding him resting a little more peacefully than before.

"You have a lovely daughter. She's entertaining the nurses at the nurses' station right now. I was wondering if there's someone I can call to take care of her for you. I'm sure you don't usually leave her alone when you're at work."

"No," was his raspy reply. "There's no one but Tenille and me. Her mother died several years ago and I have no family. She's in school when I'm at work. A neighbor brings her home and watches her until I get there. Yesterday, the neighbor told me she would need to leave before I would get home. So, I told her to make sure that Tenille was locked in safely. I thought I'd be there within a few minutes, but I didn't make it. What will happen to her while I'm in here?"

"Children's Protective Services will be called and they will place her with a foster family until you are well again."

Immediately, Mr. Ryans became visibly upset. He kept shaking his head and saying, *"No!"*

"Calm down, now, or I'll be forced to further sedate you. You're hurting yourself by reacting so violently. Try to tell me what I can do to help you."

Settling down somewhat, the severely injured man struggled to tell his story of foster care abuse. He grew up an orphan, and he just couldn't handle knowing his little girl was facing that prospect. Remmie's mind was filled with memories from the past, memories of days spent with strangers when she was only six. Her heart ached at the thought of making the call and seeing Tenille taken away for what might well be the rest of her life. She knew all too well that Mr. Ryans might not pull through. How could she cope with seeing this child put into a system she loathed! Suddenly, a thought entered her mind and without hesitation she asked, "Do you attend church? Perhaps your pastor can be of some help?"

"Yes," he answered. He struggled to give the name and number. As soon as Remmie had it, away she went to call for what she hoped would be a rescue for a child in a bad situation. The pastor said he would come immediately. Remmie waited with Tenille at her father's bedside. His condition worsened by the hour. He was losing ground. Apparently his lungs were badly burned, which caused them to fill with fluid. He looked very bloated, but he was hanging on by sheer determination. He must make suitable arrangements for his daughter.

In forty-five minutes from the call, the pastor arrived. Remmie felt his concern was genuine, since he was so prompt and seemed so compassionate. She had hoped he would bring his wife, but he didn't.

The pastor spent the first part of his visit with Jeremy Ryans. The two men prayed together before the pastor asked Remmie to step into the hall with him. Once outside the room, he wanted the specifics. He knew they needed a miracle in order for his friend to survive. Remmie confirmed that Mr. Ryans was in a life-threatening situation. She explained the next twenty-four to forty-eight hours would be crucial, and she told the pastor that he was worsening. If they could successfully battle infections and his lungs could start healing, he might actually have a fighting chance.

"Do you believe in prayer, doctor?"

"Yes, pastor, I certainly do. I've been relying on my faith and prayer most of my life."

"That's all I can do for Jeremy, and I'll do it without ceasing. But I can't help him with his little girl."

"Why! He is going to take it really hard if Tenille goes to foster care. I was in hopes you and your wife could..."

"I'm not married. I have no wife, and I can't see myself taking care of a six year old child. I don't know a thing about children anyway. I hate to let him down, but I wouldn't be a good sitter for his little girl. Perhaps you could take her," said the preacher with a huge question mark in his voice.

The statement echoed in Remmie's head again and again, *Perhaps you can take her, perhaps you can...* Her head was saying, *No!* Her heart was saying, *Yes!* Which was the right answer?

The young minister saw the perplexity in her eyes. Taking her by the arm, he led her into the lounge across the hall. "Doctor Remington, I feel strongly that this situation did not simply happen on your shift. It happened at this time because you are able to help this man with his child."

"I beg your pardon. You don't know me. Why would say that to me?"

That's very true, but I believe I heard the Lord's voice while I was talking to Jeremy. I believe the Lord told me that you are an advocate for children, that you have a heart for children in need."

Lord, are You telling this man what he says You are? I'm the one to take this child? Tell me, Father. Tell me. Remmie whispered frantically. "Pastor, this has caught me completely off guard. I don't know what to do."

"I believe you sincerely want to do it, but you are struggling with fear. Let go of the fear, and let God do whatever it is He wants to do in your life. I would even venture to say this is an old war that goes on and on. You can end it right now."

Fear was an understatement; she was petrified. The minister was right; it was an old war, and she was battle weary. She had waged a valiant war against a poorly run system, and even in victory she had been defeated. Fear was the destroyer. Fear had paralyzed her. Fear of loving and losing nameless, faceless children, children she had not seen, children she did not know. Fear was the victor!

Now, when she least expected it, God was dealing with her fear. He had revealed it so clearly through a perfect stranger. It wasn't the system, the lawyer, or the judge. No, it was her fear of being hurt. *How selfish I am,* she thought, *thinking only of myself when I could be helping this child.*

"You are so right, pastor. I have longed to help children all of my adult life. I grew up in foster care, so I know all the bad things, and to be honest, they haunt me. I've seen myself as their rescuer, but obstacles have arisen, producing fear of failure in me. Now, without warning, I am face to face with a beautiful little girl who needs me desperately, and I am so afraid to make this commitment."

"Dr. Remington, the Lord is making the choice for you. Obey Him. He will handle the fear. You are this child's rescuer, at least temporarily. Her father may recover. We can't know that, only God does. All I can say to you is what I feel impressed in my spirit to say, obey the Lord and He'll take care of the rest."

At that moment, Remmie became very calm. She was at peace. The decision was made. She would offer to care for Tenille. "Thank you, Pastor Somersly. You have more wisdom than you realize. I should get back to Tenille."

Remmie returned to Mr. Ryans' room to find Tenille there with a nurse. Tenille spoke softly with her father, reassuring him that she would take care of him. Mr. Ryans gripped his daughter's tiny hand as he nodded his head to let her know that he could hear her. It was a touching scene, almost more than Remmie could handle. She motioned for the nurse to take Tenille out of the room.

"Mr. Ryans, I know you are very tired, but I must discuss Tenille's care with you. I was hoping your pastor would be able to take her, but that isn't possible. I'll take her home with me, if you will permit it. I will need your signature on some kind of statement, giving me temporary custody of Tenille. That will protect me, as well as allow me to get medical care for her if it is needed. I was recently granted the right to adopt children in this state, even though I am not married. I have a companion who is wonderful with children. She will come into the city and help with Tenille while I work. We will take good care of her. She'll be just fine."

Struggling to speak, Jeremy Ryans said, "Get the statement prepared, I'll sign it. Tenille is very special. She is my life. Please, please don't let her worry about me. If I don't make it, you will have to do what you feel is right for her. I have no where else to turn for help. I'm at your mercy, doctor, in more ways than one."

The statement was drafted within a few minutes and delivered to Remmie. Mr. Ryans signed it. It was done. Remmie was temporary guardian of Tenille Ryans.

Shortly after the statement was signed, Mr. Ryans slipped into a coma. The prognosis was grim. Remmie didn't know what the morning would bring. It was up to the Lord now. Medical science had done all it could.

CHAPTER TWENTY-SIX

The sun was just coming up when Remmie carried a sleepy little girl to the car. Driving through the streets of the city, Remmie thought about the little child lying on the seat beside her. What would be her future? No one knew. Would Mr. Ryans be alive when the sun spread its golden glow over the sprawling city? She didn't have an answer. She only knew she had an awesome responsibility riding in the car beside her, a tender, innocent child who was facing life with the odds working against her.

What can I do for this child? I can house her, feed her, and keep her clean and warm. I can love her and educate her, but I can never replace the love she shares with her father. How will I help her face the loss, should her father die? Dear Lord, I need Your help! Give me courage and wisdom.

Tenille slept very late. Remmie waited by the phone, expecting an update on Mr. Ryans' condition. The phone finally rang at 11:30 a.m. Jeremy Ryans was slipping away. There seemed to be nothing that could be done.

"What will I tell her? How do you explain death to a six year old? I need some help with this. Sarah, it's me. I need you to come into the city. I have a small house guest, and I could really use your help."

"A small guest? What is it, Jesse's cat? You know how I feel about that cat. I don't like him, and he *don't* like me. He'll rip up your *purty* furniture. I can't believe Jesse talked *ya* into *keepin'* that crazy cat."

"It's not a cat. It's…I mean she's six, and her father is critically ill. He may not live through the day. He gave me temporary custody. Sarah, I need you here, now!"

"Well why didn't *ya* say that to start with? I'm *packin'* right this minute. Stuart will drive me in this afternoon. I should be there by four o'clock. I'll stay as long as *ya* need me."

"Thanks, Sarah. I love you. Good-bye."

"Bye, *chil'*."

Just as Remmie placed the phone on the cradle, Tenille appeared, rubbing her eyes in an effort to wake up.

"Good morning, Tenille. How are you today," asked Remmie.

"I'm okay. How's my daddy?"

This was the question she really didn't want to answer. Breathing a silent prayer, Remmie replied, "Your father isn't doing well. He's very sick. The doctors are doing everything they can to make him better. We just have to wait now."

The sleepy-eyed little girl looked deep into Remmie's eyes and saw the truth she was trying to hide from her. "Is my daddy going to die?"

Every fiber of Remmie's body tightened. Her heart pounded. "Come here, Tenille, and sit beside me."

Tenille seemed to glide across the thick, white carpet in her long, flowery pink gown. Once seated beside Remmie, she looked intently at her, awaiting an answer to her question.

Choosing her words carefully, Remmie began to speak. "Tenille, I don't know you well enough to know if you understand what death really is. Death is a part of life. It's something everyone will face. Some people live to be very old, while others live only a short time. God is the only one who knows how long each person has on this earth. If we live our lives for the Lord, He prepares a wonderful place after our life is over. We pass from this life into the next with God as our Guide. We will never be alone. God will be right beside us all the way to our new home with Him in Heaven."

"Is my daddy going to heaven today?"

"That is possible. He isn't getting any better. He may go to heaven soon."

"My daddy isn't afraid to die. He told me he knew he would be alright. He said he was going to try really, really hard to get well, but if God sent angels to get him, it would be okay. I'm not afraid of angels. They are our friends. My daddy told me all about them. He said they are all around us, protecting us. Daddy's angel must have looked away for a minute, and that's when he got hurt. I'll bet she feels really bad about what happened to my daddy."

Tears sprang to the rim of Remmie's eyes, spilling quickly down her cheeks. *Oh, God, please help me. This child is losing her only relative. Her life will never be the same again. Spare her father's life. Heal him now!*

At that instant, the doorbell rang. Remmie left Tenille on the sofa to answer the door. Standing there was John David Somersly, Jeremy's pastor. The look on his face was revealing. "May I come in, Dr. Remington? I've just left Jeremy. The hospital told me how to find you. I thought perhaps I could be of some help."

Remmie motioned for him to come in. She was still struggling to keep her composure. "How is he now? Has there been any change?"

"Only for the worse. They're losing him. He's putting up a valiant fight, but it appears this may be his time to go. Only God knows."

"Tenille is in the living room, asking questions that are difficult to answer. She knows all about angels. She just told me her Daddy's angel must have looked away for a second, that's when her Daddy got hurt. She said she bets his angel feels really bad about that." Again the tears came. Remmie fought to keep control.

The young minister took her by the shoulders and embraced her, whispering in her ear a prayer for strength. He also asked God to heal Jeremy Ryans. Leaving Remmie in the hall, the minister walked toward the living room to find Tenille. When she saw him, she jumped from the sofa and went running into his arms. Just seeing a familiar face meant a lot to her.

"Have you been to see my Daddy?"

"Yes, Tenille, I have. Your daddy's very sick."

"Yes, I know. Dr. Remington told me. He may go to heaven today. You know my daddy would like that. The only thing that will bother him is leaving me. We don't have any other family. Who will take care of me?"

The strong, young minister waged his own war with emotion. In his mind, he reached out to God with this haunting question, the age old question – why? *Dear God, You see the plight of this lovely little girl. No one can replace her father. They have been inseparable. She'll never know a blood relative if Jeremy dies. Please, please, God, spare him for Tenille.*

Taking hold of Tenille's tiny hand, Reverend Somersly spoke by faith and not by what his intellect told him. "Tenille, God will take care of you just as He takes care of me and everyone else. I believe your father will be around to see you grow up. Let's just practice having faith."

The huge brown eyes looked at him inquisitively. "Do you mean pretend? I've been pretending that my daddy was well, and we were back at our house, but then I remember that I'm here, and he's in the hospital."

"Faith isn't pretending. It's trusting and believing for something even when you can't see it or touch it. God gives us hope in times like this. Hope helps us feel encouraged. Let's hope for life for your daddy."

"I can do that." Tenille folded her hands, closed her eyes, turned her face upward, and said, "Lord, I hope You will let my daddy stay here with me. I hope, I hope, I hope!!"

The minister hugged Tenille, offering all the comfort he could. Remmie busied herself in the kitchen, making lunch for Tenille. It was something to do while the time crawled by. Rev. Somersly joined Tenille and Remmie for lunch.

At four o'clock on the dot, Sarah rushed in, with Stuart bringing up the rear. He was carrying enough suitcases to contain everything Sarah owned. Stuart followed Sarah dutifully down the hall to the room she always used. After all the bags were put away, Stuart and Sarah had lunch before Stuart returned to River Oaks. Sarah sat about winning the heart of their small, sad, house guest.

The shadows stretched across the living room as late afternoon came to the city. Sarah and Tenille were reading a book. Remmie and Reverend Somersly sat chatting over a cup of tea. The phone rang, breaking the solitude of the room.

Hesitantly, Remmie answered the phone. It was the hospital. The young minister stood beside Remmie. Sarah took Tenille upon her lap. All were frozen in their tracks as they anticipated the worse. Remmie listened to the voice of her colleague as he gave a new report on Jeremy Ryans' condition. A cautious, but obvious look of relief came across her face. It was not what she had expected to hear at all. Apparently, Jeremy had begun to respond to treatment. He was holding his own for now. This was a very hopeful sign.

Tenille read the look immediately as she responded, "He's better. I know it. Hoping really works. My daddy is going to get well. I'm never going to stop hoping."

Sarah hugged her as she whispered in her ear, "Hope's all we've got these days. God has rewarded *yore* faith, little one, and don't *ya* ever forget it."

Remmie exchanged a few private words with Reverend Somersly before he left for the hospital. Remmie, Sarah and Tenille made plans to go to the Ryans' home to pick up some things Tenille needed. It took about twenty-five minutes to get to their home. Sarah and Tenille chatted excitedly all the way. Remmie drove without saying much. Her mind reflected over the events of the last twenty-four hours. *How quickly lives change*, she thought.

Only hours ago, it appeared that Jeremy Ryans would not survive the injuries he had received. Now, he was gaining ground. And here she was temporary guardian of a child she hardly knew. Yes, indeed, life is totally unpredictable, but that makes it all the more interesting. Not to mention John David Somersly, who she found most attractive. And he had asked her out. *What does the future hold*? She thought.

~~~~~~~~~~~~~~~~~~~~

"Tenille, come eat your breakfast before it gets cold," called Remmie. "Tenille, do you hear me?"

'Yes, I hear you, and I'm coming, but first I must finish the poem I am writing about Auntie Sarah. See how this sounds---

I have a new, old friend who lives by the river.
She stays there even when winter makes her shiver.
She says the river is her oldest friend.
Well, I have a new friend, too,
And it, Auntie Sarah, is you."

Remmie burst out laughing to Tenille's bewilderment. "What is so funny, Remmie?"

"Calling Sarah old isn't the smartest thing you've ever done, young lady. Your poem is fine, but you better think twice before reading it to Auntie Sarah. Come on now and eat so I drive you to school."

Tenille hurriedly ate her breakfast in-between all the things she had to talk about. Her main concern was whether or not she could see her father. Remmie assured her she would see her father after school. Once breakfast was over, Tenille brushed her teeth. Then she began the task of brushing her long, thick hair. Remmie offered her assistance, and together they agreed on the right bow to accent her new pink outfit Remmie had bought. Finally, all the finishing touches were done, and Tenille looked as perfect as a store mannequin.

Tenille talked all the way to her school. Remmie nodded or gave an occasional "uh huh," but mostly she listened. Once Tenille was safely at school, Remmie headed for the hospital.

It had been wonderful having Tenille around. Remmie had taken her shopping, to the movies, and they had attended several school activities together. All the things Remmie had dreamt of doing with her own child,
~~~~~~~~~~~~~~~~~~~~

she had been able to do with Tenille. Each night they said their prayers together before sharing a goodnight hug. Tenille had said that she never went to sleep without a goodnight hug from her dad. Since he had not been around, Remmie had to fill in for him, of course.

Jeremy Ryans' recovery was slow and painful. He had had three surgeries, plus several skin grafts. It would be some time before he would leave the hospital. His hands were so permanently damaged that he would never work at his chosen profession again. He was very fortunate to be alive, and he knew it. Each day was a small victory for him. Tenille's daily visits, personally drawn cards, and words of encouragement were the fuel that caused Jeremy to push through the hours of rehabilitation.

Remmie visited Jeremy every day. They had become quite close. She had learned he was not widowed, as he had originally told her, but in fact, his wife disappeared when Tenille was two. Jeremy lived with the hope that she would return to be the wife and mother he and Tenille desperately needed. He had never divorced her. All his attempts to find her had failed. There had been absolutely no trace of her.

Remmie pondered these things deep in her heart. How could a mother leave a child? Why do women like that seem to be able to give birth every nine months, while others never conceive? Her final conclusion was to do the best for Tenille that she could, but to be prepared to give her up when the time came.

Sarah also had formed a bond with Jeremy and his little girl. She stayed in the city on weekends to help Remmie. They had taken Tenille to River Oaks a couple of times. Sarah had been deeply touched by the black-haired child of a million words and boundless energy. The atmosphere at River Oaks changed when Tenille was there. The house seemed more alive; the gardens seemed cheerier. Sarah dreamed of a day River Oaks would be home to little ones like Tenille. She was enthralled with the dark-haired, energized child running freely through the halls and gardens of a house that had long been too silent and too orderly.

"Auntie Sarah, let's go to the barn so I can see the baby goats. I want to see how big they are now. Can I still hold them?"

"Sure *nuf, chil'*. We'll go as soon as I get this pie in the oven. Here, *hep* me roll out this crust. Nice, even strokes, now. You don't want a thick crust on one side *whiles* the other side is thin."

"Auntie Sarah, why do you live here in this great big house all by yourself? Aren't you scared, being way out here?"

"Why, no, little missy. I love *livin'* here on the river. It's my home. What do *ya* think I should be afraid of?"

"Oh, I guess just being alone when it's dark. I've never liked the dark. My daddy never left me alone in the dark. I sleep with a night light. Do you think that makes me a baby?"

"No, of course not. But I hope you'll get over being afraid. The darkness is a natural *thang*. God created it to allow *everthin'* to rest. The sun visits the other side of our world while we refresh ourselves with sleep. The earth cools down as it prepares to begin another day. It's all a part of God's creative work. There's *nothin'* to be frightened *bout*, little missy," said Sarah as she touched Tenille's beautiful hair. "God don't want *ya* to be afraid of *nothin'* He created."

"Well, I am! I'm scared of lions and bears, too. God should've thought about me before He made big, old, scary looking animals."

Sarah burst out in laughter. "*Ya* are *somethin'*, little missy. God thought about *ya*. He gave *ya* that quick *thinkin'* mind and that beautiful face. One of these days, He'll take *yore* fears away. Let's go see the baby goats while my pie's *bakin'*."

Once inside the barn, Tenille carefully opened the gate to the stall. Nanny and her twins were sleeping in the far corner of the straw-laden stall. Tenille gently picked up the tiny black and white baby goat. Cradling the baby like one of her favorite baby dolls, she sat down in the straw, patting the baby's head. "He's so pretty and so soft. I wish he could come home with me. But he wouldn't like the city. What shall we name him, Auntie Sarah?"

"Oh, let's see now. He's black and white...what can *ya* think of that's black and white?"

Thinking really hard, Tenille said, "Penguins, Dalmatians, and my checker board. I know, let's call him Checkers! That's a good name for him, Auntie Sarah."

"It sure is, little missy! Checkers it is. *Purty* soon he'll be *jumpin'* round all over the place."

"I'll see you tomorrow, Checkers. Maybe we'll think of a good name for your sister. Be good now. Stay close to your mother. She'll keep you safe. Don't be afraid of the dark. Auntie Sarah says God doesn't want us to be afraid of anything He created. Isn't that right, Auntie Sarah?"

"That's right, little missy, and that goes for *ya*, too. Come on, I smell my pie *gettin'* done."

"How can you smell a pie getting done?"

"That's easy, with your nose," said Sarah jokingly.

"I'm serious, Auntie Sarah."

"Well, let's see here. The aroma gets stronger when the crust browns to just the right stage. It takes years of practice in the kitchen to develop *yore* sense of smell."

Tenille took a deep breath and held it in for several seconds. "Um, I think I know what a pie smells like getting done. It smells like you want to eat it all up!"

Chuckling to herself, Sarah squeezed the adorable little girl. "*Ya* are a fast learner, little missy. I think that's a *real* good way to tell when a pie's done. Stuart thinks my pie is done, too. Here he comes to the house."

Tenille ran ahead, jumping into Stuart's waiting arms. "Did Auntie Sarah teach you how to smell if a pie is done?"

"Do you mean how to tell when a pie is done?"

"No, Auntie Sarah said she can smell when a pie is done and I can, too!"

"Is that a fact? In that case, I'd say that pie in the oven is definitely done. What about you, Tenille, do you think it's done?"

"Uh huh, it sure is. I'm ready to eat it right now!"

CHAPTER TWENTY-SEVEN

The hands of the clock mocked Remmie as she watched each second linger far too long. "Come on, come on! Sarah is right, a watched pot never boils. And a watched clock doesn't tick! Oh, Colin, hurry! I've waited so long to know about my brother."

Remmie's mind was racing around all the scattered facts she knew about her twin brother - the old nun's shocking revelation, and the seemingly impossible realization that he, too, was a product of the dysfunctional foster care system. She was frantic for Colin to arrive with more information.

"Will he want to know the truth about himself? Will he know anything about his past? What will his profession be? Is he married? Am I an aunt?" *Stop it, girl! Colin will be here any second now and you'll have all the answers.*

The chime of the doorbell brought Remmie back to reality. She hurried across the room to open the door, expecting to see Colin. It wasn't Colin – it was J.D. Somersly.

"Well, I can tell by that look you weren't expecting me. I'm sorry to disappoint you. Can I come in anyway?"

"I'm sorry, J.D. Yes, please come in. I am expecting someone, though. He should be here momentarily."

"Should I come some other time? I guess I should have called first, but I was hoping to take you to dinner. It was a spur of the moment decision, and a bad one, I suppose."

"No not at all. This is a business associate. He's my attorney, Colin Forrester. It is rather personal information he's bringing me, but if you want to be a part of this, I would like you to be. You should be warned there's plenty about me you don't know yet. I'm not your typical little Sunday School teacher."

"Well, I'm not your typical preacher, either. I guess that puts us in the unordinary category. I am eager to learn all I can about you, Remmie. I want to share everything with you."

Okay, preacher, you are about to hear one of the missing pieces of my life. I have a twin brother that probably has no idea that I exist. I didn't know about him until just before my father died. How's that for soap opera drama?"

"I'd have to say that's a pretty good opening line. You must be so excited, Remmie. You've been waiting all this time to hear about him?"

"Yes, I have. It's thrilling to know that he's really alive somewhere, and hopefully I'll be seeing him soon."

J.D. embraced Remmie. "You are something, lady. You are truly remarkable. I hope this turns out exactly the way you want it to." Standing embracing each other for a long moment, Remmie and J.D. waited for the news to arrive---news that very possibly could change Remmie's life forever.

Finally, the chime rang. This time it was Colin. He greeted Remmie warmly, kissing her cheek while moving steadily toward the living room. "I know how anxious you are, Remmie, but I couldn't get out of my office any sooner." As Colin rounded the corner, entering the living room, his voice trailed off. He and J.D. were standing face to face. It was an awkward moment. Extending his hand, J.D. introduced himself. Colin returned the gesture, but moved on to the dining table where he spread out papers from his brief case. J.D. stood near the window while Remmie walked to the table, anxious to see what he had laid out.

"Colin, I should have introduced you to John David. I momentarily forgot my manners. I have been seeing J.D. for several months. I've asked him to be here."

In his most professional demeanor, Colin nodded as he continued shuffling the papers. He didn't make eye contact with J.D. or respond to Remmie's introduction.

Remmie sat down beside Colin on the huge white sofa. Colin began showing one document after the other. Each paper traced her brother's life in America, from South Florida to Central Florida, to Mobile, and finally to Atlanta.

"He's in Atlanta," screamed Remmie, clutching a document. "My brother is four hours from here. Isn't that incredible?"

"Hold on, there's more," stated Colin. He was obviously excited about Remmie's response, and obviously enjoying Remmie's undivided attention.

J.D. watched intently from his vantage point behind the sofa. He carefully observed Colin. To J.D., Colin's actions revealed more than a professional interest in Remmie.

"What else, Colin, tell me!!"

"This will really amaze you, Remmie. He's a doctor."

"Are you kidding me? My twin brother is a doctor? Can you believe that, J.D.?"

Remmie ran around the sofa into J.D.'s arms. She was much like a teenager receiving the keys to a shiny new car. J.D. shared her excitement. "It's wonderful news, Remmie. I couldn't be happier for you."

Colin was now the outsider. He saw the mutual affection between them. He was taken aback by Remmie's openness with J.D.

"Tell me more! Is he married? Does he have children? Oh, my goodness, I don't even know his name! Colin, what's his name?"

"This is another uncanny one, Remmie. His name is Roberto Elezar Ramirez."

"You are serious, aren't you?"

"Yes, I am. The same initials as yours, well, the same until your adopted name was added."

"I am absolutely amazed! We've never met, but this person and I share a profession, and the same initials. We'll be great friends, I'm sure of it! When can I meet him?"

"Not so fast or so simple. He has no idea about you. He was adopted when very young. He doesn't remember that he's adopted. His parents want it to stay that way. They are opposed to you telling him the truth."

"You have to be kidding? What right do they have to keep this truth from a grown man?"

"Remmie slow down a minute. Try to put yourself in their place. They raised this child to adulthood. They have educated him, and now to have their relationship with him threatened is very hard for them to conceive. They are uneducated, working people. They've poured everything into this son, their only child. Your entrance into his life must be with their consent. You must be their friend first."

"Colin, I've waited my whole life to fill in all the blanks. I will not be stopped now. I'm too close. I'm not into playing games with people who want to control my future with my only living relative."

Realizing a major confrontation was looming, John David stepped in. "Remmie, you are letting your emotions rule right now. Calm down, and take an objective look at this. Colin is probably right about this. You should approach them as a friend. How they feel about you may determine how your brother feels, also. He has no knowledge of the past as you do. Be careful, move cautiously, do this exactly right."

Remmie's posture changed quickly. She walked to the window, gazing out into the darkness of the night as she pondered the logical statements J.D. had made. She turned to face both men, tears filling her green eyes. "I'm so close. It's hard to be patient. I've waited so long. You're both right. I'll do as you say."

Colin breathed a deep sigh of relief. J.D. rewarded Remmie with a hug. Regaining her composure, Remmie wiped away the unwanted tears as she asked Colin when she could see the parents of her brother. He asked for a couple of days. A couple of days seemed like such a long time. Remmie dreaded the thought of more waiting. Knowing she really didn't have a choice, she nodded her consent.

"You will call me as soon as a meeting is set," asked Remmie.

"You know I will. I'm not trying to make this hard for you, Remmie. It's the safest route we can take. We are better safe than sorry, kiddo."

"It's getting late, Colin. You are welcome to the guest room. You can drive back to Atlanta in the morning."

"Thanks, Remmie, but I have an early appointment. I should go tonight."

Remmie walked Colin to the door. When they were alone in the entry hall out of J.D.'s sight, Colin seized the moment. He put his arm around Remmie as if to console, but then without warning he kissed her firmly on the lips. Remmie responded, and they kissed again and again.

Remmie realized what she was doing and tried to pull herself free from Colin's embrace. He did not release her. Forcing her to the wall, Colin continued kissing her. Remmie pushed him, and motioned for him to stop.

"Colin, please, I don't want to do this."

"I don't believe you. I felt you return my kisses. You aren't being true to yourself or to me. I let you go without a fight once, but I won't do it again. I've been in love with you since we first met. I am the right man for you. You know I'm right. Be true to yourself, Remmie. I can make you happy."

"Stop it, Colin. I am being honest. You are mistaken. Now, I'll hear no more of this. Please don't ever take charge of me in that manner again. I will reject your advances."

"Come on, Remmie! You aren't engaged to this man. You can change your mind."

"J.D. has nothing to do with my rejection of your advances. The truth is I had strong feelings for you once. I still find you very attractive, but my feelings have changed. I'm sorry for kissing you like that. I was caught up with emotion. I made a foolish mistake. It is nothing more, Colin. It won't happen again. You are a dependable friend. You are my attorney, but that ends it. I will not admit to feelings I do not have."

Unaffected by the deliberate statements Remmie had just made, Colin opened the door to walk out, but before the door closed, he looked into Remmie's sea foam green eyes and said, "I'll not give up! You are the woman I've been searching for." With that he walked away.

Astounded by what had just occurred, Remmie leaned her head against the door. *How in the world do I get myself into such fixes,* she pondered. *Oh mercy, I hope J.D. didn't hear any of this. What will he think of me?*

Gathering herself, Remmie walked back into the living room to find J.D. on the balcony. He was looking out over the city with a whimsical, faraway look in his eyes. Realizing she was present, J.D. reached out his hand to her. Taking his hand, Remmie walked up beside him.

"What is it out there that has so captured your attention?"

Returning his gaze to the maze of flickering lights, J.D. shrugged his shoulders as if to say he didn't know. "This has been quite an eventful evening for you. I am pleased you allowed me to share it with you. Thanks."

"You are welcome. I guess I thought it about time for my story to be revealed. You are taking this news in stride. I suppose being a Minister you have heard plenty of bizarre stories."

"That is true, but somehow I knew there was a mystery to be unraveled about you. I felt it from the first date we had."

"Is that a fact?"

"It is and what's more, I knew I fit into the mystery somewhere. Strange, isn't it? Just how do you think I fit in, Remmie?" Turning sharply to face J.D., Remmie stared into his eyes, not knowing how to answer his question.

"Don't look so concerned. I really don't expect you to answer that now. I'll let you know when I want an answer." J.D. put his strong, warm arm around her shoulder, pulling her close as he patted her reassuringly. "You'll have plenty of time to answer that one. By the way, you do know your attorney is in love with you?"

Again J.D. startled Remmie. Maybe he had overheard what happened at the door. Remmie paused.

"You aren't that naive, Remmie. Colin is head-over-heels for you. I could see it all over his face every time he looked at you. Was there more than a professional relationship?"

"Wait a minute! I am not in the habit of loving 'em and leaving' em. If you are forming some sleezy opinion of me, you are dead wrong," retorted Remmie.

"Now it's your turn to hold on! I merely asked a question. I'm not forming any opinions until I get the facts, ma'am," replied J.D.

"Okay, okay, I dated Colin briefly almost two years ago. I felt strongly about him then. Things got in the way, my father's death, a new understanding of who I really am, Jesse's accident, and well, we drifted apart. I did nothing to fix it, so Colin gave up after a while. He's a genuinely fine man, and a valued friend, but that's all."

"I believe you, Remmie, but Colin hasn't gotten you out of his system yet. How are you going to deal with that?"

"Why do I have to deal with it at all? It's his problem. He'll have to deal with it."

"You certainly can simplify things. It may not be that easy. Colin may decide to fight for you. What then?"

"Oh, please, J.D. Are you suggesting a dual at sun up? Don't you think we have over- dramatized this a wee bit? I've made my position crystal clear to Colin so, that's that!"

The next two days crawled by. Remmie busied herself with trivial things, allowing as little idle time as she could. Her thoughts made frequent visits to her brother and how he would react to the truth about himself. Each visit was more vivid than the one before, each one more exciting, more joyful, but every once in a while, she would have a negative visit---a visit without a happy ending.

John David called daily to check on her. His calls were a welcomed break from waiting to hear from Colin. They talked about the weather reports, what was happening with her work, or his work. They talked about everything. Remmie had come to depend on J.D. heavily. His strong, confident manner was comforting to her. He knew everything, now there were no secrets between them.

Jesse called, too. She was as anxious as Remmie. Jesse inwardly feared Roberto would reject Remmie. That was something she didn't want to see her best friend go through.

Sarah was calling every hour almost. She could hardly stand the wait. She too, worried that rejection might be a hurdle that even Remmie couldn't get over.

In all the waiting and speculating, Remmie did a lot of self-examination. She knew there was a possibility her brother would not want a relationship with her. She came to terms with that privately. She turned that prospect over to God. That was her way of handling everything about herself. When she felt things were out of control, she made sure she was letting God be in control. Finally, without realizing it, Remmie was going about her daily routine again. She wasn't just waiting anymore. Like so many other times in her life, Remmie found peace in the middle of a tough situation, God's peace.

Unfortunately, Sarah, Jesse, and J.D. didn't find that peace. They were now calling each other with their worries about Remmie. They couldn't help themselves. They all loved her very much.

CHAPTER TWENTY-EIGHT

Colin's call didn't come in two days. In fact, after a week went by, Remmie decided to call him. Considering what had happened between them that evening, she felt Colin might be dragging his feet just a little bit. To her amazement, Colin's office said he had not been in for several days. This made Remmie very anxious again. Where could he be? Colin had never failed to keep his word before. This was certainly out of character for him.

John David came over for dinner that evening. Remmie had Italian food catered. When she told him about Colin, he was surprised, too. But in his own special way, he consoled her.

Jesse and Sarah were as mad as wet hens. They fussed and fumed to each other about Colin. How could he treat Rem this way? They were fit to be tied. But to Remmie, they were cool as cucumbers, never letting on how angry they were.

One afternoon, J.D. received a call at the church from Colin. Colin asked if he could come by to talk with him about Remmie. J.D. agreed to the meeting. Colin was there in less than 15 minutes, looking disheveled and fatigued.

"Please excuse my appearance. I've spent the last five hours on a plane, which is one of my least favorite activities."

"You said you needed to speak to me about Remmie. What is it? You do know she has been waiting to hear from you?"

Colin's demeanor told J.D. something was terribly wrong.

"I've done an awful thing to Remmie. I let my feelings for her overrule my judgment." There was a long, weary pause between the two men.

Finally, J.D. broke the silence. "You don't know where her brother is, do you?" Again, silence. Colin sat with his head down.

J.D.'s patience ran out. "Answer my question! You don't know about her brother, do you?"

Raising his eyes to meet J.D.'s, Colin began to speak. "I do know his name was Roberto Elezar Ramirez. I do know he was a doctor. That much is true. But he died in an airplane crash when he was an intern. He's been dead five years. You are a minister. Can you help me?"

"My reaction to what you've done to the woman I love isn't ministerial. I'm outraged! How could you lead her on? How long have you known?"

Colin rose to his feet, facing the man who loved Remmie. "I've known for almost the entire time we've been searching for him. At first, I couldn't bring myself to tell her. Then I became bitter when our relationship failed, so I didn't tell her. When I found out she was seeing someone, I was overcome with jealousy. So, I decided to renew the search, hoping to put myself back in her life."

"You are an educated man. You had to know your luck would run out. How did you plan to bring this deception to a conclusion?"

"I was going to blame it on my investigators, saying they had misled me to stay on my payroll. Oh, I had it all figured out. It's true what they say about lying. You have to keep telling them. There's no way out."

"Well, you're wrong about that. There's one way out – the truth. You can tell Remmie the truth. That will set you both free. You must set this straight immediately. Remmie has waited long enough to know the truth. Give it to her."

"But what if she can't handle it? I mean she has high hopes of finding a living relative. How will this affect her emotionally?"

"Remmie is the strongest woman I've ever known. She'll handle it. You'll have a more difficult time handling what you've done. I imagine it to be totally out of character for you. Colin, you must seek Remmie's forgiveness, God's forgiveness, and then the hardest thing of all, your own forgiveness. If you want this lie to be over, you must tell Remmie the truth---now!"

John David picked up the phone, dialed Remmie's number, and waited for her to answer. He greeted her calmly, and then asked if she would come to the church office right away. He told her Colin was there, waiting to see her. Remmie said to give her thirty minutes. After hanging up the phone, J.D. told Colin he would be in the sanctuary praying while they spoke. If he was needed, he would be there. Colin paced the office from one side to the other. Every tick of the big, old clock on J.D.'s desk seemed like an explosion inside his head. Suddenly, Remmie burst through the door with expectancy on her beautiful face.

"Colin, I've been worried about you. Where have you been? What is it? You look dreadful."

Colin took Remmie by the hand and led her to the sofa. They sat side by side. Colin took her hand in both of his and patted it gently. Remmie was rigid. She felt something was very, very wrong.

"Where's J.D.?"

"He's in the church. He'll be here soon. Remmie, I made a horrible mistake for which I need to ask your forgiveness."

"Oh, Colin, if you are talking about what happened in the hallway…"

"No, I'm not talking about that. It happened way before that. Remmie, I've been in love with you since we first met. I've never felt this way about anyone. When I realized our relationship was falling apart, it almost killed me. My only tie to you has been my search for your brother."

Remmie stood up, and walked across the office with her back to Colin. Turning to face him, her stare was with filled with horror.

"Continue, Colin. What are you telling me?"

Colin walked toward her, but she put up her hand to stop him.

"No, stay there – you're close enough. Finish this – now!"

"Okay, Remmie, but please try to find it in your heart to forgive me. Within a month of beginning my search, I found out about Roberto. I didn't want to hurt you again so soon after losing your father, so I waited. Then we grew apart. I was angry and bitter, so I deliberately kept my secret. When I found out from Sarah about J.D., I made the decision to renew the search in order to be closer to you."

Remmie sat down at J.D.'s desk. "Go on, Colin, finish it."

"I'd hoped and prayed we could renew our relationship. When I found J.D. at your house, I knew I had to make my move or lose you forever. Oh, Remmie, I…"

Remmie again stopped him. "I don't want to hear that, I want to know about my brother. That's all!"

Colin mustered every ounce of courage he had, and as he straightened himself and looked into Remmie's eyes, he said, "Roberto died in a plane crash five years ago. Your brother is dead."

Remmie stared into space. "Roberto is dead? You've known all along? You let me believe I had a brother in Atlanta? All the while he was dead?

Colin, what has happened to you? The man I cared for would not have done this despicable thing. Tell me, was Roberto a doctor?"

"He was an intern. From my investigation, he was a very brilliant surgeon like you."

"Does he have family as you said?"

"Yes, that is true. They are still grieving for him. He was their only child."

Colin expected an angry outburst, but it didn't come. Without any further discussion, Remmie stood, wiped away a tear, and walked out of the office. Colin was left with the words he had just spoken echoing in his head.

Remmie walked into the sanctuary and knelt at the altar. Great sobs began way down deep inside her, coming out in waves of pain, anguish, grief, loss, and sorrow. Tears made dark circles in the red carpet. Remmie prayed, lamented, and released all the hurt she felt for herself, and yes, for Colin. She laid it all out before her Heavenly Father.

J.D. was kneeling a few rows from the altar and he heard everything. In his heart, he knew what a special woman he had found. He prayed his own prayer. It was a petition to God, asking for Remmie to be his wife.

"Dear Heavenly Father, this is the helpmate I've waited for. She is the one to make my life complete. Since her earthly father is dead, I ask You for her hand in marriage. I seek Your approval as her heavenly Father. Grant it, I pray. Please help me comfort her. Amen."

Rising from his prayer, he approached Remmie, who was still kneeling. Putting his kind, strong hands on her shoulders, he prayed aloud, "Dear Lord, You alone know her pain. Help her come to terms with the tragic news she has received. Keep her from bitterness and un-forgiveness. Let her feel Your love and mine. Grant it, I pray, Amen."

Remmie placed both her hands on the altar as she pushed herself to a standing position. She felt as if she had been kicked in the gut by a horse. Her emotions were frayed. Every nerve in her body twitched uncontrollably. She was exhausted.

J.D. maintained his position right behind her with his hands lying on her shoulders. He wanted so much to be able to relieve her pain, but he knew that was impossible. All he could do was wait for her to react, so he could offer support to her in this unthinkable situation. He had prayed for her to forgive, yet inside, he was boiling with disgust for Colin. He needed to heed his own advice.

Remmie eventually turned to face J.D., her face streaked by tears and make-up. Her beautiful features were distorted by the pain raging inside her. She wanted to scream, to vomit, to somehow be free from the internal turmoil she felt. As she looked into J.D.'s eyes, she saw her pain reflected in his eyes. There was nothing to say. All she could do was cry as she repeated the one word everyone has on the tips of their tongues during times like this---------*WHY*???

"How could Colin do this? I just cannot fathom him being so cruel. I have never experienced a betrayal that wounded me more deeply. He was my friend, my confidant, and my attorney. He's someone who knows all about me and now, he has invaded my private sanctuary, where I live, where I feel, where I love; he has ripped away a part of my very soul. How will I be able to trust him again? I'm so overwhelmed by this---by him. I can't see him now. I can't discuss this anymore right now. J.D., please send him away. Tell him we will meet again in a few days. I will let him know what I decide to do about his betrayal. Please, please don't linger with him, just send him away!"

"I will, Remmie. I agree that you shouldn't deal with this now. We will see him soon to settle this. I'll be back. Don't leave this room. I will come back for you in just a couple of minutes. Sit down."

J.D. walked quickly from the sanctuary back into his office where Colin sat with his head in his hands. When Colin heard J.D. enter the office, he jumped to his feet, as if standing at attention.

"Is she alright? Can I see her and explain…."

"No, you cannot see her. Before you say anything else, let me be extremely frank with you. She is not going to discuss this any further today. We will be in touch with you soon, at which time we will meet to let you know what Remmie plans to do about your betrayal, and your failure in your duties as her attorney. Please leave through that door right now, and do not call either of us. We will contact you when Remmie is ready."

Colin took one step forward as he tried to say something, but J.D. put his hand up in the stop position and pointed to the door. Colin left without another attempt to speak. J.D. watched as Colin drove away. Then he ran back to the sanctuary, to Remmie.

CHAPTER TWENTY-NINE

Remmie woke up in her darkened room alone, feeling like she had just experienced a death in her family. Grief lay on her chest like an anchor, impeding her movements. She reached for the remote that opened the drapes to see if the sun was up or if it, like she, had decided to stay hidden today. Steadily, the drapes folded away from the center of the glass panels until they disappeared behind the cornice on each side of the window. She was right, no sun today. The sky was gray and heavy looking. It looked as if God would release heaven's tears at any second. She wondered if the cleansing rain would help wash the earth free of all betrayers, all liars, all hurts, and all wounds. She thought that if a deluge of pounding rain would just come, maybe she would feel clean on the inside. Maybe she would feel free from the stagnating anxiety that had flooded her inmost being. *What makes our insides hurt so much*, she pondered. *Oh, to be at peace again. To know everything is alright. To have confidence in myself again.*

A soft knock came at the bedroom door. "Remmie, honey, are you up yet? I've taken the liberty of making breakfast for you. May I come in?"

Remmie sat up, brushing her thick tousled hair with her fingers and rubbing sleep from her swollen red eyes. "Yes, you can come in. I hope you aren't expecting much because I look a fright."

Cautiously, the door opened, and J.D. peeped around with a smile on his face. "Not so bad. You are always beautiful to me. I've brought you some cold tea bags for those swollen eyes. They'll help, you know?"

"I've heard that, and right now I'll try anything. I suppose I've overreacted terribly. I'm a mess, aren't I?"

"I don't think you've overreacted at all. I think you responded normally to a very emotional situation. It's always best to deal with our hurts rather than recoil, locking things inside where they fester, wounding us even more. This trial will pass. You have learned new things about yourself - things that will make your stronger in the years ahead."

"Were you here all night?"

"I was. I hope I haven't over stepped myself. I just couldn't leave you alone. It was too late to get Jesse, so I made myself at home on the sofa so I would hear you if you needed me. I slept rather well, if that's possible with one eye open. I was concerned about you, Remmie. How are you this morning?"

Looking away to the gray sky out the window, Remmie considered her answer. "I feel as if I have lost a loved one. I want to wake up and realize it's a bad dream. Colin has been a most trusted friend since my father died. I had so much confidence in him. I would have never expected a betrayal from him. I feel like something important is missing today. Does that make sense?"

"Yes, of course it makes sense. Your relationship with Colin was deeply personal. He has access to information about you that no one else has except Sarah and Jesse. He was part of your inner-circle. There's no way you could feel anything but what you feel. He did betray you. Now, the question is, what will you do about it?"

"That's the question alright, but I don't have the answer. I don't know what my options are. I need to talk to Jesse. She is about to take her bar exam. She should know what I legally need to do about Colin. After that, I have to decide how to proceed personally."

"Colin wants to talk to you. That's the last thing he said before I showed him out. I told him we would be in touch, but until then not to call either of us."

"I can't let this drag on, John David. I have to make a decision; I have to move on. My relationship with Colin is over. That much I know. It's how to handle the transition and who will be my attorney that I'm unsure about."

"Well, okay. If that's what you want, that's what you should do. I'm sure you will have no trouble finding a new attorney in a city full of them. Do you know any other attorneys?"

"No, and I don't want one here in the city, either. I liked having my attorney in Atlanta. It gave me some anonymity by using a firm in another state. I can't just let my fingers do the walking through the yellow pages. Jesse should be able to help me with this. I'll call her in a while."

J.D. saw an opportunity to change the subject. "How about that breakfast now? I worked hard on it."

"As a matter of fact, I am feeling hungry. I didn't eat anything last night, did I?"

"You didn't. So, let's go have breakfast together and make a plan for today?"

"Fine. Just give me a moment to freshen up. I'll be right along." Remmie turned on the water, adjusting the temperature to warm to wash her face. She rubbed her day cream carefully into her olive skin that seemed dry this morning. She liberally applied concealer to the dark circles under her eyes. In her closet, she found her favorite pink robe and matching slippers with ostrich feathers on them. As she applied her perfume to her wrist and her neck, she scrutinized her face in the mirror. "Once I had no idea who you were, but today I know all about you. I also know I can face this disappointment; I can face the loss of a brother I never knew because of my faith in my God. I have to do the right thing about Colin. Forgiving him will ultimately set me free from this turmoil. Lord, I forgive Colin. I ask You to bless him and give him good success. I set him free to be the man You have called him to be. Amen."

In the kitchen, J.D. fussed around, setting the table with the pretty blue china he found. A clear blue pitcher held orange juice, a clear blue platter held his made-from-scratch biscuits, and a matching bowl was filled with strawberries, blueberries, kiwi, and grapes. He placed blueberry syrup and fig preserves next to the platter of biscuits. The coffee was nearby in a carafe to keep it hot.

"Wow! You have outdone yourself, Reverend Somersby. This looks delicious."

"Thank you Miss Remington. Do have a seat here so you have a view of the morning sky. It's no longer gray. It's blue, and the sun is warming the glass panels nicely. If you listen closely, you'll hear them crackle every now and then."

"Oh J.D., this is so good. You made these biscuits from scratch? They are just as light and fluffy as Sarah's. I adore hot biscuits topped with warm blueberry syrup. Not to mention piping hot coffee. You really nailed my favorites."

Smiling to himself, J.D. had a little secret. He had asked Sarah what Remmie liked for breakfast, and she talked him through making the biscuits. He was "right proud of himself" as they say in the South…"right proud."

"So, what should we do today? We can take a ride up to Oak Mountain, we can take a long walk in the park, eat a late lunch downtown, or we can stay here, and get Jesse over later to discuss your legal issues. Which will it be?"

"Let's see, I like the drive up the mountain a lot, but I need the exercise that a walk in the park would give me, and last but not least, I do need to talk with Jesse right away. I think we should stay here and call Jesse. But, we may have time later for a nice walk."

"Okay, here's the phone. Let's get this show on the road. You call while I clean up the kitchen," J.D. said as he headed into the kitchen with his arms full of dishes.

As Remmie dialed Jess's number, she wondered how this would affect her best friend, and then there was Sarah. What in the world was she going to do when she heard this? Sarah liked Colin very much. She had really encouraged Remmie's relationship with him. Remmie was in deep thought when Jesse answered------

"Good morning and how are you today?"

"Hey, Jess. I'm okay. How are you?"

"Busy, but always time to talk to you. I spoke with Sarah earlier. She said she hasn't heard from you since day before yesterday and she's about ready to bring Tenille back to the city."

"I'll just bet she is. Tenille's break week is almost over. I will ask Stuart to bring her back this afternoon. Jess, can you come over? I need to talk to you."

"Sounds like I should have left five minutes ago. What's going on? Is Jeremy okay? Or is it the Rev. Somersly?"

"Neither one. Just come as soon as you can. I really don't want to talk about this on the phone. I need your advice. I just need you, Jess. Please come?"

"Give me fifteen minutes, and I'll be on my way. Sit tight. I'm coming."

"Don't drive wild. It's not an emergency. J.D. is here. I think you may have the answers to some questions that have come up rather suddenly. I'll be expecting you. Bye."

"So, is she on her way?"

"She will be in a few minutes. I should get dressed and try to look a little better. I'll be right out. And thanks again for that breakfast, J.D. It was delicious."

Remmie fumbled through her closet looking for something comfortable to wear. Her mind was occupied with questions to ask Jess. She picked out a cozy purple sweater with navy leggings. As she brushed her tangled locks, she considered how Colin must have been feeling today. As she pulled her thick hair into a ponytail with a scrunchy, she felt lonely somehow. Colin had been there for her since her father died. It wasn't going to be easy to find another person she could trust. Maybe she never would trust anyone the way she did Colin. Not wishing to let the loneliness take charge, she turned her thoughts to the Lord.

Lord Jesus, I need Your help. I do forgive Colin. I have no desire to cause trouble for him. I want this spirit of grief to go, in Your Holy Name. Take this need to grieve away from me. You have given me so many wonderful people with whom to share my life. I don't want to waste another minute feeling grief or depression. Amen.

As soon as "Amen" left her lips, she felt a warming sensation race over her. It was a good feeling, rather calming. She turned her eyes heavenward, and whispered, "Thanks."

As John David opened the door, Jesse rushed in. "Good morning to you too, Jesse. Come in. Would you like a cup of coffee?" J.D. was talking to the breeze Jesse left as she rushed straight into Remmie's room.

"Remmie, are you in here? Hey, where are you, girl?"

"Right here, Jess. Settle down, I'm alright. Let's go back to the living room with J.D. I need to talk with you."

Jesse had a rather confused look on her face as she followed her friend into the living room. J.D. brought in a tray with three cups of hot coffee. After serving the ladies, he took his cup and sat down next to Remmie on the sofa. Jesse sat in a chair on the other side of Remmie. There was a tense silence until Remmie decided how she wanted to begin this sorted tail of betrayal.

"Jesse, I'm about to tell you something that will be shocking, but I want you to know ahead of time, that I am fine. I've already dealt with my emotions, and I have settled this with myself and with the Lord."

Jesse scooted to the edge of her seat. "Well, go on. What is it?"

"We had a meeting with Colin yesterday about the search for my brother. Jess, Colin knew where my brother was almost from the beginning of his search...."

"He knew, and didn't tell you? What in the name of heaven was he thinking?"

"Just let me tell this my way. My brother, Roberto Elezar Ramirez, died in a plane crash five years ago. He was a surgical intern who lived in Atlanta with his adoptive parents."

Remmie paused to allow herself a moment to maintain her composure. She held her hand up toward Jesse to keep her quiet until she was ready to proceed. "Colin didn't tell me the truth because he hoped to use the 'investigation' to his advantage with me. He found out from Sarah that I am seeing J.D., so, he decided to try to resume our relationship. When I rejected his advances, he knew he had to tell me the truth. He feels just terrible about what he's done and I feel terrible for him."

That was all Jesse could take. Standing to her feet, she blurted out, "You feel terrible for him. Well, I don't know how I feel about him right this minute. I can hardly believe what I am hearing. Colin must have lost his mind to do such a thing. I mean, you trusted him completely. What a jerk!"

"Jess, please try to be calm. He made an awful mistake that hurt me deeply, but I can't let my hurt cause me to be bitter. That solves nothing. Please let me finish what I need to say."

Jesse plopped down in her chair with arms folded across her chest.

"I know exactly how you feel. I felt like that last night, but this morning, I realized how much pain the anger was causing me. It's not worth it, Jess. When I woke up this morning, I felt as if a truck was parked on my chest. My head ached, my nerves were on edge, and my heart was broken. All I wanted to do was lie in my bed and feel sorry for myself. But I prayed, and I know that God doesn't want me feeling that way. His love is big enough to cover everything that hurts us, and His love is big enough to cover everyone that causes hurts to us.

"If I don't forgive Colin, I am tied to that offense; I can't move on. By forgiving him, I am free to be what God wants me to be. Colin is free, too. Jess, he's wrong for what he's done, but God still loves him and has plans for him. I don't have the right to hold on to the offense. That would trap both of us in guilt and bitterness. I want to be free, Jesse! I want Colin to be free so he can move on with his life. Do you understand?"

Tears poured from Jesse's dark eyes as her chin quivered. "I forgive him, Rem. I forgive him. What else could I possibly do after what you just said? I definitely don't want myself tied to Colin Forrester because I can't forgive."

"Thank you, Jesse. That is so important to me. God has taught me what forgiveness is, and I know in my spirit it's absolutely the right thing to do. I will not keep him as my attorney, but I forgive him. I have no intention of making any of this public, or contacting his firm, or anything else. It is finished for me. I do need a new attorney. I'm hoping you can help me with that."

Jesse explained what needed to happen and how to go about expediting the change. She was comfortable recommending to Remmie one of her law professors. She said she would see if he would be willing to be interim attorney until a replacement was found. That sounded good to Remmie.

So, it was decided that Jesse would make the contact with Professor Lane Brady as soon as she could. If that went well, Professor Brady would contact Colin to bring about the necessary changes. Hopefully, Remmie and Colin wouldn't have to see each other again. Remmie wasn't sure if she wanted to see Colin or not, but for now, she was pleased with the plans.

CHAPTER THIRTY

John David saw Jesse to the door. Returning to the living room, he sat down on the sofa very close to Remmie. He kissed her neck. He fiddled with her ponytail. Remmie moved closer to J.D. She laid her head on his shoulder, enjoying being held. An intense feeling of belonging swept over her. She took great pleasure in being near him, in touching him, and in letting him touch her. The smell of his cologne on his skin was very alluring to her. The way his eyes sparkled when he looked at her, his smile, the way he combed his hair, the silver watch on his wrist against his tan skin---everything about him was attractive, and attracting.

Remmie knew these were feelings she had not had before, not even with Colin. She never wanted John David Somersly to leave her. When he said good night, the words made her feel lonely. She felt compelled to have their next date set before he left. She wondered if he had any idea how she felt about him. He had indicated his strong interest in her, but she wondered if he really felt the way she did.

How do you know these things, she pondered. *How do you know someone loves you as much as you love them?*

"Are you asleep? Let's take that walk in the park and get an early supper at one of those little places downtown? Does that sound good?"

Remmie nodded that it sounded good. Following an impulse, which was something she rarely did, she put her hands on either side of J.D.'s handsome face and kissed him. Then all of a sudden, she heard a familiar voice say, "I love you."

It was Remmie's voice. Had she really said those three little words? Words she had never before said to any man, except her father? Caught totally off guard, she didn't know what to say or do. She just hugged J.D. tighter, and waited for the reply she prayed would come.

Pulling her arms from around his neck, J.D. looked straight into Remmie's eyes. "Did you say what I think you said?"

"Yes, I believe that was me. I've never said that to any man, except my father. J.D., I love you. I want to know how you feel about me."

John David Somersly beamed with joy. Fixing his eyes on Remmie's lovely face, he spoke with a slight tremor in his voice. "I have loved you with my whole heart since I met you in the hospital. I have always counseled couples against believing in love at first sight. But Remmie, I fell in love with you the instant I saw you. It was a God thing, honey. I saw you, I saw your spirit; I think God let me glimpse your soul, and I knew you were the woman I have waited for all my life. I love you. I want to spend the rest of my life loving you. I want to marry you."

Embracing each other, crying tears of joy, the couple sat for a long time. Supper was forgotten. They were lost in the moment, and nothing was important enough to cause them to move an inch away from one another. Time stood still as two hearts were being melted into one.

~~~

Sarah's key went into the lock. As the door opened just a crack, in ran the impetuous little Tenille. "Remmie, are you here? Where is everybody? I'm home!!"

J.D. and Remmie jumped to their feet in a start. They looked like the two cats that swallowed the canary. Sarah was quick to pick up that something was definitely going on with them.

Tenille ran all the way to the study and was on her way back before she saw them. She headed straight into Remmie's arms then into J.D.'s arms. She was very excited to be back from River Oaks. Her little mouth was full of stories to tell. The goats, the calves, the pies, and how to smell when they are done, they all came flowing out in one long continuous sentence.

Everyone except Sarah had taken their eyes and minds off Remmie and J.D.. Stuart took the bags into the guest room before making his way to the study to watch a ball game. After all, he had heard Tenille's stories all week. Tenille chattered on and on for a while longer, but eventually, she settled into playing a new game on her Nintendo. Then, Sarah was able to pursue her suspicions that something unusual had been going on when they arrived.
~~~

"Well, missy girl, what's new around here? *Ya* look a bit tired to me. J.D., *ya* look like *ya* have found a treasure map or *somethin'*. Aren't *y'all goin'* to let me in on your secret?"

"What secret, Sarah? I really have no idea what you mean. We were resting on the sofa where we fell asleep for a few minutes when in rushed Tenille. That's it."

"Yeah, right and I just fell off a turnip truck. *Ya ain't foolin'* me. So, whenever *ya're* ready, I'll be interested in *hearin'* what *ya* got to say. Seems I did hear *ya* finally heard from Colin about your brother. What took him so long?"

"I would rather wait on that story until Tenille is settled for the night. Are you and Stuart staying over or returning to River Oaks?"

"I thought we would stay a spell if that's good with *ya*. I need to do a little *shoppin'* first *thang* in the *mornin'*. Stuart has *somethin'* he needs to see *bout*, too. We *ain't gonna* be no trouble now. Just do *what'ja* need to do, and don't mind us none."

"That's fine, Sarah. You know you guys are always welcome here. I'll set up the study for Stuart. That way he'll have a television nearby. You can stay in with Tenille. She'll love a sleep over with you. I need to get her bathed and ready for bed. She has school tomorrow. Come help me, J.D."

Remmie wanted to get J.D. alone for a moment to be sure he knew it would be best if Sarah was kept in the dark a little longer about what had happened between them. He understood, but made it clear he would go along for a short time only. Remmie agreed as she handed him the linens for Stuart's bed in the study. She headed to her bathroom with Tenille.

After Tenille fell asleep, it was time for Sarah to hear the story that Remmie really didn't want to tell again, but knew she must. J.D. took the lead, getting the ball rolling. Remmie waited for the fireworks. Sarah didn't disappoint. Boom! She blew a gasket! J.D. reasoned with her, calming her down as best as he could.

"I *wus* wrong *bout* that man. Thank the Lord above *ya* didn't listen to me, missy. I can't imagine Colin doing such a backward *thang* to *ya*. He *wus* always so proper, and *gen-u-ine*. Goes to show, even the best judge of character can be wrong."

"I'm not so sure we were wrong, Sarah. Colin let himself down, too. I believe he's a good person who made a big mistake that he's paying for now."

"*You's payin'*, too. He *should'a* thought of that before he did such a awful *thang*. I hope I get the chance to give him my *thanking* on what he done."

"I hope you can just let it be. There's no need to tell him. He knows, and he's reaping from the sowing he did. I believe we should forgive him and let it go. I'm alright."

"*Ya* fascinate me, Remmie. You *shorely* do. Well, if that's *what'ja* want, that's what *ja'll* get from me. K-sir-ra-sir-ra. Or however you say that."

"We all have the potential to do awful things to each other. The Lord Jesus and the Holy Spirit's power make the difference in how we treat others. However, there are times we just don't listen to Him, and that's when mistakes happen. It's not that we desire to hurt one another, we just make poor decisions. Colin made a poor decision because he was jealous of my relationship with J.D. He was betrayed once by someone he loved and intended to marry. And although we had grown apart, he still cared for me. When he heard that I was seeing J.D., he was desperate to re-enter my life. His search for Roberto was the vehicle he had at his disposal. Without considering that I would feel betrayed, he jumped into his ill thought-out plan to keep looking for my brother, as a way to be near and hopefully renew our courtship. Colin was a perfect gentleman with me. He respected my values. He honored my wishes completely. I can't help but feel compassion for him, now."

"I understand what *yore tellin'* me, *chil'*. I'll get my attitude right. It just makes me hopping mad when someone *thanks* so little of how they're *a treatin' ya*. It *ain't* the first time neither. *Ya* are too nice. But, I know the Lord would be pleased if I kept my mouth shut on this subject. So, I'll give it my best shot. Now is that the only *thang ya* need to talk to me about? If it is, I'm *goin'* to say *nighty-night* to *ya*. This old body is tuckered out. I still have to go *shoppin'* at that mall in the *mornin'*."

"Yep, that is all, Sarah. I hope you sleep well. I'll fix breakfast for the two of you before you go. Let's plan to eat at eight-thirty?"

"Sounds fine. Good night again, and sweet dreams."

Sarah walked slowly down the hall, rubbing her back and scratching her head, while yawning like a sleepy puppy dog. As she disappeared into the guestroom, Remmie relaxed her tight muscles. She knew Sarah was still suspicious, but for now she wanted to have her secret love, so to speak. J.D., on the other hand, wasn't going to be easy to muscle for long. Just when or how to tell the world how much in love she was, Remmie didn't know just yet. She wanted to savor the realization of being in love, really in love for the first time in her thirty-one years of life.

"I need to go, too, honey. This has been an eventful day for both of us. I must say you were quite a surprise to me earlier, but it is the best surprise of my life. How long are you going to make me keep our secret?"

Walking nearer to J.D., Remmie put her arms around his neck, laid her head on his chest, and enjoyed his presence for a few seconds more. "Not long. I don't think I can keep this secret myself, but I want to ponder it in my heart for a few days. I've never been in love before. I want to cherish every minute of the beginning of our love. Does that seem silly?"

"No, not silly, just girlie. I don't know if I ponder or not, but I certainly won't forget today. You have made me extremely happy. I had no idea you were ready to tell me how you feel about me. I knew it in my heart, but for you to say it out loud in front of God and all His angels was glorious! Don't make me keep this secret long."

They walked arm in arm to the door. As they kissed good night, J.D. whispered in her ear, "I have a surprise for you, too. When you have finished your pondering let me know because I'm ready to surprise you, too. Good night. I'll call you in the morning."

Tenille was up early, eager to have all the house guests up. She found Remmie in the kitchen preparing breakfast. Sarah was on the balcony enjoying the breezy morning air, but Stuart hadn't come out of his room yet. Although Remmie had asked Tenille to be quiet until everyone was up, she was finding that a challenge. She didn't want to appear disobedient, so she went into her room and gathered up an arm full of toys. These particular toys if accidentally dropped would make quite a noise. Carrying them out into the hall, she made it all the way to Stuart's door before the "accident" happened and all the noisy toys and gadgets hit the hardwood floor, bounced around, banged the walls, and even hit the door. It was a commotion that got everyone's attention. Remmie came from the kitchen, Sarah from the balcony, and Stuart appeared, looking somewhat drowsy.

"Tenille, what are you doing with all this stuff out in the hall? I asked you to be quiet for a while longer. Now, look what you've done to poor Stuart. I believe you should apologize for waking him up so abruptly," scolded Remmie.

Half-heartedly to say the least, Tenille looked up into Stuart's eyes and said, "I'm so sorry I woke you up, but I hope you will play with me before breakfast gets ready."

Everyone laughed, especially Stuart, and the incident was soon forgotten. After breakfast, as everyone was busy getting ready for the day, Remmie helped Tenille get dressed for school. Sarah and Stuart readied themselves for their return trip to River Oaks. Good-byes were said, and everyone was off to take care of the business of the day.

CHAPTER THIRTY-ONE

It was almost ten o'clock when Remmie checked in at the trauma center. Connie, the triage nurse, was handling the walk-ins, which appeared to be going smoothly. Connie was a twenty-two year veteran, who knew her way around the trauma unit. She had earned the respect of the doctors, as well as the other nurses.

Remmie recalled her first day at the hospital six years ago. Connie was one of the first people she had met, and she had bonded with her right away. They had been friends ever since. Connie was one of those people who could be trusted. She knew her stuff when it came to trauma medicine, and as a doctor, that meant a whole lot to Remmie.

"Well, if you can't get here on time, just get here when you can, Doc," said Connie in her dry sense of humor.

"Good advice, Connie. That's exactly what I'm doing. How are things going so far?"

"Actually, very well. It's been steady, but not chaotic. You have a good team of doctors on your staff. That's not to say that we don't need you, but we get along nicely in your absence."

"Thank you, Connie. I think? You do have a way with words. I was reminded today of when we first met. The Medical Center did well the day they hired you. When I write my evaluations for Human Resources, I make a point of letting administration know how valuable you are in the unit. I've been blessed having great nurses to work with."

"Wow! Are you trying to butter me up or something? What's up, Doc? That's a bit gushy coming from you. Are you about to ask me to take a cut in pay or retire early?"

"Absolutely none of the above. I just feel especially fortunate, no, I feel blessed today. I want you to know how important you are here at work, and how I personally feel about you. That's it."

"In that case, thank you from the bottom of my heart. We aren't often privileged to have one of the doctors say such kind things to us. I want you to know, you are a class act in my book, as well as the best doctor with whom I have ever worked."

"Okay, enough is enough of this. We sound like we are starting our own mutual admiration society," said Remmie.

"It may sound corny Dr. Remington, but your comments really mean a lot to me."

Remmie reached across the counter, patted Connie's shoulder, and gave her a smile. Then she swiped her card in the security system, which opened the doctor's door to the trauma unit.

Dr. Archer and his nurse, Bonnie, sat completing paperwork in the lull of the mid- morning shift. Dr. Warren was working on a patient who was getting stitches in his hand, and Dr. Amy Hicks was examining an elderly man who had arrived on foot at the trauma center, complaining of chest pain. Greeting everyone, Remmie was quickly brought up to speed on the events of the morning. As reported by Connie, things had been steady, but not chaotic. That was about to change, however.

A message from an ambulance in route to the hospital let the teams know a stabbing victim was on his way. Time is always of the essence with patients who have been shot, stabbed, or severely injured resulting in excessive blood loss. Seconds can make the difference between life and death. Everyone on the team was keenly aware of this.

Hearing the siren approaching, the team waited for the patient to be brought in by the paramedics. The doors flew open and the paramedics were shouting out vital signs. When the young man's clothes were removed, a small puncture wound was seen near his mid-chest on the left side.

Dr. Hicks took charge by ordering a chest tube to be inserted between his ribs to remove blood that was putting pressure on his heart and lungs. The man moaned as he writhed in pain. His side was deadened with an injection, a cut was made, and the tube was pushed into his chest cavity. Needless to say, the local anesthetic did not take care of the pain, causing the man to yell loudly. No one paid attention to his yells to stop; everyone was focused on their role in this fast moving saga that could well mean life or death for the unfortunate young man.

As soon as the tube reached the chest cavity, blood poured out on the floor. The man's struggling let up a little. The team typed and matched his blood, a cat scan was performed, and soon the man was rushed to surgery where Dr. Remington and Dr. Hicks waited to repair his damaged heart.

Dr. Hicks opened the chest in one long, careful draw of the scalpel from just below his collar bone to the end of the breastbone. Expanders were used to open the chest, revealing the heart. The heart continued pumping, even though the blood was gushing out of the stab wound, filling the chest cavity with each beat. Blood was hung, and as each bag drained into the vein of the young man, another quickly replaced it. The bleeding had to be controlled. Dr. Hicks worked fast to get the man on the bypass machine.

Once the heart was stopped, the wound was repaired quickly. Then his chest cavity was suctioned out so that any other damage could be spotted. Waiting a few seconds to observe for more bleeding, young Dr. Hicks made the decision to transfer from the bypass machine, which allowed the heart to start up again. With no additional leakage observed, the closing team was ready to get the young man put back together and on his way to the Critical Care Unit.

The two doctors left the operating room together. As they changed their scrubs, they talked about the procedure. "That was a clean surgery, doctor. Your instincts were on target. I couldn't have done any better myself. I'm proud to see such skill in a young surgeon. You have a bright future here."

"Thanks, Dr. Remington. Coming from you that means a great deal to me. I have admired you from afar. I often observed your surgeries when I was an intern here. Your techniques are very interesting to me. I've used them many times. We were fortunate today. Everything was textbook. The man has a strong heart, so it was ready to go again. He has a lot to be thankful for. I hope he will be."

"Now, I remember you, Amy. I heard Dr. McKinley expressing how very happy he is that you came back here after your residency. He sees big things ahead for you. I will let him know how well things went today. Keep up the good work."

"Oh, I intend to. This has been a long, hard road for me. I don't plan on messing up now. I want to be the best surgeon I can be. Who knows, I may get your job when you retire. Uh, I didn't mean to sound boastful. I hope you are around a long time. But when you do go, I want to be in a position to advance. That's all I meant to say."

"Hey, that's not a problem for me, Amy. That's smart thinking on your part. Keep your head in the game and you will advance. Who knows, someone may leave before I do, then you'll be ready to move up. That's the way I like to hear our young surgeons talk. Be a little boastful now and then. Show your confidence to your co-workers…and to yourself."

"I'll do it…and thanks again. You are a good motivator. When you retire, you should become a motivational speaker, encouraging young doctors to succeed. You'd be the bomb…"

At that moment, a man came running into the emergency area, screaming to the top of his lungs. "Help, Help, my wife, my wife…in the car…in the car..."

Tyrell Jackson, the nurse assigned to Remmie, bolted for the door to assist with whatever emergency the man's wife was having. Reaching a mini-van with Remmie right behind him, they discovered a young woman in hard labor with water spewing and a tiny head already visible. The two went to work. Tyrell followed each direction given by Remmie without asking questions. Soon, with one more push from his mother, the tiny baby boy was born. But that wasn't the end. Another tiny baby followed the first, and soon, he too was free from his mother's body.

Tyrell held the first, wrapping him in a blanket provided by the nurses who had come with supplies. Remmie cut the first cord. Then she cut the second cord, and clipped them both. Both babies were placed in isolettes before being rushed into the trauma unit for examination. They were obviously pre-mature, but they seemed strong and healthy.

Now Remmie's attention turned to the young mother. With Tyrell's help, they moved her to a gurney for her short trip into the hospital. The woman, whose name turned out to be Alyssa, was thoroughly examined before she was sent to a room near the nursery where her sons were being evaluated by a pediatrician. The distraught husband named Ben was reunited with his wife so he could begin enjoying the arrival of his twins, as unorthodox as the delivery had been.

"I need a cup of coffee and a few minutes to regroup. How about you, Tyrell?"

"Oh yeah, me too. That was exciting. I've never delivered a baby, let alone two at once."

"Well, can I share a secret with you? Neither have I. We did great. Don't you think?"

"Dr. Remington, are you saying you have never delivered a baby before?"

"I have... but only with assistance from a more experienced doctor, and for sure never twins. I have studied deliveries, both natural and C-section, but it just never happened on my watch until today."

"Wow, well with that said, we did a really good job. God smiled on us and on that lady today. I'll not forget seeing those little guys come into this world."

"Nor will I, Tyrell. It was indeed a blessing to be a part of such an arrival into this world. Only our Creator could come up with such a miracle. We should work together more often. Are you usually on evenings? I think I remember seeing you when I worked mid-nights a couple of years ago."

"That's me alright. I worked evening shift while I was finishing up college. Then I got married and my wife likes having me home evenings."

"What were you taking in college," asked Remmie just before taking another sip of her double mocha coffee.

"I finished my Bachelor of Science Degree. I took the RN course first, with the help of my parents. Then I got a job so I could work myself through the other two years for the BS degree. I just felt it was important to get the BS because I'm considering going on to be a Physician's Assistant or a Nurse Anesthetists, which would give me a Masters Degree."

"You are very wise, Tyrell. Both of those fields are wide open, and very profitable. How does your wife feel about you going back to school?"

"She's fine with it. She is a Physical Therapist with a home health group. Her income could keep us going if I couldn't work while getting the extra training. I hope I can work here, but I haven't officially spoken with Dr. McKinley. I really like working here. Dr. Mac is a wonderful boss."

"That's for sure. He's been good to me through some ups and downs in my life. I think he will be happy for you to get your Masters while working here. The Medical Center should help you financially with that, too. You need to talk to him ASAP. Never put off today..."

"I know. My wife says that too. I'll do it today. Thanks, Dr. Remington for your encouragement. Thanks for not telling me while the births were happening that you had never done it before. I may have freaked out on you."

"Somehow, Tyrell, I doubt that. Let's try to get on the same team again soon? I like working with you, plus, I want to keep up with your progress," Remmie said while rising slightly to shake hands with the handsome young nurse.

"That'd be great, doctor. I'll look forward to our next shift together," replied Tyrell while shaking Remmie's hand. "I better get back to the unit. I have an inkling this shift hasn't shown us all its challenges just yet."

Tyrell's inkling didn't let him down. The remainder of the shift was borderline chaotic for everyone. Connie was hopping in triage, while all three doctors kept busy treating the patients Connie sent through for immediate care. The nurses--well, they were moving so fast that they were leaving vapor trails. The good news was--there were no deaths or serious injuries in the remaining hours of the first shift. But the minor injuries, the sicknesses, and the people who just come to the hospital emergency room when they get bored were enough to make every staff person eager to go home.

Remmie, as well as Dr. Archer, Dr. Warren, and Dr. Hicks, stayed late to make sure the transition went smoothly with the doctors coming in on the second shift. Most of the patients had been admitted and moved to rooms, but there were a few who would remain in the trauma unit overnight. Some needed fluids, others needed to be observed for a few more hours, and still others were having tests done that were not completed. Satisfied that everything was under control, Remmie and her colleagues left the Medical Center. Each carried a sense of accomplishment that he or she had done their jobs to the best of their ability that day.

CHAPTER THIRTY-TWO

Driving home, Remmie recapped her conversations with Dr. Hicks and Tyrell Jackson. She saw a lot of herself in young Amy Hicks. Her determination and confidence were definitely traits needed in the world of trauma medicine. Tyrell seemed settled and thoughtful. Remmie felt those qualities to be important for young nurses who work in the trauma unit.

Way too often, she had seen the hot shot personality in trauma nurses, which turned out to be a warning sign of bad things to come. Remembering all the way back to medical school, she thought about one of her professors who called that type of personality the *lone wolf*, which interpreted means: doesn't need anyone, can handle everything without help, and sees doctors as major nuisances. Over her years of practice, she was thankful to have only encountered a few such nurses. However, the ones she had encountered had left some major damage in their wakes. She concluded that the difference between a lone wolf and a Tyrell Jackson was his level head, along with his thoughtfulness. Defining those two characteristics as caring more about the patient than how much praise was received and knowing yourself and being happy with who you are.

Yeah, she was sure she would hear more about Dr. Amy Hicks and Tyrell Jackson. And it would all be very good.

Hand in hand, Tenille and Remmie walked down the hall of the rehabilitation hospital toward Jeremy Ryans' room. Tenille chattered about the picture she had drawn and was bringing to her dad. Remmie nodded her head as she listened to the precocious little girl she had come to love so much. In her mind, she thought, *our time together is almost over, little one, and I'm not looking forward to giving you up. I know this is how it should be, but I can't help loving you so much.* Her thoughts were interrupted by Tenille skipping along beside her, singing a song to the top of her lungs.

At the sound of Tenille's singing, Jeremy came from his room into the hallway. When Tenille saw her father she pulled free from Remmie and ran full speed ahead into his waiting arms. What a joyful moment to see a father and child embrace and kiss each other over and over again. It was always such a glorious reunion between them, even though she saw him every day.

"You look great, Jeremy. How do you feel?" asked Remmie as she approached the two of them.

"I feel really good for the first time in a long, long time. My energy is returning. I just want to get home with Tenille. I believe I'm ready. What do you think, Dr. Remington?"

"I think you are, too. I'm so pleased to see the changes in you come so quickly."

"This little bundle of joy motivates me every day to get better. I can never tell you what you have done for me, Remmie - taking on a stranger's child. You had no clue if I would survive and no financial support from me at all. There aren't many people who would do this. God put us together. There's no doubt about it. I am forever in your debt."

Putting her hand up like a stop sign, Remmie wanted to stop Jeremy from speaking. He took her hand and held it while he finished what he felt compelled to say. His gratitude was heart-felt. Without Remmie's intervention, Tenille would have gone into foster care. Jeremy would never forget her generosity.

"Okay, I'm finished now," Jeremy said as he released Remmie's hand. "I had to get it said. It's that important to me. You are a God-send into our lives. I don't believe she has been adversely affected at all by what could have been a traumatic, life changing event. You didn't miss a beat with her. She was in school. Her schoolwork was done. She was in church with her friends because you took her. You made all the PTO meetings. She even had great visits in the country with Sarah. I can't wait to see River Oaks for myself. Oh, I'm babbling on again when I said I was finished."

"It's alright, Jeremy. But let me say a few things to you. Can we sit down first?" Remmie could see Jeremy was tiring.

Once they were settled, Remmie spoke about the experience of having Tenille in her home for all these months. She agreed with Jeremy that this was a God-thing for her, too. "Tenille has been joy personified to me. She has brightened every day for me. I have learned a lot about young children, their likes and dislikes, plus, I have a new found appreciation for parents. I would not trade the pleasure of having Tenille with me for anything else in this world. Thank you for allowing me to be blessed by your daughter. She is remarkable in every way."

Tenille, having sat quietly for the few moments Remmie had been speaking, grew restless and blurted out, "Why don't you marry my daddy instead of the preacher, so we can be a family?"

Jeremy and Remmie were caught off guard for the moment. They both laughed, but each had a big question rumbling around in their heads. Remmie questioned: how did Tenille know she was marrying the preacher? Jeremy questioned: has J.D. asked Remmie to marry him? Tenille laughed too.

Remmie cut the visit short, using school for the excuse. She really didn't want the previous subject to come again tonight. *What must Jeremy be thinking? Tenille is the most perceptive little thing. Her mind must grab information particles out of the air somehow.* She knew she had never spoken about her personal relationship with J.D. in front of Tenille. *How in the world could she have realized J.D. was courting her?*

Then it hit her like a bolt out of the blue. *Sarah, it's Sarah! That's it for sure. She probably pumped the child for information. I should've known right away where this came from.* At least, she could stop worrying that Tenille had seen her kiss J.D. or overheard one of their conversations. No, it all made sense now. It was Sarah.

As soon as Tenille was tucked into bed, Remmie called J.D. with her news flash. J.D. got a big kick out Tenille's suggestion to his dear friend Jeremy. He agreed that Sarah must be the key to Tenille's wisdom about their relationship. But J.D. was convinced that Jeremy would be pleased with their courtship. Remmie felt much better after talking with J.D.

J.D. had also seen Jeremy that day. He told Remmie that Jeremy would be ready to go home within a week to ten days. He would continue therapy on his hands for some time to come, but he would be able to begin his career search right away. Jeremy had indicated to J.D. he was looking to advance his computer knowledge and brush up on graphic art design, which had always interested him.

"If we had written a book together, we couldn't have fashioned a better ending for the chapter about Jeremy and Tenille," mused Remmie.

"I can only think of one thing that would have enhanced this happy ending."

"Oh? And what would that be?" asked Remmie.

"For Tenille's mom to come home. For them to be a real family again. That would be the ultimate happy ending for my friend. As a matter of fact, I want to state that as a prayer to our Heavenly Father."

"Amen." Remmie said softly.

CHAPTER THIRTY-THREE

The next week flew by for Remmie. She was extremely busy at work, as well as at home with Tenille. She helped her with her school work, took her to visit her father, plus helped J.D. plan the huge welcome home party for Jeremy. Remmie had little time to think about the closing chapter of this intriguing saga of which she had been a part for almost a year. Occasionally however, her thoughts would turn to how she would release Tenille to her father…how she would find a new way to be a part of Tenille's life.

It had to go smoothly without any hoopla. The transition of power back to Jeremy Ryans must be done without any emotional display on her part. After all, this was the miracle outcome she had prayed for. Jeremy Ryans' survival was indeed a miracle. And now, the time was near for the Ryans family to be reunited. Remmie would relinquish all legal rights to Tenille. Then she would assume her new role as a friend.

As the party drew near, Remmie and Tenille were more excited than ever. Tenille had helped choose the decorations, the menu, the music, and of course, what she was wearing. The outfit Tenille and Remmie had picked out together was a pink and blue Polka-dotted tunic over solid blue pants. She had new shoes and a new bow for her long dark hair. Remmie said the blue was perfect with her hair, skin, and eyes. She could hardly wait to wear her new party outfit.

Tenille had been able to keep the secret so far, but some days she had to be careful not to let it slip. It was going to be wonderful to surprise her dad. But more than anything else, it was going to be wonderful for them to be together again.

The day of the party arrived. It was Saturday and it was cold outside. Although the sun was shining, the temperature was in the forties. No rain in the forecast. That was really good news, since the garage and backyard were decorated for the party, as were the living room, dining room, kitchen, and breakfast area.

The whole house looked like a motorcycle gang had ridden through. Jeremy loved his Harley, so Tenille and Remmie decided that would be a great theme for the party. There were lights strung across the backyard, the garage featured the Harley, plus there was plenty of fresh seafood served out of a small rowboat filled with crushed ice. The fried fish and shrimp were served in galvanized buckets placed on the workbench and tool shelves. Remmie had brought in heaters for the garage, as well as outdoor heaters for the backyard.

Inside, the house was filled with balloons floating on the ceiling and stand-up cut-outs of all kinds of motorcycles, especially Harleys. The dining room had a punch fountain with deep red punch flowing down. All the sweet stuff was in the dining room. The kitchen was stocked with chips and dips, meatballs, little smokies, and plenty of iced tea. The barbeque pork and grilled chicken were out back. The whole neighborhood smelled like one of those barbeque shacks found on a side road down South, somewhere off the beaten path.

Everyone worked to put the finishing touches on everything before J.D. arrived with Jeremy. Jesse, Stuart, and Sarah busily made final preparations. Tenille stood peeping out the side lights of the door, watching to see the guests arriving. The doorbell sounded and the house filled with neighbors, church friends, people from Jeremy's work, and people from the hospitals. It was a massive crowd. Now, all they could do was watch for Jeremy to make his appearance.

Tenille watched as each set of car lights came down the street. Finally, she watched as a car pulled into the drive and flashed its lights, which was the signal J.D. set up with her. "He's home, he's home!" shouted Tenille. "Everyone be quiet. He's coming to the door, get ready!"

"SURPRISE!!" came the shouts as Jeremy entered his home for the first time in almost a year. Instantly, Tenille was in his arms. Jeremy was boggled for a few seconds. Faces, faces everywhere! Slowly the look on his face became more relaxed, and then the smile came and never left. It was a great party. The crew Remmie brought in to serve took over making sure things went like clockwork.

Remmie and J.D. were able to mingle with the guests, especially those from the church. J.D. was very proud to introduce Remmie to members of his congregation.

Jeremy greeted guests for over an hour. Each person seemed to have a heartfelt word for him. He was most gracious. Tenille had her friends there, too. They had a blast playing games and dancing to the music of the band that was playing on the back patio.

Toward the end of the evening, J.D. found a moment when the band played a slow song to ask Remmie for a dance. It was romantic to waltz under the stars on a chilly night in the arms of the one he loved. Closer and closer they danced until someone tapped J.D. on the shoulder. They thought he wanted to cut in, but all he wanted was to let them know the music had stopped. It hadn't stopped for them. The music went on and on--in their heads.

"That was embarrassing, J.D."

"Forget it. We are in love. Love takes over. We can't be held responsible for that."

"J.D., you are a minister. I should think we need to adapt a...a..."

"A what, Remmie?"

"Well, a more formal... or a more... Oh, I don't know. But we should be more casual with each other in public. Yes, casual. That's it."

"Which is it then, casual or formal? And would you demonstrate casual and formal for me?" asked J.D. with an air of formality to his voice.

Realizing he was making fun of her, Remmie hit him on the shoulder as she shook her head as if to say, hopeless. They finished their next waltz together, being more careful not to be too formal, but not to be too casual.

When the last guest was escorted to the door and the house was quiet, Remmie and Jeremy had a moment to express to one another how grateful they each were to the other. The expressions of gratitude were overwhelming and try as she did, Remmie couldn't keep a tear from slipping down her cheek. Jeremy shed a tear or two himself. Remmie took the papers that Jeremy had signed, giving her guardianship of Tenille from her purse. Jeremy took the papers ending their agreement from his coat pocket. Each handed the papers to the other. Remmie opened the legal document, read it briefly, and then signed it. This officially ended her oversight of Tenille.

"Dr. Remington, you are forever a part of this family. You are welcome to see to Tenille any time you like. I hope we can spend holidays together. Perhaps even work on a family vacation in the future after you and J.D.

are married. I know Tenille has your cell number, but I warn you, it may not be the wisest idea. She will miss you terribly, so she will probably call you a lot."

"First, if we are family, then my name is Remmie. Second, Tenille can have the number. I will explain to her how, and when to use it. Third, holidays and a family vacation sound marvelous to me. And finally, how long have you known J.D. and I are getting married?"

"Since I saw the way he looks at you and since all he can talk about is you. It was pretty obvious to me that he had finally met the woman he's waited for so long. You can't do any better than J.D., Remmie. He's one of a kind in all the right ways."

"Oh, how well I know that, Jeremy. He has already endeared himself to me in many, many ways. I have waited a long time to find him, too. God has doubly blessed us."

Jeremy moved close enough to give Remmie a quick hug and a kiss on the cheek. "You remember what I said, we are family now. I need family just as I believe you need family, too. J.D. is all the family Tenille and I had until we met you. Thank you for everything. May God's richest blessings be yours."

CHAPTER THIRTY-FOUR

It was a cold November day. The wind whipped up leaves from the front lawn of River Oaks. The windows were frosted in the kitchen where Sarah busily worked making a special meal for Remmie, J.D., Jesse, and Lane Brady. Today was the day that Remmie and Colin would finalize their business. It was a day that Remmie had dreaded for quite a while.

"Stuart, Stuart where are *ya*?" yelled Sarah into the intercom on the wall near the stove. "*Git yoreself* down here to *hep* me for a minute. Well *tarnations*, where is that man when *ya* need him! Stuart!"

"Hang on, Miss Sarah. Don't push that button slam through the wall. I'm here. What can I do for you?" said Stuart as he entered the kitchen door. "I thought from the sound of you, you must have set the place on fire."

"Oh, don't mind me now. I'm just over excited, I *reckon*. Remmie and J.D., Jesse, and that lawyer professor or whatever he is, will be here shortly for lunch, and I'm running a bit behind. Can *ya* get the tea made and set the dining room table with the *everday* china for me? I'll have the biscuits whipped out in five more minutes, but I don't want *'em* to see the table not set."

"Why, Miss Sarah, you know I'd do about anything for you, especially when you're making biscuits for lunch. What else have you got over there in those pots?"

"Just a few homemade mashed potatoes, smothered fried chicken with gravy, squash casserole, and a blackberry cobbler. Remember *pickin'* those berries this summer? Well, I put *'em* to good use. That cobbler will make *yore* tongue slap *yore* brains out."

Stuart just had to laugh out loud. "You are a character, Miss Sarah. Yes, indeedy, a character for sure. I don't mean to be assuming, but am I having lunch with y'all?"

"Of course, *ya* are. Set that table for six. Use the good china like I said before."

"Miss Sarah, you said everyday china before, so which is it?"

"I did? Have you already set it? If you have, then leave it like it is. The *everday* china is good enough for anyone. I don't know this *fellar whose a comin'*, but he can eat on *everday* china or chinette, whichever he wants."

Laughing again, Stuart chuckled his way back to the kitchen to make the tea for Sarah. "I thought her lawyer was coming today. Colin, I believe is his name."

"He won't be her lawyer after today. Unfortunate *thangs* happen, and Mr. Colin Forrester *shore nuff* messed up his situation. Well, it *ain't* my place to tell that story. Colin is coming later in the afternoon, but he *ain't comin'* for lunch."

"Got it. Won't ask any more questions about that. Which glasses do you want to use?"

"The crystal stems in the cabinet with the china *ya* used are fine. Be sure to get the tea as cool as *ya* can, so the ice won't water it down."

"Sure thing, Miss Sarah. All taken care of. I'll be back at noon, but if you need me just holler," called Stuart as he closed the door behind him. He immediately wished he had not said holler. Sarah was a menace on that intercom.

J.D. turned into the massive entry gate, punched in the code, and waited as the gates begin to open for their passage into the beautiful country estate of the late Dr. Benjamin Remington. The trees laden with Spanish moss bowed as the vehicle moved along the drive toward the sprawling cedar and stone house nestled in the trees. Only a few plants displayed their blooms against the winter landscape. Camellias displayed their beautiful blooms in colors of pink, red, white, and combinations of the three. The wind was stiff directly out of the east. The trees swayed as leaves billowed toward the ground. Soon, most of the trees would be bare, making the harshness of the season visible to all.

Sarah was waiting just inside the kitchen door. She was always excited when Remmie came home. Today her feelings were a bit mixed because she had always liked Colin so much. She knew Remmie dreaded the finality of today, too. She also knew that J.D. and Jesse would be on hand to make sure Remmie was alright. So, even though it would be a difficult day in some ways, it was still a welcome home day right now.

Soon, introductions were made with everyone gathered in the warm parlor near the dining room, waiting for lunch to be served. Remmie asked Jesse and Professor Brady to sit on the left side of the table directly across from J.D. and herself. Sarah and Stuart would sit at either end of the table. But first, Sarah, assisted by Stuart, brought the food to the table and filled the glasses with ice before pouring the tea. When everyone had been served, J.D. prayed a prayer of blessing over the meal. Later, coffee was served, along with the decadent blackberry cobbler. Sarah had lived up to her reputation, and then some.

Colin arrived at the gate at two o'clock, prompt as always. Stuart answered the buzzer and then opened the gate. In five minutes, Colin and Remmie would be face to face for the first time since he had told her of his deception. As Colin approached the main entrance to the house, his stomach was in knots. Nausea caused hot water to fill his mouth. He swallowed hard, trying to deny the urge to vomit. *How could I have done something so despicable, something so low and calculating? Oh Remmie, if only you knew how much I love you, maybe you could find some understanding in your heart. How sick is that thinking? I did it for love. I can't believe myself. Who in his right mind could do something so deceptive and explain it by saying I did it for love?*

The gnawing in the pit of his stomach suddenly turned to a violent heave. Colin opened the car door quickly, just before throwing up on himself. Wiping his ashen face with his handkerchief and straightening his tie and shirt, Colin closed the door, driving on to meet his destiny with Remmie.

J.D. opened the door, greeting Colin in a professional manner. No pleasantries or small talk...just, "Come in and wait in the parlor, please." Colin couldn't sit down. He stood by the window, looking far away, and wishing he was far away from River Oaks.

Remmie, Jess, and Lane Brady were in the dark paneled study waiting for J.D. to let them know Colin had arrived. "You haven't changed a thing in here," remarked Jesse as she gazed around the large room.

Books lined the walls on two sides of the room. Huge windows facing the woods and the river let in the warm glow of the sun on the south side of the room, and Dr. Remington's massive carved wood desk sat on the other wall. On the desk were his pipe and his favorite wintergreen tobacco, as though he would soon arrive to use them again. "Um, I still smell his tobacco. Maybe the wood paneling captured the aroma," said a reflective Jesse.

"I see no reason to change things in here. This is the way Dad liked it. It all reminds me of him. I come here often to collect my thoughts. It's so peaceful in here. I enjoy the view toward the river. I find my own peace just sitting here with his things all around me, and memories of our times together in this room."

Lane Brady sat quietly in a large brown leather chair. He contemplated his new role as Remmie's attorney. Even though the role was only temporary, he felt there were lessons he could learn from this very interesting young woman. At any rate, he was intrigued to see how she would handle the situation they would be facing at any moment now.

Footsteps came toward the study. J.D. entered and walked directly to Remmie. "He's here, honey. I want us to pray before we meet with Colin. He doesn't look well, Remmie. Dear Father, cover this meeting with your peace, give us all wisdom, but most of all let us part as friends. Amen."

J.D. reassuringly kissed Remmie, patting her arms. Then he walked swiftly down the hall. Everyone was quiet as they waited to hear footsteps in the hall again. The steps were slower as they came nearer and nearer until J.D. and Colin entered the study. Remmie moved toward them, extending her hand toward Colin, greeting him kindly. Colin, in turn, shook her hand. Her smile was genuine. The knot in his stomach let up just a little bit. He felt his shoulders relax as they moved lower to a more natural position.

Lane Brady moved to stand next to Remmie, who had taken a seat at the desk. Jesse shook hands with Colin and then stood on the other side of Remmie. J.D. sat down by the window, leaving Colin standing in front of the desk and Remmie.

Remmie introduced Lane Brady to Colin. She asked them to proceed with the business at hand. Colin placed a brief case on the desk, opened it, and pulled out an envelope. Mr. Brady took the envelope, opened it, and thumbed through the documents. He picked out a couple of the documents, placing them in front of Remmie. Reading them carefully, Remmie struggled to keep her mind on the business instead of the relationship that would end today.

She remembered the first time she met Colin. The day her father died in this very room. She recalled how many times Colin had been a rock for her in the weeks following her father's death. The memories were bitter sweet, because she also remembered his confession about leading her on about her brother. "Mr. Brady, are the documents in order?" asked Remmie with a stern voice.

"Yes, I believe everything we need is here."

"Colin, Mr. Brady will be acting as my attorney until Jesse takes her bar exam in a few months, then she will represent me and my father's estate. I appreciate everything you have done for me over the last two years. I'm grateful for your help in the weeks following my father's death when I had so many decisions to make. Your guidance was very helpful to me. Thank you for all you have done."

"Thank you, Remmie. You have been more gracious than I deserve, considering what I've done to you. If I have overlooked anything you need, just call. I will get it to you immediately. Mr. Brady, I am at your disposal. Good evening to you all."

Colin turned, walking quickly out of the room. His heart was pounding in his ears as each step took him nearer the door. He just wanted to get out of this place that held so many memories. As his fingertips touched the door handle, a voice called out, "Colin, don't leave like this. Wait please."

Freezing in his tracks with his face still toward the door, Colin stood like a statue. "Colin, come with me into the parlor, please," said Remmie as she walked quickly toward the parlor. J.D. was right behind her.

"I don't believe I can let our relationship end with so much tension between us. Colin, I forgive you for letting me believe my brother was alive. I was very angry with you, and extremely hurt. I don't feel that way anymore. I have forgiven you. I don't want you leaving here carrying a burden of guilt. It's over, it's over today. I've let it go, and I want you to let it go. Tell me that you have forgiven yourself. Tell me this episode is over for you, too."

Colin straightened his posture, turned his eyes to meet Remmie's, and said, "I've tried to do what you are asking. I have. So far, I haven't been successful, but I have repented to the Lord Jesus and now, I repent to you. I want to be free from this cloak of guilt. My whole life has been affected by what I did to you. I failed the Lord, you, and myself. I don't feel like the same person anymore. I feel like a stranger to myself. What can I do to put this behind me, to be free again?"

J.D. took Remmie's and Colin's hands as he bowed his head. "Dear Father, Your Word says that where two or three are gathered in Your name, You will be in the midst of them. We gather together in Your Holy Name to find a peaceful solution to a situation none of us can change. Colin has repented to You, and to Remmie. Remmie has already forgiven him. For some reason, Colin still feels the heaviness of his failure, but desires to be free from this weight. We ask You, Father, to remove the weight of the sin that is already forgiven and set Colin free to live his life in harmony with himself, as well as with You. We ask for an immediate manifestation that will affirm to Colin he is forgiven and restored. In the name of our Lord and Savior, Jesus Christ. Amen."

Still holding hands, Colin, Remmie, and J.D. stood with their heads bowed. J.D. felt in his spirit that the Father was about to manifest Himself to Colin in a powerful way. Remmie also sensed something meaningful was about to happen.

Colin released his grip on their hands, and then slowly raised his hands toward heaven. He turned his face heavenward and stood in silence for several minutes. At last, he lowered his hands as he opened his eyes. "I can't explain it, but I know I'm free from the guilt that has plagued me since this all began. I'm free. I'm at peace for the first time since I lied to you, Remmie. It's over, just like you said earlier. It's really over. Thank you, Lord.

"J.D., I appreciate that prayer so much. I also appreciate the way you have handled yourself throughout this whole ordeal. Remmie, I fully understand your decision, and I agree that I should no longer represent you or your father's estate. I will remember this time fondly with deep admiration for you. Thank you both for helping me to find freedom and peace in my spirit again. I will never forget your kindness."

"You have been a devoted friend, as well as a skillful attorney. You handled the adoption case wonderfully. I will always be grateful. I can honestly say that I still consider you my friend. Good-bye, Colin and blessings always."

"Good-bye and thank you both."

Embracing each other, Remmie and J.D. watched as Colin drove away from River Oaks. They were reminded of J.D.'s prayer before the meeting. He had asked for peace and wisdom, but more than anything he had asked that everyone would part as friends. God heard and God answered.

CHAPTER THIRTY-FIVE

The smell of coffee drifted into Remmie's room before the first beams of sunlight peaked over the horizon. Remmie stood gazing out into the darkness. The wind howled slightly as it blew around the side of the house. Touching the window pane, Remmie could tell it was getting colder. The coffee smelled so inviting. She decided to get her day started early by joining Sarah in the kitchen.

"Good morning, Sarah. How are you this beautiful morning?"

"What in the world are *ya doin'* up at this hour? Are *ya* sick or *somethin'*?"

"No, I'm fine. Just so thankful---so thankful, Sarah. God has blessed me so much. I don't want to waste a single moment that I could be thanking Him for all He's done. I feel incredibly thankful this morning."

"*Ya* are blessed, *chil'*. No doubt *'bout* it. It's good to count *yore* blessings. It's good to be humble, to recognize without the Lord, we *ain't* much."

"Humble......yes...that's how I feel right now. I feel humble, in awe of the God who created everything, and still has time for me. He never forgets His children. He knows where we are, and He cares. That's humbling."

"I reckon it is, *chil'*. God can seem so big and far away at times, but the fact is, He's as close as our breath. All we have to do is breathe His name.... and He's right there. Umm, that's truly a wonderful *feelin'* when *ya* know God is as near as *yore* next breath. That makes me want to shout--*GLORY*!"

"Sarah, you'll wake up the whole house," cautioned Remmie.

"That's okay. They may need to get up to feel some of what I'm *feelin'* right this minute. God's presence *ain't* like *nothin'* else. The joy it brings... the anticipation of *somethin'* great about to happen is....well, it's just *WONDERFUL!*"

Remmie hugged Sarah very tightly as she put her hand over her mouth to muffle any further shouts that might be lingering. "I know Sarah. He's my joy, my peace, my contentment, my fulfillment...he's everything to me. I can't imagine living a single day without Him," Remmie whispered.

Suddenly, the thought popped into Remmie's head that she had not told Sarah or Jesse that she had made a commitment to marry J.D. *I must fix this quickly. Since we are all here, this is the time to tell my family my good news. Yes, I'll speak with J.D. as soon as I can, and we will make the announcement.*

The mist from the river lay close to the ground as the sun climbed a bit higher in the morning sky. Birds foraged for their breakfast, and ground critters scampered about finding the feast God provided in abundance for them.

Stuart hurriedly finished feeding all the animals. Then he gathered up special cut logs for the large fireplace in the family room. This wood had been cured for several months before it was brought to the house in order to minimize the popping.

Stuart carried in several armloads of the wood, stacking it neatly by the large stone fireplace. First he put down the kindling, which was pine wood with plenty of sap in it so it would burn easily. Carefully Stuart set the kindling on fire, nurturing the small fire until it was burning well. The smell from kindling was especially pleasant on cold mornings. Next Stuart put down the pecan wood, which took a little longer to get going. But soon the fire was rolling and crackling as heat began to fill the room. The fragrance of the wood burning drew everyone into the family room - Jesse and Remmie each with a piping hot cup of coffee, J.D. with the newspaper, and Sarah with a bowl of potatoes she was about to peel.

Remmie sat on the hearth, staring into the fire. Jesse threw a large pillow on the floor near the hearth and became a fire watcher, too. J.D. was enthralled with the newspaper. Sarah was humming *What a Friend* while peeling potatoes. It was a cozy scene for sure.

Stuart came back in with his large mug of coffee and sat down in an arm chair near the rolling fire. "It's cold outside this morning. This fire feels mighty good to my bones right now. It's going to warm up some later, I think. When the mist is lying so close to the ground like it is, it usually warms up in the afternoon," said Stuart in his slow drawl.

"I hope it does. I want to go for a walk later if it's warm enough," Remmie remarked while still gazing into the fire.

"I can't take that cold wind myself," said Jesse. "I'll stay here and help Sarah with lunch."

"That's mighty nice of *ya*, Jesse. I plan to cook a beef brisket with potatoes and carrots. I thought I might make a pot of black-eyed peas, and a pone of cornbread. I can use *yore hep*," replied Sarah.

"That menu might get me to help in the kitchen this morning, that is if men are allowed in your kitchen, Sarah," injected J.D., turning his attention from the paper.

"Oh, they are allowed alright. Just come on in. I'll put *ya* to work. Jesse and *me* work right fine together. We'll see how *ya* work out."

"J.D. is a great cook. He fixed breakfast for me and it was delicious. He had my favorites, including homemade biscuits with warm blueberry syrup," said Remmie.

"Well imagine that. Tell me, Reverend, just *how'd ya* know Remmie's favorites like that?" questioned a naughty Sarah.

Jesse caught the look exchanged between Sarah and J.D. and she knew immediately J.D. had help with that delicious breakfast. "Don't suppose you had anything to do with that delicious breakfast, Sarah?"

Remmie turned from gazing into the fire to look at J.D. His eyes gave him away. "Oh, it's true. Sarah talked me through making the biscuits, and she told me exactly how you like everything. Sorry honey, I'm not as perfect as you thought."

"You are, too, even more than I thought. But I should have known you had a collaborator."

"If I may have your attention, I have an announcement to make. As you know, I have been seeing Remmie for about eight months now. For a long time, I have desired to find the woman God has prepared for me. I understand from talking with Remmie that she, too, has waited a long time to find the man God has prepared for her. Well, to shorten this saga, we have found each other. We believe God has ordained us to be together forever."

"Remmie, will you please stand up." As Remmie stood to her feet, J.D. knelt on one knee and took her hands. "Remmie, I fell in love with you the moment I saw you at the hospital when Jeremy was injured. I have counseled many couples to try their love, and not base a relationship on love at first sight. But I knew almost immediately that you are the woman God created for my wife. After eight months of getting to know each other under various circumstances, my feelings for you have deepened and I cannot envision my life without you. Rebecca Elizabeth Melissa, will you marry me?"

Remmie absolutely beamed with joy. "I will marry you, John David Somersly. I will."

From his pocket, J.D. took a small velvet box and opened it. "Do you remember the day you committed to me? I told you I had a surprise for you. I saw this a few months into our relationship and I bought it. I've had the hardest time keeping it from you. Every time we were together I wanted to give it to you." J.D. took a gorgeous diamond ring from the box. It was dainty, elegant, but stunning. The center stone was a square three carat diamond surrounded by two rows of smaller diamonds. The smaller stones extended around the band. Carefully he placed the ring on Remmie's finger. Then he stood, embraced her, and kissed her. Suddenly the couple was startled by loud applause and shouting.

Sarah, Jesse, and Stuart were applauding and Sarah was also shouting like a school girl. Jesse was crying---then clapping---then crying some more. Stuart was the first to shake J.D.'s hand and kiss the bride-to-be on the cheek, followed closely by Sarah and Jesse.

It was a wonderful moment in front of the big rolling fire, in the family room at River Oaks on a frosty winter morning. Sarah felt such joy inside. She knew in her heart that this was right for Remmie. Sarah also knew if Remmie's father had been there, he would have had some remarks to punctuate this memorable occasion. "Now, I *ain't* much of a speaker, but this moment deserves some words spoken. If Benjamin and Melissa had lived to see this day, I can't begin to tell *y'all* how gloriously happy they would be. Remmie *ya* are the closest *thang* to a daughter I'll ever have. My love for *ya* is as real as if I had brought *ya* into this world myself.

"*Ya* have been a *blessin'* since the first day *ya* came here as an eleven year old girl, full of doubt and fear. I watched as *ya* turned into a woman of character and of faith. *Ya* gave your parents pure joy *everday* they lived. *Ya* never disappointed *'em* in any way. Their greatest desire for *ya,* other than *servin'* the Lord, was that *ya* would marry a Godly man, and have a good life. J.D., *ya* are the man the Remingtons prayed for a long, long time ago. God never forgets our prayers.

"This is a great day at River Oaks. I give *ya* my blessings, since *yore* folks *ain't* here to give theirs. I can tell *ya* without a doubt, if they know this in heaven, they are *rejoicin'* with the angels right now."

After saying her peace, Sarah walked out into the cold winter air. Once she was alone, Sarah turned her face to heaven, lifted her hands, and said out loud, "Thank you, Father God, our heiress has found her prince."

THE END

Every year in the United States there are over three million reports of child abuse or neglect. These statistics involve an estimated six million children. It is my desire to bring attention to this epidemic by addressing it in my first novel.

Each day more than five children die because of abuse or neglect and eighty percent of those children who die are age four or under. These young Americans should not die in vain. I am making it a priority to keep this national tragedy before the eyes of my reading public.

Child abuse occurs at every socioeconomic background, across all ethnic and cultural lines, within all religions and at all levels of education. Children are not safe in their homes, at school, churches, daycare, Foster-care and on and on.

More than 90% of juvenile sexual abuse victims know their perpetrators. About 30% of abused children will abuse their own children, continuing the horrible cycle of abuse. Statistics say that 80% of twenty-one year olds that were abused as children have at least one psychological disorder. The estimated cost related to child abuse each year in America is 104 million dollars.

Those are the hard cold facts about abuse. The victims of the abuse are young, tender, innocent children. They deserve so much more from their lives. I asked myself what I could do. I decided that I could touch the hearts of my readers by including stories (fictional stories) about the silent cries of the children. Please ask yourself what can you do?

CPSIA information can be obtained at www.ICGtesting.com
Printed in the USA
LVOW090149300312

275193LV00002B/3/P